U0854627

XIFANG WENLUN YUANDIAN DAODU

西方文论原典导读

窦可阳◎主编

北京师范大学出版集团
BEIJING NORMAL UNIVERSITY PUBLISHING GROUP
北京师范大学出版社

图书在版编目（CIP）数据

西方文论原典导读 / 窦可阳主编. —北京：北京师范大学出版社，2021.4

新世纪高等学校教材. 文学理论系列教材

ISBN 978-7-303-26764-4

Ⅰ. ①西… Ⅱ. ①窦… Ⅲ. ①文学理论—西方国家—高等学校—教材 Ⅳ. ①I0

中国版本图书馆 CIP 数据核字（2021）第 016545 号

营　销　中　心　电　话　010-58807651

北师大出版社高等教育分社微信公众号　新外大街拾玖号

XIFANG WENLUN YUANDIAN DAODU

出版发行：北京师范大学出版社　www.bnup.com

北京市西城区新街口外大街 12-3 号

邮政编码：100088

印　　刷：天津旭非印刷有限公司

经　　销：全国新华书店

开　　本：787 mm×1092 mm　1/16

印　　张：25.5

字　　数：640 千字

版　　次：2021 年 4 月第 1 版

印　　次：2021 年 4 月第 1 次印刷

定　　价：49.80 元

策划编辑：周劲含　　责任编辑：陈　倩

美术编辑：李向昕　　装帧设计：李向昕

责任校对：康　悦　　责任印制：马　洁

版权所有 侵权必究

反盗版、侵权举报电话：010-58800697

北京读者服务部电话：010-58808104

外埠邮购电话：010-58808083

本书如有印装质量问题，请与印制管理部联系调换。

印制管理部电话：010-58805079

Contents

1. 导读

本教材是基于在线课程“西方文论原典导读”而编写的。“西方文论原典导读”是我在2014年开设的双语专业课程。我特意选取了14~16篇颇具权威性和代表性的西方文论原典，精心设计了师生互动和一系列特别的全英文讲座，并建立了良好的分享、讨论、问答机制，经过不断调整、改进，最后将其建设成一门混合式教学双语在线课程。该课程于2016年上线，并在2018年被评为“国家精品在线课程”。目前，此课程在爱课程“中国大学MOOC”、超星“学银在线”、超星“泛雅”和“智慧树”等在线教学平台每年开放一期。该课程的设计初衷是拓宽学生的理论视野，提升学生的专业外语水平，尤其中文专业的学生在学习了“西方文论”或“西方文学批评”这门课后，精读西方文论原典就成了他们强化理论认识、加深知识接受度的必要功课。但是，如果说西方文论的中文译本算作“二手文献”，是一种“转述”的话，大约只有诵读了原汁原味的西方文论原典，才会有更直观、更真切的体会。另外，在各高校建设“双一流”、与国际密切接轨的今天，专业外语水平的提升，也成了当下中文专业本科生、研究生教育必须面对的课题。因此，这门双语课程虽然有一定难度，但作为各类在线教学平台上唯一中英双语教学的西方文论“原典导读”，它的受众群体一直在扩大，不单单中文专业的学生，外语专业的学生和各年龄段的外国文学、外国文论爱好者都可以从本门课程中获益。

本教材所选的原典素材，与“西方文论原典导读”在线课程的素材基本一致，除了“弗吉尼亚·伍尔芙”一章为原课程所无（但未来也会被补录进在线课程的视频素材中）。这些课文的原作者，大多数都来自英语国家，包括塞缪尔·约翰逊、威廉·华兹华斯、奥斯卡·王尔德、弗吉尼亚·伍尔芙、T. S. 艾略特、威廉·燕卜荪、M. H. 艾布拉姆斯、苏姗·桑塔格和爱德华·赛义德等；伊波利特·丹纳虽然是法国人，但他的材料来自他的《英国文学史》；H. R. 姚斯虽然是德国人，但他本身也是一位英国文学的研究者。至于其他课文，也都有醇厚优雅的英文译本。本课程所选材料也基本是这些文论家或批评家的经典之作，详见下表：

Plato（柏拉图）	*Ion*（《伊安篇》）
Aristotle（亚里士多德）	*Poetics*（《诗学》）
Samuel Johnson（塞缪尔·约翰逊）	*Preface to The Plays of William Shakespeare*（《莎士比亚戏剧·序》）
William Wordsworth（威廉·华兹华斯）	*Preface to Lyrical Ballads* (2nd Edition)（《抒情歌谣集序言(第 2 版)》）
Hippolyte Taine（伊波利特·丹纳）	*Preface to History of English Literature*（《英国文学史·序》）
Oscar Wilde（奥斯卡·王尔德）	*Preface to The Picture of Dorian Gray*（《道林格雷的画像·序》）
Sigmund Freud（西格蒙德·弗洛伊德）	*Development of the Libido and Sexual Organization*（《力比多和性器官的演化》）
Virginia Woolf（弗吉尼亚·伍尔芙）	*Modern Fiction*（《当代小说》）
T. S. Eliot（艾略特）	*Tradition and the Individual Talent*（《传统与个人天赋》）
Mikhail Bakhtin（米哈伊尔·巴赫金）	*Epic and Novel*（《史诗与小说》）
William Empson（威廉·燕卜荪）	*Seven Types of Ambiguity*（《含混的七种形态》）
M. H. Abrams（艾布拉姆斯）	*The Mirror and the Lamp*（《镜与灯》）
H. R. Jauss（姚斯）	*Literary History as a Challenge to Literary Theory*（《文学史对文学理论的挑战》）
Susan Sontag（苏姗·桑塔格）	*Against Interpretation*（《反对阐释》）
Edward Said（爱德华·赛义德）	*Orientalism*（《东方学》）

全书除了“导读”，共 15 篇课文，它们围绕每一篇素材构成了本教材的一章。每一章共分 4 节，第一节一般为“导入”(Lead-in)，对本章的文论家和所选素材做一般性的介绍；第二节为“正文”(Text)，即所选素材；第三节为“关键词”(Key Words)，对与本节素材相关的 7~10 个重要概念做一般性的说明；第四节为思考题(Extensive Explorations)，包含了和本节素材直接相关的若干问题。因为本教材主要用于配合在线课程，所以各部分尽量简练、直观，很多问题的拓展探讨，可以在作为“慕课”的“西方文论原典导读”中进一步了解，甚至参与进来。

2. Plato' s *Ion*

2.1 Lead-in

Plato (427 B.C.E.–347 B.C.E.) was an ancient Greek philosopher during the classical period, widely considered as one of the first major figures in the history of ancient Greek and Western philosophy. Along with his master, Socrates (苏格拉底), and his most famous student, Aristotle (亚里士多德), they are generally referred as the Three Heroes of Ancient Greece (古希腊三杰). As the founder of the Platonist school of thought, and establisher of the Academy in Athens, Plato is also constantly cited as one of the founders of Western religion and spirituality.

Plato is believed to be the innovator of the written dialogue and dialectic forms in philosophy. Plato is also considered the founder of Western political philosophy. His most famous contribution is the Theory of Forms (形式) known by pure reason, in which Plato presents a solution to the problem of universals known as Platonism. Unlike the works of nearly all of his contemporaries, Plato's entire body of work is well preserved and is believed to have survived intact for over 2,400 years. Although their popularity has fluctuated over the years, the works of Plato have never been without readers since the time they were written.

As the best-known collection of Plato's works ever in history, *The Dialogues of Plato* (《柏拉图对话录》), which consisted of about 40 pieces of dialogues, discussed a wide range of politics, ethics, philosophy and especially aesthetic topics which would be introduced in this textbook. *The Dialogues of Plato* include famous pieces such as *Ion* (《伊安篇》), *Hippias* (《希庇阿斯篇》), *Protagoras* (《普罗泰戈拉篇》), *Phaedo* (《斐多篇》), *Republic* (《理想国》), *Phaedrus* (《斐德若篇》), *Symposium* (《会饮篇》) and so forth. These dialogues were generally ascribed to Plato, but the speaker in almost all pieces is Socrates. Plato never appeared in the discussions, leaving us a myth of the authentic and exact view of Plato. The "Socratic Humor," also caused troubles in the understanding of the philosophy of Plato. In the dialogues, Socrates would pretend to be a learner or listener of the rival, next he may harshly burlesque the opponent after figuring out the errors and weaknesses in their speech. Though this skill of debating is excellent, it's always a tough mission to outline the exact idea of Socrates or Plato. Some dialogues do not even give a final solution, or bring out contradictive conclusions, making the apprehension even harder.

However, in the overall study of *The Dialogues of Plato*, the aesthetic theory of Plato is quite clear, and *Ion* is one of the most representative pieces. In *Ion*, Socrates discusses with the titular character, a professional rhapsode who also lectures on Homer, the question of whether the rhapsode, a performer of poetry, gives his performance on account of his skill and knowledge or by virtue of divine possession. It is one of the shortest of Plato's dialogues. Ion was a singer of *Homer Epics*, a rhapsode. And his duty is to sing and perform *Homer Epics*. The text of *Ion* is about a discussion between Socrates and Ion on the origin of technics and inspiration of poets. Ion has just won a laurel before the discussion and therefore he considered himself as a great poet. Through discussion, Socrates concluded that Ion's glory was on account of divine grace which is actually inspiration which was explained as nimbus in the universe. Plato also explained inspiration as an out-of-body experience in *Phaedo* when spirit got into heaven it would regain his memories of the past. In a word, *Ion* is still significant and it does suggest the way of talking in Plato's dialogues.

2.2 Text

ION

PERSONS OF THE DIALOGUE: Socrates, Ion.

SOCRATES: Welcome, Ion. Are you from your native city of Ephesus?

ION: No, Socrates; but from Epidaurus, where I attended the festival of Asclepius.

SOCRATES: And do the Epidaurians have contests of rhapsodes at the festival?

ION: O yes; and of all sorts of musical performers.

SOCRATES: And were you one of the competitors—and did you succeed?

ION: I obtained the first prize of all, Socrates.

SOCRATES: Well done; and I hope that you will do the same for us at the Panathenaea.

ION: And I will, please heaven.

SOCRATES: I often envy the profession of a rhapsode, Ion; for you have always to wear fine clothes, and to look as beautiful as you can is a part of your art. Then, again, you are obliged to be continually in the company of many good poets; and especially of Homer, who is the best and most divine of them; and to understand him, and not merely learn his words by rote, is a thing greatly to be envied. And no man can be a rhapsode who does not understand the meaning of the poet. For the rhapsode ought to interpret the mind of the poet to his hearers, but how can he interpret him well unless he knows what he means? All this is greatly to be envied.

ION: Very true, Socrates; interpretation has certainly been the most laborious part of my art; and I believe myself able to speak about Homer better than any man; and that neither Metrodorus of Lampsacus, nor Stesimbrotus of Thasos, nor Glaucon, nor any one else who ever was, had as good ideas about Homer as I have, or as many.

SOCRATES: I am glad to hear you say so, Ion; I see that you will not refuse to acquaint me with them.

ION: Certainly, Socrates; and you really ought to hear how exquisitely I render Homer. I think that the Homeridae should give me a golden crown.

SOCRATES: I shall take an opportunity of hearing your embellishments of him at some other time. But just now I should like to ask you a question: Does your art extend to Hesiod and Archilochus, or to Homer only?

ION: To Homer only; he is in himself quite enough.

SOCRATES: Are there any things about which Homer and Hesiod agree?

ION: Yes; in my opinion there are a good many.

SOCRATES: And can you interpret better what Homer says, or what Hesiod says, about these matters in which they agree?

ION: I can interpret them equally well, Socrates, where they agree.

SOCRATES: But what about matters in which they do not agree?—for example, about divination, of which both Homer and Hesiod have something to say,—

ION: Very true:

SOCRATES: Would you or a good prophet be a better interpreter of what these two poets say about divination, not only when they agree, but when they disagree?

ION: A prophet.

SOCRATES: And if you were a prophet, would you not be able to interpret them when they disagree as well as when they agree?

ION: Clearly.

SOCRATES: But how did you come to have this skill about Homer only, and not about Hesiod or the other poets? Does not Homer speak of the same themes which all other poets handle? Is not war his great argument? And does he not speak of human society and of intercourse of men, good and bad, skilled and unskilled, and of the gods conversing with one another and with mankind, and about what happens in heaven and in the world below, and the generations of gods and heroes? Are not these the themes of which Homer sings?

ION: Very true, Socrates.

SOCRATES: And do not the other poets sing of the same?

ION: Yes, Socrates; but not in the same way as Homer.

SOCRATES: What, in a worse way?

ION: Yes, in a far worse.

SOCRATES: And Homer in a better way?

ION: He is incomparably better.

SOCRATES: And yet surely, my dear friend Ion, in a discussion about arithmetic, where many people are speaking, and one speaks better than the rest, there is somebody who can judge which of them is the good speaker?

ION: Yes.

SOCRATES: And he who judges of the good will be the same as he who judges of the bad speakers?

ION: The same.

SOCRATES: And he will be the arithmetician?

ION: Yes.

SOCRATES: Well, and in discussions about the wholesomeness of food, when many persons are speaking, and one speaks better than the rest, will he who recognizes the better speaker be a different person from him who recognizes the worse, or the same?

ION: Clearly the same.

SOCRATES: And who is he, and what is his name?

ION: The physician.

SOCRATES: And speaking generally, in all discussions in which the subject is the same and many men are speaking, will not he who knows the good know the bad speaker also? For if he does not know the bad, neither will he know the good when the same topic is being discussed.

ION: True.

SOCRATES: Is not the same person skillful in both?

ION: Yes.

SOCRATES: And you say that Homer and the other poets, such as Hesiod and Archilochus, speak of the same things, although not in the same way; but the one speaks well and the other not so well?

ION: Yes; and I am right in saying so.

SOCRATES: And if you knew the good speaker, you would also know the inferior speakers to be inferior?

ION: That is true.

SOCRATES: Then, my dear friend, can I be mistaken in saying that Ion is equally skilled in Homer and in other poets, since he himself acknowledges that the same person will be a good judge of all those who speak of the same things; and that almost all poets do speak of the same things?

ION: Why then, Socrates, do I lose attention and go to sleep and have absolutely no ideas of the least value, when any one speaks of any other poet; but when Homer is mentioned, I wake up at once and am all attention and have plenty to say?

SOCRATES: The reason, my friend, is obvious. No one can fail to see that you speak of Homer without any art or knowledge. If you were able to speak of him by rules of art, you would have been able to speak of all other poets; for poetry is a whole.

ION: Yes.

SOCRATES: And when anyone acquires any other art as a whole, the same may be said of them. Would you like me to explain my meaning, Ion?

ION: Yes, indeed, Socrates; I very much wish that you would: for I love to hear you wise men talk.

SOCRATES: O that we were wise, Ion, and that you could truly call us so; but you rhapsodes and actors, and the poets whose verses you sing, are wise; whereas I am a common man, who only speak the truth. For consider what a very commonplace and trivial thing is this which I have said—a thing which any man might say: that when a man has acquired a knowledge of a whole art, the enquiry into good and bad is one and the same. Let us consider this matter; is not the art of painting a whole?

ION: Yes.

SOCRATES: And there are and have been many painters good and bad?

ION: Yes.

SOCRATES: And did you ever know any one who was skillful in pointing out the excellences and defects of Polygnotus the son of Aglaophon, but incapable of criticizing other painters; and when the work of any other painter was produced, went to sleep and was at a loss, and had no ideas; but when he had to give his opinion about Polygnotus, or whoever the painter might be, and about him only, woke up and was attentive and had plenty to say?

ION: No indeed, I have never known such a person.

SOCRATES: Or did you ever know of any one in sculpture, who was skillful in expounding the merits of Daedalus the son of Metion, or of Epeius the son of Panopeus, or of Theodorus the Samian, or of any individual sculptor; but when the works of sculptors in general were produced, was at a loss and went to sleep and had nothing to say?

ION: No indeed; no more than the other.

SOCRATES: And if I am not mistaken, you never met with any one among flute-players or harp-players or singers to the harp or rhapsodes who was able to discourse of Olympus or Thamyras or Orpheus, or Phemius the rhapsode of Ithaca, but was at a loss when he came to speak of Ion of Ephesus, and had no notion of his merits or defects?

ION: I cannot deny what you say, Socrates. Nevertheless I am conscious in my own self, and the world agrees with me in thinking that I do speak better and have more to say about Homer than any other man. But I do not speak equally well about others—tell me the reason of this.

SOCRATES: I perceive, Ion; and I will proceed to explain to you what I imagine to be the reason of this. The gift which you possess of speaking excellently about Homer is not an art, but, as I was just saying, an inspiration; there is a divinity moving you, like that contained in the stone which Euripides calls a magnet, but which is commonly known as the stone of Heraclea. This stone not only attracts iron rings, but also imparts to them a similar power of attracting other rings; and sometimes you may see a number of pieces of iron and rings suspended from one another so as to form quite a long chain: and all of them derive their power of suspension from the original stone. In like manner the Muse first of all inspires men herself; and from these inspired persons a chain of other persons is suspended, who take the inspiration. For all good poets, epic as well as lyric, compose their beautiful poems not by art, but because they are inspired and possessed. And as the Corybantian revellers when they dance are not in their right mind, so the lyric poets are not in their right mind when they are composing their beautiful strains: but when falling under the power of music and metre they are inspired and possessed; like Bacchic maidens who draw milk and honey from the rivers when they are under the influence of Dionysus but not when they are in their right mind. And the soul of the lyric poet does the same, as they themselves say; for they tell us that they bring songs from honeyed fountains, culling them out of the gardens and dells of the Muses; they, like the bees, winging their way from flower to flower. And this is true. For the poet is a light and winged and holy thing, and there is no invention in him until he has been inspired and is out of his senses, and the mind is no longer in him: when he has not attained to this state, he is powerless and is unable to utter his oracles. Many are the noble words in which poets speak concerning the actions of men; but like yourself when speaking about Homer, they do not speak of them by any rules of art: they are simply inspired to utter that to which the Muse impels them, and that only; and when inspired, one of them will make dithyrambs, another hymns of praise, another choral strains, another epic or iambic verses—and he who is good at one is not good at any other kind of verse: for not by art does the poet sing, but by power divine. Had he learned by rules of art, he would have known how to speak not of one theme only, but of all; and therefore God takes away the minds of poets, and uses them as his ministers, as he also uses diviners and holy prophets, in order that we who hear them may know them to be speaking not of themselves who utter these priceless words in a state of unconsciousness, but that God himself is the speaker, and that through them he is conversing with us. And Tynnichus the Chalcidian affords a striking instance of what I am saying: he wrote nothing that any one would care to remember but the famous paean which is in every one's mouth, one of the finest poems ever written, simply an invention of the Muses, as he himself says. For in this way the God would seem to indicate to us and not allow us to doubt that these beautiful poems are not human, or the work of man, but divine and the work of God; and that the poets are only the interpreters of the Gods by whom they are severally possessed. Was not this the lesson which the God intended to teach when by the mouth of the worst of poets he sang the best of songs? Am I not right, Ion?

ION: Yes, indeed, Socrates, I feel that you are; for your words touch my soul, and I am persuaded that good poets by a divine inspiration interpret the things of the Gods to us.

SOCRATES: And you rhapsodists are the interpreters of the poets?

ION: There again you are right.

SOCRATES: Then you are the interpreters of interpreters?

ION: Precisely.

SOCRATES: I wish you would frankly tell me, Ion, what I am going to ask of you: When you produce the greatest effect upon the audience in the recitation of some striking passage, such as the apparition of Odysseus leaping forth on the floor, recognized by the suitors and casting his arrows at his feet, or the description of Achilles rushing at Hector, or the sorrows of Andromache, Hecuba, or Priam,—are you in your right mind? Are you not carried out of yourself, and does not your soul in an ecstasy seem to be among the persons or places of which you are speaking, whether they are in Ithaca or in Troy or whatever may be the scene of the poem?

ION: That proof strikes home to me, Socrates. For I must frankly confess that at the tale of pity my eyes are filled with tears, and when I speak of horrors, my hair stands on end and my heart throbs.

SOCRATES: Well, Ion, and what are we to say of a man who at a sacrifice or festival, when he is dressed in holiday attire, and has golden crowns upon his head, of which nobody has robbed him, appears weeping or panic-stricken in the presence of more than twenty thousand friendly faces, when there is no one despoiling or wronging him;—is he in his right mind or is he not?

ION: No indeed, Socrates, I must say that, strictly speaking, he is not in his right mind.

SOCRATES: And are you aware that you produce similar effects on most of the spectators?

ION: Only too well; for I look down upon them from the stage, and behold the various emotions of pity, wonder, sternness, stamped upon their countenances when I am speaking: and I am obliged to give my very best attention to them; for if I make them cry I myself shall laugh, and if I make them laugh I myself shall cry when the time of payment arrives.

SOCRATES: Do you know that the spectator is the last of the rings which, as I am saying, receive the power of the original magnet from one another? The rhapsode like yourself and the actor are intermediate links, and the poet himself is the first of them. Through all these the God sways the souls of men in any direction which he pleases, and makes one man hang down from another. Thus there is a vast chain of dancers and masters and under-masters of choruses, who are suspended, as if from the stone, at the side of the rings which hang down from the Muse. And every poet has some Muse from whom he is suspended, and by whom he is said to be possessed, which is nearly the same thing; for he is taken hold of. And from these first rings, which are the poets, depend others, some deriving their inspiration from Orpheus, others from Musaeus; but the greater number are possessed and held by Homer. Of whom, Ion, you are one, and are possessed by Homer; and when any one repeats the words of another poet you go to sleep, and know not what to say; but when any one recites a strain of Homer you wake up in a moment, and your soul leaps within you, and you have plenty to say; for not by art or knowledge about Homer do you say what you say, but by divine inspiration and by possession; just as the Corybantian revellers too have a quick perception of that strain only which is appropriated to the God by whom they are possessed, and have plenty of dances and words for that, but take no heed of any other. And you, Ion, when the name of Homer is mentioned have plenty to say, and have nothing to say of others. You ask, 'Why is this?' The answer is that you praise Homer not by art but by divine inspiration.

ION: That is good, Socrates; and yet I doubt whether you will ever have eloquence enough to persuade me that I praise Homer only when I am mad and possessed; and if you could hear me speak of him I am sure you would never think this to be the case.

SOCRATES: I should like very much to hear you, but not until you have answered a question which I have to ask. On what part of Homer do you speak well?—not surely about every part.
ION: There is no part, Socrates, about which I do not speak well: of that I can assure you.
SOCRATES: Surely not about things in Homer of which you have no knowledge?
ION: And what is there in Homer of which I have no knowledge?
SOCRATES: Why, does not Homer speak in many passages about arts? For example, about driving; if I can only remember the lines I will repeat them.
ION: I remember, and will repeat them.
SOCRATES: Tell me then, what Nestor says to Antilochus, his son, where he bids him be careful of the turn at the horserace in honour of Patroclus.
ION: 'Bend gently,' he says, 'in the polished chariot to the left of them, and urge the horse on the right hand with whip and voice; and slacken the rein. And when you are at the goal, let the left horse draw near, yet so that the nave of the well-wrought wheel may not even seem to touch the extremity; and avoid catching the stone (Il.).'
SOCRATES: Enough. Now, Ion, will the charioteer or the physician be the better judge of the propriety of these lines?
ION: The charioteer, clearly.
SOCRATES: And will the reason be that this is his art, or will there be any other reason?
ION: No, that will be the reason.
SOCRATES: And every art is appointed by God to have knowledge of a certain work; for that which we know by the art of the pilot we do not know by the art of medicine?
ION: Certainly not.
SOCRATES: Nor do we know by the art of the carpenter that which

we know by the art of medicine?

ION: Certainly not.

SOCRATES: And this is true of all the arts;—that which we know with one art we do not know with the other? But let me ask a prior question: You admit that there are differences of arts?

ION: Yes.

SOCRATES: You would argue, as I should, that when one art is of one kind of knowledge and another of another, they are different?

ION: Yes.

SOCRATES: Yes, surely; for if the subject of knowledge were the same, there would be no meaning in saying that the arts were different,—if they both gave the same knowledge. For example, I know that here are five fingers, and you know the same. And if I were to ask whether I and you became acquainted with this fact by the help of the same art of arithmetic, you would acknowledge that we did?

ION: Yes.

SOCRATES: Tell me, then, what I was intending to ask you,—whether this holds universally? Must the same art have the same subject of knowledge, and different arts other subjects of knowledge?

ION: That is my opinion, Socrates.

SOCRATES: Then he who has no knowledge of a particular art will have no right judgment of the sayings and doings of that art?

ION: Very true.

SOCRATES: Then which will be a better judge of the lines which you were reciting from Homer, you or the charioteer?

ION: The charioteer.

SOCRATES: Why, yes, because you are a rhapsode and not a charioteer.

ION: Yes.

SOCRATES: And the art of the rhapsode is different from that of the charioteer?

ION: Yes.

SOCRATES: And if a different knowledge, then a knowledge of different matters?

ION: True.

SOCRATES: You know the passage in which Hecamede, the concubine of Nestor, is described as giving to the wounded Machaon a posset, as he says,

'Made with Pramnian wine; and she grated cheese of goat's milk with a grater of bronze, and at his side placed an onion which gives a relish to drink (Il.).'

Now would you say that the art of the rhapsode or the art of medicine was better able to judge of the propriety of these lines?

ION: The art of medicine.

SOCRATES: And when Homer says,

'And she descended into the deep like a leaden plummet, which, set in the horn of ox that ranges in the fields, rushes along carrying death among the ravenous fishes (Il.),'—

will the art of the fisherman or of the rhapsode be better able to judge whether these lines are rightly expressed or not?

ION: Clearly, Socrates, the art of the fisherman.

SOCRATES: Come now, suppose that you were to say to me: 'Since you, Socrates, are able to assign different passages in Homer to their corresponding arts, I wish that you would tell me what are the passages of which the excellence ought to be judged by the prophet and prophetic art'; and you will see how readily and truly I shall answer you. For there are many such passages, particularly in the Odyssee; as, for example, the passage in which Theoclymenus the prophet of the house of Melampus says to the suitors:—

'Wretched men! What is happening to you? Your heads and your faces and your limbs underneath are shrouded in night; and the voice of lamentation bursts forth, and your cheeks are wet with tears. And the vestibule is full, and the court is full, of ghosts descending into the darkness of Erebus, and the sun has perished out of heaven, and an evil mist is spread abroad (Od.).'

And there are many such passages in the Iliad also; as for example in the description of the battle near the rampart, where he says:—

'As they were eager to pass the ditch, there came to them an omen: a soaring eagle, holding back the people on the left, bore a huge bloody dragon in his talons, still living and panting; nor had he yet resigned the strife, for he bent back and smote the bird which carried him on the breast by the neck, and he in pain let him fall from him to the ground into the midst of the multitude. And the eagle, with a cry, was borne afar on the wings of the wind (Il.).'

These are the sort of things which I should say that the prophet ought to consider and determine.

ION: And you are quite right, Socrates, in saying so.

SOCRATES: Yes, Ion, and you are right also. And as I have selected from the Iliad and Odyssee for you passages which describe the office of the prophet and the physician and the fisherman, do you, who know Homer so much better than I do, Ion, select for me passages which relate to the rhapsode and the rhapsode's art, and which the rhapsode ought to examine and judge of better than other men.

ION: All passages, I should say, Socrates.

SOCRATES: Not all, Ion, surely. Have you already forgotten what you were saying? A rhapsode ought to have a better memory.

ION: Why, what am I forgetting?

SOCRATES: Do you not remember that you declared the art of the rhapsode to be different from the art of the charioteer?

ION: Yes, I remember.

SOCRATES: And you admitted that being different they would have different subjects of knowledge?

ION: Yes.

SOCRATES: Then upon your own showing the rhapsode, and the art of the rhapsode, will not know everything?

ION: I should exclude certain things, Socrates.

SOCRATES: You mean to say that you would exclude pretty much the subjects of the other arts. As he does not know all of them, which of them will he know?

ION: He will know what a man and what a woman ought to say, and what a freeman and what a slave ought to say, and what a ruler and what a subject.

SOCRATES: Do you mean that a rhapsode will know better than the pilot what the ruler of a sea-tossed vessel ought to say?

ION: No; the pilot will know best.

SOCRATES: Or will the rhapsode know better than the physician what the ruler of a sick man ought to say?

ION: He will not.

SOCRATES: But he will know what a slave ought to say?

ION: Yes.

SOCRATES: Suppose the slave to be a cowherd; the rhapsode will know better than the cowherd what he ought to say in order to soothe the infuriated cows?

ION: No, he will not.

SOCRATES: But he will know what a spinning-woman ought to say about the working of wool?

ION: No.

SOCRATES: At any rate he will know what a general ought to say when exhorting his soldiers?

ION: Yes, that is the sort of thing which the rhapsode will be sure to know.

SOCRATES: Well, but is the art of the rhapsode the art of the general?

ION: I am sure that I should know what a general ought to say.

SOCRATES: Why, yes, Ion, because you may possibly have a

knowledge of the art of the general as well as of the rhapsode; and you may also have a knowledge of horsemanship as well as of the lyre: and then you would know when horses were well or ill managed. But suppose I were to ask you: By the help of which art, Ion, do you know whether horses are well managed, by your skill as a horseman or as a performer on the lyre—what would you answer?

ION: I should reply, by my skill as a horseman.

SOCRATES: And if you judged of performers on the lyre, you would admit that you judged of them as a performer on the lyre, and not as a horseman?

ION: Yes.

SOCRATES: And in judging of the general's art, do you judge of it as a general or a rhapsode?

ION: To me there appears to be no difference between them.

SOCRATES: What do you mean? Do you mean to say that the art of the rhapsode and of the general is the same?

ION: Yes, one and the same.

SOCRATES: Then he who is a good rhapsode is also a good general?

ION: Certainly, Socrates.

SOCRATES: And he who is a good general is also a good rhapsode?

ION: No; I do not say that.

SOCRATES: But you do say that he who is a good rhapsode is also a good general.

ION: Certainly.

SOCRATES: And you are the best of Hellenic rhapsodes?

ION: Far the best, Socrates.

SOCRATES: And are you the best general, Ion?

ION: To be sure, Socrates; and Homer was my master.

SOCRATES: But then, Ion, what in the name of goodness can be the reason why you, who are the best of generals as well as the best of rhapsodes in all Hellas, go about as a rhapsode when you might be a general? Do you think that the Hellenes want a rhapsode with his golden crown, and do not want a general?

ION: Why, Socrates, the reason is, that my countrymen, the Ephesians, are the servants and soldiers of Athens, and do not need a general; and you and Sparta are not likely to have me, for you think that you have enough generals of your own.

SOCRATES: My good Ion, did you never hear of Apollodorus of Cyzicus?

ION: Who may he be?

SOCRATES: One who, though a foreigner, has often been chosen their general by the Athenians: and there is Phanosthenes of Andros, and Heraclides of Clazomenae, whom they have also appointed to the command of their armies and to other offices, although aliens, after they had shown their merit. And will they not choose Ion the Ephesian to be their general, and honour him, if he prove himself worthy? Were not the Ephesians originally Athenians, and Ephesus is no mean city? But, indeed, Ion, if you are correct in saying that by art and knowledge you are able to praise Homer, you do not deal fairly with me, and after all your professions of knowing many glorious things about Homer, and promises that you would exhibit them, you are only a deceiver, and so far from exhibiting the art of which you are a master, will not, even after my repeated entreaties, explain to me the nature of it. You have literally as many forms as Proteus; and now you go all manner of ways, twisting and turning, and, like Proteus, become all manner of people at once, and at last slip away from me in the disguise of a general, in order that you may escape exhibiting your Homeric lore. And if you have art, then, as I was saying, in falsifying your promise that you would exhibit Homer, you are not dealing fairly with me. But if, as I believe, you have no art, but speak all these beautiful words about Homer unconsciously under his inspiring influence, then I acquit you of dishonesty, and shall only say that you are inspired. Which do you prefer to be thought, dishonest or inspired?

ION: There is a great difference, Socrates, between the two alternatives; and inspiration is by far the nobler.

SOCRATES: Then, Ion, I shall assume the nobler alternative; and attribute to you in your praises of Homer inspiration, and not art.

2.3 Key Words

① Socrates 苏格拉底

Socrates (469 B.C.E.–399 B.C.E.) was a classical Greek (Athenian) philosopher credited as one of the founders of Western philosophy, and as the first moral philosopher of the Western ethical tradition of thought. Plato's dialogues are among the most comprehensive accounts of Socrates to survive from antiquity, from which Socrates has become renowned for his contributions to the fields of ethics and epistemology. It is this Platonic Socrates who lends his name to the concepts of Socratic irony and the Socratic methods, or elenchus. However, questions remain regarding the distinction between the real-life Socrates and Plato's portrayal of Socrates in his dialogues. Socrates exerted a strong influence on philosophers in later antiquity and in the modern era. Depictions of Socrates in art, literature and popular culture have made him one of the most widely known figures in the Western philosophical tradition.

② Homer Epics 荷马史诗

Homer is the semi-legendary author of *Iliad* (《伊利亚特》) and *Odyssey* (《奥德赛》), two epic poems which are the central works of ancient Greek literature. *Iliad* is set during the Trojan War, the ten-year siege of the city of Troy by a coalition of Greek kingdoms. It focuses on a quarrel between King Agamemnon and the warrior Achilles lasting a few weeks during the last year of the war. *Odyssey* focuses on the ten-year journey home of Odysseus, king of Ithaca, after the fall of

Troy. Many accounts of Homer's life circulated in classical antiquity, the most widespread being that he was a blind bard from Ionia (爱奥尼亚), a region of central coastal Anatolia (安纳托利亚) in present-day Turkey. Modern scholars consider these accounts legendary.

③ Idealism 理想主义；唯心主义，唯心论

In philosophy, idealism is the diverse group of metaphysical philosophy which asserts that "reality" is in some way indistinguishable or inseparable from human understanding and/or perception; that it is in some sense mentally constituted, or otherwise closely connected to ideas. It comes via Latin idea from the ancient Greek idea (ἰδέα) from idein (ἰδεῖν), meaning "to see." Plato's Theory of Forms or "ideas" describes ideal forms (for example the platonic solids in geometry or abstracts like Goodness and Justice), as universals existing independently of any particular instance.

④ Platonism 柏拉图主义

Platonism is the philosophy of Plato and philosophical systems closely derived from it, though contemporary platonists do not necessarily accept all of the doctrines of Plato. Platonism has a profound effect on Western thought. Platonism at least affirms the existence of abstract objects, which are asserted to exist in a third realm distinct from both the sensible external world and from the internal world of consciousness, and is the opposite of Nominalism. This can apply to properties, types, prepositions, meanings, numbers, sets, truth values, and so on. Philosophers who affirm the existence of abstract objects are sometimes called platonists; those who deny their existence are sometimes called nominalists. The terms "Platonism" and "Nominalism" also have established senses in the history of philosophy, where they denote positions that have little to do with the modern notion of an abstract object.

⑤ Euripides 欧里庇得斯（希腊的悲剧诗人）

Euripides (480 B.C.E.–406 B.C.E.) is a tragedian of classical Athens, and one of the three ancient Greek tragedians. [The other two are Aeschylos (埃斯库罗斯) and Sophocles (索福克勒斯), a significant number of whose plays have survived.] 18 or 19 of his plays have survived more or less complete and there are also fragments, some substantial, of most of the other plays. In the Hellenistic Age (希腊化时代), he is regarded as a cornerstone of ancient literary education, along with Homer, Demosthenes (德摩斯梯尼), and Menander (米南德). His most famous work is *Medea*, based upon the myth of Jason and Medea and first produced in 431 B.C.E.

⑥ Classical Greece 古典希腊

Classical Greece is an era that began with the Greco-Persian Wars, lasting from the 5th to 4th centuries B.C.E. The most prosperous and leading Hellenic city states or polis were Athens and Sparta, with Corinth, Thebes, Miletus, Argos and so on that appeared quite often in history. Classical Greek culture, especially philosophy, had a powerful influence on ancient Rome, and for this reason, it is generally considered to be the seminal culture which provided the foundation of modern Western culture and is considered the cradle of Western civilization.

⑦ Rhapsode 吟游诗人

A rhapsode or, in modern usage, rhapsodist, refers to a classical Greek professional performer of epic poetry in the classical Greece. Rhapsodes notably performed the epics of Homer but also the wisdom and catalogue poetry of Hesiod and the satires of Archilochus and others. *Ion*, in which Socrates confronts a star player rhapsode, remains the most coherent source of information on these artists. Often, rhapsodes are depicted in Greek art, wearing their signature cloak and carrying a staff. This equipment is also characteristic of travelers in general, implying that rhapsodes were itinerant performers, moving from town to town.

2.4 Extensive Explorations

① In what way and at what length did classical Greek civilizaiton influence Plato's idealism?

② As a rhapsode, what is the attitude of Ion towards poetry according to the text?

③ Can you pick out any typical examples of Socrates' humor in the dialogue with Ion?

④ How much do you know about Plato's "bed"? Can you discuss about the theoretical idea indicated in *Ion* with reference of the example of bed in Plato's theory?

⑤ Can you give a description about the ecstasy introduced by Socrates in the dialogue? Do you know any typical instance in modern works of literature depicting ecstasy?

⑥ What do you know about the poetic inspiration? Did you feel the infiltration of the inspiration when you create a piece of literary work?

⑦ What do you think about the skills of poetic creation of the discussion between Ion and Socrates? Are the skills similar to those of the craftsmen?

3. Aristotle's *Poetics*

3.1 Lead-in

Aristotle (384 B.C.E.–322 B.C.E.) was a Greek philosopher and scientist born in the Macedonian city of Stagira (斯塔吉拉), Chalkidice, on the northern periphery of classical Greece.

Aristotle was appointed as the head of the royal academy of Macedon (马其顿). During that time he served as tutor to Alexander, who later conquered the Greek world and the whole Persian Empire (波斯帝国). Aristotle encouraged Alexander toward Eastern conquest and his attitude towards Persia was unabashedly ethnocentric. In one famous example, he counsels Alexander to be "a leader to the Greeks and a despot to the barbarians, to look after the former as after friends and relatives, and to deal with the latter as with beasts or plants." By 335 B.C.E., Aristotle had returned to Athens, establishing his own school there known as the Lyceum. Aristotle conducted courses at the school for the next twelve years.

His writings cover many subjects — including physics, biology, zoology, metaphysics, logic, ethics, aesthetics, poetry, theater, music, rhetoric, linguistics, politics and government — and constitute the first comprehensive system of Western philosophy. In this sense, Aristotle was regarded as one of the earliest polymaths (博学家) in the history of human culture. *Poetics* is specifically concerned with drama. At some point, Aristotle's original work was divided into two parts, each "book" written on a separate roll of papyrus. Only the first part which focuses on tragedy and epic survives. The lost second part addressed comedy. Some other scholars indicate that "tragedy" is a very misleading translation for the Greek tragoidos, which seems to have meant "goat-song" originally.

In this textbook, we picked the 1st, 4th and 9th chapter of *Poetics* introducing Aristotle's imitation theory. In the 1st chapter, Aristotle clearly stated that both poetry and play can be grouped as works of imitation. However, Aristotle's imitation theory is apparently different from Plato's. In *Republic* Plato outlined the "bed" theory in 3 layers. First the concrete bed, and a bed is only an authentic bed when it accords with the idea of bed, so Plato said that the real bed is actually not a bed. The idea of bed is the real bed. That is the measure of bed — the truth. Here Plato applied a word "Eidos." A physical bed is merely an imitation of the idea: the second layer. What artists imitated is the 3rd layer, the imitation of the physical bed which makes the 3 layers away from the truth. Though this calculation is doubtable, for in our view there are only 2 layers away. When it comes to Aristotle, he couldn't agree that artists are so distant away from the truth. On the contrary, art is the imitation of ultimate truth. It was a process, which Aristotle systematically and technologically interpreted the idea of imitation in *Poetics*. Another difference between Aristotle and Plato in imitation theory is, the former also believes that there are two origins of art as imitation: One is human's instinct of imitation, and the other is that human naturally adore rhythm and harmony. Therefore, for Aristotle, poetry as imitation is not fraud and to be expelled as was stated in *Republic*. On the contrary, art as imitation is the nearest thing to the truth, one that touches the deepest intuition of the soul of humans.

3.2 Text

The Poetics of Aristotle

(Chapter 1, 4, 6, 9)

I.'Imitation' the Common Principle of the Arts of Poetry

I propose to treat of Poetry in itself and of its various kinds, noting the essential quality of each; to inquire into the structure of the plot as requisite to a good poem; into the number and nature of the parts of which a poem is composed; and similarly into whatever else falls within the same inquiry. Following, then, the order of nature, let us begin with the principles which come first.

Epic poetry and Tragedy, Comedy also and dithyrambic poetry, and the music of the flute and of the lyre in most of their forms, are all in their general conception modes of imitation. They differ, however, from one another in three respects,—the medium, the objects, the manner or mode of imitation, being in each case distinct.

For as there are persons who, by conscious art or mere habit, imitate and represent various objects through the medium of colour and form, or again by the voice; so in the arts above mentioned, taken as a whole, the imitation is produced by rhythm, language, or 'harmony,' either singly or combined.

Thus in the music of the flute and the lyre, 'harmony' and rhythm alone are employed; also in other arts, such as that of the shepherd's pipe, which are essentially similar to these. In dancing, rhythm alone is used without 'harmony'; for even dancing imitates character, emotion, and action, by rhythmical movement. There is another art which imitates by means of language alone, and that either in prose or verse—which, verse, again, may either combine different metres or consist of but one kind—but this has hitherto been without a name.

For there is no common term we could apply to the mimes of Sophron and Xenarchus and the Socratic dialogues on the one hand; and, on the other, to poetic imitations in iambic, elegiac, or any similar metre. People do, indeed, add the word 'maker' or 'poet' to the name of the metre, and speak of elegiac poets, or epic (that is, hexameter) poets, as if it were not the imitation that makes the poet, but the verse that entitles them all indiscriminately to the name. Even when a treatise on medicine or natural science is brought out in verse, the name of poet is by custom given to the author; and yet Homer and Empedocles have nothing in common but the metre, so that it would be right to call the one poet, the other physicist rather than poet. On the same principle, even if a writer in his poetic imitation were to combine all metres, as Chaeremon did in his Centaur, which is a medley composed of metres of all kinds, we should bring him too under the general term poet. So much then for these distinctions.

There are, again, some arts which employ all the means above mentioned,—namely, rhythm, tune, and metre. Such are dithyrambic and nomic poetry, and also Tragedy and Comedy; but between them the difference is, that in the first two cases these means are all employed in combination, in the latter, now one means is employed, now another.

Such, then, are the differences of the arts with respect to the medium of imitation.

IV. The Origin and Development of Poetry

Poetry in general seems to have sprung from two causes, each of them lying deep in our nature. First, the instinct of imitation is implanted in man from childhood, one difference between him and other animals being that he is the most imitative of living creatures; and through imitation he learns his earliest lessons; and no less universal is the pleasure felt in things imitated. We have evidence of this in the facts of experience. Objects which in themselves we view with pain, we delight to contemplate when reproduced with minute fidelity: such as the forms of the most ignoble animals and of dead bodies. The cause of this again is, that to learn gives the liveliest pleasure, not only to philosophers but to men in general; whose capacity, however, of learning is more limited. Thus the reason why men enjoy seeing a likeness is, that in contemplating it they find themselves learning or inferring, and saying perhaps, 'Ah, that is he.' For if you happen not to have seen the original, the pleasure will be due not to the imitation as such, but to the execution, the colouring, or some such other cause.

Imitation, then, is one instinct of our nature. Next, there is the instinct for 'harmony' and rhythm, metres being manifestly sections of rhythm. Persons, therefore, starting with this natural gift developed by degrees their special aptitudes, till their rude improvisations gave birth to Poetry.

Poetry now diverged in two directions, according to the individual character of the writers. The graver spirits imitated noble actions, and the actions of good men. The more trivial sort imitated the actions of meaner persons, at first composing satires, as the former did hymns to the gods and the praises of famous men. A poem of the satirical kind cannot indeed be put down to any author earlier than Homer; though many such writers probably there were. But from Homer onward, instances can be cited,—his own Margites, for example, and other similar compositions. The appropriate metre was also here introduced; hence the measure is still called the iambic or lampooning measure, being that in which people lampooned one another. Thus the older poets were distinguished as writers of heroic or of lampooning verse.

As, in the serious style, Homer is pre-eminent among poets,

standing alone not only in the excellence, but also in the dramatic form of his imitations, so he too first laid down the main lines of Comedy, by dramatizing the ludicrous instead of writing personal satire. His Margites bears the same relation to Comedy that the Iliad and Odyssey do to Tragedy. But when Tragedy and Comedy came to light, the two classes of poets still followed their natural bent: the lampooners became writers of Comedy, and the Epic poets were succeeded by Tragedians, since the drama was a larger and higher form of art.

Whether Tragedy has as yet perfected its proper types or not; and whether it is to be judged in itself, or in relation also to the audience,—this raises another question. Be that as it may, Tragedy—as also Comedy—was at first mere improvisation. The one originated with the leaders of the dithyramb, the other with those of the phallic songs, which are still in use in many of our cities. Tragedy advanced by slow degrees; each new element that showed itself was in turn developed. Having passed through many changes, it found its natural form, and there it stopped.

Aeschylus first introduced a second actor; he diminished the importance of the Chorus, and assigned the leading part to the dialogue. Sophocles raised the number of actors to three, and added scene-painting. It was not till late that the short plot was discarded for one of greater compass, and the grotesque diction of the earlier satyric form for the stately manner of Tragedy. The iambic measure then replaced the trochaic tetrameter, which was originally employed when the poetry was of the satyric order, and had greater affinities with dancing. Once dialogue had come in, Nature herself discovered the appropriate measure. For the iambic is, of all measures, the most colloquial: we see it in the fact that conversational speech runs into iambic form more frequently than into any other kind of verse; rarely into hexameters, and only when we drop the colloquial intonation. The number of 'episodes' or acts was also increased, and the other embellishments added, of which tradition tells. These we need not here discuss; to enter into them in detail would, doubtless, be a large undertaking.

VI. Definition of Tragedy

Of the poetry which imitates in hexameter verse, and of Comedy, we will speak hereafter. Let us now discuss Tragedy, resuming its formal definition, as resulting from what has been already said.

Tragedy, then, is an imitation of an action that is serious, complete, and of a certain magnitude; in language embellished with each kind of artistic ornament, the several kinds being found in separate parts of the play; in the form of action, not of narrative; through pity and fear effecting the proper purgation of these emotions. By 'language embellished,' I mean language into which rhythm, 'harmony,' and song enter. By 'the several kinds in separate parts,' I mean, that some parts are rendered through the medium of verse alone, others again with the aid of song.

Now as tragic imitation implies persons acting, it necessarily follows, in the first place, that Scenic equipment will be a part of Tragedy. Next, Song and Diction, for these are the medium of imitation. By 'Diction' I mean the mere metrical arrangement of the words: as for 'Song,' it is a term whose sense every one understands.

Again, Tragedy is the imitation of an action; and an action implies personal agents, who necessarily possess certain distinctive qualities both of character and thought. It is these that determine the qualities of actions themselves; these—thought and character—are the two natural causes from which actions spring: on these causes, again, all success or failure depends. Hence, the Plot is the imitation of the action:—for by plot I here mean the arrangement of the incidents. By Character I mean that in virtue of which we ascribe certain qualities to the agents. Thought is required wherever a statement is proved, or, it may be, a general truth enunciated. Every Tragedy, therefore, must have six parts, which parts determine its quality—namely, Plot, Character, Diction, Thought, Scenery, Song. Two of the parts constitute the medium of imitation, one the manner, and three the objects of imitation. And these complete the list. These elements have been employed, we may say, by the poets to a man; in fact, every play contains Scenic accessories as well as Character, Plot, Diction, Song, and Thought.

IX. (Plot continued.) Dramatic Unity

It is, moreover, evident from what has been said, that it is not the function of the poet to relate what has happened, but what may happen,—what is possible according to the law of probability or necessity. The poet and the historian differ not by writing in verse or in prose. The work of Herodotus might be put into verse, and it would still be a species of history, with metre no less than without it. The true difference is that one relates what has happened, the other what may happen. Poetry, therefore, is a more philosophical and a higher thing than history: for poetry tends to express the universal, history the particular. By the universal, I mean how a person of given character will on occasion speak or act, according to the law of probability or necessity; and it is this universality at which poetry aims in the names she attaches to the personages. The particular is—for example—what Alcibiades did or suffered. In Comedy this is already apparent: for here the poet first constructs the plot on the lines of probability, and then inserts characteristic names;—unlike the lampooners who write about particular individuals. But tragedians still keep to real names, the reason being that what is possible is credible: what has not happened we do not at once feel sure to be possible: but what has happened is manifestly possible; otherwise it would not have happened. Still there are some tragedies in which there are only one or two well-known names, the rest being fictitious. In others, none are well known, —as in Agathon's Flower, where incidents and names alike are fictitious, and yet they give none the less pleasure. We must not, therefore, at all costs keep to the received legends, which are the usual subjects of Tragedy. Indeed, it would be absurd to attempt it; for even familiar subjects are familiar only to a few, and yet give pleasure to all. It clearly follows that the poet or 'maker' should be the maker of plots rather than of verses; since he is a poet because he imitates, and what he imitates are actions. And even if he chances to take an historical subject, he is none the less a poet; for there is no reason why some events that have actually happened should not conform to the law of the probable and possible, and in virtue of that quality in them he is their poet or maker.

Of all plots and actions the epeisodic are the worst. I call a plot 'epeisodic' in which the episodes or acts succeed one another without probable or necessary sequence. Bad poets compose such pieces by their own fault, good poets, to please the players; for, as they write show pieces for competition, they stretch the plot beyond its capacity, and are often forced to break the natural continuity.

But again, Tragedy is an imitation not only of a complete action, but of events terrible and pitiful. Such an effect is best produced when the events come on us by surprise; and the effect is heightened when, at the same time, they follow from one another. The tragic wonder will then be greater than if they happened of themselves or by accident; for even coincidences are most striking when they have an air of design. We may instance the statue of Mitys at Argos, which fell upon his murderer while he was a spectator at a festival, and killed him. Such events seem not to be due to mere chance. Plots, therefore, constructed on these principles are necessarily the best.

3.3 Key Words

① Dithyramb 酒神赞美歌

The dithyramb was an ancient Greek hymn sung and danced in honour of Dionysus (迪奥尼索斯), the god of wine and fertility; the term was also used as an epithet of the god: Plato, in *The Laws*, while discussing various kinds of music mentions "the birth of Dionysus, called, I think, the dithyramb." Plato also remarks in *Republic* that dithyrambs are the clearest example of poetry in which the poet is the only speaker.

② (Platonic) Academy (柏拉图) 阿卡德米

The Academy was founded by Plato in c. 387 B.C.E. in Athens. Aristotle studied there for twenty years (367 B.C.E.–347 B.C.E.) before founding his own school, the Lyceum. The Academy persisted throughout the Hellenistic period as a skeptical school, until coming to an end after the death of Philo of Larissa (拉里萨) in 83 B.C.E. The Platonic Academy was destroyed by the Roman dictator Sulla (苏拉) in 86 B.C.E.

③ Lyceum 兰西姆 (古希腊地名)

The Lyceum or Lycaeum was a temple dedicated to Apollo Lyceus ("Apollo the wolf-god"). It was best known for the Peripatetic school of philosophy founded there by Aristotle in 334 B.C.E. Aristotle fled Athens in 323 B.C.E., but the school continued to function under a series of leaders until the Roman general Sulla destroyed it during his assault on Athens in 86 B.C.E. The remains of the Lyceum were discovered in modern Athens in 1996 in a park behind the Hellenic Parliament.

④ Imitation 模仿

Imitation is an advanced behavior whereby an individual observes and replicates another's behavior. In Plato and Aristotle's theoretical system, it always refers to the act of literary creation.

⑤ Chaeremon's *Centaur* 开瑞蒙的《人马》

A centaur, or occasionally hippocentaur, is a creature from Greek mythology with the upper body of a human and the lower body and legs of a horse. Centaurs are thought of in many Greek myths as being as wild as untamed horses, and were said to have inhabited the region of Magnesia and Mount Pelion in Thessaly (塞萨利), the Foloi oak forest in Elis, and the Malean peninsula in southern Laconia. Centaurs are subsequently featured in Roman mythology, and were familiar figures in the medieval bestiary. They remain a staple of modern fantastic literature. Chaeremon was an Athenian dramatist of the first half of the 4th century B.C.E. Aristotle said his works were intended for reading, not for representation. His *Centaur* (or *Centaurus*) is described by Aristotle as a rhapsody in all kinds of metres.

⑥ Agathon's *Antheus* 阿伽通的《花》

Antheus or *Anthos* (*Flower*) is a play by the 5th century B.C.E. Athenian dramatist Agathon. The play has been lost. The play is mentioned by Aristotle in his *Poetics* as an example of a tragedy with a plot which gives pleasure despite the incidents and characters being entirely made up. *Anthos* is the only known Greek tragedy play whose plot was entirely invented by the poet. Other 5th-century tragedies were based on myth, or less frequently on actual history.

3.4 Extensive Explorations

① How much do you know about Aristotle's *Poetics*?

② What's the difference between Plato and Aristotle in metaphysical theory?

③ Can you outline the relationship between Aristotle's metaphysics and his poetics?

④ What's the difference between Plato and Aristotle's imitation theory?

⑤ Give a talk on poetry and philosophy.

⑥ Give examples on classic comedies and tragedies you know.

⑦ What do you think about the "Spirit of Dionysus" mentioned by Nietzsche (尼采) and Aristotle's discussion on tragedy?

4. Samuel Johnson's *Preface to The Plays of William Shakespeare*

4.1 Lead-in

Samuel Johnson (1709–1784), often referred to as Dr. Johnson, was an English writer who made lasting contributions to English literature as a poet, playwright, essayist, moralist, literary critic, biographer, editor, and lexicographer. Religiously, he was a devout Anglican (英格兰教会教徒), and politically a committed Tory (托利党员). *Oxford Dictionary of National Biography* describes Johnson as "arguably the most distinguished man of letters in English history," and he was also described by Walter Jackson Bate as "the most famous single work of biographical art in the whole of literature." Johnson was a tall and robust man. His odd gestures and tics were disconcerting to some on first meeting him. He died in 1784, and was buried in Westminster Abbey (威斯敏斯特教堂).

Johnson was born in a family of book seller in Lichfield, Staffordshire. He attended Pembroke College, Oxford, for just over a year, but a lack of funds forced him to leave. After working as a teacher, he moved to London, where he began to write for *The Gentleman's Magazine*. After nine years of work, Johnson's *A Dictionary of the English Language* was published in 1755. It had a far-reaching effect on modern English and has been acclaimed as "one of the greatest single achievements of scholarship." This work brought Johnson popularity and success. Until the completion of *Oxford English Dictionary* 150 years later, Johnson's was the pre-eminent British dictionary. His later works included essays, an influential annotated edition of *The Plays of William Shakespeare*, and the widely read tale *The History of Rasselas, Prince of Abissinia* (阿比西尼亚). Towards the end of his life, he produced the massive and influential *Lives of the Most Eminent English Poets*, a collection of biographies and evaluations of 17th-and-18th-century poets.

The Plays of William Shakespeare was an 18th-century edition of the dramatic works of William Shakespeare, edited by Samuel Johnson and George Steevens. Johnson announced his intention to edit Shakespeare's plays in his *Miscellaneous Observations on The Tragedy of Macbeth* (1745), and a full proposal for the edition was published in 1756. The edition was finally published in 1765.

As we know, Samuel Johnson's era was when English Philosophy came on a rise. David Hume (大卫·休谟), Edmund Burke (埃德蒙·伯克) displayed their influence on Samuel Johnson. Besides, living at the end of the age of classicism criticism, Johnson persisted the tradition of classicism criticism, meanwhile he was open-minded. His criticism on Shakespearean drama seemed quite different from classicism criticism. Today, we consider him as the master of neoclassicism (新古典主义) on account of his great difference from classicism and Romanticism. Johnson's preface showed his great difference from Voltaire (伏尔泰) and Dryden (德莱顿), which is one of the reasons why he was criticized by his contemporaries. Besides, he wasn't that persistent on his theory. For example, he shared both high admiration and cruel criticism for Shakespeare. First, Johnson's comment on Shakespeare, *The Plays of William Shakespeare* is unique. As was commented by Johnson, Shakespeare is above all writers, at least above all modern writers. His characters are not modified by the customs of particular places unpracticed by the rest of the world, by the peculiarities of studies or professions which can operate but upon small numbers or by the accidents of transient fashions or temporary opinions. Such comments given by Johnson show the complexity of his criticism. The reason why he acclaimed so highly of Shakespeare is that Shakespeare depicted a universal humanity rather than certain specific special occasional humanity. This universal humanity suggests a criticism method of classicism. He praised Shakespeare on shaping characters and setting rules on types. But on the contrary, the plays repress personal character as well. Typification in criticism rejects personalities and particularities as well. Apart from this, though Johnson gave the highest remark on Shakespeare, he never spoke unclear of Shakespeare's drawbacks. Now we can see that in the preface, Johnson justifies trying to determine the original language of the Shakespearean plays. To benefit the reading audience, he added explanatory notes to various passages. Later editors followed Johnson's lead and sought to determine an authoritative text of Shakespeare.

The 2 excerpts were believed to be the best piece of critics on Shakespeare in the 18th century. The major features of the styles of Johnson's criticism are both typical in the 2 excerpts, one is about the excellency of Shakespeare, and the other about Shakespeare's faults.

4.2 Text

Preface to The Plays of William Shakespeare

(Abridged)

[*Shakespeare's Excellence, General Nature*]

That praises are without reason lavished on the dead, and that the honours due only to excellence are paid to antiquity, is a complaint likely to be always continued by those who, being able to add nothing to truth, hope for eminence from the heresies of paradox; or those who, being forced by disappointment upon consolatory expedients, are willing to hope from posterity what the present age refuses, and flatter themselves that the regard which is yet denied by envy, will be at last bestowed by time.

Antiquity, like every other quality that attracts the notice of mankind, has undoubtedly votaries that reverence it, not from reason, but from prejudice. Some seem to admire indiscriminately whatever has been long preserved, without considering that time has sometimes cooperated with chance; all perhaps are more willing to honour past than present excellence; and the mind contemplates genius through the shades of age, as the eye surveys the sun through artificial opacity. The great contention of criticism is to find the faults of the moderns, and the beauties of the ancients. While an author is yet living we estimate his powers by his worst performance, and when he is dead we rate them by his best.

To works, however, of which the excellence is not absolute and definite, but gradual and comparative; to works not raised upon principles demonstrative and scientific, but appealing wholly to observation and experience, no other test can be applied than length of duration and continuance of esteem. What mankind have long possessed they have often examined and compared, and if they persist to value the possession, it is because frequent comparisons have confirmed opinion in its favour. As among the works of nature no man can properly call a river deep or a mountain high, without the knowledge of many mountains and many rivers; so in the productions of genius, nothing can be styled excellent till it has been compared with other works of the same kind. Demonstration immediately displays its power, and has nothing to hope or fear from the flux of years; but works tentative and experimental must be estimated by their proportion to the general and collective ability of man, as it is discovered in a long succession of endeavours. Of the first building that was raised, it might be with certainty determined that it was round or square, but whether it was spacious or lofty must have been referred to time. The Pythagorean scale of numbers was at once discovered to be perfect; but the poems of Homer we yet know not to transcend the common limits of human intelligence, but by remarking, that nation after nation, and century after century, has been able to do little more than transpose his incidents, new name his characters, and paraphrase his sentiments.

The reverence due to writings that have long subsisted arises therefore not from any credulous confidence in the superior wisdom of past ages, or gloomy persuasion of the degeneracy of mankind, but is the consequence of acknowledged and indubitable positions, that what has been longest known has been most considered, and what is most considered is best understood.

The poet, of whose works I have undertaken the revision, may now begin to assume the dignity of an ancient, and claim the privilege of established fame and prescriptive veneration. He has long outlived his century, the term commonly fixed as the test of literary merit. Whatever advantages he might once derive from personal allusions, local customs, or temporary opinions, have for many years been lost; and every topic of merriment or motive of sorrow, which the modes of artificial life afforded him, now only obscure the scenes which they once illuminated. The effects of favour and competition are at an end; the tradition of his friendships and his enmities has perished; his works support no opinion with arguments, nor supply any faction with invectives; they can neither indulge vanity nor gratify malignity, but are read without any other reason than the desire of pleasure, and are therefore praised only as pleasure is obtained; yet, thus unassisted by interest or passion, they have past through variations of taste and changes of manners, and, as they devolved from one generation to another, have received new honours at every transmission.

But because human judgment, though it be gradually gaining upon certainty, never becomes infallible; and approbation, though long continued, may yet be only the approbation of prejudice or fashion; it is proper to inquire by what peculiarities of excellence Shakespeare has gained and kept the favour of his countrymen.

Nothing can please many, and please long, but just representations of general nature. Particular manners can be known to few, and therefore few only can judge how nearly they are copied. The irregular combinations of fanciful invention may delight awhile, by that novelty of which the common satiety of life sends us all in quest; but the pleasures of sudden wonder are soon exhausted, and the mind can only repose on the stability of truth.

Shakespeare is above all writers, at least above all modern writers, the poet of nature; the poet that holds up to his readers a faithful mirror of manners and of life. His characters are not modified by the customs of particular places, unpractised by the rest of the world; by the peculiarities of studies or professions, which can operate but upon small numbers; or by the accidents of transient fashions or temporary opinions: they are the genuine progeny of common humanity, such as the world will always supply and observation will always find. His persons act and speak by the influence of those general passions and principles by which all minds are agitated, and the whole system of life is continued in motion. In the writings of other poets a character is too often an individual; in those of Shakespeare it is commonly a species.

It is from this wide extension of design that so much instruction is derived. It is this which fills the plays of Shakespeare with practical axioms and domestic wisdom. It was said of Euripides, that every verse was a precept; and it may be said of Shakespeare, that from his works may be collected a system of civil and economical prudence. Yet his real power is not shown in the splendour of particular passages, but by the progress of his fable, and the tenor of his dialogue; and he that tries to recommend him by select quotations, will succeed like the pedant in Hierocles, who, when he offered his house to sale, carried a brick in his pocket as a specimen.

It will not easily be imagined how much Shakespeare excels in accommodating his sentiments to real life, but by comparing him with other authors. It was observed of the ancient schools of declamation, that the more diligently they were frequented, the more was the student disqualified for the world, because he found nothing there which he should ever meet in any other place. The same remark may be applied to every stage but that of Shakespeare. The theatre, when it is under any other direction, is peopled by such characters as were never seen, conversing in a language which was never heard, upon topics which will never arise in the commerce of mankind. But the dialogue of this author is often so evidently determined by the incident which produces it, and is pursued with so much ease and simplicity, that it seems scarcely to claim the merit of fiction, but to have been gleaned by diligent selection out of common conversation, and common occurrences.

Upon every other stage the universal agent is love, by whose power all good and evil is distributed, and every action quickened or retarded. To bring a lover, a lady, and a rival into the fable; to entangle them in contradictory obligations, perplex them with oppositions of interest, and harass them with violence of desires inconsistent with each other; to make them meet in rapture and part in agony; to fill their mouths with hyperbolical joy and outrageous sorrow; to distress them as nothing human ever was distressed; to deliver them as nothing human ever was delivered, is the business of a modern dramatist. For this probability is violated, life is misrepresented, and language is depraved. But love is only one of many passions, and as it has no great influence upon the sum of life, it has little operation in the dramas of a poet, who caught his ideas from the living world, and exhibited only what he saw before him. He knew that any other passion, as it was regular or exorbitant, was a cause of happiness or calamity.

Characters thus ample and general were not easily discriminated and preserved, yet perhaps no poet ever kept his personages more distinct from each other. I will not say with Pope, that every speech may be assigned to the proper speaker, because many speeches there are which have nothing characteristical; but, perhaps, though some may be equally adapted to every person, it will be difficult to find any that can be properly transferred from the present possessor to another claimant. The choice is right, when there is reason for choice.

Other dramatists can only gain attention by hyperbolical or aggravated characters, by fabulous and unexampled excellence or depravity, as the writers of barbarous romances invigorated the reader by a giant and a dwarf; and he that should form his expectations of human affairs from the play or from the tale, would be equally deceived. Shakespeare has no heroes; his scenes are occupied only by men, who act and speak as the reader thinks that he should himself have spoken or acted on the same occasion. Even where the agency is supernatural the dialogue is level with life. Other writers disguise the most natural passions and most frequent incidents; so that he who contemplates them in the book will not know them in the world: Shakespeare approximates the remote, and familiarizes the wonderful; the event which he represents will not happen, but if it were possible, its effects would be probably such as he has assigned; and it may be said, that he has not only shown human nature as it acts in real exigencies, but as it would be found in trials to which it cannot be exposed.

This therefore is the praise of Shakespeare, that his drama is the mirror of life; that he who has mazed his imagination, in following the phantoms which other writers raise up before him, may here be cured of his delirious ecstasies, by reading human sentiments in human language; by scenes from which a hermit may estimate the transactions of the world, and a confessor predict the progress of the passions.

[*Shakespeare's Faults, the Three Dramatic Unities*]

Shakespeare with his excellencies has likewise faults, and faults sufficient to obscure and overwhelm any other merit. I shall show them in the proportion in which they appear to me, without envious malignity or superstitious veneration. No question can be more innocently discussed than a dead poet's pretensions to renown; and little regard is due to that bigotry which sets candour higher than truth.

His first defect is that to which may be imputed most of the evil in books or in men. He sacrifices virtue to convenience, and is so much more careful to please than to instruct, that he seems to write without any moral purpose. From his writings indeed a system of social duty may be selected, for he that thinks reasonably must think morally; but his precepts and axioms drop casually from him; he makes no just distribution of good or evil, nor is always careful to show in the virtuous a disapprobation of the wicked; he carries his persons indifferently through right and wrong, and at the close dismisses them without further care, and leaves their examples to operate by chance. This fault the barbarity of his age cannot extenuate; for it is always a writer's duty to make the world better, and justice is a virtue independent on time or place.

The plots are often so loosely formed, that a very slight consideration may improve them, and so carelessly pursued, that he seems not always fully to comprehend his own design. He omits opportunities of instructing or delighting which the train of his story seems to force upon him, and apparently rejects those exhibitions which would be more affecting, for the sake of those which are more easy.

It may be observed, that in many of his plays the latter part is evidently neglected. When he found himself near the end of his work, and, in view of his reward, he shortened the labour to snatch the profit. He therefore remits his efforts where he should most vigorously exert them, and his catastrophe is improbably produced or imperfectly represented.

He had no regard to distinction of time or place, but gives to one age or nation, without scruple, the customs, institutions, and opinions of another, at the expense not only of likelihood, but of possibility. These faults Pope has endeavoured, with more zeal than judgment, to transfer to his imagined interpolators. We need not wonder to find Hector quoting Aristotle, when we see the loves of Theseus and Hippolyta combined with the Gothic mythology of fairies. Shakespeare, indeed, was not the only violator of chronology, for in the same age Sidney, who wanted not the advantages of learning, has, in his *Arcadia*, confounded the pastoral with the feudal times, the days of innocence, quiet, and security, with those of turbulence, violence, and adventure.

In his comic scenes he is seldom very successful when he engages his characters in reciprocations of smartness and contest of sarcasm; their jests are commonly gross, and their pleasantry licentious; neither his gentlemen nor his ladies have much delicacy, nor are sufficiently distinguished from his clowns by any appearance of refined manners. Whether he represented the real conversation of his time is not easy to determine; the reign of Elizabeth is commonly supposed to have been a time of stateliness, formality, and reserve, yet perhaps the relaxations of that severity were not very elegant. There must, however, have been always some modes of gaiety preferable to others, and a writer ought to choose the best.

In tragedy his performance seems constantly to be worse as his labour is more. The effusions of passion which exigency forces out are for the most part striking and energetic; but whenever he solicits his invention, or strains his faculties, the offspring of his throes is tumour, meanness, tediousness, and obscurity.

In narration he affects a disproportionate pomp of diction and a wearisome train of circumlocution, and tells the incident imperfectly in many words, which might have been more plainly delivered in few. Narration in dramatic poetry is, naturally tedious, as it is unanimated and inactive, and obstructs the progress of the action; it should therefore always be rapid, and enlivened by frequent interruption. Shakespeare found it an encumbrance, and instead of lightening it by brevity, endeavoured to recommend it by dignity and splendour.

His declamations or set speeches are commonly cold and weak, for his power was the power of nature; when he endeavoured, like other tragic writers, to catch opportunities of amplification, and instead of inquiring what the occasion demanded, to show how much his stores of knowledge could supply, he seldom escapes without the pity or resentment of his leader.

It is incident to him to be now and then entangled with an unwieldy sentiment, which he cannot well express, and will not reject; he struggles with it awhile, and if it continues stubborn, comprises it in words such as occur, and leaves it to be disentangled and evolved by those who have more leisure to bestow upon it.

Not that always where the language is intricate the thought is subtle, or the image always great where the line is bulky; the equality of words to things is very often neglected, and trivial sentiments and vulgar ideas disappoint the attention to which they are recommended by sonorous epithets and swelling figures.

But the admirers of this great poet have more reason to complain when he approaches nearest to his highest excellence and seems fully resolved to sink them in dejection, and mollify them with tender emotions by the fall of greatness, the danger of innocence, or the crosses of love. What he does best, he soon ceases to do. He is not long soft and pathetic without some idle conceit, or contemptible equivocation. He no sooner begins to move, than he counteracts himself; and terror and pity, as they are rising in the mind, are checked and blasted by sudden frigidity.

A quibble is to Shakespeare, what luminous vapours are to the traveler; he follows it at all adventures, it is sure to lead him out of his way, and sure to engulf him in the mire. It has some malignant power over his mind, and its fascinations are irresistible. Whatever be the dignity or profundity of his disquisition, whether he be enlarging knowledge or exalting affection, whether he be amusing attention with incidents, or enchaining it in suspense, let but a quibble spring up before him, and he leaves his work unfinished. A quibble is the golden apple for which he will always turn aside from his career, or stoop from his elevation. A quibble, poor and barren as it is, gave him such delight, that he was content to purchase it, by the sacrifice of reason, propriety, and truth. A quibble was to him the fatal Cleopatra for which he lost the world, and was content to lose it.

It will be thought strange that, in enumerating the defects of this writer, I have not yet mentioned his neglect of the unities; his violation of those laws which have been instituted and established by the joint authority of poets and of critics.

For his other deviations from the art of writing, I resign him to critical justice, without making any other demand in his favour, than that which must be indulged to all human excellence; that his virtues be rated with his failings: But, from the censure which this irregularity may bring upon him, I shall, with due reverence to that learning which I must oppose, adventure to try how I can defend him.

His histories, being neither tragedies nor comedies, are not subject to any of their laws; nothing more is necessary to all the praise which they expect, than that the changes of action be so prepared as to be understood, that the incidents be various and affecting, and the characters consistent, natural, and distinct. No other unity is intended, and therefore none is to be sought.

In his other works he has well enough preserved the unity of action. He has not, indeed, an intrigue regularly perplexed and regularly unravelled; he does not endeavour to hide his design only to discover it, for this is seldom the order of real events, and Shakespeare is the poet of nature. But his plan has commonly what Aristotle requires, a beginning, a middle, and an end; one event is concatenated with another, and the conclusion follows by easy consequence. There are perhaps some incidents that might be spared, as in other poets there is much talk that only fills up time upon the stage; but the general system makes gradual advances, and the end of the play is the end of expectation.

To the unities of time and place he has shown no regard, and perhaps a nearer view of the principles on which they stand will diminish their value, and withdraw from them the veneration which, from the time of Corneille, they have very generally received by discovering that they have given more trouble to the poet, than pleasure to the auditor.

The necessity of observing the unities of time and place arises from the supposed necessity of making the drama credible. The critics hold it impossible, that an action of months or years can be possibly believed to pass in three hours; or that the spectator can suppose himself to sit in the theatre, while ambassadors go and return between distant kings, while armies are levied and towns besieged, while an exile wanders and returns, or till he whom they saw courting his mistress, shall lament the untimely fall of his son. The mind revolts from evident falsehood, and fiction loses its force when it departs from the resemblance of reality.

From the narrow limitation of time necessarily arises the contraction of place. The spectator, who knows that he saw the first act at Alexandria, cannot suppose that he sees the next at Rome, at a distance to which not the dragons of Medea could, in so short a time, have transported him; he knows with certainty that he has not changed his place; and he knows that place cannot change itself; that what was a house cannot become a plain; that what was Thebes can never be Persepolis.

Such is the triumphant language with which a critic exults over the misery of an irregular poet, and exults commonly without resistance or reply. It is time therefore to tell him, by the authority of Shakespeare, that he assumes, as an unquestionable principle, a position which, while his breath is forming it into words, his understanding pronounces to be false. It is false, that any representation is mistaken for reality; that any dramatic fable in its materiality was ever credible, or, for a single moment, was ever credited.

The objection arising from the impossibility of passing the first hour at Alexandria, and the next at Rome, supposes, that when the play opens the spectator really imagines himself at Alexandria, and believes that his walk to the theatre has been a voyage to Egypt, and that he lives in the days of Antony and Cleopatra. Surely he that imagines this, may imagine more. He that can take the stage at one time for the palace of the Ptolemies, may take it in half an hour for the promontory of Actium. Delusion, if delusion be admitted, has no certain limitation; if the spectator can be once persuaded that his old acquaintance are Alexander and Caesar, that a room illuminated with candles is the plain of Pharsalia or the bank of Granicus, he is in a state of elevation above the reach of reason, or of truth, and from the heights of empyrean poetry, may despise the circumscriptions of terrestrial nature. There is no reason why a mind thus wandering in ecstasy should count the clock, or why an hour should not be a century in that calenture of the brains that can make the stage a field.

The truth is, that the spectators are always in their senses, and know, from the first act to the last, that the stage is only a stage, and that the players are only players. They come to hear a certain number of lines recited with just gesture and elegant modulation. The lines relate to some action, and an action must be in some place; but the different actions that complete a story may be in places very remote from each other; and where is the absurdity of allowing that space to represent first Athens, and then Sicily, which was always known to be neither Sicily nor Athens, but a modern theatre?

By supposition, as place is introduced, time may be extended; the time required by the fable elapses for the most part between the acts; for, of so much of the action as is represented, the real and poetical duration is the same. If, in the first act, preparations for war against Mithridates are represented to be made in Rome, the event of the war may, without absurdity, be represented, in the catastrophe, as happening in Pontus; we know that there is neither war, nor preparation for war; we know that we are neither in Rome nor Pontus; that neither Mithridates nor Lucullus are before us. The drama exhibits successive imitations of successive actions, and why may not the second imitation represent an action that happened years after the first; if it be so connected with it, that nothing but time can be supposed to intervene? Time is, of all modes of existence, most obsequious to the imagination; a lapse of years is as easily conceived as a passage of hours. In contemplation we easily contract the time of real actions, and therefore willingly permit it to be contracted when we only see their imitation.

It will be asked, how the drama moves, if it is not credited. It is credited with all the credit due to a drama. It is credited, whenever it moves, as a just picture of a real original; as representing to the auditor what he would himself feel, if he were to do or suffer what is there feigned to be suffered or to be done. The reflection that strikes the heart is not that the evils before us are real evils, but that they are evils to which we ourselves may be exposed. If there be any fallacy, it is not that we fancy the players, but that we fancy ourselves unhappy for a moment; but we rather lament the possibility than suppose the presence of misery, as a mother weeps over her babe, when she remembers that death may take it from her. The delight of tragedy proceeds from our consciousness of fiction; if we thought murders and treasons real, they would please no more.

Imitations produce pain or pleasure, not because they are mistaken for realities, but because they bring realities to mind. When the imagination is recreated by a painted landscape, the trees are not supposed capable to give us shade, or the fountains coolness; but we consider, how we should be pleased with such fountains playing beside us, and such woods waving over us. We are agitated in reading the history of *Henry the Fifth*, yet no man takes his book for the field of Agincourt. A dramatic exhibition is a book recited with concomitants that increase or diminish its effect. Familiar comedy is often more powerful on the theatre, than in the page; imperial tragedy is always less. The humour of Petruchio may be heightened by grimace; but what voice or what gesture can hope to add dignity or force to the soliloquy of Cato.

A play read affects the mind like a play acted. It is therefore evident that the action is not supposed to be real, and it follows that between the acts a longer or shorter time may be allowed to pass, and that no more account of space or duration is to be taken by the auditor of a drama, than by the reader of a narrative, before whom may pass in an hour the life of a hero, or the revolutions of an empire.

Whether Shakespeare knew the unities, and rejected them by design, or deviated from them by happy ignorance, it is, I think, impossible to decide, and useless to inquire. We may reasonably suppose that, when he rose to notice, he did not want the counsels and admonitions of scholars and critics, and that he at last deliberately persisted in a practice which he might have begun by chance. As nothing is essential to the fable but unity of action, and as the unities of time and place arise evidently from false assumptions, and, by circumscribing the extent of the drama, lessen its variety, I cannot think it much to be lamented that they were not known by him, or not observed. Nor, if such another poet could arise, should I very vehemently reproach him, that his first act passed at Venice, and his next in Cyprus. Such violations of rules merely positive become the comprehensive genius of Shakespeare, and such censures are suitable to the minute and slender criticism of Voltaire:

Non usque adeo permiscuit imis
Longus summa dies, ut non, si voce Metelli
Serventur leges, malint a Caesare tolli.

Lucan, *Pharsalia*, III. 138–140

Nor time, nor chance breed such confusions yet,
Nor are the mean so rais'd, nor sunk the great;
But laws themselves would rather chuse to be
Suppress'd by Caesar, than preserved by thee.

transl. Nicholas Rowe

Yet when I speak thus slightly of dramatic rules, I cannot but recollect how much wit and learning may be produced against me; before such authorities I am afraid to stand, not that I think the present question one of those that are to be decided by mere authority, but because it is to be suspected that these precepts have not been so easily received but for better reasons than I have yet been able to find. The result of my enquiries, in which it would be ludicrous to boast of impartiality, is, that the unities of time and place are not essential to a just drama, that though they may sometimes conduce to pleasure, they are always to be sacrificed to the nobler beauties of variety and instruction; and that a play, written with nice observation of critical rules, is to be contemplated as an elaborate curiosity, as the product of superfluous and ostentatious art, by which is shown rather what is possible, than what is necessary.

He that, without diminution of any other excellence, shall preserve all the unities unbroken, deserves the like applause with the architect, who shall display all the orders of architecture in a citadel, without any deduction from its strength; but the principal beauty of a citadel is to exclude the enemy; and the greatest graces of a play, are to copy nature and instruct life.

4.3 Key Words

① William Shakespeare 威廉·莎士比亚

William Shakespeare (1564–1616) was an English poet, playwright, and actor, widely regarded as the greatest writer in the English language and the world's greatest dramatist. He is often called England's national poet and the "Bard of Avon." His extant works, including collaborations, consist of some 39 plays, 154 sonnets, two long narrative poems, and a few other verses, some of uncertain authorship. His plays have been translated into every major living language and are performed more often than those of any other playwright.

② Voltaire 伏尔泰

François-Marie Arouet de Voltaire (1694–1778) was a French

Enlightenment writer, historian, and philosopher. Voltaire was a versatile and prolific writer, and had written more than 20,000 letters and 2,000 books and pamphlets. He was an outspoken advocate of civil liberties, and was at constant risk from the strict censorship laws of the Catholic French monarchy. His polemics witheringly satirized intolerance, religious dogma, and the French institutions of his day.

③ Alexander Pope 亚历山大·蒲柏

Alexander Pope (1688–1744) was regarded as one of the greatest English poets, and the foremost poet of the early 18th century. He is best known for his satirical and discursive poetry, including *The Rape of the Lock*, *The Dunciad*, and *An Essay on Criticism*, as well as for his translation of Homer.

④ The Reign of Elizabeth 伊丽莎白时代

Queen Elizabeth Ⅰ (1533–1603) was Queen of England and Ireland from 1558 until her death in 1603. Elizabeth was the last monarch of the House of Tudor, which was replaced by her nephew, James Ⅰ (1566–1625) of House of Stuart (斯图亚特王朝). Shakespeare lived in the reign of Queen Elizabeth Ⅰ with other world famous scholars and poets such as Edmund Spencer, Issac Newton and Francis Bacon. Elizabethan era is generally regarded as one of the most important periods in the history of the rise of England, in commerce, science and naval expansion.

⑤ Philip Sidney 悉尼爵士

Sir Philip Sidney (1554–1586) was an English poet, courtier and scholar in the Elizabethan age. His works include *Astrophel and Stella*, *The Defence of Poesy* and *The Countess of Pembroke's Arcadia*.

⑥ Ptolemies 托勒密

Ptolemies, name of a Macedonian dynasty that reigned ancient Egypt from the 3rd century B.C.E. to the 1st century B.C.E., after a general under Alexander the Great. Cleopatra (克莱奥帕特拉), the famous queen of the dynasty was the last of the house.

4.4 Extensive Explorations

① How many plays of Shakespeare's have you read? Can you list the comedies, histories or tragedies in your memory?

② According to the text, how do you define antiquity? What's Johnson's attitude toward it?

③ How does human judgment work in Shakespeare's plays according to Johnson?

④ Did you notice the term "imitation" in Johnson's text? What's the difference between Johnson and ancient Greek philosophers?

⑤ In Elizabethan era, how does the unity of place and time work in plays?

⑥ What do you think, with reference to the text, of the roles of playwrights, players and spectators?

⑦ How do you describe the influence of the spectators on the plays?

⑧ On your modern knowledge, at what points do you agree or disagree with Johnson's view on plays in his time?

5. William Wordsworth's *Preface to Lyrical Ballads* (2nd Edition)

5.1 Lead-in

William Wordsworth

William Wordsworth (1770–1850) was an English Romantic poet. He was born in what is now named Wordsworth House in Cockermouth, Cumberland, part of the scenic region in northwestern England known as the Lake District. He was one of the Lake Poets.

Wordsworth made his debut as a writer in 1787 when he published a sonnet in *The European Magazine*. In that same year he attended St. John's College, Cambridge. He received his BA degree in 1791. In 1793 he had the first publication of poems in the collections *An Evening Walk* and *Descriptive Sketches*. In 1795 he received a legacy and became a professional poet. Together, Wordsworth and Coleridge produced *Lyrical Ballads* (1798), which was believed to launch the Romantic Age in English literature.

Wordsworth's magnum opus (masterpiece) is generally considered to be *The Prelude*, a semi-autobiographical poem of his early years that he revised and expanded a number of times. It was posthumously titled and published by his wife in the year of his death, before which it was generally known as "the poem to Coleridge." Wordsworth was Britain's poet laureate from 1843 until his death from pleurisy in 1850.

Lyrical Ballads, is a collection of poems by William Wordsworth and Samuel Taylor Coleridge. As was introduced above, it was first published in 1798 and generally considered to have marked the beginning of the English Romantic movement in literature. The immediate effect on critics was modest, but it became and remains a landmark, changing the course of English literature and poetry. Most of the poems in the 1798 edition were written by Wordsworth, with Coleridge contributing only four poems to the collection, including one of his most famous works, *The Rime of the Ancient Mariner.* Of course, the 4 poems occupied over a quarter of the whole length.

A second edition was published in 1800, in which Wordsworth included additional poems and a preface detailing the pair's avowed poetical principles. The text we selected in this textbook is the preface for the 2nd edition. For another edition, published in 1802, Wordsworth added an appendix titled *Poetic Diction* in which he expanded the ideas set forth in the preface, and a fourth edition was published in 1805. There are two main versions of *Preface to Lyrical Ballads.* The first is that of 1800 and the second that of 1802, which is the basis of Wordsworth's final version of 1805. The main difference between the two versions is the addition in the 1802 text of the passage which discusses the question, "What is a Poet?" The purpose of the preface was to defend the poets, and Wordsworth's famous saying "Poetry is the spontaneous overflow of powerful feelings." is also reflected in the text. Besides "What is a Poet," Wordsworth also discussed important topics such as "the subjects and language of poetry" and "emotions recollected in poetry."

5.2 Text

Preface to Lyrical Ballads (2nd Edition)[①]

The first volume of these Poems has already been submitted to general perusal. It was published, as an experiment, which, I hoped, might be of some use to ascertain, how far, by fitting to metrical arrangement a selection of the real language of men in a state of vivid sensation, that sort of pleasure and that quantity of pleasure may be imparted, which a Poet may rationally endeavor to impart.

I had formed no very inaccurate estimate of the probable effect of those Poems: I flattered myself that they who should be pleased with them would read them with more than common pleasure: and, on the other hand, I was well aware, that by those who should dislike them, they would be read with more than common dislike. The result has differed from my expectation in this only, that a greater number have been pleased than I ventured to hope I should please.

Several of my Friends are anxious for the success of these Poems, from a belief, that, if the views with which they were composed were indeed realized, a class of Poetry would be produced, well adapted to interest mankind permanently, and not unimportant in the quality, and in the multiplicity of its moral relations: and on this account they have advised me to prefix a systematic defence of the theory upon which the Poems were written. But I was unwilling to undertake the task, knowing that on this occasion the Reader would look coldly upon my arguments, since I might be suspected of having been principally influenced by the selfish and foolish hope of *reasoning* him into an approbation of these particular poems: and I was still more unwilling to undertake the task, because, adequately to display

---

① The preface to the second edition of *Lyrical Ballads* was first published in 1800. Wordsworth subsequently revised it, and the final version appeared in the edition of his poems published in 1849–1850. The text follows is that version.

the opinions, and fully to enforce the arguments, would require a space wholly disproportionate to a preface. For, to treat the subject with the clearness and coherence of which it is susceptible, it would be necessary to give a full account of the present state of the public taste in this country, and to determine how far this taste is healthy or depraved; which, again, could not be determined, without pointing out in what manner language and the human mind act and react on each other, and without retracing the revolutions, not of literature alone, but likewise of society itself. I have therefore altogether declined to enter regularly upon this defense; yet I am sensible, that there would be something like impropriety in abruptly obtruding upon the Public, without a few words of introduction, Poems so materially different from those upon which general approbation is at present bestowed.

It is supposed, that by the act of writing in verse an Author makes a formal engagement that he will gratify certain known habits of association; that he not only thus apprises the Reader that certain classes of ideas and expressions will be found in his book, but that others will be carefully excluded. This exponent or symbol held forth by metrical language must in different eras of literature have excited very different expectations: for example, in the age of Catullus, Terence and Lucretius, and that of Statius or Claudian; and in our own country, in the age of Shakespeare and Beaumont and Fletcher, and that of Donne and Cowley, or Dryden, or Pope.[①] I will not take upon me to determine the exact import of the promise which, by the

① Caius Valerius Catullus (84 B.C.E.–54 B.C.E.), Publius Terentius Afer (c. 185 B.C.E.–c. 159 B.C.E.), Titus Lucretius Carus (c.99 B.C.E.–c. 55 B.C.E.), Publius Popinius Statius (c.40–c.96), and Claudius Claudianus (d. 408), are all Roman writers. William Shakespeare, Francis Beaumont, John Fletcher are all English dramatists. John Donne and Abraham Cowley (1618–1667), John Dryden (1931–1700), Alexander Pope (1688–1744) are all English poets.

act of writing in verse, an Author in the present day makes to his reader: but it will undoubtedly appear to many persons that I have not fulfilled the terms of an engagement thus voluntarily contracted. They who have been accustomed to the gaudiness and inane phraseology of many modern writers, if they persist in reading this book to its conclusion, will, no doubt, frequently have to struggle with feelings of strangeness and awkwardness: they will look round for poetry, and will be induced to inquire by what species of courtesy these attempts can be permitted to assume that title. I hope therefore the Reader will not censure me for attempting to state what I have proposed to myself to perform; and also (as far as the limits of a preface will permit) to explain some of the chief reasons which have determined me in the choice of my purpose: that at least he may be spared any unpleasant feeling of disappointment, and that I myself may be protected from one of the most dishonourable accusations which can be brought against an Author, namely, that of an indolence which prevents him from endeavouring to ascertain what is his duty, or, when his duty is ascertained, prevents him from performing it.

The principal object, then, proposed in these Poems was to choose incidents and situations from common life, and to relate or describe them, throughout, as far as was possible in a selection of language really used by men, and, at the same time, to throw over them a certain colouring of imagination, whereby ordinary things should be presented to the mind in an unusual aspect; and further, and above all, to make these incidents and situations interesting by tracing in them, truly though not ostentatiously, the primary laws of our nature: chiefly, as far as regards the manner in which we associate ideas in a state of excitement. Humble and rustic life was generally chosen, because, in that condition, the essential passions of the heart find a better soil in which they can attain their maturity, are less under restraint, and speak a plainer and more emphatic language;

because in that condition of life our elementary feelings coexist in a state of greater simplicity, and, consequently, may be more accurately contemplated, and more forcibly communicated; because the manners of rural life germinate from those elementary feelings, and, from the necessary character of rural occupations, are more easily comprehended, and are more durable; and, lastly, because in that condition the passions of men are incorporated with the beautiful and permanent forms of nature. The language, too, of these men has been adopted (purified indeed from what appears to be its real defects, from all lasting and rational causes of dislike or disgust) because such men hourly communicate with the best objects from which the best part of language is originally derived; and because, from their rank in society and the sameness and narrow circle of their intercourse, being less under the influence of social vanity, they convey their feelings and notions in simple and unelaborated expressions. Accordingly, such a language, arising out of repeated experience and regular feelings, is a more permanent, and a far more philosophical language, than that which is frequently substituted for it by Poets, who think that they are conferring honour upon themselves and their art, in proportion as they separate themselves from the sympathies of men, and indulge in arbitrary and capricious habits of expression, in order to furnish food for fickle tastes, and fickle appetites, of their own creation.[①]

I cannot, however, be insensible to the present outcry against the triviality and meanness, both of thought and language, which some of my contemporaries have occasionally introduced into their metrical compositions; and I acknowledge that this defect where it exists, is more dishonourable to the writer's own character than false

---

① [Wordsworth] It is worthwhile here to observe that the affecting parts of Chaucer are almost always expressed in language pure and universally intelligible even to this day.

refinement or arbitrary innovation, though I should contend at the same time, that it is far less pernicious in the sum of its consequences. From such verses the Poems in these volumes will be found distinguished at least by one mark of difference, that each of them has a worthy *purpose*. Not that I always began to write with a distinct purpose formerly conceived; but habits of meditation have, I trust, so prompted and regulated my feelings, that my descriptions of such objects as strongly excite those feelings, will be found to carry along with them a *purpose*. If this opinion be erroneous, I can have little right to the name of a Poet. For all good poetry is the spontaneous overflow of powerful feelings: and though this be true, Poems to which any value can be attached were never produced on any variety of subjects but by a man who, being possessed of more than usual organic sensibility, had also thought long and deeply. For our continued influxes of feeling are modified and directed by our thoughts, which are indeed the representatives of all our past feelings; and, as by contemplating the relation of these general representatives to each other, we discover what is really important to men, so, by the repetition and continuance of this act, our feelings will be connected with important subjects, till at length, if we be originally possessed of much sensibility, such habits of mind will be produced, that, by obeying blindly and mechanically the impulses of those habits, we shall describe objects, and utter sentiments, of such a nature, and in such connexion with each other, that the understanding of the Reader must necessarily be in some degree enlightened, and his affections strengthened and purified.

It has been said that each of these poems has a purpose. Another circumstance must be mentioned which distinguishes these Poems from the popular Poetry of the day; it is this, that the feeling therein developed gives importance to the action and situation, and not the action and situation to the feeling.[①]

A sense of false modesty shall not prevent me from asserting, that the Reader's attention is pointed to this mark of distinction, far less for the sake of these particular Poems than from the general importance of the subject. The subject is indeed important! For the human mind is capable of being excited without the application of gross and violent stimulants; and he must have a very faint perception of its beauty and dignity who does not know this, and who does not further know that one being is elevated above another, in proportion as he possesses this capability. It has therefore appeared to me, that to endeavour to produce or enlarge this capability is one of the best services in which, at any period, a writer can be engaged; but this service, excellent at all times, is especially so at the present day. For a multitude of causes, unknown to former times, are now acting with a combined force to blunt the discriminating powers of the mind, and, unfitting it for all voluntary exertion, to reduce it to a state of almost savage torpor. The most effective of these causes are the great national events which are daily taking place,[②] and the increasing accumulation of men in cities, where the uniformity of their occupations produces a craving for extraordinary incident which the rapid communication of intelligence hourly gratifies. To this tendency of life and manners the literature and theatrical exhibitions of the country have conformed themselves. The invaluable works of our elder writers, I had almost said the works of Shakespeare and Milton, are driven into neglect by frantic novels,[③] sickly and stupid German Tragedies, and deluges of idle and extravagant stories in verse.—When I think upon this

---

① In contrast to Aristotle, Wordsworth does not place action (plot) first in importance.

② Among these, the war with France.

③ It refers to the popular 'gothic' novels of the time.

degrading thirst after outrageous stimulation, I am almost ashamed to have spoken of the feeble endeavour made in these volumes to counteract it; and, reflecting upon the magnitude of the general evil, I should be oppressed with no dishonourable melancholy, had I not a deep impression of certain inherent and indestructible qualities of the human mind, and likewise of certain powers in the great and permanent objects that act upon it, which are equally inherent and indestructible; and were there not added to this impression a belief, that the time is approaching when the evil will be systematically opposed, by men of greater powers, and with far more distinguished success.

Having dwelt thus long on the subjects and aim of these Poems, I shall request the Reader's permission to apprise him of a few circumstances relating to their *style*, in order, among other reasons, that he may not censure me for not having performed what I never attempted. The Reader will find that personifications of abstract ideas rarely occur in these volumes; and are utterly rejected, as an ordinary device to elevate the style, and raise it above prose.① My purpose was to imitate, and, as far as possible, to adopt the very language of men; and assuredly such personifications do not make any natural or regular part of that language. They are, indeed, a figure of speech occasionally prompted by passion, and I have made use of them as such; but have endeavoured utterly to reject them as a mechanical device of style, or as a family language which writers in meter seem to lay claim to by prescription. I have wished to keep the Reader in the company of flesh and blood, persuaded that by so doing I shall interest him. Others who pursue a different track will interest him likewise; I do not interfere with their claim, but wish to prefer a claim

① Here Wordsworth is allied with other writers of the time who denigrate what they call allegory.

of my own. There will also be found in these volumes little of what is usually called poetic diction; as much pains has been taken to avoid it as is ordinarily taken to produce it; this has been done for the reason already alleged, to bring my language near to the language of men; and further, because the pleasure which I have proposed to myself to impart, is of a kind very different from that which is supposed by many persons to be the proper object of poetry. Without being culpably particular, I do not know how to give my Reader a more exact notion of the style in which it was my wish and intention to write, than by informing him that I have at all times endeavoured to look steadily at my subject; consequently, there is I hope in these Poems little falsehood of description, and my ideas are expressed in language fitted to their respective importance. Something must have been gained by this practice, as it is friendly to one property of all good poetry, namely, good sense: but it has necessarily cut me off from a large portion of phrases and figures of speech which from father to son have long been regarded as the common inheritance of Poets. I have also thought it expedient to restrict myself still further, having abstained from the use of many expressions, in themselves proper and beautiful, but which have been foolishly repeated by bad poets, till such feelings of disgust are connected with them as it is scarcely possible by any art of association to overpower.

If in a poem there should be found a series of lines, or even a single line, in which the language, though naturally arranged, and according to the strict laws of meter, does not differ from that of prose, there is a numerous class of critics, who, when they stumble upon these prosaisms, as they call them, imagine that they have made a notable discovery, and exult over the Poet as over a man ignorant of his own profession. Now these men would establish a canon of criticism which the Reader will conclude he must utterly reject, if he wishes to be pleased with these volumes. And it would be a most easy task to prove to him, that not only the language of a large portion of every good poem, even of the most elevated character, must necessarily, except with reference to the meter, in no respect differ from that of good prose, but likewise that some of the most interesting parts of the best poems will be found to be strictly the language of prose when prose is well written. The truth of this assertion might be demonstrated by innumerable passages from almost all the poetical writings, even of Milton himself. To illustrate the subject in a general manner, I will here adduce a short composition of Gray, who was at the head of those who, by their reasonings, have attempted to widen the space of separation betwixt Prose and Metrical composition, and was more than any other man curiously elaborate in the structure of his own poetic diction.

In vain to me the smiling mornings shine,
And reddening Phoebus lifts his golden fire:
The birds in vain their amorous descant join,
Or cheerful fields resume their green attire.
These ears, alas! for other notes repine;
A different object do these eyes require;
My lonely anguish melts no heart but mine;
And in my breast the imperfect joys expire;
Yet morning smiles the busy race to cheer,
And new-born pleasure brings to happier men;
The fields to all their wonted tribute bear;
To warm their little loves the birds complain.
I fruitless mourn to him that cannot hear,
And weep the more because I weep in vain.[①]

---

① Thomas Gray (1716–1771), *Sonnet on the Death of Mr. Richard West.*

It will easily be perceived, that the only part of this Sonnet which is of any value is the lines printed in Italics; it is equally obvious, that, except in the rhyme, and in the use of the single word 'fruitless' for fruitlessly, which is so far a defect, the language of these lines does in no respect differ from that of prose.

By the foregoing quotation it has been shown that the language of Prose may yet be well adapted to Poetry; and it was previously asserted, that a large portion of the language of every good poem can in no respect differ from that of good prose. We will go further. It may be safely affirmed, that there neither is, nor can be, any *essential* difference between the language of prose and metrical composition. We are fond of tracing the resemblance between Poetry and Painting, and, accordingly, we call them Sisters:[①] but where shall we find bonds of connexion sufficiently strict to typify the affinity betwixt metrical and prose composition? They both speak by and to the same organs; the bodies in which both of them are clothed may be said to be of the same substance, their affections are kindred, and almost identical, not necessarily differing even in degree; Poetry[②] sheds no tears 'such as Angels weep,' but natural and human tears; she can boast of no celestial choir that distinguishes her vital juices from those of prose; the same human blood circulates through the veins of them both.

---

① The term 'sister arts' was widely used in the eighteenth century to denote the relations among the arts of poetry, painting, sculpture, and music.

② [Wordsworth] I here use the word 'Poetry' (though against my own judgment) as opposed to the word 'Prose,' and synonymous with metrical composition. But much confusion has been introduced into criticism by this contradiction of Poetry and Prose, instead of the more philosophical one of Poetry and Matter of Fact, or Science. The only strict antithesis to Prose is Meter, nor is this, in truth, a strict antithesis, because lines and passages of meter so naturally occur in writing prose, that it would be scarcely possible to avoid them, even were it desirable.

If it be affirmed that rhyme and metrical arrangement of themselves constitute a distinction which overturns what has just been said on the strict affinity of metrical language with that of prose, and paves the way for other artificial distinctions which the mind voluntarily admits, I answer that the language of such Poetry as is here recommended is, as far as is possible, a selection of the language really spoken by men; that this selection, wherever it is made with true taste and feeling, will of itself form a distinction far greater than would at first be imagined, and will entirely separate the composition from the vulgarity and meanness of ordinary life; and, if meter be superadded thereto, I believe that a dissimilitude will be produced altogether sufficient for the gratification of a rational mind. What other distinction would we have? Whence is it to come? And where is it to exist? Not, surely, where the Poet speaks through the mouths of his characters: it cannot be necessary here, either for elevation of style, or any of its supposed ornaments: for, if the Poet's subject be judiciously chosen, it will naturally, and upon fit occasion, lead him to passions the language of which, if selected truly and judiciously, must necessarily be dignified and variegated, and alive with metaphors and figures. I forbear to speak of an incongruity which would shock the intelligent Reader, should the Poet interweave any foreign splendor of his own with that which the passion naturally suggests: it is sufficient to say that such addition is unnecessary. And surely it is more probable that those passages which with propriety abound with metaphors and figures, will have their due effect, if, upon other occasions where the passions are of a milder character, the style also be subdued and temperate.

But, as the pleasure which I hope to give by the Poems now presented to the Reader must depend entirely on just notions upon this subject, and, as it is in itself of high importance to our taste and moral feelings, I cannot content myself with these detached remarks.

And if, in what I am about to say, it shall appear to some that my labour is unnecessary, and that I am like a man fighting a battle without enemies, such persons may be reminded, that, whatever be the language outwardly holden by men, a practical faith in the opinions which I am wishing to establish is almost unknown. If my conclusions are admitted, and carried as far as they must be carried if admitted at all, our judgments concerning the works of the greatest Poets both ancient and modern will be far different from what they are at present, both when we praise, and when we censure; and our moral feelings influencing and influenced by these judgments will, I believe, be corrected and purified.

Taking up the subject, then, upon general grounds, let me ask, what is meant by the word Poet? What is a Poet? To whom does he address himself? And what language is to be expected from him? —He is a man speaking to men: a man, it is true, endowed with more lively sensibility, more enthusiasm and tenderness, who has a greater knowledge of human nature, and a more comprehensive soul, than are supposed to be common among mankind; a man pleased with his own passions and volitions, and who rejoices more than other men in the spirit of life that is in him; delighting to contemplate similar volitions and passions as manifested in the goings-on of the Universe, and habitually impelled to create them where he does not find them. To these qualities he has added a disposition to be affected more than other men by absent things as if they were present; an ability of conjuring up in himself passions, which are indeed far from being the same as those produced by real events, yet (especially in those parts of the general sympathy which are pleasing and delightful) do more nearly resemble the passions produced by real events, than anything which, from the motions of their own minds merely, other men are accustomed to feel in themselves:—whence, and from practice, he has acquired a greater readiness and power in expressing what he thinks and feels, and especially those thoughts and feelings which, by his own choice, or from the structure of his own mind, arise in him without immediate external excitement.

But whatever portion of this faculty we may suppose even the greatest Poet to possess, there cannot be a doubt that the language which it will suggest to him, must often, in liveliness and truth, fall short of that which is uttered by men in real life, under the actual pressure of those passions, certain shadows of which the Poet thus produces, or feels to be produced, in himself.

However exalted a notion we would wish to cherish of the character of a Poet, it is obvious, that while he describes and imitates passions, his employment is in some degree mechanical, compared with the freedom and power of real and substantial action and suffering. So that it will be the wish of the Poet to bring his feelings near to those of the persons whose feelings he describes, nay, for short spaces of time, perhaps, to let himself slip into an entire delusion, and even confound and identify his own feelings with theirs; modifying only the language which is thus suggested to him by a consideration that he describes for a particular purpose, that of giving pleasure. Here, then, he will apply the principle of selection which has been already insisted upon. He will depend upon this for removing what would otherwise be painful or disgusting in the passion; he will feel that there is no necessity to trick out or to elevate nature; and, the more industriously he applies this principle, the deeper will be his faith that no words which *his* fancy or imagination can suggest, will be to be compared with those which are the emanations of reality and truth.

But it may be said by those who do not object to the general spirit of these remarks, that, as it is impossible for the Poet to produce upon all occasions language as exquisitely fitted for the passion as that which the real passion itself suggests, it is proper that he should consider himself as in the situation of a translator, who does not scruple to substitute excellencies of another kind for those which are unattainable by him; and endeavours occasionally to surpass his original, in order to make some amends for the general inferiority to which he feels that he must submit. But this would be to encourage idleness and unmanly despair. Further, it is the language of men who speak of what they do not understand; who talk of Poetry as of a matter of amusement and idle pleasure; who will converse with us as gravely about a *taste* for Poetry, as they express it, as if it were a thing as indifferent as a taste for rope-dancing, or Frontiniac or Sherry. Aristotle, I have been told, has said, that Poetry is the most philosophic of all writing:[①] it is so: its object is truth, not individual and local, but general,[②] and operative; not standing upon external testimony, but carried alive into the heart by passion; truth which is its own testimony, which gives competence and confidence to the tribunal to which it appeals, and receives them from the same tribunal. Poetry is the image of man and nature. The obstacles which stand in the way of the fidelity of the Biographer and Historian, and of their consequent utility, are incalculably greater than those which are to be encountered by the Poet who comprehends the dignity of his art. The Poet writes under one restriction only, namely, the necessity of giving immediate pleasure to a human Being possessed of that information which may be expected from him, not as a lawyer, a physician, a mariner, an astronomer, or a natural philosopher, but as a Man. Except this one restriction, there is no object standing between the Poet and the image of things; between this, and the Biographer and Historian, there are a thousand.

---

① Aristotle says that poetry is more philosophical than history on the ground that history addresses particulars and poetry universals.

② Wordworth's use of 'general' here rather than 'universal' indicates the influence of Locke's empiricism.

Nor let this necessity of producing immediate pleasure be considered as a degradation of the Poet's art. It is far otherwise. It is an acknowledgment of the beauty of the universe, an acknowledgment the more sincere, because not formal, but indirect; it is a task light and easy to him who looks at the world in the spirit of love: further, it is a homage paid to the native and naked dignity of man, to the grand elementary principle of pleasure, by which he knows, and feels, and lives, and moves. We have no sympathy but what is propagated by pleasure: I would not be misunderstood; but wherever we sympathize with pain, it will be found that the sympathy is produced and carried on by subtle combinations with pleasure. We have no knowledge, that is, no general principles drawn from the contemplation of particular facts, but what has been built up by pleasure, and exists in us by pleasure alone. The Man of science, the Chemist and Mathematician, whatever difficulties and disgusts they may have had to struggle with, know and feel this. However painful may be the objects with which the Anatomist's knowledge is connected, he feels that his knowledge is pleasure; and where he has no pleasure he has no knowledge. What then does the Poet? He considers man and the objects that surround him as acting and reacting upon each other, so as to produce an infinite complexity of pain and pleasure; he considers man in his own nature and in his ordinary life as contemplating this with a certain quantity of immediate knowledge, with certain convictions, intuitions, and deductions, which from habit acquire the quality of intuitions; he considers him as looking upon this complex scene of ideas and sensations, and finding everywhere objects that immediately excite in him sympathies which, from the necessities of his nature, are accompanied by an overbalance of enjoyment.

To this knowledge which all men carry about with them, and to these sympathies in which, without any other discipline than that of our daily life, we are fitted to take delight, the Poet principally directs his attention. He considers man and nature as essentially adapted to each other, and the mind of man as naturally the mirror of the fairest and most interesting properties of nature. And thus the Poet, prompted by this feeling of pleasure, which accompanies him through the whole course of his studies, converses with general nature, with affections akin to those, which, through labour and length of time, the Man of science has raised up in himself, by conversing with those particular parts of nature which are the objects of his studies. The knowledge both of the Poet and the Man of science is pleasure; but the knowledge of the one cleaves to us as a necessary part of our existence, our natural and unalienable inheritance; the other is a personal and individual acquisition, slow to come to us, and by no habitual and direct sympathy connecting us with our fellow-beings. The Man of science seeks truth as a remote and unknown benefactor; he cherishes and loves it in his solitude: the Poet, singing a song in which all human beings join with him, rejoices in the presence of truth as our visible friend and hourly companion. Poetry is the breath and finer spirit of all knowledge; it is the impassioned expression which is in the countenance of all Science. Emphatically may it be said of the Poet, as Shakespeare hath said of man, "that he looks before and after." He is the rock of defence for human nature; an upholder and preserver, carrying everywhere with him relationship and love. In spite of difference of soil and climate, of language and manners, of laws and customs; in spite of things silently gone out of mind, and things violently destroyed; the Poet binds together by passion and knowledge the vast empire of human society, as it is spread over the whole earth, and over all time. The objects of the Poet's thoughts are everywhere; though the eyes and senses of man are, it is true, his favourite guides, yet he will follow wheresoever he can find an atmosphere of sensation in which to move his wings. Poetry is the first and last of all knowledge—it is as immortal as the heart of man. If the labours of Men of science should ever create any material revolution, direct or indirect, in our condition, and in the impressions which we habitually receive, the Poet will sleep then no more than at present; he will be ready to follow the steps of the Man of science, not only in those general indirect effects, but he will be at his side, carrying sensation into the midst of the objects of the science itself. The remotest discoveries of the Chemist, the Botanist, or Mineralogist, will be as proper objects of the Poet's art as any upon which it can be employed, if the time should ever come when these things shall be familiar to us, and the relations under which they are contemplated by the followers of these respective sciences shall be manifestly and palpably material to us as enjoying and suffering beings. If the time should ever come when what is now called science, thus familiarized to men, shall be ready to put on, as it were, a form of flesh and blood, the Poet will lend his divine spirit to aid the transfiguration, and will welcome the Being thus produced, as a dear and genuine inmate of the household of man. — It is not, then, to be supposed that any one who holds that sublime notion of Poetry which I have attempted to convey, will break in upon the sanctity and truth of his pictures by transitory and accidental ornaments, and endeavour to excite admiration of himself by arts, the necessity of which must manifestly depend upon the assumed meanness of his subject.①

What has been thus far said applies to Poetry in general; but especially to those parts of composition where the Poet speaks through the mouths of his characters; and upon this point it appears to authorize the conclusion that there are few persons of good sense,

① In this long paragraph, the old classical contrast of poetry with history and philosophy is replaced by the modern contrast of poetry to science, which dominates criticism into the middle of the twentieth century. It expresses a new anxiety about poetry's cultural position.

who would not allow that the dramatic parts of composition are defective, in proportion as they deviate from the real language of nature, and are coloured by a diction of the Poet's own, either peculiar to him as an individual Poet or belonging simply to Poets in general; to a body of men who, from the circumstance of their compositions being in meter, it is expected will employ a particular language.

It is not, then, in the dramatic parts of composition that we look for this distinction of language; but still it may be proper and necessary where the Poet speaks to us in his own person and character. To this I answer by referring the Reader to the description before given of a Poet. Among the qualities there enumerated as principally conducing to form a Poet, is implied nothing differing in kind from other men, but only in degree. The sum of what was said is, that the Poet is chiefly distinguished from other men by a greater promptness to think and feel without immediate external excitement, and a greater power in expressing such thoughts and feelings as are produced in him in that manner. But these passions and thoughts and feelings are the general passions and thoughts and feelings of men. And with what are they connected? Undoubtedly with our moral sentiments and animal sensations, and with the causes which excite these; with the operations of the elements, and the appearances of the visible universe; with storm and sunshine, with the revolutions of the seasons, with cold and heat, with loss of friends and kindred, with injuries and resentments, gratitude and hope, with fear and sorrow. These, and the like, are the sensations and objects which the Poet describes, as they are the sensations of other men, and the objects which interest them. The Poet thinks and feels in the spirit of human passions. How, then, can his language differ in any material degree from that of all other men who feel vividly and see clearly? It might be proved that it is impossible. But supposing that this were not the case, the Poet might then be allowed to use a peculiar language when expressing his feelings for his own gratification, or that of men like himself. But Poets do not write for Poets alone, but for men. Unless therefore, we are advocates for that admiration which subsists upon ignorance, and that pleasure which arises from hearing what we do not understand, the Poet must descend from this supposed height; and, in order to excite rational sympathy, he must express himself as other men express themselves. To this it may be added, that while he is only selecting from the real language of men, or, which amounts to the same thing, composing accurately in the spirit of such selection, he is treading upon safe ground, and we know what we are to expect from him. Our feelings are the same with respect to meter; for, as it may be proper to remind the Reader, the distinction of meter is regular and uniform, and not, like that which is produced by what is usually called poetic diction, arbitrary, and subject to infinite caprices upon which no calculation whatever can be made. In the one case, the Reader is utterly at the mercy of the Poet, respecting what imagery or diction he may choose to connect with the passion; whereas, in the other, the meter obeys certain laws, to which the Poet and Reader both willingly submit because they are certain, and because no interference is made by them with the passion, but such as the concurring testimony of ages has shown to heighten and improve the pleasure which coexists with it.

It will now be proper to answer an obvious question, namely, why, professing these opinions, have I written in verse? To this, in addition to such answer as is included in what has been already said, I reply, in the first place, because however I may have restricted myself, there is still left open to me what confessedly constitutes the most valuable object of all writing, whether in prose or verse; the great and universal passions of men, the most general and interesting of their occupations, and the entire world of nature before me—to supply endless combinations of forms and imagery. Now, supposing for a moment that whatever is interesting in these objects may be as vividly described in prose, why should I be condemned for attempting to superadd to such description the charm which, by the consent of all nations, is acknowledged to exist in metrical language? To this, by such as are yet unconvinced, it may be answered that a very small part of the pleasure given by Poetry depends upon the meter, and that it is injudicious to write in meter, unless it be accompanied with the other artificial distinctions of style with which meter is usually accompanied, and that, by such deviation, more will be lost from the shock which will thereby be given to the Reader's associations than will be counterbalanced by any pleasure which he can derive from the general power of numbers. In answer to those who still contend for the necessity of accompanying meter with certain appropriate colours of style in order to the accomplishment of its appropriate end, and who also, in my opinion, greatly underrate the power of meter in itself, it might, perhaps, as far as relates to these Volumes, have been almost sufficient to observe, that poems are extant, written upon more humble subjects, and in a still more naked and simple style, which have continued to give pleasure from generation to generation. Now, if nakedness and simplicity be a defect, the fact here mentioned affords a strong presumption that poems somewhat less naked and simple are capable of affording pleasure at the present day; and what I wish *chiefly* to attempt, at present, was to justify myself for having written under the impression of this belief.

But various causes might be pointed out why, when the style is manly, and the subject of some importance, words metrically arranged will long continue to impart such a pleasure to mankind as he who proves the extent of that pleasure will be desirous to impart. The end of Poetry is to produce excitement in coexistence with an overbalance of pleasure; but, by the supposition, excitement is an unusual and irregular state of the mind; ideas and feelings do not, in that state, succeed each other in accustomed order. If the words, however, by which this excitement is produced be in themselves powerful, or the images and feelings have an undue proportion of pain connected with them, there is some danger that the excitement may be carried beyond its proper bounds. Now the copresence of something regular, something to which the mind has been accustomed in various moods and in a less excited state, cannot but have great efficacy in tempering and restraining the passion by an intertexture of ordinary feeling, and of feeling not strictly and necessarily connected with the passion. This is unquestionably true; and hence, though the opinion will at first appear paradoxical, from the tendency of meter to divest language, in a certain degree, of its reality, and thus to throw a sort of half-consciousness of unsubstantial existence over the whole composition, there can be little doubt but that more pathetic situations and sentiments, that is, those which have a greater proportion of pain connected with them, may be endured in metrical composition, especially in rhyme, than in prose. The meter of the old ballads is very artless; yet they contain many passages which would illustrate this opinion; and, I hope, if the following Poems be attentively perused, similar instances will be found in them. This opinion may be further illustrated by appealing to the Reader's own experience of the reluctance with which he comes to the reperusal of the distressful parts of *Clarissa Harlowe*, or *The Gamester*;① while Shakespeare's writings, in the most pathetic scenes, never act upon us, as pathetic, beyond the bounds of pleasure—an effect which, in a much greater degree than might at first be imagined, is to be ascribed to small, but continual and regular impulses of pleasurable surprise from the metrical arrangement.—On the other hand (what it must be allowed

① *Clarissa Harlowe* was written by Samuel Richardson (1689–1761); *The Gamester* was written by Edward Moore (1712–1757).

will much more frequently happen) if the Poet's words should be incommensurate with the passion, and inadequate to raise the Reader to a height of desirable excitement, then (unless the Poet's choice of his meter has been grossly injudicious) in the feelings of pleasure which the Reader has been accustomed to connect with meter in general, and in the feeling, whether cheerful or melancholy, which he has been accustomed to connect with that particular movement of meter, there will be found something which will greatly contribute to impart passion to the words, and to effect the complex end which the Poet proposes to himself.

If I had undertaken a systematic defense of the theory here maintained, it would have been my duty to develop the various causes upon which the pleasure received from metrical language depends. Among the chief of these causes is to be reckoned a principle which must be well known to those who have made any of the Arts the object of accurate reflection; namely, the pleasure which the mind derives from the perception of similitude in dissimilitude. This principle is the great spring of the activity of our minds, and their chief feeder. From this principle the direction of the sexual appetite, and all the passions connected with it, take their origin: it is the life of our ordinary conversation; and upon the accuracy with which similitude in dissimilitude, and dissimilitude in similitude are perceived, depend our taste and our moral feelings. It would not be a useless employment to apply this principle to the consideration of meter, and to show that meter is hence enabled to afford much pleasure, and to point out in what manner that pleasure is produced. But my limits will not permit me to enter upon this subject, and I must content myself with a general summary.

I have said that poetry is the spontaneous overflow of powerful feelings: it takes its origin from emotion recollected in tranquility: the emotion is contemplated till, by a species of reaction, the tranquility gradually disappears, and an emotion, kindred to that which was before the subject of contemplation, is gradually produced, and does itself actually exist in the mind. In this mood successful composition generally begins, and in a mood similar to this it is carried on; but the emotion, of whatever kind, and in whatever degree, from various causes, is qualified by various pleasures, so that in describing any passions whatsoever, which are voluntarily described, the mind will, upon the whole, be in a state of enjoyment. If Nature be thus cautious to preserve in a state of enjoyment a being so employed, the Poet ought to profit by the lesson held forth to him, and ought especially to take care, that, whatever passions he communicates to his Reader, those passions, if his Reader's mind be sound and vigorous, should always be accompanied with an overbalance of pleasure. Now the music of harmonious metrical language, the sense of difficulty overcome, and the blind association of pleasure which has been previously received from works of rhyme or meter of the same or similar construction, an indistinct perception perpetually renewed of language closely resembling that of real life, and yet, in the circumstance of meter, differing from it so widely—all these imperceptibly make up a complex feeling of delight, which is of the most important use in tempering the painful feeling always found intermingled with powerful descriptions of the deeper passion. This effect is always produced in pathetic and impassioned poetry; while, in lighter compositions, the ease and gracefulness with which the Poet manages his numbers are themselves confessedly a principal source of the gratification of the Reader. All that it is *necessary* to say, however, upon this subject, may be effected by affirming, what few persons will deny, that, of two descriptions, either of passions, manners, or characters, each of them equally well executed, the one in prose and the other in verse, the verse will be read a hundred times where the prose is read once.

Having thus explained a few of my reasons for writing in verse, and why I have chosen subjects from common life, and endeavoured to bring my language near to the real language of men, if I have been too minute in pleading my own cause, I have at the same time been treating a subject of general interest; and for this reason a few words shall be added with reference solely to these particular poems, and to some defects which will probably be found in them. I am sensible that my associations must have sometimes been particular instead of general, and that, consequently, giving to things a false importance, I may have sometimes written upon unworthy subjects; but I am less apprehensive on this account, than that my language may frequently have suffered from those arbitrary connexions of feelings and ideas with particular words and phrases, from which no man can altogether protect himself. Hence I have no doubt that, in some instances, feelings, even of the ludicrous, may be given to my Readers by expressions which appeared to me tender and pathetic. Such faulty expressions, were I convinced they were faulty at present, and that they must necessarily continue to be so, I would willingly take all reasonable pains to correct. But it is dangerous to make these alterations on the simple authority of a few individuals, or even of certain classes of men; for where the understanding of an Author is not convinced, or his feelings altered, this cannot be done without great injury to himself: for his own feelings are his stay and support; and, if he set them aside in one instance, he may be induced to repeat this act till his mind shall lose all confidence in itself, and become utterly debilitated. To this it may he added, that the critic ought never to forget that he is himself exposed to the same errors as the Poet, and, perhaps in a much greater degree: for there can be no presumption in saying of most Readers, that it is not probable they will be so well acquainted with the various stages of meaning through which words have passed, or with the fickleness or stability of the relations of particular ideas to each other; and, above all, since they are so much less interested in the subject, they may decide lightly and carelessly.

Long as the Reader has been detained, I hope he will permit me to caution him against a mode of false criticism which has been applied to Poetry, in which the language closely resembles that of life and nature. Such verses have been triumphed over in parodies, of which Dr. Johnson's stanza is a fair specimen: —

I put my hat upon my head
And walked into the Strand,
And there I met another man
Whose hat was in his hand.

Immediately under these lines let us place one of the most justly admired stanzas of the "Babes in the Wood."[①]

These pretty Babes with hand in hand
Went wandering up and down;
But never more they saw the Man
Approaching from the town.

In both these stanzas the words, and the order of the words, in no respect differ from the most unimpassioned conversation. There are words in both, for example, 'the Strand,' *and* 'the town,' connected with none but the most familiar ideas; yet the one stanza we admit as admirable, and the other as a fair example of the superlatively contemptible. Whence arises this difference? Not from the meter, not from the language, not from the order of the words; but the *matter* expressed in Dr. Johnson's stanza is contemptible. The proper method

① An anonymous ballad.

of treating trivial and simple verses, to which Dr. Johnson's stanza would be a fair parallelism, is not to say, this is a bad kind of poetry, or, this is not poetry; but, this wants sense; it is neither interesting in itself nor can *lead* to anything interesting; the images neither originate in that sane state of feeling which arises out of thought, nor can excite thought or feeling in the Reader. This is the only sensible manner of dealing with such verses. Why trouble yourself about the species till you have previously decided upon the genus? Why take pains to prove that an ape is not a Newton, when it is self-evident that he is not a man?

One request I must make of my Reader, which is, that in judging these Poems he would decide by his own feelings genuinely, and not by reflection upon what will probably be the judgment of others. How common is it to hear a person say, I myself do not object to this style of composition, or this or that expression, but, to such and such classes of people it will appear mean or ludicrous! This mode of criticism, so destructive of all sound unadulterated judgment, is almost universal: let the Reader then abide, independently, by his own feelings, and, if he finds himself affected, let him not suffer such conjectures to interfere with his pleasure.

If an Author, by any single composition, has impressed us with respect for his talents, it is useful to consider this as affording a presumption that on other occasions where we have been displeased, he, nevertheless, may not have written ill or absurdly; and further, to give him so much credit for this one composition as may induce us to review what has displeased us, with more care than we should otherwise have bestowed upon it. This is not only an act of justice, but, in our decisions upon poetry especially, may conduce, in a high degree, to the improvement of our own taste; for an *accurate* taste in poetry, and in all the other arts, as Sir Joshua Reynolds has observed, is an *acquired* talent, which can only be produced by thought and a long-continued intercourse with the best models of composition.[①] This is mentioned, not with so ridiculous a purpose as to prevent the most inexperienced Reader from judging for himself (I have already said that I wish him to judge for himself), but merely to temper the rashness of decision, and to suggest, that, if Poetry be a subject on which much time has not been bestowed, the judgment may be erroneous; and that, in many cases, it necessarily will be so.

Nothing would, I know, have so effectually contributed to further the end which I have in view, as to have shown of what kind the pleasure is, and how that pleasure is produced, which is confessedly produced by metrical composition essentially different from that which I have here endeavoured to recommend: for the Reader will say that he has been pleased by such composition; and what more can be done for him? The power of any art is limited; and he will suspect, that, if it be proposed to furnish him with new friends, that can be only upon condition of his abandoning his old friends. Besides, as I have said, the Reader is himself conscious of the pleasure which he has received from such composition, composition to which he has peculiarly attached the endearing name of Poetry; and all men feel an habitual gratitude, and something of an honourable bigotry, for the objects which have long continued to please them: we not only wish to be pleased, but to be pleased in that particular way in which we have been accustomed to be pleased. There is in these feelings enough to resist a host of arguments; and I should be the less able to combat them successfully, as I am willing to allow, that, in order entirely to enjoy the Poetry which I am recommending, it would be necessary to give up much of what is ordinarily enjoyed. But, would my limits have permitted me to point out how this pleasure is produced, many obstacles might have been removed, and the Reader assisted in

---

① See Discourse VII (*Critical Theory Since Plato*, p. 398ff.).

perceiving that the powers of language are not so limited as he may suppose; and that it is possible for poetry to give other enjoyments, of a purer, more lasting, and more exquisite nature. This part of the subject has not been altogether neglected, but it has not been so much my present aim to prove, that the interest excited by some other kinds of poetry is less vivid, and less worthy of the nobler powers of the mind, as to offer reasons for presuming, that if my purpose were fulfilled, a species of poetry would be produced which is genuine poetry, in its nature well adapted to interest mankind permanently, and likewise important in the multiplicity and quality of its moral relations.

From what has been said, and from a perusal of the Poems, the Reader will be able clearly to perceive the object which I had in view: he will determine how far it has been attained; and, what is a much more important question, whether it be worth attaining: and upon the decision of these two questions will test my claim to the approbation of the Public.

5.3 Key Words

① The Lake Poets 湖畔诗人

The Lake Poets were a group of English poets who all lived in the Lake District of England, United Kingdom, in the first half of the nineteenth century. As a group, the title "Lake Poets" was named by *Edinburgh Review*, and they are considered part of the Romantic movement. The three main figures of what has become known as the Lake School were William Wordsworth, Samuel Taylor Coleridge, and Robert Southey. They were associated with several other poets and writers, including Dorothy Wordsworth, Charles Lamb, Mary Lamb, Charles Lloyd, Hartley Coleridge, John Wilson, and Thomas De Quincey.

② Samuel Taylor Coleridge 柯尔律治

Samuel Taylor Coleridge (1772–1834) was an English poet, literary critic, philosopher and theologian who, with his friend William Wordsworth, was a founder of the Romantic movement in England and a member of the Lake Poets. He wrote the poems *The Rime of the Ancient Mariner* and *Kubla Khan*, as well as the major prose work *Biographia Literaria*. His critical work, especially on William Shakespeare, was highly influential, and he helped introduce German idealist philosophy to English-speaking culture. He had a major influence on Ralph Waldo Emerson and American transcendentalism.

③ the Romantic movement 浪漫主义运动

The Romantic movement was an artistic, literary, musical and intellectual movement that originated in Europe towards the end of the 18th century. In English literature, the key figures of the Romantic movement are considered to be the group of poets including William Wordsworth, Samuel Taylor Coleridge, John Keats, Lord Byron, Percy Bysshe Shelley and so forth.

④ Ballad 歌谣

A ballad is a form of verse, often a narrative set to music. Ballads derive from the medieval French chanson originally defined as "dance songs." Ballads were particularly characteristic of the popular poetry and song of Britain and Ireland from the later medieval period until the 19th century. Ballads are often 13 lines with an ABABBCBC form, consisting of couplets (two lines) of rhymed verse, each of 14 syllables. Another common form is ABAB or ABCB repeated, in alternating 8- and 6-syllable lines.

⑤ Poetic diction（诗歌）辞藻

Poetic diction refers to the linguistic style, the vocabulary, and the metaphors used in the writing of poetry. In the Western tradition, all these elements were thought of as properly different in poetry and prose up to the time of the Romantic revolution, when William

Wordsworth challenged the distinction in his Romantic manifesto, the preface to the second edition of *Lyrical Ballads*. Wordsworth proposed that "a language near to the language of men" was as appropriate for poetry as it was for prose. This idea was very influential, though more in theory than practice: a special "poetic" vocabulary and mode of metaphor persisted in 19th-century poetry. It was deplored by the modernist poets of the 20th century, who again proposed that there was no such thing as a "prosaic" word unsuitable for poetry.

5.4 Extensive Explorations

① Have you heard of Lake Poets in China? Who are the members of the Chinese Lake Poets? What's the difference between the Lake Poets in England and in China?

② What do you know about ballads? Can you compare the ballads in China and those in *Lyrical Ballads*?

③ For whom and what are Wordsworth defending in his preface?

④ What do you think of Wordsworth's famous statement, "Poetry is the spontaneous overflow of powerful feelings"? Can you pick out any similar example in the history of literature in China?

⑤ Can you find the similarities of Coleridge and Wordsworth by analyzing the poems of theirs?

⑥ What is the influence of the Industrial Revolution that was going on in England on the Lake Poets?

⑦ What is the essential feature of the diction in poetry?

⑧ What do you think of the role of emotions in poetry?

6. Hippolyte Taine's *Preface to History of English Literature*

6.1 Lead-in

Hippolyte Adolphe Taine (1828–1893) is a French critic and historian. In the 19th century, he was the chief source of theoretical influence on French Naturalism, a major proponent of Sociological Positivism and one of the first practitioners of Historicist Criticism. Literary Historicism as a critical movement has been said to originate with him. Taine is also remembered for his attempts to provide a scientific account of literature.

Taine was born in Vouziers, Ardennes. He excelled in his studies and in 1847 obtained two Baccalauréat degrees (Science and Philosophy) and received the honorary prize of the concours. He was awarded a first in the entrance examination of the letters section of École Normale Supérieure (巴黎高等师范学院), to which he was admitted in 1848. The École is the major birthplace for numerous celebrities in science, arts and politics in modern France. For his excellency in study and research, he acquired great success and good fame in Europe, not only to live by his pen, but also to be named professor of the History of Art and Aesthetics at the School of Fine Arts and at Saint-Cyr (圣西尔学院). He also taught at Oxford, and in 1878, he was elected member of the French Academy. Taine was interested in many subjects, including art, literature, but especially history. Deeply shaken by the defeat of 1870 against the Prussians (普鲁士), as well as by the insurrection (and violent repression) of the

Paris Commune (巴黎公社), Taine became fully devoted to his major historical work, *The Origins of Contemporary France* (1875–1893), on which he worked until his death in 1893.

Taine's influence on French intellectual culture and literature was significant. As we know, Taine is a philosopher and scholar in the middle 1800s when the Industrial Revolution was booming, which greatly inspired the study of humanities at that time. In his *Preface* to *History of English Literature*, he said "... there was an attempt to relate scientific method to literary creation and criticism." In the middle of the 19th century, Charles Darwin's (查尔斯·达尔文) *On the Origin of Species* (《物种起源》) was published. Darwin's scientific perspective at human's evolution was one of the attempts of scientific methods probed into the domain of literary research in a dynamic way, pounding on the basis of Taine's theory. Taine's most famous statement is in part Ⅴ of the preface, partly as a summarization of the dynamic principle of the evolution of literature. Three elements, the race, the surroundings and the epoch are accelerating the development of literature and art. Taine came up with his three-factor theory under the influence of Sainte-Beuve's contention which is to take artists' biography as a significant factor in literary criticism, but Taine also pointed out that Sainte-Beuve only focused on artists' internal environment, which has come to the theoretical limit of explaining the ultimate dynamic forces of evolution. Because from the perspective of science, scientific research should focus on external environment motivation and physical causes. Taine pointed out that Sainte-Beuve gave too much attention to artists' inner life neglecting what was behind artists' personal experience, character and writing style. Another important source of influence came from a French female critic back in Napoleon's time (拿破仑时期): Madame de Staël (斯塔尔夫人). Madame de Staël liked to discuss how Mediterranean (地中海) climate influenced Greek and Italian artists and how the gloomy rainy days in North Europe influenced Nordic and German artists. The influence can be seen in the epics and myths as well as the following poetries and proses written by artists of different races. Obviously, Taine was also influenced by Madame de Staël. Because in Europe, people were pretty sensitive about how different climates and environments affected people especially when transportation advanced due to the development of industry. It might take only less than a day to go to Nordic region from Mediterranean region by train or in a carriage. So it was easier to discover surroundings' influence on art in Taine's time. Of course, if we give a close study of the three elements, we can see that, both the race and the epoch can be included theoretically into the fact of surroundings, because they all provided synthesized impacts on the development of literature, and the neglect of the internal or spiritual facts is apparent.

In today's view, Taine's theory might not be persuasive enough. But what we have to understand is that his theory, in his time, is strongly innovative for it enlightened people to pay close attention to external factors which had great influence on art. Taine's theory fits the way ancient even modern Europeans think which reflects the fact of scientific methods being used in the research of art. Taine's scientific methods and his pursuing for accuracy is a great advancement in his time. He also reminds us that criticism only focusing on internal factors is no good criticism.

The text selected from *Preface to History of English Literature* is excerpted from the 5th chapter to the end. We would focus on Taine's discussion on the three elements, and the 5th chapter made a concentrative introduction of the three elements and deployed further discussion in the following chapters.

6.2 Text

Preface to History of English Literature

(Chapter 5-8)

V

Three different sources contribute to produce this elementary moral state—the race, the surroundings, and the epoch. What we call the *race* are the innate and hereditary dispositions which man brings with him to the light, and which, as a rule, are united with the marked differences in the temperament and structure of the body. They vary with various peoples. There is a natural variety of men, as of oxen and horses, some brave and intelligent, some timid and dependent, some capable of superior conceptions and creations, some reduced to rudimentary ideas and inventions, some more specially fitted to special works, and gifted more richly with particular instincts, as we meet with species of dogs better favored than others—these for hunting, these for fighting, these for the chase, these again for house dogs or shepherds' dogs. We have here a distinct force—so distinct, that amidst the vast deviations which the other two motive forces produce in him, one can recognize it still; and a race, like the old Aryans, scattered from the Ganges as far as the Hebrides, settled in every clime, spread over every grade of civilization, transformed by thirty centuries of revolutions, nevertheless manifests in its tongues, religions, literatures, philosophies, the community of blood and of intellect which to this day binds its offshoots together. Different as they are, their parentage is not obliterated; barbarism, culture and grafting, differences of sky and soil, fortunes good and bad, have labored in vain: the great marks of the original model have remained, and we find again the two or three principal lineaments of the primitive imprint underneath the secondary imprints which time has stamped above them. There is nothing astonishing in this extraordinary tenacity. Although the vastness of the distance lets us but half perceive—and by a doubtful light—the origin of species,① the events of history sufficiently illumine the events anterior to history, to explain the almost immovable steadfastness of the primordial marks. When we meet with them, fifteen, twenty, thirty centuries before our era, in an Aryan, an Egyptian, a Chinese, they represent the work of several myriads of centuries. For as soon as an animal begins to exist, it has to reconcile itself with its surroundings; it breathes after a new fashion, renews itself, is differently affected according to the new changes in air, food, temperature. Different climate and situation bring it various needs, and consequently a different course of actions; and this, again, a different set of habits; and still again, a different set of aptitudes and instincts. Man, forced to accommodate himself to circumstances, contracts a temperament and a character corresponding to them; and his character, like his temperament, is so much more stable, as the external impression is made upon him by more numerous repetitions, and is transmitted to his progeny by a more ancient descent. So that at any moment we may consider the character of a people as an abridgment of all its preceding actions and sensations; that is, as a quantity and as a weight, not infinite,② since everything in nature is finite, but disproportioned to the rest, and almost impossible to lift, since every moment of an almost infinite past has contributed to increase it, and because, in order to raise the scale, one must place in the opposite scale a still greater number of actions and sensations. Such is the first and richest source of these master faculties from which historical events take their rise; and one

---

① [Taine] Darwin, *The Origin of Species*. Prosper Lucas, *De l'hérédité* (*On Heredity*).

② [Taine] Spinoza, *Ethics*, Part IV. Axiom.

sees at the outset, that if it be powerful, it is because this is no simple spring, but a kind of lake, a deep reservoir wherein other springs have, for a multitude of centuries, discharged their several streams.

Having thus outlined the interior structure of a race, we must consider the surroundings in which it exists. For man is not alone in the world: nature surrounds him, and his fellow men surround him; accidental and secondary tendencies come to place themselves on his primitive tendencies, and physical or social circumstances disturb or confirm the character committed to their charge. In course of time the climate has had its effect. Though we can follow but obscurely the Aryan peoples from their common fatherland to their final countries, we can yet assert that the profound differences which are manifest between the German races on the one side, and the Greek and Latin on the other arise for the most part from the difference between the countries in which they are settled: some in cold moist lands, deep in black marshy forests or on the shores of a wild ocean, caged in by melancholy or violent sensations, prone to drunkenness and gluttony, bent on a fighting, blood-spilling life; others, again, within a lovely landscape, on a bright and laughing seacoast, enticed to navigation and commerce, exempt from gross cravings of the stomach, inclined from the beginning to social ways, to a settled organization of the state, to feelings and dispositions such as develop the art of oratory, the talent for enjoyment, the inventions of science, letters, arts. Sometimes the state policy has been at work, as in the two Italian civilizations: the first wholly turned to action, conquest, government, legislation, by the original site of its city of refuge, by its borderland emporium, by an armed aristocracy, who, by inviting and drilling the strangers and the conquered, presently set face to face two hostile armies, having no escape from its internal discords and its greedy instincts but in systematic warfare; the other, shut out from unity and any great political ambition by the stability of its municipal character, the cosmopolitan condition of its pope, and the military intervention of neighboring nations, directed the whole of its magnificent, harmonious bent towards the worship of pleasure and beauty. Sometimes the social conditions have impressed their mark, as eighteen centuries ago by Christianity, and twenty-five centuries ago by Buddhism, when around the Mediterranean, as in Hindustan, the extreme results of Aryan conquest and civilization induced an intolerable oppression, the subjugation of the individual, utter despair, a curse upon the world, with the development of metaphysics and myth, so that man in this dungeon of misery, feeling his heart softened, begot the idea of abnegation, charity, tender love, gentleness, humility, brotherly love — there, in a notion of universal nothingness, here under the fatherhood of God. Look around you upon the regulating instincts and faculties implanted in a race — in short, the mood of intelligence in which it thinks and acts at the present time: you will discover most often the work of some one of these prolonged situations, these surrounding circumstances, persistent and gigantic pressures, brought to bear upon an aggregation of men who, singly and together, from generation to generation, are continually molded and modeled by their action; in England, a political establishment of eight centuries, which keeps a man erect and respectful, in independence and obedience, and accustoms him to strive unitedly, under the authority of the law; in France, a Latin organization, which, imposed first upon docile barbarians, then shattered in the universal crash, is reformed from within under a lurking conspiracy of the national instinct, is developed under hereditary kings, ends in a sort of egality republic, centralized, administrative, under dynasties exposed to revolution. These are the most efficacious of the visible causes which mold the primitive man: they are to nations what education, career, condition, abode, are to individuals; and they seem to comprehend everything, since they comprehend all external powers which shape human matter, and by which the external acts on the internal.

There is yet a third rank of causes; for, with the forces within and without, there is the work which they have already produced together, and this work itself contributes to produce that which follows. Beside the permanent impulse and the given surroundings, there is the acquired momentum. When the national character and surrounding circumstances operate, it is not upon a *tabula rasa*,① but on a ground on which marks are already impressed. According as one takes the ground at one moment or another, the imprint is different; and this is the cause that the total effect is different. Consider, for instance, two epochs of a literature or an art—French tragedy under Corneille and under Voltaire, the Greek drama under Aeschylus and under Euripides, Italian painting under da Vinci and under Guido.② Truly, at either of these two extreme points the general idea has not changed; it is always the same human type which is its subject of representation or painting; the mold of verse, the structure of the drama, the form of body has endured. But among several differences there is this, that the one artist is the precursor, the other the successor; the first has no model, the second has; the first sees objects face to face, the second sees them through the first; that many great branches of art are lost, many details are perfected, that simplicity and grandeur of impression have diminished, pleasing and refined forms have increased—in short, that the first work has outlived the second. So it is with a people as with a plant; the same sap, under the same temperature, and in the same soil, produces, at different steps of its

---

① Blank tablet.

② Corneille (*Critical Theory Since Plato*. p.244); François Marie Arouet de Voltaire (1694–1778), French philosopher; Aeschylus (525 B.C.E.–456 B.C.E.) and Euripides (c. 485 B.C.E.–406 B.C.E.), Greek tragic dramatists; Leonardo da Vinci (1452–1519), Italian artist and scientist; Guido Reni (1575–1642), Italian painter and engraver.

progressive development, different formations, buds, flowers, fruits, seed vessels, in such a manner that the one which follows has slways the first for its condition, and grows from its death. And if now you consider no longer a brief epoch, as our own time, but one of those wide intervals which embrace one or more centuries, like the Middle Ages, or our last classic age, the conclusion will be similar. A certain dominant ideas has had sway; men, for two, for five hundred years, have taken to themselves a certain ideal model of man: in the Middle Ages, the knight and the monk; in our classic age, the courtier, the man who speaks well. This creative and universal idea is displayed over the whole field of action and thought; and after covering the world with its works, involuntarily systematic, it has faded, it has died away, and lo, a new idea springs up, destined to a like domination, and the like number of creations. And here remember that the second depends in part upon the first, and that the first, uniting its effect with those of national genius and surrounding circumstances, imposes on each new creation its bent and direction. The great historical currents are formed after this law—the long dominations of one intellectual pattern, or a master idea, such as the period of spontaneous creations called the Renaissance, or the period of oratorical models called the Classical Age, or the series of mystical compositions called the Alexandrian and Christian eras, or the series of mythological efflorescences which we meet with in the infancy of the German people, of the Indian and the Greek. Here as elsewhere we have but a mechanical problem; the total effect is a result, depending entirely on the magnitude and direction of the producing causes. The only difference which separates these moral problems from physical ones is that the magnitude and direction cannot be valued or computed in the first as in the second. If a need or a faculty is a quantity, capable of degrees, like a pressure or a weight, this quantity is not measurable like the pressure or the weight. We cannot define it in an exact or approximative formula; we cannot have more, or give more, in respect of it, than a literary impression; we are limited to marking and quoting the salient points by which it is manifested, and which indicate approximately and roughly the part of the scale which is its position. But though the means of notation are not the same in the moral and physical sciences, yet as in both the matter is the same, equally made up of forces, magnitudes, and directions, we may say that in both the final result is produced after the same method. It is great or small, as the fundamental forces are great or small and act more or less exactly in the same sense, according as the distinct effects of race, circumstance, and epoch combine to add the one to the other, or to annul one another. Thus are explained the long impotences and the brilliant triumphs which make their appearance irregularly and without visible cause in the life of a people; they are caused by internal concords or contrarieties. There was such a concord when in the seventeenth century the sociable character and the conversational aptitude, innate in France, encountered the drawing room manners and the epoch of oratorical analysis; when in the nineteenth century the profound and elastic genius of Germany encountered the age of philosophical compositions and of cosmopolitan criticism. There was such a contrariety when in the seventeenth century the rude and lonely English genius tried blunderingly to adopt a novel politeness; when in the sixteenth century the lucid and prosaic French spirit tried vainly to cradle a living poetry. That hidden concord of creative forces produced the finished urbanity and the noble and regular literature under Louis XIV and Bossuet, the grand metaphysics and broad critical sympathy of Hegel and Goethe.① That hidden contrariety of creative forces produced the imperfect literature, the scandalous

① Louis XIV of France reigned from 1638 to 1715; Jacques Benigne Bossuet (1627–1704), French prelate.

comedy, the abortive drama under Dryden and Wycherley,① the vile Greek importations, the groping elaborate efforts, the scant half-graces under Ronsard and the Pleiad.② So much we can say with confidence, that the unknown creations towards which the current of the centuries conducts us, will be raised up and regulated altogether by the three primordial forces; that if these forces could be measured and computed, one might deduce from them as from a formula the specialties of future civilization; and that if, in spite of the evident crudeness of our notations, and the fundamental inexactness of our measures, we try now to form some idea of our general destiny, it is upon an examination of these forces that we must ground our prophecy. For in enumerating them, we traverse the complete circle of the agencies; and when we have considered race, circumstance, and epoch, which are the internal mainsprings, the external pressure, and the acquired momentum, we have exhausted not only the whole of the actual cause, but also the whole of the possible causes of motive.

VI

It remains for us to examine how these causes, when applied to a nation or an age, produce their results. As a rivulet falling from a height spreads its streams, according to the depth of the descent, stage after stage, until it reaches the lowest level of the soil, so the disposition of intellect or soul impressed on a people by race, circumstance, or epoch, spreads in different proportions and by regular descents, down the diverse orders of facts which make up

① Dryden (*Critical Theory Since Plato*, p.253); William Wycherley (1640?–1716), English comic dramatist.

② Pierre de Ronsard (1524?–1585), French poet, leader of the Pleiad, a group of poets advocating writing in French rather than Latin.

its civilization.[①] If we arrange the map of a country, starting from the watershed, we find that below this common point the streams are divided into five or six principal basins, then each of these into several secondary basins, and so on, until the whole country with its thousand details is included in the ramifications of this network. So, if we arrange the psychological map of the events and sensations of a human civilization, we find first of all five or six well-defined provinces—religion, art, philosophy, the state, the family, the industries; then in each of these provinces natural departments; and in each of these, smaller territories, until we arrive at the numberless details of life such as may be observed within and around us every day. If now we examine and compare these diverse groups of facts, we find first of all that they are made up of parts, and that all have parts in common. Let us take first the three chief works of human intelligence—religion, art, philosophy. What is a philosophy but a conception of nature and its primordial causes, under the form of abstractions and formularies? What is there at the bottom of a religion or of an art but a conception of this same nature and of these same causes, under form of symbols more or less concise, and personages more or less marked; with this difference, that in the first we believe that they exist, in the second we believe that they do not exist? Let the reader consider a few of the great creations of the intelligence in India, Scandinavia, Persia, Rome, Greece, and he will see that, throughout, art is a kind of philosophy made sensible, religion a poem taken for true, philosophy an art and a religion dried up, and reduced to simple ideas. There is therefore, at the core of each of these three groups, a common element, the conception of

① [Taine] For this scale of coordinate effects consult Renan, *Langues Sémetiques* (*General History of the Semitic Languages*). Chapter I; Mommsen, *Comparison Between Greek and Roman Civilizations*, third edition, Vol. I, Chapter 2; and Tocqueville, *Consequences of Democracy in America*, Vol. III.

the world and its principles; and if they differ among themselves, it is because each combines with the common, a distinct element: now the power of abstraction, again the power to personify and to believe, and finally the power to personify and not believe. Let us now take the two chief works of human association, the family and the state. What forms the state but a sentiment of obedience, by which the many unite under the authority of a chief? And what forms the family but the sentiment of obedience, by which wife and children act under the direction of a father and husband? The family is a natural state, primitive and restrained, as the state is an artificial family, ulterior and expanded; and amongst the differences arising from the number, origin, and condition of its members, we discover in the small society as in the great, a like disposition of the fundamental intelligence which assimilates and unites them. Now suppose that this element receives from circumstance, race, or epoch certain special marks, it is clear that all the groups into which it enters, will be modified proportionately. If the sentiment of obedience has its root in the instinct of order, sociality, and honor, you will find, as in France, a perfect military organization, a fine administrative hierarchy, a want of public spirit with occasional jerks of patriotism, ready docility of the subject with a revolutionary impatience, the cringing courtier with the counter-efforts of the genuine man, the refined sympathy between conversation and society on the one hand, and the worry at the fireside and among the family on the other, the equality of the married with the incompleteness of the married state, under the necessary constraint of the law. If, again, the sentiment of obedience has its root in the instinct of subordination and the idea of duty, you will find, as among the Germans, security and happiness in the household, a solid basis of domestic life, a tardy and incomplete development of society, an innate respect for established dignities, a superstitious reverence for the past, the keeping up of social inequalities, natural and habitual regard for the law. So in a race, according as the aptitude for general ideas varies, religion, art, and philosophy vary. If man is naturally inclined to the widest universal conceptions, and apt to disturb them at the same time by the nervous delicacy of his oversensitive organization, you will find, as in India, an astonishing abundance of gigantic religious creations, a glowing outgrowth of vast and transparent epic poems, a strange tangle of subtle and imaginative philosophies, all so well interwoven, and so penetrated with a common essence, as to be instantly recognized, by their breadth, their coloring, and their want of order, as the products of the same climate and the same intelligence. If, on the other hand, a man naturally staid and balanced in mind limits of his own accord the scope of his ideas, in order the better to define their form, you will find, as in Greece, a theology of artists and tale-tellers; distinctive gods, soon considered distinct from things, and transformed, almost at the outset, into recognized personages; the sentiment of universal unity all but effaced, and barely preserved in the vague notion of destiny; a philosophy rather close and delicate than grand and systematic, confined to a lofty metaphysics,① but incomparable for logic, sophistry, and morals; poetry and arts superior for clearness, spirit, scope, truth, and beauty to all that have ever been known. If, once more, man, reduced to narrow conceptions, and deprived of all speculative refinement, is at the same time altogether absorbed and straitened by practical occupations, you will find, as in Rome, rudimentary deities, mere hollow names, serving to designate

① [Taine] The Alexandrian philosophy had its birth from the West. The metaphysical notions of Aristotle are isolated; moreover, with him as with Plato, they are but a sketch. By way of contrast consider the systematic vigor of Plotinus, Procius, Schelling, and Hegel, or the admirable boldness of Brahminica and Buddhist speculation.

the trivial details of agriculture, generation, household concerns, etiqueties in fact of marriage, of the farm, producing a mythology, a philosophy, a poetry, either worth nothing or borrowed. Here, as elsewhere, the law of mutual dependence① comes into play. A civilization forms a body, and its parts are connected with each other like the parts of an organic body. As in an animal, instincts, teeth, limbs, osseous structure, muscular envelope, are mutually connected, so that a change in one produces a corresponding change in the rest, and a clever naturalist can by a process of reasoning reconstruct out of a few fragments almost the whole body; even so in a civilization, religion, philosophy, the organization of the family, literature, the arts, make up a system in which every local change induces a general change, so that an experienced historian, studying some particular part of it, sees in advance and half predicts the character of the rest. There is nothing vague in this interdependence. In the living body the regulator is, first, its tendency to manifest a certain primary type; then its necessity for organs whereby to satisfy its wants, and for harmony with itself in order that it may live. In a civilization, the regulator is the presence, in every great human creation, of a productive element, present also in other surrounding creations—to wit, some faculty, aptitude, disposition, effective and discernible, which, being possessed of its proper character, introduces it into all the operations in which it assists, and, according to its variations, causes all the works in which it cooperates to vary also.

VII

At this point we can obtain a glimpse of the principal features of human transformations, and begin to search for the general laws

① [Taine] I have endeavored on several occasions to give expression to this law notably in the *Preface to Essais de critique et d'histoire* (*Critical and Historical Essays*).

which regulate, not events only, but classes of events, not such and such religion or literature, but a group of literatures or religions. If, for instance, it were admitted that a religion is a metaphysical poem, accompanied by a belief; and remarking at the same time that there are certain epochs, races, and circumstances in which belief, the poetical and metaphysical faculty, are combined with an unwanted vigor; if we consider that Christianity and Buddhism were produced at periods of grand productions, and amid such miseries as raised up the fanatics of the Cévennes; if we recognize, on the other hand, that primitive religions are born at the awakening of human reason, during the richest blossoming of human imagination, at a time of the fairest artlessness and the greatest credulity; if we consider, also, that Mohammedanism appeared with the dawning of poetic prose, and the conception of national unity, amongst a people destitute of science, at a period of sudden development of the intellect, we might then conclude that a religion is born, declines, is reformed and transformed according as circumstances confirm and combine with more or less exactitude and force its three generative instincts; and we should understand why it is endemic in India, amidst imaginative, philosophic, eminently fanatic brains; why it blossomed forth so strangely and grandly in the Middle Ages, amidst an oppressive organization, new tongues and literatures; why it was aroused in the sixteenth century with a new character and heroic enthusiasm, amid universal regeneration, and during the awakening of the German races; why it breaks out into eccentric sects amid the rude American democracy, and under the bureaucratic Russian despotism; why, in fine, it is spread, at the present day, over Europe in such different dimensions and such various characteristics, according to the differences of race and civilization. And so for every kind of human production—for literature, music, the fine arts, philosophy, science, statecraft, industries, and the rest. Each of these has for its direct cause a moral disposition, or a combination of moral dispositions: the cause given, they appear; the cause withdrawn, they vanish: the weakness or intensity of the cause measures their weakness or intensity. They are bound up with their causes, as a physical phenomenon with its condition, as the dew with the fall of the variable temperature, as dilatation with heat. There are such dualities in the moral as in the physical world, as rigorously bound together, and as universally extended in the one as in the other. Whatever in the one case produces, alters, suppresses the first term, produces, alters, suppresses the second as a necessary consequence. Whatever lowers the temperature, deposits the dew. Whatever develops credulity side by side with poetical thoughts, engenders religion. Thus phenomena have been produced; thus they will be produced. As soon as we know the sufficient and necessary condition of one of these vast occurrences, our understanding grasps the future as well as the past. We can say with confidence in what circumstances it will reappear, foresee without rashness many portions of its future history, and sketch with care some features of its ulterior development.

VIII

History is now upon, or perhaps almost upon this footing, that it must proceed after such a method of research. The question propounded nowadays is of this kind. Given a literature, philosophy, society, art, group of arts, what is the moral condition which produced it? What the conditions of race, epoch, circumstance, the most fitted to produce this moral condition? There is a distinct moral condition for each of these formations, and for each of their branches; one for art in general, one for each kind of art—for architecture, painting, sculpture, music, poetry; each has its special germ in the wide field of human psychology; each has its law, and it is by virtue of this law that we see it raised, by chance, as it seems, wholly alone, amid the miscarriage of its neighbors, like painting in Flanders and Holland in the seventeenth century, poetry in England in the sixteenth, music in Germany in the eighteenth. At this moment, and in these countries, the conditions have been fulfilled for one art, not for others, and a single branch has budded in the general barrenness. For these rules of human growth must history search; with the special psychology of each special formation it must occupy itself; the finished picture of these characteristic conditions it must now labor to compose. No task is more delicate or more difficult; Montesquieu[①] tried it, but in his time history was too new to admit of his success; they had not yet even a suspicion of the road necessary to be traveled, and hardly now do we begin to catch sight of it. Just as in its elements astronomy is a mechanical and physiology a chemical problem, so history in its elements is a psychological problem. There is a particular inner system of impressions and operations which makes an artist, a believer, a musician, a painter, a wanderer, a man of society; and of each the affiliation, the depth, the independence of ideas and emotions, are different: each has its moral history and its special structure, with some governing disposition and some dominant feature. To explain each, it would be necessary to write a chapter of esoteric analysis, and barely yet has such a method been rudely sketched. One man alone, Stendhal,[②] with a singular bent of mind and a singular education, has undertaken it, and to this day the majority of readers find his books paradoxical and obscure: his talent and his ideas were premature; his admirable divinations were not understood, any more than his profound sayings thrown out cursorily, or the astonishing justness of

① Charles Louis de Secondat, Baron de la Bréde Montesquieu (1689–1755), French political philosopher.

② Stendhal (Marie Henri Beyle, 1783–1842), French novelist.

his perception and of his logic. It was not perceived that, under the exterior of a conversationalist and a man of the world, he explained the most complicated of esoteric mechanisms; that he laid his finger on the mainsprings; that he introduced into the history of the heart scientific processes, the art of notation, decomposition, deduction; that he first marked the fundamental causes of nationality, climate, temperament; in short, that he treated of sentiments as they should be treated — in the manner of the naturalist, namely, and of the natural philosopher, who constructs classifications and weighs forces. For this very reason he was considered dry and eccentric: he remained solitary, writing novels, voyages, notes, for which he sought and obtained a score of readers. And yet we find in his books at the present day essays the most suitable to open the path which I have endeavored to describe. No one has better taught us how to open our eyes and see, to see first the men that surround us and the life that is present, then the ancient and authentic documents, to read between the black and white lines of the pages, to recognize under the old impression, under the scribbling of a text, the precise sentiment, the movement of ideas, the state of mind in which they were written. In his writings, in Sainte-Beuve, in the German critics, the reader will see all the wealth that may be drawn from a literary work: when the work is rich, and one knows how to interpret it, we find there the psychology of a soul, frequently of an age, now and then of a race. In this light, a great poem, a fine novel, the confessions of a superior man, are more instructive than a heap of historians with their histories. I would give fifty volumes of charters and a hundred volumes of state papers for the memoirs of Cellini, the epistles of St. Paul, the table-talk of Luther, or the comedies of Aristophanes.① In this consists the importance of literary works: they are instructive because they are beautiful; their

① Aristophanes (c. 448 B.C.E.–after 388 B.C.E.), Greek comic dramatist.

utility grows with their perfection; and if they furnish documents, it is because they are monuments. The more a book represents visible sentiments, the more it is a work of literature; for the proper office of literature is to take note of sentiments. The more a book represents important sentiments, the higher is its place in literature; for it is by representing the mode of being of a whole nation and a whole age, that a writer rallies round him the sympathies of an entire age and an entire nation. This is why, amid the writings which set before our eyes the sentiments of preceding generations, a literature, and notably a grand literature, is incomparably the best. It resembles that admirable apparatus of extraordinary sensibility, by which physicians disentangle and measure the most recondite and delicate changes of a body. Constitutions, religions, do not approach it in importance; the articles of a code and of a catechism only show us the spirit roughly and without delicacy. If there are any writings in which politics and dogma are full of life, it is in the eloquent discourses of the pulpit and the tribune, memoirs, unrestrained confessions; and all this belongs to literature: so that, in addition to itself, it has all the advantage of other works. It is then chiefly by the study of literatures that one may construct a moral history, and advance toward the knowledge of psychological laws, from which events spring.

I am about to write the history of a literature, and to seek in it for the psychology of a people: if I have chosen this one in particular, it is not without a reason. I had to find a people with a grand and complete literature, and this is rare: there are few nations who have, during their whole existence, really and written. Among the ancients, the Latin literature is worth nothing at the outset, then borrowed and imitative. Among the moderns, German literature is almost wanting for two centuries.① Italian literature and Spanish literature end at the middle

① [Taine] From 1550–1750.

of the seventeenth century. Only ancient Greece, modern France and England, offer a complete series of great significant monuments. I have chosen England, because being yet alive, and subject to direct examination, it may be better studied than a destroyed civilization, of which we retain but the scraps, and because, being different from France, it has in the eyes of a Frenchman a more distinct character. Besides, there is a peculiarity in this civilization, that apart from its spontaneous development, it presents a forced deviation, it has suffered the last and most effectual of all conquests, and that the three grounds whence it has sprung, race, climate, the Norman invasion, may be observed in its remains with perfect exactness; so well, that we may examine in this history the two most powerful moving springs of human transformation, natural bent and constraining force, and we may examine them without uncertainty or gap, in a series of authentic and unmutilated memorials. I have endeavored to define these primary springs, to exhibit their gradual effects, to explain how they have ended by bringing to light great political, religious, and literary works, and by developing the recondite mechanism whereby the Saxon barbarian has been transformed into the Englishman of today.

6.3 Key Words

① École Normale Supérieure 巴黎高等师范学院

École Normale Supérieure (ENS) is one of the most selective and prestigious graduate schools in Paris, France. It is one of the French grandes écoles and a constituent member of PSL University. Initially conceived during the French Revolution, the principal goal of ENS is the training of professors, researchers and public administrators. Among its alumni there are 14 Nobel Prize Laureates, 12 Fields Medalists, more than half the recipients of the CNRS's Gold Medal (France's highest scientific prize), several hundred members of the

Institut de France, and scores of politicians and statesmen. The school has achieved particular recognition in the fields of mathematics and physics as one of France's foremost scientific training grounds, along with notability in the human sciences as the spiritual birthplace of authors such as Julien Gracq, Jean Giraudoux, Assia Djebar, and Charles Péguy, philosophers such as Henri Bergson (亨利·柏格森), Jean-Paul Sartre (让-保罗·萨特), Louis Althusser, Simone Weil, Maurice Merleau-Ponty (莫里斯·梅洛-庞蒂) and Alain Badiou (阿兰·巴迪欧), social scientists such as Émile Durkheim, Raymond Aron, and Pierre Bourdieu, and "French theorists" such as Michel Foucault (米歇尔·福柯) and Jacques Derrida (雅克·德里达).

② Sainte-Beuve 圣-勃夫

Charles Augustin Sainte-Beuve (1804–1869) was a French literary critic. He used to study medicine, and served in St. Louis Hospital. Beginning in 1824, he contributed literary articles, and later became friend of Victor Hugo (维克多·雨果). Sainte-Beuve published collections of poems and the partly autobiographical novel *Volupté* in 1834. His articles and essays were collected in the volumes *Port-Royal* and *Portraits littéraires*.

③ Madame de Staël 斯塔尔夫人

Anne Louise Germaine de Staël-Holstein (1766–1817), commonly known as Madame de Staël, was a woman of letters and political theorist. Known as a witty and brilliant conversationalist, she stimulated the political and intellectual life of her time, a time witnessing the great revolution and Napoleon. Her works, whether novels, travel literature or polemics, emphasized individuality and passion made a lasting mark on European thought. Her most influential works included *Lettres sur le caractère et les écrits de J.-J. Rousseau* (《论卢梭的性格与作品》) in 1788, *De la littérature dans ses rapports avec les institutions sociales* (《论文学与社会制度的关系》) in 1799, and *De l'Allemagne* (《论德意志》) in 1813.

④ the Industrial Revolution 工业革命

In our text, the Industrial Revolution generally refers to the First Industrial Revolution, which was the transition to new manufacturing processes in Europe and the United States, in the period from about 1760 to sometime between 1820 and 1840. It began in England, and greatly changed the world by providing new technologies and scientific views of the world which had never appeared ever in history.

⑤ Milieu 环境

Milieu in French or the social environment, social context, sociocultural context refers to the immediate physical and social setting in which people live or in which something happens or develops. It includes the culture that the individual was educated or lives in, and the people and institutions with whom they interact. The interaction may be in person or through communication media, even anonymous or one-way, and may not imply equality of social status. The social environment is a broader concept than that of social class or social circle.

6.4 Extensive Explorations

① How much do you know about the Industrial Revolution in the 19th century? How did it change the way of thought of human beings?

② Have you read Taine's *The Philosophy of Art* (《艺术哲学》)? Is there any correlation with the three elements mentioned in *Preface to History of English Literature*?

③ What do you think of the influence of the fact of races on literature? Make an example to verify your idea.

④ What do you know about the geographical surroundings in Europe? Is there any similar example you can analyze in China?

⑤ Wang Guowei (王国维) once said, each era possesses their own typical literature (一代有一代之文学). Can you compare this with Taine's element of epoch?

⑥ Which is the most influential fact between external and internal impacts on literature? Why?

⑦ Do you agree with Taine's discussion on the dynamic forces on the evolution of literature? If not, provide the reason for disagreement.

⑧ Is Taine's theory still beneficial for today's literary study?

7. Oscar Wilde's *Preface to The Picture of Dorian Gray*

7.1 Lead-in

Oscar Fingal O'Flahertie Wills Wilde (1854–1900) was an Irish poet and playwright. He became one of the most popular playwrights in early 1890s in London. He is best remembered for his epigrams and plays, his novel *The Picture of Dorian Gray* (《道林·格雷的画像》), and the circumstances of his criminal conviction for "gross indecency," imprisonment, and early death at age of 46.

Wilde received the best education in his youth and learned to speak fluent French and German. He went to Trinity College Dublin (都柏林圣三一学院), then to Oxford. At college he was deeply attracted by the emerging philosophy of aestheticism, influenced by Walter Pater and John Ruskin. He was very active in the cultural life in London and lectured in North America on the new "English Renaissance in Art" and interior decoration, and then returned to London where he worked prolifically as a journalist. Known for his biting wit, flamboyant dress and glittering conversational skill, Wilde acquired great popularity in his day. At the turn of the 1890s, he refined his ideas about the supremacy of art in a series of dialogues and essays, and incorporated themes of decadence, duplicity, and beauty into what would be his only novel, *The Picture of Dorian Gray* (1890). The opportunity to construct aesthetic details precisely, and combine them with larger social themes, drew Wilde to write dramas. He wrote *Salome* (1891) in French while in Paris but it was refused a license for

England due to an absolute prohibition on the portrayal of Biblical subjects on the English stage. Unperturbed, Wilde produced four society comedies in the early 1890s, which made him one of the most successful playwrights of late-Victorian London.

When enjoying high level of success in his career, Wilde had legal disputes with the Marquess of Queensberry (昆斯伯里侯爵) who was the father of Wilde's lover, Lord Alfred Douglas. This dispute caused him two years' hard labour, the maximum penalty, and was jailed from 1895 to 1897. During this time, he wrote *De Profundis* (published posthumously in 1905), and his last work, *The Ballad of Reading Gaol* (1898), a long poem commemorating the harsh rhythms of prison life, was finished on his release.

Oscar Wilde's fairy tale, *The Selfish Giant* (《自私的巨人》), was once selected in our middle school textbooks. He is called "Prince of Fairy Tales" for two famous fairy-tale selections. The material we've chosen for the textbook is the preface to a controversial novel in his time, *The Picture of Dorian Gray*. The preface of 2 pages is the shortest of the 15 pieces of material in the textbook, which is basically made up of mottos and versicles, which is similar to a declaration of his attitude on literature and aesthetics.

As a genius in his time, Oscar Wilde presented his views of aestheticism which was formed at college in the story, *The Picture of Dorian Gray*. Dorian Gray was a handsome kind young man from London. One time he saw the portrait a painter Basil Hallward created for him and discovered his own beauty. Dorian listens to Lord Henry espousing his hedonistic world view and wish that the painted image of himself would age in his stead and take all the consequences of his evil. He didn't think much of it at first. Then after fooling the actress Sibyl with love and causing her suicide, Dorian notices that the portrait has changed. The man in the portrait bears a subtle sneer of cruelty. Dorian though scared didn't restrain himself but indulged ever more. His beauty lasted while the portrait got more and more ugly. 18 years later, Dorian murdered the painter of the portrait Basil Hallward for Dorian loathed his own sin. The actress's brother found Dorian but was deceived by his words. He ended up dead. His death woke Dorian. Dorian stabbed the portrait only to find himself dead as a result, his face aged and ugly while the portrait reverted to its original beauty. There are some other details to add. The novel launched intense discussion at the time. Many of the reasons were not mentioned in what I've just said. Abusing, murder and many other awful deeds were described, including destroying bodies to cover the evidence.

Such story aroused harsh response on the first release. Even after the story was rewritten for many times, it was still strictly criticized even after mass modification. Apart from that, the story was also profoundly sarcastic. The ugliness of upper class and how modern science obliterated art was revealed. In the novel, after Dorian Gray killed the painter, he forced a chemist to burn the body with a specific kind of chemical. The novel also exposed the disguise of morality which stimulated the crowd. His wish for immortality and youth was everything against his morality. The more he wish to be mortal, the more he indulge himself. And during that process, he did countless crimes which were revealed by the ugliness of the changing portrait. In Oscar Wilde's time, the novel is relatively obscure, but still unacceptable, morally and aesthetically. Oscar Wilde simply held the view that pure aestheticism, for example, a face that never age could only cause fallen morality. In the pursuit of beauty, one should procure the balance between beauty and morality. This is how the intense, even perverted story of Oscar Wilde's enlightens us. The above are Oscar Wilde's tendency of aesthetics and literature criticism theory.

7.2 Text

The Picture of Dorian Gray

(The Preface)

The artist is the creator of beautiful things.

To reveal art and conceal the artist is art's aim.

The critic is he who can translate into another manner or a new material his impression of beautiful things.

The highest, as the lowest, form of criticism is a mode of autobiography.

Those who find ugly meanings in beautiful things are corrupt without being charming. This is a fault.

Those who find beautiful meanings in beautiful things are the cultivated. For these there is hope. They are the elect to whom beautiful things mean only Beauty.

There is no such thing as a moral or an immoral book. Books are well written, or badly written. That is all.

The nineteenth-century dislike of Realism is the rage of Caliban seeing his own face in a glass.

The nineteenth-century dislike of Romanticism is the rage of Caliban not seeing his own face in a glass.

The moral life of man forms part of the subject matter of the artist, but the morality of art consists in the perfect use of an imperfect medium.

No artist desires to prove anything. Even things that are true can be proved.

No artist has ethical sympathies. An ethical sympathy in an artist is an unpardonable mannerism of style.

No artist is ever morbid. The artist can express everything.

Thought and language are to the artist instruments of an art.

Vice and virtue are to the artist materials for an art.

From the point of view of form, the type of all the arts is the art of the musician. From the point of view of feeling, the actor's craft is the type.

All art is at once surface and symbol.

Those who go beneath the surface do so at their peril.

Those who read the symbol do so at their peril.

It is the spectator, and not life, that art really mirrors.

Diversity of opinion about a work of art shows that the work is new, complex, and vital.

When critics disagree the artist is in accord with himself.

We can forgive a man for making a useful thing as long as he does not admire it. The only excuse for making a useless thing is that one admires it intensely.

All art is quite useless.

7.3 Key Words

① Playwright 剧作家

The word "play" is from Middle English pleye, in the meaning of game, drama or applause. The word "wright" is an archaic English term for a craftsman or builder (as in a wheelwright or cartwright). The words combine to indicate a person who has "wrought" words, themes, and other elements into a dramatic form—a play. The first recorded use of the term "playwright" is from 1605, 73 years before the first written record of the term "dramatist." It appears to have been first used in a pejorative sense by Ben Jonson to suggest a mere tradesman fashioning works for the theatre.

② Trinity College Dublin 都柏林圣三一学院

Trinity College, officially College of the Holy and Undivided Trinity of Queen Elizabeth near Dublin, is the sole constituent college of the University of Dublin, a research university located in Dublin, Ireland. The college was founded in 1592 by Queen Elizabeth I (伊

丽莎白一世) as “the mother of a university” but only one college was ever established; as such, the designations “Trinity College” and “University of Dublin” are usually synonymous for practical purposes. The university is a member of the League of European Research Universities (LERU), a list of 23 institutions that excel in academic research, and is the only Irish university in the group. The university has educated some of Ireland’s most famous poets, playwrights and authors, including Oscar Wilde, Jonathan Swift, Bram Stoker, William Trevor, Oliver Goldsmith and William Congreve, Nobel Laureates Samuel Beckett, Ernest Walton and William Cecil Campbell, former Presidents of Ireland, including Mary McAleese, Douglas Hyde and Mary Robinson, philosophers including George Berkeley and Edmund Burke, and mathematician — William Rowan Hamilton.

③ Aestheticism 唯美主义

Aestheticism (also the Aesthetic Movement) is an intellectual and art movement supporting the emphasis of aesthetic values more than social-political themes for literature, fine art, music and other arts. This meant that art from this particular movement focused more on being beautiful rather than having a deeper meaning — “art for art’s sake” (为艺术而艺术). It was particularly prominent in Europe during the late 19th century, supported by notable figures such as Walter Pater and Oscar Wilde, the latter was the pupil of Pater at Oxford. More contemporary critics are also associated with the movement, such as Harold Bloom, who argued against projecting social and political ideology onto literary works, which he believes has been a growing problem in humanities departments over the 20th century.

④ *Salome* (play)《莎乐美》

Salome is a tragedy by Oscar Wilde. The original 1891 version of the play was in French. Three years later an English translation was published. The play tells in one act the Biblical story of Salome, stepdaughter of the tetrarch Herod Antipas, who, to her stepfather's dismay but to the delight of her mother Herodias, requests the head of Jokanaan (John the Baptist) on a silver platter as a reward for dancing the dance of the seven veils.

⑤ Caliban 卡利班

Caliban, son of the witch Sycorax, is an important character in William Shakespeare's play *The Tempest* (《暴风雨》). His character is one of the few Shakespearean figures to take on a life of its own "outside" Shakespeare's own work; as Russell Hoban put it, "Caliban is one of the hungry ideas, he's always looking for someone to word him into being ... Caliban is a necessary idea."

⑥ Lord Alfred Douglas 阿尔弗雷德·道格拉斯勋爵

Lord Alfred Bruce Douglas (1870–1945) was a British poet and journalist best known as the lover of Oscar Wilde. While studying at Oxford, he edited an undergraduate journal, *The Spirit Lamp*, which carried a homoerotic subtext, and met Wilde, with whom he started a close but stormy relationship. Douglas' father, the Marquess of Queensberry, disapproved strongly of the affair, and set out to humiliate Wilde, publicly accusing him of homosexuality. Wilde sued him for criminal libel, but some of his intimate notes were discovered, and he was duly jailed. On his release, Wilde briefly lived with Douglas in Naples, but they were separated by the time Wilde died in 1900.

⑦ Criminal libel 刑事诽谤

Criminal libel is a legal term, of English origin, which may be used with one of two distinct meanings in those common law jurisdictions where it is still used. It is also used as a collective term for all offences which consist of the publication of some prohibited matter in a libel (in permanent form), namely defamatory libel, seditious libel, blasphemous libel and obscene libel.

⑧ Autobiography 自传

An autobiography is a self-written account of the life of oneself. The word "autobiography" was first used deprecatingly by William Taylor in 1797 in the English periodical *The Monthly Review*, when he suggested the word as a hybrid, but condemned it as "pedantic." Despite only being named early in the 19th century, first-person autobiographical writing originates in antiquity. While biographers generally rely on a wide variety of documents and viewpoints, autobiography may be based entirely on the writer's memory. The memoir form is closely associated with autobiography but it tends, as Pascal claims, to focus less on the self and more on others during the autobiographer's review of his or her life.

7.4 Extensive Explorations

① Have you read any of Wilde's fairy tales? Try to repeat the story.

② Watch the movie titled *The Picture of Dorian Gray* and review Wilde's ideas in the preface.

③ How do you comment on Dorian Gray's ambition or appetence?

④ What do you think of Wilde's "The highest as the lowest form of criticism is a mode of autobiography"? If you are to write your own autobiography, how would you depict your experiences?

⑤ Think about the moral factors in a book in English literature and compare it with Wilde's idea. What does the morality work in a story?

⑥ What does Wilde mean when he said "No artist has ethical sympathies"?

⑦ Do you have any similar experience in going beneath the surface and symbol when encountering a piece of work of art?

⑧ Why did Wilde say "All art is quite useless"?

8. Sigmund Freud's *Development of the Libido and Sexual Organization*

8.1 Lead-in

Sigmund Freud (1856–1939) was an Austrian neurologist, born in a Jewish family in Freiburg. He qualified as a doctor of medicine in 1881 at the University of Vienna and became founder of psychoanalysis (精神分析), which is a clinical method for treating psychopathology through dialogue between a patient and a psychoanalyst. As the founding pioneer of psychoanalysis, he developed therapeutic techniques such as the use of free association and discovered transference, establishing its central role in the analytic process. Freud's redefinition of sexuality to include its infantile forms led him to formulate the Oedipus complex (俄狄浦斯情结) as the central tenet of psychoanalytical theory. His analysis of dreams as wish-fulfillments provided him with models for the clinical analysis of symptom formation and the underlying mechanisms of repression. On this basis Freud elaborated his theory of the unconscious and went on to develop a model of psychic structure comprising id, ego and super-ego. Freud postulated the existence of libido (力比多), a sexualized energy with which mental processes and structures are invested and which generates erotic attachments, and a death drive, the source of compulsive repetition, hate, aggression and neurotic guilt. In his later works, Freud developed a wide-ranging interpretation and critique of religion and culture.

As we know, Freud was not a professional literature critic. He was known to the world as a psychiatrist. However, he displayed great impact in the history of literary criticism, especially Western literary theory. He spent 8 years studying in University of Vienna as a student of Brentano (布伦塔诺), the famous philosopher and foregoer of psychology research. Since late 19th century was a time for the transition of literary theory and aesthetical theory, as well as the transition of hermeneutics from Dilthey (狄尔泰) to Heidegger (海德格尔), from pre-modern to modern. Brentano had yet several well-known students on philosophy, and Edmund Husserl (埃德蒙·胡塞尔) was one of them. Husserl was also a German Jewish philosopher, who established phenomenology in consequence of his disagreement with Brentano. Phenomenology is exactly a retort towards psychoanalysis.

The text we selected for the textbook is excerpted from *Introductory Lectures on Psycho-Analysis*. This material is part of the 21st lecture which analyzes the pattern and development of libido. Freud's another masterpiece, *The Interpretation of Dreams* (《梦的解析》) enlightened literature development, as a key to analyzing literary creation. This text we selected is different from those Freudian essays which analyze literary phenomena through psychoanalysis such as the Oedipus complex and its appearance in *Hamlet* (《哈姆雷特》) and *Sons and Lovers* (《儿子与情人》). It mainly analyzes through scientific pattern and talks about the meaning of libido and development of human mind. The purpose of this text in the textbook is, on the contrary, simply forming the basis for the original analysis of libido.

In Freud's realm of psychoanalysis theory, literature had its origin in sexual desire of human. However, libido is not simply sex. It's exactly the pleasure gained by satisfying human desire. In Freud's view, human desire comes from libido. It is the source power of human desire, which is human nature as well. Human mind would not develop itself unless desire is satisfied, or it will be terribly blocked and irregular phenomenon will happen. And this is one of Freud's sources on analyzing literary phenomena. Furthermore, Freud divided human development into five stages on account of sexual organism development. These five phases start from one's childhood, or rather, infant time. In Freud's perspective, an infant has touched its mother's sexual organ. And human's sexual mind starts to change during this minute. In Freud's theory, human development is divided into oral stage (口唇期), anal stage (肛门期), phallia stage (性器官期), latancy stage (潜伏期) and genital stage (生殖期). Human sexual organs have different aspects of satisfaction during these stages. In his view, if human desire isn't satisfied, these stage will be stuck, or even go back. The former usually means emotional waves and the latter, for example, one in anal stage may get back to his oral stage and one in his latancy stage may get back to his phallia stage. It is usually showed by emotional shock such as smoke addiction, alcohol addiction or childish behaviours. And such phenomena are also well proved in some literary works.

Freud's libido and his five stages can interpret some special literary phenomena well, especially those concerned with huge emotional waves. For example, the Oedipus complex is one of those classic ones. Oedipus, the ancient Greek hero, his own fate was exactly the effect of libido. In Freud's view, Oedipus depressed himself during his infant time. And his effort to relieve his stress finally contributed to the later tragedy. Freud's theory not only impacts literary research through these five stages. For example, his interpretations on day dream and unconsciousness are also key facts in the psychoanalysis on literature. In this sense, to understand Freud well, intensive reading of *The Interpretation of Dreams* and *Introductory Lectures on Psycho-Analysis* are strongly recommended.

8.2 Text

Development of the Libido and Sexual Organization[①]

[Freud begins this lecture with a return to the subject of perversions and its importance for his theory of sexuality, with particular emphasis upon infantile sexuality, especially as children seek "gratification in the genital organs." He introduces the idea of a "latency period" that may be absent, but usually appears from about the sixth to the eighth year, though the period of "greatest interest" for "libido-development" comes earlier, usually before the third year. The rapid development of the libido in early childhood carries forward, from an early "oral phase" to a period of "genital organization" which subordinates the "libido-function" to "the primacy of the genital zone."]

* * *

Today we will follow up another aspect of this development—namely, the relation of the sexual component-impulses to an *object*; or, rather, we will take a fleeting glimpse over this development so that we may spend more time upon a comparatively late result of it. Certain of the component-impulses of the sexual instinct have an object from the very beginning and hold fast to it: such are the impulses to mastery (sadism), to gazing (skoptophilia) and curiosity. Others, more plainly

---

① From TWENTY-FIRST LECTURE: DEVELOPMENT OF THE LIBIDO AND SEXUAL ORGANIZATION, which was first given in a series of lectures in Vienna, 1915–1917, and first published in 1920, revised edition, 1935. Reprinted from *A General Introduction to Psychoanalysis*, authorized English translation of the revised edition by Joan Riviere (New York: Liveright Publishing Corporation, 1935).

connected with particular erotogenic areas in the body, only have an object in the beginning, so long as they are still dependent upon the non-sexual functions, and give it up when they become detached from these later. Thus the first object of the oral component of the sexual instinct is the mother's breast which satisfies the infant's need for nutrition. In the act of sucking for its own sake the erotic component, also gratified in sucking for nutrition, makes itself independent, gives up the object in an external person, and replaces it by a part of the child's own person. The oral impulse becomes auto-erotic, as the anal and other erotogenic impulses are from the beginning. Further development has, to put it as concisely as possible, two aims: first, to renounce auto-erotism, to give up again the object found in the child's own body in exchange again for an external one; and secondly, to combine the various objects of the separate impulses and replace them by one single one. This naturally can only be done if the single object is again itself complete, with a body like that of the subject; nor can it be accomplished without some part of the auto-erotic impulse-excitations being abandoned as useless.

The processes by which an object is found are rather involved, and have not so far received comprehensive exposition. For our purposes, it may be emphasized that, when the process has reached a certain point in the years of childhood before the latency period, the object adopted proves almost identical with the first object of the oral pleasure impulse, adopted by reason of the child's dependent relationship to it; it is, namely, the mother, although not the mother's breast. We call the mother the first love-object. We speak of "love" when we lay the accent upon the mental side of the sexual impulses and disregard, or wish to forget for a moment, the demands of the fundamental physical or "sensual" side of the impulses. At about the time when the mother becomes the love-object, the mental operation of repression has already begun in the child and has withdrawn from him the knowledge of some part of his sexual aims. Now with this choice of the mother as love-object is connected all that which, under the name of "the Oedipus complex," has become of such great importance in the psychoanalytic explanation of the neuroses and which has had a perhaps equally important share in causing the opposition against psychoanalysis.

Here is a little incident which occurred during the present war.[①] One of the staunch adherents of psychoanalysis was stationed in his medical capacity on the German front in Poland; he attracted the attention of his colleagues by the fact that he occasionally effected an unexpected influence upon a patient. On being questioned, he admitted that he worked with psychoanalytic methods and with readiness agreed to impart his knowledge to his colleagues. So every evening the medical men of the corps, his colleagues and superiors, met to be initiated into the mysteries of psychoanalysis. For a time all went well; but when he had introduced his audience to the Oedipus complex a superior officer rose and announced that he did not believe this, it was the behaviour of a cad for the lecturer to relate such things to brave men, fathers of families who were fighting for their country, and he forbade the continuation of the lectures. This was the end; the analyst got himself transferred to another part of the front. In my opinion however, it is a bad outlook if a victory for German arms depends upon an "organization" of science such as this, and German science will not prosper under any such organization.

Now you will be impatiently waiting to hear what this terrible Oedipus complex comprises. The name tells you: you all know the Greek myth of King Oedipus; whose destiny was to slay his father and to wed his mother, who did all in his power to avoid the fate prophesied by the oracle, and who in self-punishment blinded himself

① That is World War I.

when he discovered that in ignorance he had committed both these crimes. I trust that many of you have yourselves experienced the profound effect of the tragic drama fashioned by Sophocles from this story. The Attic poet's work portrays the gradual discovery of the deed of Oedipus, long since accomplished, and brings it slowly to light by skillfully prolonged enquiry, constantly fed by new evidence; it has thus a certain resemblance to the course of a psychoanalysis. In the dialogue the deluded mother-wife, Jocasta, resists the continuation of the enquiry; she points out that many people in their dreams have mated with their mothers, but that dreams are of no account. To us dreams are of much account, especially typical dreams which occur in many people; we have no doubt that the dream Jocasta speaks of is intimately related to the shocking and terrible story of the myth.

It is surprising that Sophocles' tragedy does not call forth indignant remonstrance in its audience; this reaction would be much better justified in them than it was in the blunt army doctor. For at bottom it is an immoral play; it sets aside the individual's responsibility to social law, and displays divine forces ordaining the crime and rendering powerless the moral instincts of the human being which would guard him against the crime. It would be easy to believe that an accusation against destiny and the gods was intended in the story of the myth; in the hands of the critical Euripides, at variance with the gods, it would probably have become such an accusation. But with the reverent Sophocles there is no question of such an intention; the pious subtlety which declares it the highest morality to bow to the will of the gods, even when they ordain a crime, helps him out of the difficulty. I do not believe that this moral is one of the virtues of the drama, but neither does it detract from its effect; it leaves the hearer indifferent; he does not react to this, but to the secret meaning and content of the myth itself. He reacts as though by self-analysis he had detected the Oedipus complex in himself, and had recognized the will of the gods and the oracle as glorified disguises of his own unconscious; as though he remembered in himself the wish to do away with his father and in his place to wed his mother, and must abhor the thought. The poet's words seem to him to mean: "In vain do you deny that you are accountable, in vain do you proclaim how you have striven against these evil designs. You are guilty, nevertheless; for you could not stifle them; they still survive unconsciously in you." And psychological truth is contained in this; even though man has repressed his evil desires into his Unconscious and would then gladly say to himself that he is no longer answerable for them, he is yet compelled to feel his responsibility in the form of a sense of guilt for which he can discern no foundation.

There is no possible doubt that one of the most important sources of the sense of guilt which so often torments neurotic people is to be found in the Oedipus complex. More than this: in 1913, under the title of *Totem and Tabu,* I published a study of the earliest forms of religion and morality in which I expressed a suspicion that perhaps the sense of guilt of man kind as a whole, which is the ultimate source of religion and morality, was acquired in the beginnings of history through the Oedipus complex. I should much like to tell you more of this, but I had better not; it is difficult to leave this subject when once one begins upon it, and we must return to individual psychology.

Now what does direct observation of children, at the period of object-choice before the latency period, show us in regard to the Oedipus complex? Well, it is easy to see that the little man wants his mother all to himself, finds his father in the way, becomes restive when the latter takes upon himself to caress her, and shows his satisfaction when the father goes away or is absent. He often expresses his feelings directly in words and promises his mother to marry her; this may not seem much in comparison with the deeds of Oedipus, but it is enough in fact; the kernel of each is the same. Observation is often rendered puzzling by the circumstance that the same child on other occasions at this period will display great affection for the father; but such contrasting — or, better, *ambivalent* — states of feeling, which in adults would lead to conflicts, can be tolerated alongside one another in the child for a long time, just as later on they dwell together permanently in the unconscious. One might try to object that the little boy's behaviour is due to egoistic motives and does not justify the conception of an erotic complex; the mother looks after all the child's needs and consequently it is to the child's interest that she should trouble herself about no one else. This too is quite correct; but it is soon clear that in this, as in similar dependent situations, egoistic interests only provide the occasion on which the erotic impulses seize. When the little boy shows the most open sexual curiosity about his mother, wants to sleep with her at night, insists on being in the room while she is dressing, or even attempts physical acts of seduction, as the mother so often observes and laughingly relates, the erotic nature of this attachment to her is established without a doubt. Moreover, it should not be forgotten that a mother looks after a little daughter's needs in the same way without producing this effect; and that often enough a father eagerly vies with her in trouble for the boy without succeeding in winning the same importance in his eyes as the mother. In short, the factor of sex preference is not to be eliminated from the situation by any criticisms. From the point of view of the boy's egoistic interests it would merely be foolish if he did not tolerate two people in his service rather than only one of them.

As you see, I have only described the relationship of a boy to his father and mother; things proceed in just the same way, with the necessary reversal, in little girls. The loving devotion to the father, the need to do away with the superfluous mother and to take her place, the early display of coquetry and the arts of later womanhood, make up a particularly charming picture in a little girl, and may cause us to forget its seriousness and the grave consequences which may later result from this situation. Let us not fail to add that frequently the parents themselves exert a decisive influence upon the awakening of the Oedipus complex in a child, by themselves following the sex attraction where there is more than one child; the father in an unmistakable manner prefers his little daughter with marks of tenderness, and the mother, the son; but even this factor does not seriously impugn the spontaneous nature of the infantile Oedipus complex. When other children appear, the Oedipus complex expands and becomes a family complex. Reinforced anew by the injury resulting to the egoistic interests, it actuates a feeling of aversion towards these new arrivals and an unhesitating wish to get rid of them again. These feelings of hatred are as a rule much more often openly expressed than those connected with the parental complex. If such a wish is fulfilled and after a short time death removes the unwanted addition to the family, later analysis can show what a significant event this death is for the child, although it does not necessarily remain in memory. Forced into the second place by the birth of another child and for the first time almost entirely parted from the mother, the child finds it very hard to forgive her for this exclusion of him; feelings which in adults we should describe as profound embitterment are roused in him, and often become the ground-work of a lasting estrangement. That sexual curiosity and all its consequences is usually connected with these experiences has already been mentioned. As these new brothers and sisters grow up the child's attitude to them undergoes the most important transformations. A boy may take his sister as love-object in place of his faithless mother; where there are several brothers to win the favour of a little sister hostile rivalry, of great importance in after life, shows itself already in the nursery. A little girl takes an older brother as a substitute for the father who no longer treats her with the same tenderness as in her earliest years;

or she takes a little sister as a substitute for the child that she vainly wished for from her father.

So much and a great deal more of a similar kind is shown by direct observation of children, and by consideration of clear memories of childhood, uninfluenced by analysis. Among other things you will infer from this that a child's position in the sequence of brothers and sisters is of very great significance for the course of his later life, a factor to be considered in every biography. What is even more important, however, is that in the face of these enlightening considerations, so easily to be obtained, you will hardly recall without smiling the scientific theories accounting for the prohibition of incest. What has not been invented for this purpose! We are told that sexual attraction is diverted from the members of the opposite sex in one family owing to their living together from early childhood; or that a biological tendency against inbreeding has a mental equivalent in the horror of incests! Whereby it is entirely overlooked that no such rigorous prohibitions in law and custom would be required if any trustworthy natural barriers against the temptation to incest existed. The opposite is the truth. The first choice of object in mankind is regularly an incestuous one, directed to the mother and sister of men, and the most stringent prohibitions are required to prevent this sustained infantile tendency from being carried into effect. In the savage and primitive peoples surviving today the incest prohibitions are a great deal stricter than with us; Theodor Reik[①] has recently shown in a brilliant work that the meaning of the savage rites of puberty which represent rebirth is the loosening of the boy's incestuous attachment to the mother and his reconciliation with the father.

Mythology will show you that incest, ostensibly so much abhorred

---

① Theodor Reik (1888–1969), Austrian psychologist who emigrated to the United States in 1938.

by men, is permitted to their gods without a thought; and from ancient history you may learn that incestuous marriage with a sister was prescribed as a sacred duty for kings (the Pharaohs of Egypt and the Incas of Peru); it was therefore in the nature of a privilege denied to the common herd.

Incest with the mother is one of the crimes of Oedipus and parricide the other. Incidentally, these are the two great offences condemned by totemism, the first social-religious institution of mankind. Now let us tum from the direct observation of children to the analytic investigation of adults who have become neurotic; what does analysis yield in further knowledge of the Oedipus complex? Well, this is soon told. The complex is revealed just as the myth relates it; it will be seen that every one of these neurotics was himself an Oedipus or, what amounts to the same thing, has become a Hamlet in his reaction to the complex. To be sure, the analytic picture of the Oedipus complex is an enlarged and accentuated edition of the infantile sketch; the hatred of the father and the death-wishes against him are no longer vague hints, the affection for the mother declares itself with the aim of possessing her as a woman. Are we really to accredit such grossness and intensity of the feelings to the tender age of childhood; or does the analysis deceive us by introducing another factor? It is not difficult to find one. Every time anyone describes anything past, even if he be a historian, we have to take into account all that he unintentionally imports into that past period from present and intermediate times, thereby falsifying it. With the neurotic it is even doubtful whether this retroversion is altogether unintentional; we shall hear later on that there are motives for it and we must explore the whole subject of the "retrogressive phantasy-making" which goes back to the remote past. We soon discover, too, that the hatred against the father has been strengthened by a number of motives arising in later periods and other relationships in life, and that the sexual desires towards the mother have been moulded into forms which would have been as yet foreign to the child. But it would be a vain attempt if we endeavoured to explain the whole of the Oedipus complex by "retrogressive phantasy-making," and by motives originating in later periods of life. The infantile nucleus, with more or less of the accretions to it, remains intact, as is confirmed by direct observation of children. The clinical fact which confronts us behind the form of the Oedipus complex as established by analysis now becomes of the greatest practical importance. We learn that at the time of puberty, when the sexual instinct first asserts its demands in full strength, the old familiar incestuous objects are taken up again and again invested by the libido. The infantile object-choice was but a feeble venture in play, as it were, but it laid down the direction for the object-choice of puberty. At this time a very intense flow of feeling towards the Oedipus complex or in reaction to it comes into force; since their mental antecedents have become intolerable, however, these feelings must remain for the most part outside consciousness. From the time of puberty onward the human individual must devote himself to the great task of *freeing himself from the parents*; and only after this detachment is accomplished can he cease to be a child and so become a member of the social community. For a son, the task consists in releasing his libidinal desires from his mother, in order to employ them in the quest of an external love-object in reality; and in reconciling himself with his father if he has remained antagonistic to him, or in freeing himself from his domination if, in the reaction to the infantile revolt, he has lapsed into subservience to him. These tasks are laid down for every man; it is noteworthy how seldom they are carried through ideally, that is, how seldom they are solved in a manner psychologically as well as socially satisfactory. In neurotics, however, this detachment from the parents is not accomplished at all; the son remains all his life in subjection to his father, and incapable of transferring his libido to a new sexual object. In the reversed relationship the daughter's fate may be the same. In this sense the Oedipus complex is justifiably regarded as the kernel of the neuroses.

You will imagine how incompletely I am sketching a large number of the connections bound up with the Oedipus complex which practically and theoretically are of great importance. I shall not go into the variations and possible inversions of it at all. Of its less immediate effects I should like to allude to one only, which proves it to have influenced literary production in a far-reaching manner. Otto Rank has shown in a very valuable work that dramatists throughout the ages have drawn their material principally from the Oedipus and incest complex and its variations and masked forms.① It should also be remarked that long before the time of psychoanalysis the two criminal offences of Oedipus were recognized as the true expressions of unbridled instinct. Among the works of the Encyclopaedist Diderot② you will find the famous dialogue, *Le neveu de Rameau*, which was translated into German by no less a person than Goethe. There you may read these remarkable words: *Si le petit sauvage était abandonné à lui-même, qu'il conserva toute son inbecillité et qu'il réunit au peu de raison de l'enfant au berceau la violence des passions de l'homme de trente ans, il tordrait le cou à son pére et coucherait avec sa mère.*③

There is yet one thing more which I cannot pass over. The mother-wife of Oedipus must not remind us of dreams in vain. Do you still

---

① Otto Rank (1884–1939), Austrian psychoanalyst. Freud refers to *in Das Inzest-Motiv in Dichtung und Sage* (*The Incest Theme in Literature and Legend*, translation published in 1992).

② Denis Diderot (*Critical Theory Since Plato*, p. 383); *Rameau's Nephew* was first published in 1762.

③ If the little savage were left to himself, preserving all of his imbecility, and joined the small reason of the infant in the cradle to the violence of the passions of a man of thirty years of age, he would wring his father's neck and sleep with his mother.

remember the results of our dream-analyses, how so often the dream-forming wishes proved perverse and incestuous in their nature, or betrayed an unsuspected enmity to near and beloved relatives? We then left the source of these evil strivings of feeling unexplained. Now you can answer this question yourselves. They are dispositions of the libido, and investments of objects by libido, belonging to early infancy and long since given up in conscious life, but which at night prove to be still present and in a certain sense capable of activity. But, since all men and not only neurotic persons have perverse, incestuous, and murderous dreams of this kind, we may infer that those who are normal today have also made the passage through the perversions and the object-investments of the Oedipus complex; and that this is the path of normal development; only that neurotics show in a magnified and exaggerated form what we also find revealed in the dream-analyses of normal people. And this is one of the reasons why we chose the study of dreams to lead up to that of neurotic symptoms.

8.3 Key Words

① Psychoanalysis 精神分析

Psychoanalysis is a set of theories and therapeutic techniques related to the study of the unconscious mind, which together form a method of treatment for mental disorders. The discipline was established in the early 1890s by Sigmund Freud, and was later developed in different directions, mostly by students of Freud, such as Alfred Adler (阿尔弗雷德·阿德勒) and his collaborator, Carl Gustav Jung (卡尔·荣格), as well as by Neo-Freudian (新弗洛伊德主义) thinkers, such as Erich Fromm, Karen Horney, and Harry Stack Sullivan. Psychoanalysis has been known to be a controversial discipline, as its validity as a science is often contested. Nonetheless, it remains a strong influence within psychiatry, more so in some quarters than others. Psychoanalytic concepts are also widely used outside the therapeutic arena, in areas such as psychoanalytic literary criticism, as well as in the analysis of film, fairy tales and other cultural phenomena.

② Oedipus 俄狄浦斯

Oedipus was a mythical Greek king of Thebes (底比斯). A tragic hero in Greek mythology, Oedipus accidentally fulfilled a prophecy that he would end up killing his father and marrying his mother, thereby bringing disaster to his city and family. The story of *Oedipus* is the subject of Sophocles' tragedy *Oedipus Rex*, which is followed in the narrative sequence by *Oedipus at Colonus* and *Antigone*. Together, these plays make up Sophocles' three Theban plays. Oedipus represents two enduring themes of Greek myth and drama: the flawed nature of humanity and an individual's role in the course of destiny in a harsh universe. Oedipus was born to King Laius and Queen Jocasta. Laius wished to thwart the prophecy, so he sent a shepherd-servant to leave Oedipus to die on a mountainside. However, the shepherd took pity on the baby and passed him to another shepherd who gave Oedipus to King Polybus and Queen Merope to raise as their own. Oedipus learned from the oracle at Delphi of the prophecy that he would end up killing his father and marrying his mother but, unaware of his true parentage, believed he was fated to murder Polybus and marry Merope, so left for Thebes. On his way he met an older man and killed him in a quarrel. Continuing on to Thebes, he found that the king of the city (Laius) had been recently killed, and that the city was at the mercy of the Sphinx. Oedipus answered the monster's riddle correctly, defeating it and winning the throne of the dead king—and the hand in marriage of the king's widow, who was also (unbeknownst to him) his mother Jocasta. Years later, to end a plague on Thebes, Oedipus searched to find who had killed Laius, and discovered that he himself was responsible. Jocasta, upon realizing that she had married her own son, hanged herself. Oedipus then seized two pins from her dress and blinded himself with them. The legend of Oedipus was used by Sigmund Freud to name and give mythic precedent to the Oedipus complex.

③ libido 力比多

Libido is a person's overall sexual drive or desire for sexual activity. Social factors, such as work and family, and internal psychological factors, such as personality and stress, can affect libido. Libido can also be affected by medical conditions, medications, lifestyle and relationship issues, and age. A person who has extremely frequent or a suddenly increased sex drive may be experiencing hyper-sexuality, while the opposite condition is hypo-sexuality. Sexual desires are often an important factor in the formation and maintenance of intimate relationships in humans. A lack or loss of sexual desire can adversely affect relationships.

④ *The Interpretation of Dreams*《梦的解析》

The Interpretation of Dreams is one of the most famous books by Sigmund Freud, first published in 1900, in which the author introduces his theory of the unconscious with respect to dream interpretation, and discusses what would later become the theory of the Oedipus complex. The book was revised at least eight times by Freud and, in the third edition, he added an extensive section which treated dream symbolism very literally, following the influence of Wilhelm Stekel. Because of the book's length and complexity, Freud also wrote an abridged version called *On Dreams*. The original text is widely regarded as one of Freud's most significant works.

⑤ the unconscious 潜意识

The unconscious (or the unconscious mind) consists of the processes in the mind which occur automatically and are not available to introspection and include thought processes, memories, interests and motivations. Even though these processes exist well under the surface of conscious awareness, they are theorized to exert an impact on behaviour. The term was coined by the 18th-century

German philosopher Friedrich Schelling (弗里德里克·谢林) and later introduced into English by the poet and essayist Samuel Taylor Coleridge. Empirical evidence suggests that unconscious phenomena include repressed feelings, automatic skills, subliminal perceptions, and automatic reactions, and possibly also complexes, hidden phobias and desires. The concept was popularized by Sigmund Freud. In psychoanalytic theory, unconscious processes are understood to be directly represented in dreams, as well as in slips of the tongue and jokes. Thus the unconscious mind can be seen as the source of dreams and automatic thoughts (those that appear without any apparent cause), the repository of forgotten memories (that may still be accessible to consciousness at some later time), and the locus of implicit knowledge (the things that we have learned so well that we do them without thinking).

⑥ the latency period 潜伏期

The latency period, or incubation period is the time elapsed between exposure to a pathogenic organism, a chemical, or radiation, and when symptoms and signs are first apparent. In a typical infectious disease, the incubation period signifies the period taken by the multiplying organism to reach a threshold necessary to produce symptoms in the host. While latent or latency period may be synonymous, a distinction is sometimes made between incubation period, the period between infection and onset of the disease, and latent period, the time from infection to infectiousness. Which is shorter depends on the disease.

⑦ Diderot 狄德罗

Denis Diderot (1713–1784) was a French philosopher, art critic, and writer, best known for serving as co-founder, chief editor, and contributor to the *Encyclopédie* along with Jean le Rond d'Alembert. He was a prominent figure during the Age of Enlightenment (启蒙运动时期).

8.4 Extensive Explorations

① Have you heard about psychology or knowledge of related fields? Do you think it necessary to popularize psychology to everyone in the society?

② Can you give examples about psychoanalysis you know?

③ What is the latent period like in Freud's depiction?

④ Can you tell stories verifying the Oedipus complex? Or, can you pick out movies or fictions in the history of art similar to this myth?

⑤ At what extent would the unconscious mind influence one's behaviour?

⑥ How did Freud define libido? What's the function of libido in psychoanalysis?

⑦ Do you agree that the dreams are reflection of one's unconscious or subconscious mind?

⑧ How are dreams depicted in literary works of art?

⑨ What does the theory of id, ego and super-ego work in *Development of the Libido and Sexual Organization*?

9. Virginia Woolf's *Modern Fiction*

9.1 Lead-in

Adeline Virginia Woolf (1882–1941) was an English writer who was honored as one of the most influential modernist literati and also a pioneering practitioner in the use of Stream of Consciousness (意识流) in her novel.

Woolf was born in South Kensington, London, home-schooled in English classics and Victorian literature. During her childhood she saw the Godrevy Lighthouse at the summer home, which was to become central in her novel *To the Lighthouse* (《到灯塔去》, 1927) which was her most typical novel applying Stream of Consciousness.

In 1897, she attended the Ladies' Department of King's College London (伦敦国王学院) where she studied classics and history and came into contact with early reformers of women's higher education and the women's rights movement. Encouraged by her father, Woolf began writing professionally in 1900. After her father's death in 1905, the family moved to Bloomsbury, where they adopted a free-spirited lifestyle. It was in Bloomsbury where, in conjunction with the brothers' intellectual friends, they formed the artistic and literary Bloomsbury Group.

In 1912, she married Leonard Woolf. They lived in Sussex and moved there permanently in 1940. Throughout her life, Woolf was troubled by her mental illness. Her first and second mental breakdown came from the loss of her parents, and she was institutionalized several times and attempted suicide at least twice.

Her illness may have been bipolar disorder, for which there was no effective intervention during her lifetime. In 1941, at age 59, Woolf died by drowning herself in the River Ouse at Lewes.

In 1915, Woolf published her first novel, *The Voyage Out*, and her best-known works include the novels *Mrs. Dalloway* (《达洛维夫人》, 1925), *To the Lighthouse* and *Orlando* (《奥兰多》, 1928). Her essay, *A Room of One's Own* (《一个人的房间》, 1929), displayed the much-quoted dictum, "A woman must have money and a room of her own if she is to write fiction." Woolf is also a key figure and topic in feminist criticism and her works have since garnered much attention and widespread commentary for "inspiring feminism."

Modern Fiction is an essay published in 1921 with a series of short stories called *Monday or Tuesday*. The essay is a criticism of Woolf's view on writers and literature. She believed a writer should write what inspires them and not follow any special method, however, the writers were constrained by the publishing market, which was very common at the rise of the novel in England since the early 19th century. For this reason, writers should write what they feel, the complexities of life, other than what society or publishers plotted them to depict. At this standard, she commented on various authors of modern fiction. In this text, Woolf considered writers should focus on the awkwardness of life and craved originality in their work to inspire modern fiction writers to write what interested them, wherever it may lead.

9.2 Text

Modern Fiction

In making any survey, even the freest and loosest, of modern fiction, it is difficult not to take it for granted that the modern practice of the art is somehow an improvement upon the old. With their simple tools and primitive materials, it might be said, Fielding did well and

Jane Austen even better, but compare their opportunities with ours! Their masterpieces certainly have a strange air of simplicity. And yet the analogy between literature and the process, to choose an example, of making motor cars scarcely holds good beyond the first glance. It is doubtful whether in the course of the centuries, though we have learnt much about making machines, we have learnt anything about making literature. We do not come to write better; all that we can be said to do is to keep moving, now a little in this direction, now in that, but with a circular tendency should the whole course of the track be viewed from a sufficiently lofty pinnacle. It need scarcely be said that we make no claim to stand, even momentarily, upon that vantage ground. On the flat, in the crowd, half-blind with dust, we look back with envy to those happier warriors, whose battle is won and whose achievements wear so serene an air of accomplishment that we can scarcely refrain from whispering that the fight was not so fierce for them as for us. It is for the historian of literature to decide; for him to say if we are now beginning or ending or standing in the middle of a great period of prose fiction, for down in the plain little is visible. We only know that certain gratitudes and hostilities inspire us; that certain paths seem to lead to fertile land, others to the dust and the desert; and of this perhaps it may be worth while to attempt some account.

Our quarrel, then, is not with the classics, and if we speak of quarrelling with Mr. Wells, Mr. Bennett, and Mr. Galsworthy, it is partly that by the mere fact of their existence in the flesh their work has a living, breathing, everyday imperfection which bids us take what liberties with it we choose. But it is also true that, while we thank them for a thousand gifts, we reserve our unconditional gratitude for Mr. Hardy, for Mr. Conrad, and in a much lesser degree for the Mr. Hudson of *The Purple Land*, *Green Mansions*, and *Far Away and Long Ago*. Mr. Wells, Mr. Bennett, and Mr. Galsworthy have excited so many hopes and disappointed them so persistently that our gratitude largely takes the form of thanking them for having shown us what they might have done but have not done; what we certainly could not do, but as certainly, perhaps, do not wish to do. No single phrase will sum up the charge or grievance which we have to bring against a mass of work so large in its volume and embodying so many qualities, both admirable and the reverse. If we tried to formulate our meaning in one word we should say that these three writers are materialists. It is because they are concerned not with the spirit but with the body that they have disappointed us, and left us with the feeling that the sooner English fiction turns its back upon them, as politely as may be, and marches, if only into the desert, the better for its soul. Naturally, no single word reaches the centre of three separate targets. In the case of Mr. Wells it falls notably wide of the mark. And yet even with him it indicates to our thinking the fatal alloy in his genius, the great clod of clay that has got itself mixed up with the purity of his inspiration. But Mr. Bennett is perhaps the worst culprit of the three, inasmuch as he is by far the best workman. He can make a book so well constructed and solid in its craftsmanship that it is difficult for the most exacting of critics to see through what chink or crevice decay can creep in. There is not so much as a draught between the frames of the windows, or a crack in the boards. And yet—if life should refuse to live there? That is a risk which the creator of *The Old Wives' Tale*, George Cannon, Edwin Clayhanger, and hosts of other figures, may well claim to have surmounted. His characters live abundantly, even unexpectedly, but it remains to ask how do they live, and what do they live for? More and more they seem to us, deserting even the well-built villa in the Five Towns, to spend their time in some softly padded first-class railway carriage, pressing bells and buttons innumerable; and the density to which they travel so luxuriously becomes more and more unquestionably an eternity of bliss spent in the very best hotel in Brighton. It can scarcely be said of Mr. Wells that he is a materialist in the sense that he takes too much delight in the solidity of his fabric. His mind is too generous in its sympathies to allow him to spend much time in making things shipshape and substantial. He is a materialist from sheer goodness of heart, taking upon his shoulders the work that ought to have been discharged by Government officials, and in the plethora of his ideas and facts scarcely having leisure to realize, or forgetting to think important, the crudity and coarseness of his human beings. Yet what more damaging criticism can there be both of his earth and of his Heaven than that they are to be inhabited here and hereafter by his Joans and his Peters? Does not the inferiority of their natures tarnish whatever institutions and ideals may be provided for them by the generosity of their creator? Nor, profoundly though we respect the integrity and humanity of Mr. Galsworthy, shall we find what we seek in his pages.

If we fasten, then, one label on all these books, on which is one word materialists, we mean by it that they write of unimportant things; that they spend immense skill and immense industry making the trivial and the transitory appear the true and the enduring.

We have to admit that we are exacting, and, further, that we find it difficult to justify our discontent by explaining what it is that we exact. We frame our question differently at different times. But it reappears most persistently as we drop the finished novel on the crest of a sigh—Is it worth while? What is the point of it all? Can it be that, owing to one of those little deviations which the human spirit seems to make from time to time, Mr. Bennett has come down with his magnificent apparatus for catching life just an inch or two on the wrong side? Life escapes; and perhaps without life nothing else is worth while. It is a confession of vagueness to have to make use of such a figure as this, but we scarcely better the matter by speaking, as critics are prone to do, of reality. Admitting the vagueness which afflicts all criticism of novels, let us hazard the opinion that for us at this moment the form of fiction most in vogue more often misses than secures the thing we seek. Whether we call it life or spirit, truth or reality, this, the essential thing, has moved off, or on, and refuses to be contained any longer in such ill-fitting vestments as we provide. Nevertheless, we go on perseveringly, conscientiously, constructing our two and thirty chapters after a design which more and more ceases to resemble the vision in our minds. So much of the enormous labour of proving the solidity, the likeness to life, of the story is not merely labour thrown away but labour misplaced to the extent of obscuring and blotting out the light of the conception. The writer seems constrained, not by his own free will but by some powerful and unscrupulous tyrant who has him in thrall, to provide a plot, to provide comedy, tragedy, love interest, and an air of probability embalming the whole so impeccable that if all his figures were to come to life they would find themselves dressed down to the last button of their coats in the fashion of the hour. The tyrant is obeyed; the novel is done to a turn. But sometimes, more and more often as time goes by, we suspect a momentary doubt, a spasm of rebellion, as the pages fill themselves in the customary way. Is life like this? Must novels be like this?

Look within and life, it seems, is very far from being 'like this.' Examine for a moment an ordinary mind on an ordinary day. The mind receives a myriad impressions—trivial, fantastic, evanescent, or engraved with the sharpness of steel. From all sides they come, an incessant shower of innumerable atoms; and as they fall, as they shape themselves into the life of Monday or Tuesday, the accent falls differently from of old; the moment of importance came not here but there; so that, if a writer were a free man and not a slave, if he could write what he chose, not what he must, if he could base his work upon his own feeling and not upon convention, there would be no plot, no comedy, no tragedy, no love interest or catastrophe in the accepted style, and perhaps not a single button sewn on as the Bond Street tailors would have it. Life is not a series of gig lamps symmetrically arranged; life is a luminous halo, a semi-transparent envelope surrounding us from the beginning of consciousness to the end. Is it not the task of the novelist to convey this varying, this unknown and uncircumscribed spirit, whatever aberration or complexity it may display, with as little mixture of the alien and external as possible? We are not pleading merely for courage and sincerity; we are suggesting that the proper stuff of fiction is a little other than custom would have us believe it.

It is, at any rate, in some such fashion as this that we seek to define the quality which distinguishes the work of several young writers, among whom Mr. James Joyce is the most notable, from that of their predecessors. They attempt to come closer to life, and to preserve more sincerely and exactly what interests and moves them, even if to do so they must discard most of the conventions which are commonly observed by the novelist. Let us record the atoms as they fall upon the mind in the order in which they fall. Let us trace the pattern, however disconnected and incoherent in appearance, which each sight or incident scores upon the consciousness. Let us not take it for granted that life exists more fully in what is commonly thought big than in what is commonly thought small. Any one who has read *The Portrait of the Artist as a Young Man* or, what promises to be a far more interesting work, *Ulysses*,[①] now appearing in the *Little Review*, will have hazarded some theory of this nature as to Mr. Joyce's intention. On our part, with such a fragment before us, it is hazarded rather than affirmed; but whatever the intention of the whole, there can be no question but that it is of the utmost sincerity and that the result, difficult or unpleasant as we may judge it, is undeniably important. In contrast with those whom we have called materialists, Mr. Joyce is spiritual;

---

① Written in April 1919.

he is concerned at all costs to reveal the flickerings of that innermost flame which flashes its messages through the brain, and in order to preserve it he disregards with complete courage whatever seems to him adventitious, whether it be probability, or coherence, or any other of these signposts which for generations have served to support the imagination of a reader when called upon to imagine what he can neither touch nor see. The scene in the cemetery, for instance, with its brilliancy, its sordidity, its incoherence, its sudden lightning flashes of significance, does undoubtedly come so close to the quick of the mind that, on a first reading at any rate, it is difficult not to acclaim a masterpiece. If we want life itself, here surely we have it. Indeed, we find ourselves fumbling rather awkwardly if we try to say what else we wish, and for what reason a work of such originality yet fails to compare, for we must take high examples, with *Youth* or *The Mayor of Casterbridge*. It fails because of the comparative poverty of the writer's mind, we might say simply and have done with it. But it is possible to press a little further and wonder whether we may not refer our sense of being in a bright yet narrow room, confined and shut in, rather than enlarged and set free, to some limitation imposed by the method as well as by the mind. Is it the method that inhibits the creative power? Is it due to the method that we feel neither jovial nor magnanimous, but centred in a self which, in spite of its tremor of susceptibility, never embraces or creates what is outside itself and beyond? Does the emphasis laid, perhaps didactically, upon indecency, contribute to the effect of something angular and isolated? Or is it merely that in any effort of such originality it is much easier, for contemporaries especially, to feel what it lacks than to name what it gives? In any case it is a mistake to stand outside examining 'methods.' Any method is right, every method is right, that expresses what we wish to express, if we are writers; that brings us closer to the novelist's intention if we are readers. This method has the merit of bringing us closer to what we were prepared to call life itself; did not the reading of *Ulysses* suggest how much of life is excluded or ignored, and did it not come with a shock to open *Tristram Shandy* or even *Pendennis* and be by them convinced that there are not only other aspects of life, but more important ones into the bargain.

However this may be, the problem before the novelist at present, as we suppose it to have been in the past, is to contrive means of being free to set down what he chooses. He has to have the courage to say that what interests him is no longer 'this' but 'that': out of 'that' alone must he construct his work. For the moderns 'that,' the point of interest, lies very likely in the dark places of psychology. At once, therefore, the accent falls a little differently; the emphasis is upon something hitherto ignored; at once a different outline of form becomes necessary, difficult for us to grasp, incomprehensible to our predecessors. No one but a modern, no one perhaps but a Russian, would have felt the interest of the situation which Tchehov has made into the short story which he calls 'Gusev.' Some Russian soldiers lie ill on board a ship which is taking them back to Russia. We are given a few scraps of their talk and some of their thoughts; then one of them dies and is carried away; the talk goes on among the others for a time, until Gusev himself dies, and looking 'like a carrot or a radish' is thrown overboard. The emphasis is laid upon such unexpected places that at first it seems as if there were no emphasis at all; and then, as the eyes accustom themselves to twilight and discern the shapes of things in a room we see how complete the story is, how profound, and how truly in obedience to his vision Tchehov has chosen this, that, and the other, and placed them together to compose something new. But it is impossible to say 'this is comic,' or 'that is tragic,' nor are we certain, since short stories, we have been taught, should be brief and conclusive, whether this, which is vague and inconclusive, should be called a short story at all.

The most elementary remarks upon modern English fiction can hardly avoid some mention of the Russian influence, and if the Russians are mentioned one runs the risk of feeling that to write of any fiction save theirs is waste of time. If we want understanding of the soul and heart where else shall we find it of comparable profundity? If we are sick of our own materialism the least considerable of their novelists has by right of birth a natural reverence for the human spirit. 'Learn to make yourself akin to people ... But let this sympathy be not with the mind—for it is easy with the mind—but with the heart, with love towards them.' In every great Russian writer we seem to discern the features of a saint, if sympathy for the sufferings of others, love towards them, endeavour to reach some goal worthy of the most exacting demands of the spirit constitute saintliness. It is the saint in them which confounds us with a feeling of our own irreligious triviality, and turns so many of our famous novels to tinsel and trickery. The conclusions of the Russian mind, thus comprehensive and compassionate, are inevitably, perhaps, of the utmost sadness. More accurately indeed we might speak of the inconclusiveness of the Russian mind. It is the sense that there is no answer, that if honestly examined life presents question after question which must be left to sound on and on after the story is over in hopeless interrogation that fills us with a deep, and finally it may be with a resentful, despair. They are right perhaps; unquestionably they see further than we do and without our gross impediments of vision. But perhaps we see something that escapes them, or why should this voice of protest mix itself with our gloom? The voice of protest is the voice of another and an ancient civilization which seems to have bred in us the instinct to enjoy and fight rather than to suffer and understand. English fiction from Sterne to Meredith bears witness to our natural delight in humour and comedy, in the beauty of earth, in the activities of the intellect, and in the splendour of the body. But any deductions that we may draw from the comparison of two fictions so immeasurably far apart are futile save indeed as they flood us with a view of the infinite possibilities of the art and remind us that there is no limit to the horizon, and that nothing—no 'method,' no experiment, even of the wildest—is forbidden, but only falsity and pretence. 'The proper stuff of fiction' does not exist; everything is the proper stuff of fiction, every feeling, every thought; every quality of brain and spirit is drawn upon; no perception comes amiss. And if we can imagine the art of fiction come alive and standing in our midst, she would undoubtedly bid us break her and bully her, as well as honour and love her, for so her youth is renewed and her sovereignty assured.

9.3 Key Words

① Stream of Consciousness 意识流

In literary criticism, Stream of Consciousness is a narrative mode or method that attempts "to depict the multitudinous thoughts and feelings which pass through the mind" of a narrator. The term was coined by Alexander Bain in 1855 in the first edition of *The Senses and the Intellect*. But it is commonly credited to William James who used it in 1890 in his *The Principles of Psychology*. In 1918, the novelist May Sinclair (1863–1946) first applied the term Stream of Consciousness in a literary context, when discussing Dorothy Richardson's (1873–1957) novels. *Pointed Roofs* (1915), the first work in Richardson's series of 13 semi-autobiographical novels titled *Pilgrimage*, is the first complete stream-of-consciousness novel published in English. For modern readers, the most renowned novels applying such skills included Woolf's *To the Lighthouse*, Proust's *À la recherche du temps perdu* (《追忆逝水年华》) and James Joyce's *Ulysses*.

② *To the Lighthouse*《到灯塔去》

To the Lighthouse is a novel by Virginia Woolf. The novel centres on the Ramsay family and their visits to the Isle of Skye in Scotland between 1910 and 1920. Following and extending the tradition of modernist novelists like Marcel Proust (马塞尔·普鲁斯特) and James Joyce, the plot of *To the Lighthouse* is secondary to its philosophical introspection. Cited as a key example of the literary technique of multiple focalizing, the novel includes little dialogue and almost no action; most of it is written as thoughts and observations. The novel recalls childhood emotions and highlights adult relationships. Among the book's many tropes and themes are those of loss, subjectivity, the nature of art and the problem of perception. In 2005, the novel was chosen by *TIME* magazine (《时代》杂志) as one of the one hundred best English-language novels since 1923.

③ Bloomsbury Group 布鲁姆兹伯里学派

The Bloomsbury Group—or Bloomsbury Set—was a group of associated English writers, intellectuals, philosophers and artists in the first half of the 20th century, including Virginia Woolf, John Maynard Keynes, E. M. Forster and Lytton Strachey. This loose collective of friends and relatives was closely associated with the University of Cambridge for the men and King's College London for the women, and they lived, worked or studied together near Bloomsbury, London. Their works and outlook deeply influenced literature, aesthetics, criticism, and economics as well as modern attitudes towards feminism, pacifism, and sexuality.

④ *A Room of One's Own*《一个人的房间》

A Room of One's Own is an extended essay by Virginia Woolf, first published in 1929. The work is based on two lectures Woolf delivered in October 1928 at Newnham College and Girton College, women's constituent colleges at the University of Cambridge. As an important feminist text, the essay is noted in its argument for both a literal and figurative space for women's writers within a literary tradition dominated by men. The essay was based on two papers Woolf read in October 1928 to two Cambridge student societies. It was published in

1929 as a book with six chapters.

⑤ Jane Austen 简·奥斯汀

Jane Austen (1775–1817) was an English novelist known primarily for her six major novels. Her plots often explore the dependence of women on marriage in the pursuit of favorable social standing and economic security. Her works critique the novels of sensibility of the second half of the 18th century and are part of the transition to the 19th-century literary realism. Her use of biting irony, along with her realism, humour, and social commentary, has long earned her acclaim among critics, scholars, and popular audiences alike. To readers in China, she is best known for *Sense and Sensibility* (1811), *Pride and Prejudice* (1813), *Mansfield Park* (1814), *Emma* (1816) and *Northanger Abbey* (1818).

⑥ James Joyce 詹姆斯·乔伊斯

James Augustine Aloysius Joyce (1882–1941) was an Irish novelist, short story writer, poet, teacher, and literary critic. He contributed to the modernist avant-garde and is regarded as one of the most influential and important authors of the 20th century. Joyce is best known for *Ulysses* (1922), a landmark work in which the episodes of Homer's *Odyssey* are paralleled in a variety of literary styles, most famously Stream of Consciousness. Other well-known works are the short-story collection *Dubliners* (1914), and the novels *A Portrait of the Artist as a Young Man* (1916) and *Finnegans Wake* (1939). His other writings include three books of poetry, a play, his published letters and occasional journalism.

⑦ *The Mayor of Casterbridge*《卡斯特桥市长》

The Mayor of Casterbridge: The Life and Death of a Man of Character is an 1886 novel by the English author Thomas Hardy（托马斯·哈代）. As one of Hardy's Wessex（韦塞克斯）novels, it is set in a fictional rustic England with Casterbridge standing in for Dorchester in Dorset where the author spent his youth. It was first published as a weekly serialization from January 1886. The novel is considered to be one of Hardy's masterpieces, although it has been criticized for incorporating too many incidents: a consequence of the author trying to include something in every weekly published instalment.

9.4 Extensive Explorations

① How much do you know about Stream of Consciousness? What are the major features of the technique of literature?

② How did Woolf's life influence the formation of her theory of novels?

③ According to Woolf's attitude towards Austen, why would she be so sure that the modern fictions made great improvement compared to the "old"?

④ How is Mr. James Joyce the most notable, from that of their predecessors?

⑤ How did Woolf indicate the Russian influence on the English fiction?

⑥ Why did Woolf say "it is impossible to say 'this is comic,' or 'that is tragic' "?

10. T. S. Eliot's *Tradition and the Individual Talent*

10.1 Lead-in

Thomas Stearns Eliot (1888–1965) was an essayist, publisher, poet, and literary critic. Born in St. Louis, Missouri (密苏里), USA, he moved to England in 1914 at the age of 25 and went on to settle, work and marry there and renounced his American citizenship, making his life a reverse edition to the majority of the New Englanders in North America.

Recognized as one of the major poets in the 20th century, Eliot was widely known to the world for his "The Waste Land" (1922), and "The Love Song of J. Alfred Prufrock" (1915), which were not only masterpieces of Eliot, but of the modernist movement in the 20th century. It was followed by some of the best-known poems in the English language, including "The Hollow Men" (1925), "Ash Wednesday" (1930), and "Four Quartets" (1943). He was also known for his seven plays, particularly *Murder in the Cathedral* (1935) and *The Cocktail Party* (1949). He was awarded the Nobel Prize in Literature in 1948.

We selected his article "Tradition and the Individual Talent" in the textbook. Eliot, as a remarkable scholar of Anglo-American New Criticism (英美新批评), had rarely any similarity with his contemporaries. For example, Eliot dived all of himself into his academic study. Unlike Wilde, Johnson or Empson, he was neither a free-lancer nor a talented playwright, for he spent most of his life time in the ivory tower. His view on the world seems more academic than the others. "Tradition and the Individual Talent" is one of the best and typical examples of this. Eliot's description on tradition is quite different from "Poetry is the spontaneous overflow of powerful feelings" by Wordsworth. His analysis on individual talent is routinely in academic style as well. As we can see, Eliot's view is convincing on account of his own identity as a poet. Eliot was well-educated at young age and consecutively, he taught in worldly top-class universities. Therefore, it's not a tough mission to understand his tradition. Eliot considered tradition a history awareness which is typical in academic style and such awareness deeply permeates poets. In this sense, Eliot's definition is different from those Romantic poets. A number of literary theoreticians and poets choose to neglect traditions because traditions were seen as chains and cliches. But Eliot's theoretical system is more flexible. He believes traditions are open and creation of poets, which was actually part of tradition, was not only shaped by traditions but also help shape traditions themselves. Besides, Eliot considered the individual talent of poets not decisive. He disagreed with Wordsworth's "Poetry is the spontaneous overflow of powerful feelings." Because the personal experiences and strong feelings cannot be transformed into literary works directly, poets need to recreate on their straight, rough feelings and it is such effect that Eliot believed individual talent really makes. Of course, Eliot also suggested poets were like catalysts. We do not need to comment on his view. Litterateurs like Eliot received nice education on science. Some of them directly learned from mathematicians and scientists. For example, Bertrand Russel was not only a philosopher but a mathematician. Empson majored in mathematics on campus. Wittgenstein, the remarkable philosopher, gained high reputation on account of his achievements on mathematics. Of course, Wittgenstein lived a little later than Eliot. Eliot finished this essay in 1917. Classified in time, this essay was Eliot's early theory work. Eliot joined Church of England in 1927, which divided his theory style into two parts. And you may read more about Eliot's later theory works.

10.2 Text

Tradition and the Individual Talent[①]

I

In English writing we seldom speak of tradition, though we occasionally apply its name in deploring its absence. We cannot refer to "the tradition" or to "a tradition"; at most, we employ the adjective in saying that the poetry of so-and-so is "traditional" or even "too traditional." Seldom, perhaps, does the word appear except in a phrase of censure. If otherwise, it is vaguely approbative, with the implication, as to the work approved, of some pleasing archaeological reconstruction. You can hardly make the word agreeable to English ears without this comfortable reference to the reassuring science of archaeology.

Certainly the word is not likely to appear in our appreciations of living or dead writers. Every nation, every race, has not only its own creative, but its own critical turn of mind; and is even more oblivious of the shortcomings and limitations of its critical habits than of those of its creative genius. We know, or think we know, from the enormous mass of critical writing that has appeared in the French language the critical method or habit of the French; we only conclude (we are such unconscious people) that the French are "more critical" than we, and sometimes even plume ourselves a little with the fact, as if the French were the less spontaneous. Perhaps they are; but we might remind ourselves that criticism is as inevitable as breathing, and that we should be none the worse for articulating what passes in our minds when we read a book and feel an emotion about it, for

---

① *Tradition and the Individual Talent* was first published in 1917. The text is from Eliot's *Selected Essays* 1917–1932 (1932).

criticizing our own minds in their work of criticism. One of the facts that might come to light in this process is our tendency to insist, when we praise a poet, upon those aspects of his work in which he least resembles anyone else. In these aspects or parts of his work we pretend to find what is individual, what is the peculiar essence of the man. We dwell with satisfaction upon the poet's difference from his predecessors, especially his immediate predecessors; we endeavour to find something that can be isolated in order to be enjoyed. Whereas if we approach a poet without this prejudice we shall often find that not only the best, but the most individual parts of his work may be those in which the dead poets, his ancestors, assert their immortality most vigorously. And I do not mean the impressionable period of adolescence, but the period of full maturity.

Yet if the only form of tradition, of handing down, consisted in following the ways of the immediate generation before us in a blind or timid adherence to its successes, "tradition" should positively be discouraged. We have seen many such simple currents soon lost in the sand; and novelty is better than repetition. Tradition is a matter of much wider significance. It cannot be inherited, and if you want it you must obtain it by great labour. It involves, in the first place, the historical sense, which we may call nearly indispensable to anyone who would continue to be a poet beyond his twenty-fifth year; and the historical sense involves a perception, not only of the pastness of the past, but of its presence; the historical sense compels a man to write not merely with his own generation in his bones, but with a feeling that the whole of the literature of Europe from Homer and within it the whole of the literature of his own country has a simultaneous existence and composes a simultaneous order. This historical sense, which is a sense of the timeless as well as of the temporal and of the timeless and of the temporal together, is what makes a writer traditional. And it is at the same time what makes a writer most acutely conscious of his place in time, of his contemporaneity.

No poet, no artist of any art, has his complete meaning alone. His significance, his appreciation is the appreciation of his relation to the dead poets and artists. You cannot value him alone; you must set him, for contrast and comparison, among the dead. I mean this as a principle of aesthetic, not merely historical, criticism. The necessity that he shall conform, that he shall cohere, is not one-sided; what happens when a new work of art is created is something that happens simultaneously to all the works of art which preceded it. The existing monuments form an ideal order among themselves, which is modified by the introduction of the new (the really new) work of art among them. The existing order is complete before the new work arrives; for order to persist after the supervention of novelty, the whole existing order must be, if ever so slightly, altered; and so the relations, proportions, values of each work of art toward the whole are readjusted; and this is conformity between the old and the new. Whoever has approved this idea of order, of the form of European, of English literature will not find it preposterous that the past should be altered by the present as much as the present is directed by the past. And the poet who is aware of this will be aware of great difficulties and responsibilities.

In a peculiar sense he will be aware also that he must inevitably be judged by the standards of the past. I say judged, not amputated, by them; not judged to be as good as, or worse or better than, the dead; and certainly not judged by the canons of dead critics. It is a judgment, a comparison, in which two things are measured by each other. To conform merely would be for the new work not really to conform at all; it would not be new, and would therefore not be a work of art. And we do not quite say that the new is more valuable because it fits in; but its fitting in is a test of its value—a test. it is true, which can only be slowly and cautiously applied, for we are none of us infallible judges of conformity. We say: it appears to conform, and is perhaps individual, or it appears individual, and may conform; but we are hardly likely to find that it is one and not the other.

To proceed to a more intelligible exposition of the relation of the poet to the past: he can neither take the past as a lump, an indiscriminate bolus, nor can he form himself wholly on one or two private admirations, nor can he form himself wholly upon one preferred period. The first course is inadmissible, the second is an important experience of youth, and the third is a pleasant and highly desirable supplement. The poet must be very conscious of the main current, which does not at all flow invariably through the most distinguished reputations. He must be quite aware of the obvious fact that art never improves,[①] but that the material of art is never quite the same. He must be aware that the mind of Europe—the mind of his own country—a mind which he learns in time to be much more important than his own private mind—is a mind which changes, and that this change is a development which abandons nothing *en route*, which does not superannuate either Shakespeare, or Homer, or the rock drawing of the Magdalenian draughtsmen. That this development, refinement perhaps, complication certainly, is not, from the point of view of the artist, any improvement. Perhaps not even an improvement from the point of view of the psychologist or not to the extent which we imagine; perhaps only in the end based upon a complication in economics and machinery. But the difference between the present and the past is that the conscious present is an awareness of the past in a way and to an extent which the past's awareness of itself cannot show.

---

① Blake (*Annotations to Reynolds' Discourses*, Discourse VI, p. 154).

Someone said: "The dead writers are remote from us because we know so much more than they did." Precisely, and they are that which we know.

I am alive to a usual objection to what is clearly part of my programme for the *métier* of poetry. The objection is that the doctrine requires a ridiculous amount of erudition (pedantry), a claim which can be rejected by appeal to the lives of poets in any pantheon. It will even be affirmed that much learning deadens or perverts poetic sensibility. While, however, we persist in believing that a poet ought to know as much as will not encroach upon his necessary receptivity and necessary laziness, it is not desirable to confine knowledge to whatever can be put into a useful shape for examinations, drawing rooms, or the still more pretentious modes of publicity. Some can absorb knowledge, the more tardy must sweat for it. Shakespeare acquired more essential history from Plutarch[①] than most men could from the whole British Museum. What is to be insisted upon is that the poet must develop or procure the consciousness of the past and that he should continue to develop this consciousness throughout his career.

What happens is a continual surrender of himself as he is at the moment to something which is more valuable. The progress of an artist is a continual self-sacrifice, a continual extinction of personality.

There remains to define this process of depersonalization and its relation to the sense of tradition. It is in this depersonalization that art may be said to approach the condition of science. I shall, therefore, invite you to consider, as a suggestive analogy, the action which takes place when a bit of finely filiated platinum is introduced into a chamber containing oxygen and sulphur dioxide.

---

① Plutarch (*Critical Theory Since Plato*, p. 119).

II

Honest criticism and sensitive appreciation are directed not upon the poet but upon the poetry. If we attend to the confused cries of the newspaper critics and the susurrus[①] of popular repetition that follows, we shall hear the names of poets in great numbers; if we seek not blue-book knowledge but the enjoyment of poetry, and ask for a poem, we shall seldom find it. In the last article I tried to point out the importance of the relation of the poem to other poems by other authors, and suggested the conception of poetry as a living whole of all the poetry that has ever been written. The other aspect of this impersonal theory of poetry is the relation of the poem to its author. And I hinted, by an analogy, that the mind of the mature poet differs from that of the immature one not precisely in any valuation of "personality," not being necessarily more interesting, or having "more to say," but rather by being a more finely perfected medium in which special, or very varied, feelings are at liberty to enter into new combinations.

The analogy was that of the catalyst. When the two gases previously mentioned are mixed in the presence of a filament of platinum, they form sulphurous acid. This combination takes place only if the platinum is present; nevertheless the newly formed acid contains no trace of platinum, and the platinum itself is apparently unaffected; has remained inert, neutral, and unchanged. The mind of the poet is the shred of platinum. It may partly or exclusively operate upon the experience of the man himself; but, the more perfect the artist, the more completely separate in him will be the man who suffers and the mind which creates; the more perfectly will the mind digest and transmute the passions which are its material.

The experience, you will notice, the elements which enter the

---

① "Muttering."

presence of the transforming catalyst, are of two kinds: emotions and feelings. The effect of a work of art upon the person who enjoys it is an experience different in kind from any experience not of art. It may be formed out of one emotion, or may be a combination of several; and various feelings, inhering for the writer in particular words or phrases or images, may be added to compose the final result. Or great poetry may be made without the direct use of any emotion whatever: composed out of feelings solely. Canto XV of the *Inferno* (Brunetto Latini) is a working up of the emotion evident in the situation; but the effect, though single as that of any work of art, is obtained by considerable complexity of detail. The last quatrain gives an image, a feeling attaching to an image, which "came," which did not develop simply out of what precedes, but which was probably in suspension in the poet's mind until the proper combination arrived for it to add itself to. The poet's mind is in fact a receptacle for seizing and storing up numberless feelings, phrases, images, which remain there until all the particles which can unite to form a new compound are present together.

If you compare several representative passages of the greatest poetry you see how great is the variety of types of combination, and also how completely any semi-ethical criterion of "sublimity" misses the mark. For it is not the "greatness," the intensity, of the emotions, the components, but the intensity of the artistic process, the pressure, so to speak, under which the fusion takes place, that counts. The episode of Paolo and Francesca employs a definite emotion, but the intensity of the poetry is something quite different from whatever intensity in the supposed experience it may give the impression of. It is no more intense, furthermore, than Canto XXVI, the voyage of Ulysses, which has not the direct dependence upon an emotion. Great variety is possible in the process of transmutation of emotion: the murder of Agamemnon, or the agony of Othello, gives an artistic effect apparently closer to a possible original than the scenes from Dante. In the *Agamemnon*, the artistic emotion approximates to the emotion of an actual spectator; in *Othello* to the emotion of the protagonist himself. But the difference between art and the event is always absolute; the combination which is the murder of Agamemnon is probably as complex as that which is the voyage of Ulysses. In either case there has been a fusion of elements. The ode of Keats contains a number of feelings which have nothing particular to do with the nightingale, but which the nightingale, partly, perhaps, because of its attractive name, and partly because of its reputation, served to bring together.

The point of view which I am struggling to attack is perhaps related to the metaphysical theory of the substantial unity of the soul: for my meaning is, that the poet has, not a "personality" to express, but a particular medium, which is only a medium and not a personality, in which impressions and experiences combine in peculiar and unexpected ways. Impressions and experiences which are important for the man may take no place in the poetry, and those which become important in the poetry may play quite a negligible part in the man, the personality.

I will quote a passage which is unfamiliar enough to be regarded with fresh attention in the light—or darkness—of these observations:

And now methinks I could e'en chide myself
For doating on her beauty, though her death
Shall be revenged after no common action.
Does the silkworm expend her yellow labours
For thee? For thee does she undo herself?
Are lordships sold to maintain ladyships
For the poor benefit of a bewildering minute?
Why does yon fellow falsify highways,

And put his life between the judge's lips,
To refine such a thing-keeps horse and men
To beat their valours for her?...[①]

In this passage (as is evident if it is taken in its context) there is a combination of positive and negative emotions: an intensely strong attraction toward beauty and an equally intense fascination by the ugliness which is contrasted with it and which destroys it. This balance of contrasted emotion is in the dramatic situation to which the speech is pertinent, but that situation alone is inadequate to it. This is, so to speak, the structural emotion, provided by the drama. But the whole effect, the dominant tone, is due to the fact that a number of floating feelings, having an affinity to this emotion by no means superficially evident, have combined with it to give us a new art emotion.

It is not in his personal emotions, the emotions provoked by particular events in his life, that the poet is in any way remarkable or interesting. His particular emotions may be simple, or crude, or flat. The emotion in his poetry will be a very complex thing, but not with the complexity of the emotions of people who have very complex or unusual emotions in life. One error, in fact, of eccentricity in poetry is to seek for new human emotions to express; and in this search for novelty in the wrong place it discovers the perverse. The business of the poet is not to find new emotions, but to use the ordinary ones and, in working them up into poetry, to express feelings which are not in actual emotions at all. And emotions which he has never experienced will serve his turn as well as those familiar to him. Consequently, we must believe that "emotion recollected in tranquility"[②] is an inexact

① Cyril Tourneur (early seventeenth century), *The Revenger's Tragedy*, 1606–1607.
② Wordsworth (*Critical Theory Since Plato*, p. 490).

formula. For it is neither emotion, nor recollection, nor, without distortion of meaning, tranquility. It is a concentration, and a new thing resulting from the concentration, of a very great number of experiences which to the practical and active person would not seem to be experiences at all; it is a concentration which does not happen consciously or of deliberation. These experiences are not "recollected," and they finally unite in an atmosphere which is "tranquil" only in that it is a passive attending upon the event. Of course this is not quite the whole story. There is a great deal, in the writing of poetry, which must be conscious and deliberate. In fact, the bad poet is usually unconscious where he ought to be conscious, and conscious where he ought to be unconscious. Both errors tend to make him "personal." Poetry is not a turning loose of emotion, but an escape from emotion; it is not the expression of personality, but an escape from personality. But, of course, only those who have personality and emotions know what it means to want to escape from these things.

III

ὀ δὲ υοῢς ἴσως θειότερόυ τι καὶ ἀτταθὲς ἐστιυ[1]

This essay proposes to halt at the frontier of metaphysics or mysticism, and confine itself to such practical conclusions as can be applied by the responsible person interested in poetry. To divert interest from the poet to the poetry is a laudable aim: for it would conduce to a juster estimation of actual poetry, good and bad. There are many people who appreciate the expression of sincere emotion in verse, and there is a smaller number of people who can appreciate technical excellence. But very few know when there is expression of *significant* emotion, emotion which has its life in the poem and not in

① "The mind may be too divine and therefore unmoved."

the history of the poet. The emotion of art is impersonal. And the poet cannot reach this impersonality without surrendering himself wholly to the work to be done. And he is not likely to know what is to be done unless he lives in what is not merely the present, but the present moment of the past, unless he is conscious, not of what is dead, but of what is already living.

10.3 Key Words

① "The Waste Land"《荒原》

"The Waste Land" is a poem by T. S. Eliot, widely regarded as one of the most important poems of the 20th century and a central work of modernist poetry. Published in 1922, the 434-line poem first appeared in the UK in the October issue of Eliot's *The Criterion* and in the United States in the November issue of *The Dial*. It was published in book form in December 1922. Among its famous phrases are "April is the cruelest month," "I will show you fear in a handful of dust," and the mantra in the Sanskrit language（梵文）"Shantih shantih shantih." The poem's structure is divided into five sections. The first section, "The Burial of the Dead," introduces the diverse themes of disillusionment and despair. The second, "A Game of Chess," employs alternating narrations, in which vignettes of several characters address those themes experientially. "The Fire Sermon," the third section, offers a philosophical meditation in relation to the imagery of death and views of self-denial in juxtaposition influenced by Augustine of Hippo and Eastern religions. After a fourth section, "Death by Water," which includes a brief lyrical petition, the culminating fifth section, "What the Thunder Said," concludes with an image of judgment.

② the modernist movement 现代主义运动

The modernist movement is both a philosophical movement and an art movement that arose from broad transformations in Western society during the late 19th and early 20th centuries. A notable characteristic of the modernist movement is self-consciousness concerning artistic and social traditions, which often led to experimentation with form, along with the use of techniques that drew attention to the processes and materials used in creating works of art.

③ canto 颂

The canto is a principal form of division in medieval and modern long poetry. The word canto is derived from the Italian word for "song" or "singing," which comes from the Latin cantus, "song," from the infinitive verb canere, "to sing." There is no specific format, construction or style for a canto and it is not limited to any type of poetry.

④ sublimity 崇高

In aesthetics, the sublimity is the quality of greatness, whether physical, moral, intellectual, metaphysical, aesthetic, spiritual, or artistic. The term especially refers to greatness beyond all possibility of calculation, measurement, or imitation.

⑤ *The adventures of Odysseus*《奥德修斯历险记》

The character of Ulysses (in Greek, Odysseus) has been explored widely in literature. The adventures of Odysseus were first recorded in Homer's *Iliad* and *Odyssey*, and Tennyson draws on Homer's narrative in the poem. Most critics, however, find that Tennyson's Ulysses recalls Dante's Ulisse in his *Inferno* (c. 1320). In Dante's retelling, Ulisse is condemned to hell among the false counsellors, both for his pursuit of knowledge beyond human bounds and for creating the deception of the Trojan horse.

⑥ Keats 济慈

John Keats (1795–1821) was an English Romantic poet. He was one of the main figures of the second generation of Romantic poets, along with Lord Byron and Percy Bysshe Shelley, despite comparatively short life of 25. Some of his most acclaimed works are "Ode to a Nightingale" (《夜莺颂》), "Sleep and Poetry" (《眠与诗》), and the famous sonnet "On First Looking into Chapman's Homer" (《初读查普曼译荷马有感》).

⑦ *Othello*《奥赛罗》

Othello is a tragedy by William Shakespeare, believed to have been written in 1603. It is based on the story *Un Capitano Moro* ("A Moorish Captain") by Cinthio (a disciple of Boccaccio), first published in 1565. The story revolves around its two central characters: Othello, a Moorish general in the Venetian army, and his treacherous ensign, Iago. Given its varied and enduring themes of racism, love, jealousy, betrayal, revenge, and repentance, *Othello* is still often performed in professional and community theatre alike, and has been the source for numerous operatic, film, and literary adaptations.

⑧ Agamemnon 阿伽门农

In Greek mythology, Agamemnon was a king of Mycenae (迈锡尼), the son, or grandson, of King Atreus and Queen Aerope of Mycenae, the brother of Menelaus. Legends make him the king of Mycenae or Argos, thought to be different names for the same area. When Menelaus's wife, Helen, was taken to Troy by Paris (帕里斯), Agamemnon commanded the united Greek armed forces in the ensuing Trojan War. Upon Agamemnon's return from Troy, he was killed by Aegisthus.

10.4 Extensive Explorations

① Have you read "The Waste Land"? What do you think of the images and ideas in the poem?

② How do you tell the difference between "Tradition" and "Traditional"?

③ How do you comment on Eliot's statement, "Every nation, every race, has not only its own creative, but its own critical turn of mind"? Do you have any typical turn of the mind of a nation in your memory?

④ What is the function of knowledge in the creation of a poem?

⑤ If it is not "the intensity of the emotions and the components" that makes the poem great, then which would be counted in this? Why?

⑥ According to Eliot, how does the personality function in a poem?

⑦ In Eliot's discussion, what is "a poet's business"?

⑧ What is Eliot's attitude toward William Wordsworth's "emotion recollected in tranquility"?

⑨ What does Eliot mean when he said "The emotion of art is impersonal"?

11. Mikhail Bakhtin's *Epic and Novel*

11.1 Lead-in

Mikhail Mikhailovich Bakhtin (1895–1975) was a Soviet Russian philosopher, literary critic and scholar. Regarded as a talent in the history of literary history, his writings, on a variety of subjects, inspired scholars working in different traditions [Marxism (马克思主义), semiotics (符号学), structuralism (结构主义), religious criticism (宗教学批评)] and in disciplines as diverse as literary criticism, history, philosophy, sociology, anthropology and psychology. Although Bakhtin was active in the debates on aesthetics and literature that took place in the Soviet Union in the 1920s, his distinctive position did not become well known until he was rediscovered by Russian scholars in the 1960s.

Bakhtin was born in Oryol (奥廖尔) to an old family of the Romanov Russia (罗曼诺夫沙皇俄国) nobility. He joined the historical and philological faculty at the local university (the Odessa University) in 1913. It is here that Bakhtin was greatly influenced by the classicist F. F. Zelinsky (泽林斯基). Then he moved to Nevel (Pskov Oblast), where the first "Bakhtin Circle" formed. The group consisted of intellectuals with varying interests, but all shared a love for the discussion of literary, religious, and political topics. In 1924, Bakhtin assumed a position at the Historical Institute and provided consulting services for the State Publishing House. In 1929, *Problems of Dostoevsky's Art* (《关于托斯妥耶夫斯基艺术诸问题》), Bakhtin's first major work was published. It is here that Bakhtin introduces the concept of dialogism. He then lived in Moscow for some years, but his theory was not favoured by Stalin (斯大林), which caused his disappearance from the academic circle for almost 30 years, and he was excluded, imprisoned and exiled. Without Gorky's (高尔基) aid, Bakhtin would have received higher level of persecution. It was by accident that he was rediscovered by a young scholar in late 1960s, which regained him world fame, however, his deteriorating health forced him to retire, and in 1969, in search of medical attention, Bakhtin moved back to Moscow where he lived until his death in 1975.

Bakhtin's achievement can be concluded into 3 aspects. First, Theory of Polyphony (复调理论); next, Theory of Dialogue (对话理论); and finally, Theory of Carnivalization (狂欢理论). The most influential and typical application of these theories is in Dostoevsky's novels. From the perspective of theory, essence critics ahead of Bakhtin have discussed about these theories already. Taking Theory of Polyphony for example, it means various consciousness occur in an equal way. I.e., novels are neither fully in control of authors nor the one-man show of the leading role. Novels equip themselves with various possibilities and magnificent scenes tend to occur in novels. He pointed out that no one actually apprehended the greatness of Dostoevsky in consequence of the neglect of Polyphonic Theory. And Theory of Dialogue is similar to Reception Aesthetic (接受美学). Theory of Dialogue means dialogues among leading roles, authors and readers in the future tend to be everywhere, and dialogues can be divided into dialogues with great background, small background, etc. Literally, it refers to minor roles that have their choice and readers who tend to intervene, which provides aesthetic reception with a direct reference. In Bakhtin's respect, Theory of Carnivalization applies to novels of Dostoevsky even further. Carnivalization actually means certain rebellion toward cliches, daily routine and moral standards. In the situation of Carnivalization, one tends to break his chains. The noble and the humble, sorrow and happiness, tend to combine with each other. Chains of status have been broken and therefore scenes of Dostoevsky's novel can be cruel, immoral, and taboo words occur in a natural way.

Bakhtin's most illuminative and influential theories are mainly presented in his essays during the 1930s and 1940s. During his disappearance in the 1950s and 1960s, Bakhtin's works weren't known to the world. "Epic and Novel," the text selected in the textbook was published in 1930s, despite some researchers hold the view that the essay was published in 1941. "Epic and Novel" is a speech script for a meeting on Gorky research. Bakhtin divided literary works into two types, epics and novels, which are closely tied with his three major theories. On the basis of distinguishing between epic and novel, he further distinguished between the meanings of epics and novels. Taking epics for example, epics are the original and monumental models of a nationality, while novels' characters define themselves as the story goes. If epics are immortal, novels are more concerned with changing reality. Epics are internalized with stigmas and religious spells while novels combine with insides and outsides, subjects and objects, or rather a variety of misrepresentations, questions and dialogues with rich possibilities.

11.2 Text

Epic and Novel: Toward a Methodology for the Study of the Novel

The study of the novel as a genre is distinguished by peculiar difficulties. This is due to the unique nature of the object itself: the novel is the sole genre that continues to develop, that is as yet uncompleted. The forces that define it as a genre are at work before our eyes: the birth and development of the novel as a genre takes place in the full light of the historical day. The generic skeleton of the novel is still far from having hardened, and we cannot foresee all its plastic possibilities.①

We know other genres, as genres, in their completed aspect, that is, as more or less fixed pre-existing forms into which one may then pour artistic experience. The primordial process of their formation lies outside historically documented observation. We encounter the epic as a genre that has not only long since completed its development, but one that is already antiquated. With certain reservations we can say the same for the other major genres, even for tragedy. The life they have in history, the life with which we are familiar, is the life they have lived as already completed genres, with a hardened and no longer flexible skeleton. Each of them has developed its own canon that operates in literature as an authentic historical force.

All these genres, or in any case their defining features, are considerably older than written language and the book, and to the present day they retain their ancient oral and auditory characteristics. Of all the major genres only the novel is younger than writing and the book: it alone is organically receptive to new forms of mute perception, that is, to reading. But of critical importance here is the fact that the novel has no canon of its own, as do other genres; only individual examples of the novel are historically active, not a generic canon as such. Studying other genres is analogous to studying dead languages; studying the novel, on the other hand, is like studying languages that are not only alive, but still young.

---

① "Epic and Novel: Toward a Methodology for the Study of the Novel" was written sometime in the 1930s. It is reprinted from *The Dialogic Imagination*, translated by Caryl Emerson and Michael Holquist. Copyright by the University of Texas Press, 1981. Reprinted with permission.
See Aristotle (*Critical Theory Since Plato*, p. 54), where Aristotle treats various genres as completed forms.

This explains the extraordinary difficulty inherent in formulating a theory of the novel. For such a theory has at its heart an object of study completely different from that which theory treats in other genres. The novel is not merely one genre among other genres. Among genres long since completed and in part already dead, the novel is the only developing genre. It is the only genre that was born and nourished in a new era of world history and therefore it is deeply akin to that era, whereas the other major genres entered that era as already fixed forms, as an inheritance, and only now are they adapting themselves—some better, some worse—to the new conditions of their existence. Compared with them, the novel appears to be a creature from an alien species. It gets on poorly with other genres. It fights for its own hegemony in literature; wherever it triumphs, the other older genres go into decline. Significantly, the best book on the history of the ancient novel—that by Erwin Rohde[①]—does not so much recount the history of the novel as it does illustrate the process of disintegration that affected all major genres in antiquity.

The mutual interaction of genres within a single unified literary period is a problem of great interest and importance. In certain eras—the Greek classical period, the Golden Age of Roman literature, the neoclassical period—all genres in "high" literature (that is, the literature of ruling social groups) harmoniously reinforce each other to a significant extent; the whole of literature, conceived as a totality of genres, becomes an organic unity of the highest order. But it is characteristic of the novel that it never enters into this whole, it does

① [Emerson and Holquist] Erwin Rohde (1845–1898), *Der Griechesche Roman und seine Vorläufer* [1876, but many later editions, most recently that published by F. Olds (Hildesheim, 1960)], one of the greatest monuments of nineteenth-century classical scholarship in Germany. It has never been superseded. But see: Ben F. Perry, *The Ancient Romances* (Berkeley, 1967), and Arthur Heiserman, *The Novel Before the Novel* (Chicago, 1977).

not participate in any harmony of the genres. In these eras the novel has an unofficial existence, outside "high" literature. Only already completed genres, with fully formed and well-defined generic contours, can enter into such a literature as a hierarchically organized, organic whole. They can mutually delimit and mutually complement each other, while yet preserving their own generic natures. Each is a unit, and all units are interrelated by virtue of certain features of deep structure that they all have in common.

The great organic poetics of the past — those of Aristotle, Horace, Boileau① — are permeated with a deep sense of the wholeness of literature and of the harmonious interaction of all genres contained within this whole. It is as if they literally hear this harmony of the genres. In this is their strength — the inimitable, all-embracing fullness and exhaustiveness of such poetics. And they all, as a consequence, ignore the novel. Scholarly poetics of the nineteenth century lack this integrity: they are eclectic, descriptive; their aim is not a living and organic fullness but rather an abstract and encyclopedic comprehensiveness. They do not concern themselves with the actual possibility of specific genres coexisting within the living whole of literature in a given era; they are concerned rather with their coexistence in a maximally complete anthology. Of course these poetics can no longer ignore the novel — they simply add it (albeit in a place of honor) to already existing genres (and thus it enters the roster as merely one genre among many; in literature conceived as a living whole, on the other hand, it would have to be included in a completely different way).

We have already said that the novel gets on poorly with other genres. There can be no talk of a harmony deriving from mutual limitation and complementariness. The novel parodies other genres

① Horace (*Critical Theory Since Plato*, p. 78); Nicolas Boileau-Despréaux (1636–1711), French poet.

(precisely in their role as genres); it exposes the conventionality of their forms and their language; it squeezes out some genres and incorporates others into its own peculiar structure, reformulating and reaccentuating them. Historians of literature sometimes tend to see in this merely the struggle of literary tendencies and schools. Such struggles of course exist, but they are peripheral phenomena and historically insignificant. Behind them one must be sensitive to the deeper and more truly historical struggle of genres, the establishment and growth of a generic skeleton of literature.

Of particular interest are those eras when the novel becomes the dominant genre. All literature is then caught up in the process of "becoming," and in a special kind of "generic criticism." This occurred several times in the Hellenic period, again during the late Middle Ages and the Renaissance, but with special force and clarity beginning in the second half of the eighteenth century. In an era when the novel reigns supreme, almost all the remaining genres are to a greater or lesser extent "novelized": drama (for example Ibsen, Hauptmann, the whole of Naturalist drama), epic poetry (for example, *Childe Harold* and especially Byron's *Don Juan*), even lyric poetry (as an extreme example, Heine's lyrical verse).① Those genres that stubbornly preserve their old canonic nature begin to appear stylized. In general any strict adherence to a genre begins to feel like a stylization, a stylization taken to the point of parody, despite the artistic intent of the author. In an environment where the novel is the dominant genre, the conventional languages of strictly canonical genres begin to sound in new ways, which are quite different from the ways they sounded in those eras when the novel was *not* included in "high" literature.

---

① Henrik Ibsen (1828–1906), Norwegian dramatist; Gerhart Hauptmann (1862–1946), German dramatist; George Gordon Lord Byron (1788–1824), English poet; Heinrich Heine (1977–1856), German poet.

Parodic stylizations of canonized genres and styles occupy an essential place in the novel. In the era of the novel's creative ascendency—and even more so in the periods of preparation preceding this era—literature was flooded with parodies and travesties of all the high genres (parodies precisely of genres, and not of individual authors or schools)—parodies that are the precursors, "companions" to the novel, in their own way studies for it. But it is characteristic that the novel does not permit any of these various individual manifestations of itself to stabilize. Throughout its entire history there is a consistent parodying or travestying of dominant or fashionable novels that attempt to become models for the genre: parodies on the chivalric romance of adventure (*Dit d'aventures*, the first such parody, belongs to the thirteenth century), on the Baroque novel, the pastoral novel (Sorel's *Le Berger extravagant*),① the Sentimental novel (Fielding, and *The Second Grandison*,② of Musäus) and so forth. This ability of the novel to criticize itself is a remarkable feature of this ever-developing genre.

What are the salient features of this novelization of other genres suggested by us above? They become more free and flexible, their language renews itself by incorporating extraliterary heteroglossia

---

① [Emerson and Holquist] Charles Sorel (1599–1674), an important figure in the reaction to the *preciosité* of such figures as Honoré d'Urfé (1567–1625), whose *L'Astrée* (1607–1627), a monstrous 5,500-page volume overflowing with high-flown language, is parodied in *Le Berger extravagant* (1627). The latter book's major protagonist is a dyed-in-the-wool Parisian who reads too many pastoral novels; intoxicated by these, he attempts to live the rustic life as they describe it—with predictably comic results.

② [Emerson and Holquist] Johann Karl August Musäus (1735–1787), along with Tieck and Brentano, one of the great collectors of German folktales and author of several *Kunstmärchen* of his own (translated into English by Carlyle). Reference here is to his *Grandison der Zweite* (1760–1762, rewritten as *Der deutsche Grandison*, 1781–1782), a satire on Richardson (English novelist, 1689–1761).

and the "novelistic" layers of literary language, they become dialogized, permeated with laughter, irony, humor, elements of self-parody and finally—this is the most important thing—the novel inserts into these other genres an indeterminacy, a certain semantic openendedness, a living contact with unfinished, still-evolving contemporary reality (the openended present). As we will see below, all these phenomena are explained by the transposition of other genres into this new and peculiar zone for structuring artistic models (a zone of contact with the present in all its openendedness), a zone that was first appropriated by the novel.

It is of course impossible to explain the phenomenon of novelization purely by reference to the direct and unmediated influence of the novel itself. Even where such influence can be precisely established and demonstrated, it is intimately interwoven with those direct changes in reality itself that also determine the novel and that condition its dominance in a given era. The novel is the only developing genre and therefore it reflects more deeply, more essentially, more sensitively and rapidly, reality itself in the process of its unfolding. Only that which is itself developing can comprehend development as a process. The novel has become the leading hero in the drama of literary development in our time precisely because it best of all reflects the tendencies of a new world still in the making; it is, after all, the only genre born of this new world and in total affinity with it. In many respects the novel has anticipated, and continues to anticipate, the future development of literature as a whole. In the process of becoming the dominant genre, the novel sparks the renovation of all other genres, it infects them with its spirit of process and inconclusiveness. It draws them ineluctably into its orbit precisely because this orbit coincides with the basic direction of the development of literature as a whole. In this lies the exceptional importance of the novel, as an object of study for the theory as well as the history of literature.

Unfortunately, historians of literature usually reduce this struggle between the novel and other already completed genres, all these aspects of novelization, to the actual real-life struggle among "schools" and "trends." A novelized poem, for example, they call a "romantic poem" (which of course it is) and believe that in so doing they have exhausted the subject. They do not see beneath the superficial hustle and bustle of literary process the major and crucial fates of literature and language, whose great heroes tum out to be first and foremost genres, and whose "trends" and "schools" are but second- or third-rank protagonists.

The utter inadequacy of literary theory is exposed when it is forced to deal with the novel. In the case of other genres literary theory works confidently and precisely, since there is a finished and already formed object, definite and clear. These genres preserve their rigidity and canonic quality in all classical eras of their development; variations from era to era, from trend to trend or school to school are peripheral and do not affect their ossified generic skeleton. Right up to the present day, in fact, theory dealing with these already completed genres can add almost nothing to Aristotle's formulations. Aristotle's poetics, although occasionally so deeply embedded as to be almost invisible, remains the stable foundation for the theory of genres. Everything works as long as there is no mention of the novel. But the existence of novelized genres already leads theory into a blind alley. Faced with the problem of the novel, genre theory must submit to a radical re-structuring.

Thanks to the meticulous work of scholars, a huge amount of historical material has accumulated and many questions concerning the evolution of various types of novels have been clarified — but the problem of the novel genre as a whole has not yet found anything like a satisfactory principled resolution. The novel continues to be seen as one genre among many; attempts are made to distinguish it as an already completed genre from other already completed genres, to discover its internal canon—one that would function as a well-defined system of rigid generic factors. In the vast majority of cases, work on the novel is reduced to mere cataloging, a description of all variants on the novel—albeit as comprehensive as possible. But the results of these descriptions never succeed in giving us as much as a hint of comprehensive formula for the novel as a genre. In addition, the experts have not managed to isolate a single definite, stable characteristic of the novel—without adding a reservation, which immediately disqualifies it altogether as a generic characteristic.

Some examples of such "characteristics with reservations" would be: the novel is a multi-layered genre (although there also exist magnificent single-layered novels); the novel is a precisely plotted and dynamic genre (although there also exist novels that push to its literary limits the art of pure description); the novel is a complicated genre (although novels are mass produced as pure and frivolous entertainment like no other genre); the novel is a love story (although the greatest examples of the European novel are utterly devoid of the love element); the novel is a prose genre (although there exist excellent novels in verse). One could of course mention a large number of additional "generic characteristics" for the novel similar to those given above, which are immediately annulled by some reservation innocently appended to them.

Of considerably more interest and consequence are those normative definitions of the novel offered by novelists themselves, who produce a specific novel and then declare it the only correct, necessary and authentic form of the novel. Such, for instance, is Rousseau's foreword to his *La Nouvelle Héloise*,[1] Wieland's to his

---

① Jean Jacques Rousseau (1712–1778).

Agathon,[1] Wezel's to his *Tobias Knouts*,[2] in such a category belong the numerous declarations and statements of principle by the Romantics on *Wilhelm Meister*; *Lucinda*[3] and other texts. Such statements are not attempts to incorporate all the possible variants of the novel into a single eclectic definition, but are themselves part and parcel of the living evolution of the novel as a genre. Often they deeply and faithfully reflect the novel's struggle with other genres and with itself (with other dominant and fashionable variants of the novel) at a particular point in its development. They come closer to an understanding of the peculiar position of the novel in literature, a position that is not commensurate with that of other genres.

Especially significant in this connection is a series of statements that accompanied the emergence of a new novel-type in the eighteenth century. The series opens with Fielding's reflections on the novel and its hero in *Tom Jones*.[4] It continues in Wieland's foreword to *Agathon*, and the most essential link in the series is Blankenburg's *Versuch über*

---

① [Emerson and Holquist] Christoph Martin Wieland (1733–1813) is the author of *Geschichte des Agathon* (1767, first of many versions), an autobiographical novel in the guise of a Greek romance, considered by many to be the first in the long line of German *Bildungsromane*.

② [Emerson and Holquist] Reference here is to Johann Carl Wezel (1747–1819), *Lebensgeschichte Tobias Knouts, des Weisen, sonst der Stammler genannt* (733), a novel that has not received the readership that it deserves. A four-volume reprint was published by Metzler (Stuttgart, Afterword by Viktor Lange) in 1971. Also see Elizabeth Holzberg-Pfenniger, *Der disorientierte Erzahler: Studien zu J. C. Wezels Lebensgeschichte des Tobias Knouts* (Bern, 1976).

③ By Johann Wolfgang von Goethe (1749–1832) and Friedrich Schlegel (*Critical Theory Since Plato*, p. 473) respectively.

④ Henry Fielding (1707–1754).

den Roman.[1] By the end of this series we have, in fact, that theory of the novel later formulated by Hegel. In all these statements, each reflecting the novel in one of its critical stages (*Tom Jones, Agathon, Wilhelm Meister*), the following prerequisites for the novel are characteristic: (1) the novel should not be "poetic," as the word "poetic" is used in other genres of imaginative literature; (2) the hero of a novel should not be "heroic" in either the epic or the tragic sense of the word: he should combine in himself negative as well as positive features, low as well as lofty, ridiculous as well as serious; (3) the hero should not be portrayed as an already completed and unchanging person but as one who is evolving and developing, a person who learns from life; (4) the novel should become for the contemporary world what the epic was for the ancient world (an idea that Blankenburg expressed very precisely, and that was later repeated by Hegel).[2]

All these positive prerequisites have their substantial and productive side—taken together, they constitute a criticism (from the novel's point of view) of other genres and of the relationship these genres bear to reality: their stilted heroizing, their narrow and unlifelike poeticalness, their monotony and abstractness, the pre-packaged and unchanging nature of their heroes. We have here, in fact, a rigorous critique of the literariness and poeticalness inherent in other genres and also in the predecessors of the contemporary novel (the heroic Baroque novel and the Sentimental novels of Richardson).

---

① [Emerson and Holquist] Friedrich von Blankenburg (1744–1796), *Versuch über den Roman* (1774), an enormous work (over 500 pages) that attempts to define the novel in terms of a rudimentary psychology, a concern for *Tugend* in the heroes. A facsimile edition was published by Metzler (Stuttgart) in 1965. Little is known about Blankenburg, who is also the author of an unfinished novel with the imposing title *Beytrage zur Geschichte deutschen Reichs und deutschen Sitten*, the first part of which appeared a year after the *Versuch* in 1775.

② Hegel (*Critical Theory Since Plato*, p. 552).

These statements are reinforced significantly by the practice of these novelists themselves. Here the novel—its texts as well as the theory connected with it—emerges consciously and unambiguously as a genre that is both critical and self-critical, one fated to revise the fundamental concepts of literariness and poeticalness dominant at the time. On the one hand, the contrast of novel with epic (and the novel's opposition to the epic) is but one moment in the criticism of other literary genres (in particular, a criticism of epic heroization); but on the other hand, this contrast aims to elevate the significance of the novel, making of it the dominant genre in contemporary literature.

The positive prerequisites mentioned above constitute one of the high-points in the novel's coming to self-consciousness. They do not yet of course provide a theory of the novel. These statements are also not distinguished by any great philosophical depth. They do however illustrate the nature of the novel as a genre no less—if perhaps no more—than do other existing theories of the novel.

I will attempt below to approach the novel precisely as a genre-in-the-making, one in the vanguard of all modern literary development. I am not constructing here a functional definition of the novelistic canon in literary history, that is, a definition that would make of it a system of fixed generic characteristics. Rather, I am trying to grope my way toward the basic structural characteristics of this most fluid of genres, characteristics that might determine the direction of its peculiar capacity for change and of its influence and effect on the rest of literature.

I find three basic characteristics that fundamentally distinguish the novel in principle from other genres: (1) its stylistic three-dimensionality, which is linked with the multi-languaged consciousness realized in the novel; (2) the radical change it effects in the temporal coordinates of the literary image; (3) the new zone opened by the novel for structuring literary images, namely, the zone of maximal contact with the present (with contemporary reality) in all its openendedness.

These three characteristics of the novel are all organically interrelated and have all been powerfully affected by a very specific rupture in the history of European civilization: its emergence from a socially isolated and culturally deaf semipatriarchal society, and its entrance into international and interlingual contacts and relationships. A multitude of different languages, cultures and times became available to Europe, and this became a decisive factor in its life and thought.

In another work[①] I have already investigated the first stylistic peculiarity of the novel, the one resulting from the active polyglossia of the new world, the new culture and its new creative literary consciousness. I will summarize here only the basic points.

Polyglossia had always existed (it is more ancient than pure, canonic monoglossia), but it had not been a factor in literary creation; an artistically conscious choice between languages did not serve as the creative center of the literary and language process. Classical Greeks had a feeling both for "languages" and for the epochs of language, for the various Greek literary dialects (tragedy is a polyglot genre), but creative consciousness was realized in closed, pure languages (although in actual fact they were mixed). Polyglossia was appropriated and canonized among all the genres.

The new cultural and creative consciousness lives in an actively polyglot world. The world becomes polyglot, once and for all and irreversibly. The period of national languages, coexisting but closed and deaf to each other, comes to an end. Languages throw light on each other: one language can, after all, see itself only in the light of another language. The naive and stubborn coexistence of "languages"

---

① [Bakhtin] Cf. The article "From the Prehistory of Novelistic Discourse" (in *The Dialogic Imagination*).

within a given national language also comes to an end — that is, there is no more peaceful coexistence between territorial dialects, social and professional dialects and jargons, literary language, generic languages within literary language, epochs in language and so forth.

All this set into motion a process of active, mutual cause-and-effect and interillumination. Words and language began to have a different feel to them; objectively they ceased to be what they had once been. Under these conditions of external and internal interillumination, each given language — even if its linguistic composition (phonetics, vocabulary, morphology, etc.) were to remain absolutely unchanged — is, as it were, reborn, becoming qualitatively a different thing for the consciousness that creates in it.

In this actively polyglot world, completely new relationships are established between language and its object (that is, the real world) — and this is fraught with enormous consequences for all the already completed genres that had been formed during eras of closed and deaf monoglossia. In contrast to other major genres, the novel emerged and matured precisely when intense activation of external and internal polyglossia was at the peak of its activity; this is its native element. The novel could therefore assume leadership in the process of developing and renewing literature in its linguistic and stylistic dimension.

In the above-mentioned work I tried to elucidate the profound stylistic originality of the novel, which is determined by its connection with polyglossia.

Let us move on to the two other characteristics, both concerned with the thematic aspect of structure in the novel as a genre. These characteristics can be best brought out and clarified through a comparison of the novel with the epic.

The epic as a genre in its own right may, for our purposes, be characterized by three constitutive features: (1) a national epic past—in Goethe's and Schiller's terminology the "absolute past"—serves as the subject for the epic;[①] (2) national tradition (not personal experience and the free thought that grows out of it) serves as the source for the epic; (3) an absolute epic distance separates the epic world from contemporary reality, that is, from the time in which the singer (the author and his audience) lives.

We will deal in more detail with each of these constitutive features of the epic.

The world of the epic is the national heroic past: it is a world of "beginnings" and "peak times" in the national history, a world of fathers and of founders of families, a world of "firsts" and "bests." The important point here is not that the past constitutes the content of the epic. The formally constitutive feature of the epic as a genre is rather the transferral of a represented world into the past, and the degree to which this world participates in the past. The epic was never a poem about the present, about its own time (one that became a poem about the past only for those who came later). The epic, as the specific genre known to us today, has been from the beginning a poem about the past, and the authorial position immanent in the epic and constitutive for it (that is, the position of the one who utters the epic word) is the environment of a man speaking about a past that is to him inaccessible, the reverent point of view of a descendent. In its style, tone and manner of expression, epic discourse is infinitely far removed from discourse of a contemporary about a contemporary

① [Emerson and Holquist] Reference here is to "Über epische und dramatische Dichtung," co-signed by Schiller and Goethe, but probably written by the latter in 1797, although not published until 1827. The actual term used by Goethe for what Bakhtin is calling "absolute past" is *Volkommen vergangen*, which is opposed not to the novel, but to drama, which is defined as *Volkommen gegenwartig*. The essay can be found in Goethe's *Sämliche Werke* [Jubiläums-Ausgabe, Stuttgart and Berlin (1902–1907)], vol. 36, pp. 149–152.

addressed to contemporaries ("Onegin, my good friend, was born on the banks of the Neva, where perhaps you were also born, or once shone, my reader...")① Both the singer and the listener, immanent in the epic as a genre, are located in the same time and on the same evaluative (hierarchical) plane, but the represented world of the heroes stands on an utterly different and inaccessible time-and-value plane, separated by epic distance. The space between them is filled with national tradition. To portray an event on the same time-and-value plane as oneself and one's contemporaries (and an event that is therefore based on personal experience and thought) is to undertake a radical revolution, and to step out of the world of epic into the world of the novel.

It is possible, of course, to conceive even "my time" as heroic, epic time, when it is seen as historically significant; one can distance it, look at it as if from afar (not from one's own vantage point but from some point in the future), one can relate to the past in a familiar way (as if relating to "my" present). But in so doing we ignore the presentness of the present and the pastness of the past; we are removing ourselves from the zone of "my time," from the zone of familiar contact with me.

We speak of the epic as a genre that has come down to us already well defined and real. We come upon it when it is already completely finished, a congealed and half-moribund genre. Its completedness, its consistency and its absolute lack of artistic naiveté bespeak its old age as a genre and its lengthy past. We can only conjecture about this past, and we must admit that so far our conjectures have been rather poor. Those hypothetical primordial songs that preceded both the epic and the creation of a generic epic tradition, songs about contemporaries that directly echoed events that had just occurred — such songs we do not know, although we must presume they existed. We can only guess

---

① A. S. Pushkin (1799–1837). *Eugene Onegjn.*

at the nature of those original aëdonic songs, or of the cantilenas. And we have no reason to assume that they are any more closely related to the later and better-known epic songs than to our topical feuilletons or popular ditties. Those heroicized epic songs about contemporaries that *are* available to us and that we *do* know existed arose only after the epic was already an established form, and arose on the basis of an already ancient and powerful epic tradition. These songs transfer to contemporary events and contemporaries the ready-made epic form; that is, they transfer to these events the time-and-value contour of the past, thus attaching them to the world of fathers, of beginnings and peak time—canonizing these events, as it were, while they are still current. In a patriarchal social structure the ruling class does, in a certain sense, belong to the world of "fathers" and is thus separated from other classes by a distance that is almost epic. The epic incorporation of the contemporary hero into a world of ancestors and founders is a specific phenomenon that developed out of an epic tradition long since completed, and that therefore is as little able to explain the origin of the epic as is, say, the neoclassical ode.

Whatever its origins, the epic as it has come down to us is an absolutely completed and finished generic form, whose constitutive feature is the transferral of the world it describes to an absolute past of national beginnings and peak times. The absolute past is a specifically evaluating (hierarchical) category. In the epic world view, "beginning," "first," "founder," "ancestor," "that which occurred earlier" and so forth are not merely temporal categories but *valorized* temporal categories, and valorized to an extreme degree. This is as true for relationships among people as for relations among all the other items and phenomena of the epic world. In the past, everything is good: all the really good things (i.e., the "first" things) occur *only* in this past. The epic absolute past is the single source and beginning of everything good for all later times as well.

In ancient literature it is memory, and not knowledge, that serves as the source and power for the creative impulse. That is how it was, it is impossible to change it: the tradition of the past is sacred. There is as yet no consciousness of the possible relativity of any past.

The novel, by contrast, is determined by experience, knowledge and practice (the future). In the era of Hellenism a closer contact with the heroes of the Trojan epic cycle began to be felt; epic is already being transformed into novel. Epic material is transposed into novelistic material, into precisely that zone of contact that passes through the intermediate stages of familiarization and laughter. When the novel becomes the dominant genre, epistemology becomes the dominant discipline.

The epic past is called the "absolute past" for good reason: it is both monochronic and valorized (hierarchical); it lacks any relativity, that is, any gradual, purely temporal progressions that might connect it with the present. It is walled off absolutely from all subsequent times, and above all from those times in which the singer and his listeners are located. This boundary, consequently, is immanent in the form of the epic itself and is felt and heard in its every word.

To destroy this boundary is to destroy the form of the epic as a genre. But precisely because it is walled off from all subsequent times, the epic past is absolute and complete. It is as closed as a circle; inside it everything is finished, already over. There is no place in the epic world for any openendedness, indecision, indeterminacy. There are no loopholes in it through which we glimpse the future, it suffices unto itself, neither supposing any continuation nor requiring it. Temporal and valorized definitions are here fused into a single inseparable whole (as they are also fused in the semantic layers of ancient languages). Everything incorporated into this past was simultaneously incorporated into a condition of authentic essence and significance, but therefore also took on conclusiveness and finality, depriving itself, so to speak, of all rights and potential for a real continuation. Absolute conclusiveness and closedness is the outstanding feature of the temporally valorized epic past.

Let us move on to tradition. The epic past, walled off from all subsequent times by an impenetrable boundary, is preserved and revealed only in the form of national tradition. The epic relies entirely on this tradition. Important here is not the fact that tradition is the factual source for the epic — what matters rather is that a reliance on tradition is immanent in the very form of the epic, just as the absolute past is immanent in it. Epic discourse is a discourse handed down by tradition. By its very nature the epic world of the absolute past is inaccessible to personal experience and does not permit an individual, personal point of view or evaluation. One cannot glimpse it, grope for it, touch it; one cannot look at it from just any point of view; it is impossible to experience it, analyze it, take it apart, penetrate into its core. It is given solely as tradition, sacred and sacrosanct, evaluated in the same way by all and demanding a pious attitude toward itself. Let us repeat: the important thing is not the factual sources of the epic, not the content of its historical events, nor the declarations of its authors — the important thing is this formal constitutive characteristic of the epic as a genre (to be more precise, the formal-substantive characteristic): its reliance on impersonal and sacrosanct tradition, on a commonly held evaluation and point of view — which excludes any possibility of another approach — and which therefore displays a profound piety toward the subject described and toward the language used to describe it, the language of tradition.

The absolute past as the subject for epic and sacrosanct tradition as its sole source also determines the nature of epic distance — that is, the third constitutive characteristic of the epic as a genre. As we have already pointed out, the epic past is locked into itself and walled off from all subsequent times by an impenetrable boundary, isolated (and this is most important) from the eternal present of children and descendents in which the epic singer and his listeners are located, which figures in as an event in their lives and becomes the epic performance. On the other hand, tradition isolates the world of the epic from personal experience, from any new insights, from any personal initiative in understanding and interpreting, from new points of view and evaluations. The epic world is an utterly finished thing, not only as an authentic event of the distant past but also on its own terms and by its own standards; it is impossible to change, to re-think, to re-evaluate anything in it. It is completed, conclusive and immutable, as a fact, an idea and a value. This defines absolute epic distance. One can only accept the epic world with reverence; it is impossible to really touch it, for it is beyond the realm of human activity, the realm in which everything humans touch is altered and rethought. This distance exists not only in the epic material, that is, in the events and the heroes described, but also in the point of view and evaluation one assumes toward them; point of view and evaluation are fused with the subject into one inseparable whole. Epic language is not separable from its subject, for an absolute fusion of subject matter and spatial-temporal aspects with valorized (hierarchical) ones is characteristic of semantics in the epic. This absolute fusion and the consequent unfreedom of the subject was first overcome only with the arrival on the scene of an active polyglossia and interillumination of languages (and then the epic became a semiconventional, semimoribund genre).

Thanks to this epic distance, which excludes any possibility of activity and change, the epic world achieves a radical degree of completedness not only in its content but in its meaning and its values as well. The epic world is constructed in the zone of an absolute distanced image, beyond the sphere of possible contact with the developing, incomplete and therefore re-thinking and re-evaluating present.

The three characteristics of the epic posited by us above are, to a greater or lesser extent, also fundamental to the other high genres of classical antiquity and the Middle Ages. At the heart of all these already completed high genres lie the same evaluation of time, the same role for tradition, and a similar hierarchical distance. Contemporary reality as such does not figure in as an available object of representation in any of these high genres. Contemporary reality may enter into the high genres only in its hierarchically highest levels, already distanced in its relationship to reality itself. But the events, victors and heroes of "high" contemporary reality are, as it were, appropriated by the past as they enter into these high genres (for example, Pindar's odes or the works of Simonides);[1] they are woven by various intermediate links and connective tissue into the unified fabric of the heroic past and tradition. These events and heroes receive their value and grandeur precisely through this association with the past, the source of all authentic reality and value. They withdraw themselves, so to speak, from the present day with all its inconclusiveness, its indecision, its openness, its potential for re-thinking and re-evaluating. They are raised to the valorized plane of the past, and assume there a finished quality. We must not forget that "absolute past" is not to be confused with time in our exact and limited sense of the word; it is rather a temporally valorized hierarchical category.

It is impossible to achieve greatness in one's own time. Greatness always makes itself known only to descendents, for whom such a quality is always located in the past (it turns into a distanced image); it has become an object of memory and not a living object that one can see and touch. In the genre of the "memorial," the poet constructs his image in the future and distanced plane of his descendents (cf.

---

① Pindar (c. 522 B.C.E.–443 B.C.E.), Greek poet; Simonides (fifth c. B.C.E.), Greek poet.

the inscriptions of oriental despots, and of Augustus). In the world of memory, a phenomenon exists in its own peculiar context, with its own special rules, subject to conditions quite different from those we meet in the world we see with our own eyes, the world of practice and familiar contact. The epic past is a special form for perceiving people and events in art. In general the act of artistic perception and representation is almost completely obscured by this form. Artistic representation here is representation *sub specie aeternitatis.*① One may, and in fact one must, memorialize with artistic language only that which is worthy of being remembered, that which should be preserved in the memory of descendents; an image is created for descendents, and this image is projected on to their sublime and distant horizon. Contemporaneity for its own sake (that is to say, a contemporaneity that makes no claim on future memory) is molded in clay; contemporaneity for the future (for descendents) is molded in marble or bronze.

The interrelationship of times is important here. The valorized emphasis is not on the future and does not serve the future, no favors are being done it (such favors face an eternity outside time); what is served here is the future memory of a past, a broadening of the world of the absolute past, an enriching of it with new images (at the expense of contemporaneity) — a world that is always opposed in principle to any *merely transitory* past.

In the already completed high genres, tradition also retains its significance — although under conditions of open and personal creativity, its role becomes more conventionalized than in the epic.

In general, the world of high literature in the classical era was a world projected into the past, on to the distanced plane of memory, but not into a real, relative past tied to the present by uninterrupted

① Under the aspect of eternity.

temporal transitions; it was projected rather into a valorized past of beginnings and peak times. This past is distanced, finished and closed like a circle. This does not mean, of course, that there is no movement within it. On the contrary, the relative temporal categories within it are richly and subtly worked out (nuances of "earlier," "later," sequences of moments, speeds, durations, etc.); there is evidence of a high level of artistic technique in matters of time. But within this time, completed and locked into a circle, all points are equidistant from the real, dynamic time of the present; insofar as this time is whole, it is not localized in an actual historical sequence; it is not relative to the present or to the future; it contains within itself, as it were, the entire fullness of time. As a consequence all high genres of the classical era, that is, its entire high literature, are structured in the zone of the distanced image, a zone outside any possible contact with the present in all its openededness.

As we have said, contemporaneity as such (that is, one that preserves its own living contemporary profile) cannot become an object of representation for the high genres. Contemporaneity was reality of a "lower" order in comparison with the epic past. Least of all could it serve as the starting point for artistic ideation or evaluation. The focus for such an idea of evaluation could only be found in the absolute past. The present is something transitory, it is flow, it is an eternal continuation without beginning or end; it is denied an authentic conclusiveness and consequently lacks an essence as well. The future as well is perceived either as an essentially indifferent continuation of the present, or as an end, a final destruction, a catastrophe. The temporally valorized categories of absolute beginning and absolute end are extremely significant in our sense of time and in the ideologies of past times. The beginning is idealized, the end is darkened (catastrophe, "the twilight of the gods"). This sense of time and the hierarchy of times described by us here permeate all the high genres of antiquity and the Middle Ages. They permeated so deeply into the basic foundation of these genres that they continue to live in them in subsequent eras—up to the nineteenth century, and even further.

This idealization of the past in high genres has something of an official air. All eternal expressions of the dominant force and truth (the expression of everything conclusive) were formulated in the valorized-hierarchical category of the past, in a distanced and distant image (everything from gesture and clothing to literary style, for all are symbols of authority). The novel, however, is associated with the eternally living element of unofficial language and unofficial thought (holiday forms, familiar speech, profanation).

The dead are loved in a different way. They are removed from the sphere of contact. One can and indeed must speak of them in a different style. Language about the dead is stylistically quite distinct from language about the living.

In the high genres all authority and privilege, all lofty significance and grandeur, abandon the zone of familiar contact for the distanced plane (clothing, etiquette, the style of a hero's speech and the style of speech about him). It is in this orientation toward completeness that the classicism of all non-novel genres is expressed.

Contemporaneity, flowing and transitory, "low," present—this "life without beginning or end" was a subject of representation only in the low genres. Most importantly, it was the basic subject matter in that broadest and richest of realms, the common people's creative culture of laughter. In the aforementioned work I tried to indicate the enormous influence exercised by this realm—in the ancient world as well as the Middle Ages—on the birth and formation of lovelistic language. It was equally significant for all other historical factors in the novelistic genre, during their emergence and early formation. Precisely here, in popular laughter, the authentic folkloric roots of the novel are to be thought. The present, contemporary life as such,

"I myself" and "my contemporaries," "my time"—all these concepts were originally the objects of ambivalent laughter, at the same time cheerful and annihilating. It is precisely here that fundamentally new attitude toward language and toward the word is generated. Alongside direct representation—laughing at living reality—there flourish parody and travesty of all high genres and of all lofty models embodied in rational myth. The "absolute past" of gods, demigods and heroes is here, in parodies and even more so in travesties, "contemporized": it is brought low, represented on a plane equal with contemporary life, in an everyday environment, in the low language of contemporaneity.

In classical times this elemental popular laughter gave rise directly to a broad and varied field of ancient literature, one that the ancients themselves expressively labeled *spoudogeloion*, that is, the field of "serio-comical." The weakly plotted mimes of Sophron,[①] all the bucolic poems, the fable, early memoir literature (the *Epidēmiai* of Ion of Chios,[②] the *Homilae* of Critias),[③] pamphlets all belong to this field;

---

① [Emerson and Holquist] Sophron (fl. fifth century B.C.E.) was probably the first writer to give literary form to the mime. He was greatly admired by Plato. The mimes were written in rhythmic prose and took as their subject matter events of everyday life.

② [Emerson and Holquist] Ion of Chios (490 B.C.E.–421 B.C.E.), a Greek poet who, when he won first for tragedy in the Great Dionysia, made a present of Chian wine to every Athenian. His memoirs have not come down to us, but Atheaeus (*q. v.*) gives long quotes, including the description of an evening Sophocles spent with him in his home on Chios. It has been said no other Greek before Socrates has been presented so vividly. The title of these *Epidēmiai* probably refers to the visits of distinguished Athenians who came to see Ion on Chios.

③ [Emerson and Holquist] Critias (460 B.C.E.–403 B.C.E.), one of the Thirty Tyrants, also active as a writer. He wrote mostly elegies and tragedies. Fragments of *Homilai* ("discussions") have come down to us. Galen is cited by the editors of the *Pauly Wissowa* (vol.II of the 1910 ed., p. 1910) as calling the two books of the original *Homilai* "aimless discussions" (*zwanglose Unterhaltungen*).

here the ancients themselves included the "Socratic dialogues" (as a genre), here belong Roman satire (Lucilius, Horace, Persius, Juvenal),① the extensive literature of the "Symposia" and finally Menippean satire② (as a genre) and dialogues of the Lucianic type. All these genres, permeated with the "serio-comical," are authentic predecessors of the novel. In addition, several of these genres are thoroughly novelistic, containing in embryo and sometimes in developed form the basic elements characteristic of the most important later prototypes of the European novel. The authentic spirit of the novel as a developing genre is present in them to an incomparably greater degree than in the socalled Greek novels (the sole ancient genre bearing the name). The Greek novel [Greek romance] had a powerful influence on the European novel precisely in the Baroque era, that is, precisely at that time when novel theory was beginning to be reworked (Abbé Huet)③ and when the very term "novel" was being tightened and made more precise. Out of all novelistic works of antiquity, the term "novel" was, therefore, attached to the Greek novel alone. Nevertheless, the serio-comical genres mentioned above anticipate the more essential historical aspects in the development of the novel in modern times, even though they lack that sturdy skeleton of plot and composition

---

① [Emerson and Holquist] Lucilius Gaius (?–102 B.C.E.), member of one of the greatest Roman families, author of several important satires, chiefly remarkable for the personal, almost autobiographical tone he introduces into them. (Horace, *Critical Theory Since Plato*, p. 78) Persius, Flaccus Aulus (34–62 A.D.), satirist heavily influenced by Stoic philosophy. [Juvenal (c. 60–c. 140 A.D.), Roman satirical poet.]

② [Emerson and Holquist] Menippus was a Greek Cynic writer of the third century B.C.E. His works are lost.

③ [Emerson and Holquist] Abbé Huet (1630–1731), Bishop of Avranches, learned scholar who write numerous works on a wide variety of subjects. His *Traité de l'origine des romans* (1670) was first published as an introduction to Mme. de Lafayette's *Zaide*, a novel written while its author was still influenced by ideas of the *précieux* society.

that we have grown accustomed to demand from the novel as a genre. This applies in particular to the Socratic dialogues, which may be called — to rephrase Friedrich Schlegel — "the novels of their time," and also to Menippean satire (including the *Satyricon* of Petronius),[1] whose role in the history of the novel is immense and as yet inadequately appreciated by scholarship. These seriocomical genres were the first authentic and essential step in the evolution of the novel as the genre of becoming.

Precisely what is this novelistic spirit in these seriocomical genres, and on what basis do we claim them as the first step in the development of the novel? It is this: contemporary reality serves as their subject, and — even more important — it is the starting point for understanding, evaluating and formulating such genres. For the first time, the subject of serious literary representation (although, it is true, at the same time comical) is portrayed without any distance, on the level of contemporary reality, in a zone of direct and even crude contact. Even where the past or myth serves as the subject of representation in these genres there is no epic distance, and contemporary reality provides the point of view. Of special significance in this process of demolishing distance is the comical origin of these genres: they derive from folklore (popular laughter). It is precisely laughter that destroys the epic, and in general destroys any hierarchical (distancing and valorized) distance. As a distanced image a subject cannot be comical; to be made comical, it must be brought close. Everything that makes us laugh is close at hand, all comical creativity works in a zone of maximal proximity. Laughter has the remarkable power of making an object come up close, of drawing it into a zone of crude contact where one can finger it familiarly on all sides, turn it upside down, inside out, peer at it from above and

① Petronius Gaius (first century A.D.), Roman satirist.

below, break open its external shell, look into its center, doubt it, take it apart, dismember it, lay it bare and expose it, examine it freely and experiment with it. Laughter demolishes fear and piety before an object, before a world, making of it an object of familiar contact and thus clearing the ground for an absolutely free investigation of it. Laughter is a vital factor in laying down that prerequisite for fearlessness without which it would be impossible to approach the world realistically. As it draws an object to itself and makes it familiar, laughter delivers the object into the fearless hands of investigative experiment—both scientific and artistic—and into the hands of free experimental fantasy. Familiarization of the world through laughter and popular speech is an extremely important and indispensable step in making possible free, scientifically knowable and artistically realistic creativity in European civilization.

The plane of comic (humorous) representation is a specific plane in its spatial as well as its temporal aspect. Here the role of memory is minimal; in the comic world there is nothing for memory and tradition to do. One ridicules in order to forget. This is the zone of maximally familiar and crude contact; laughter means abuse, and abuse could lead to blows. Basically this is uncrowning, that is, the removal of an object from the distanced plane, the destruction of epic distance, an assault on and destruction of the distanced plane in general. In this plane (the plane of laughter) one can disrespectfully walk around whole objects; therefore, the back and rear portion of an object (and also its innards, not normally accessible for viewing) assume a special importance. The object is broken apart, laid bare (its hierarchical ornamentation is removed): the naked object is ridiculous; its "empty" clothing, stripped and separated from its person, is also ridiculous. What takes place is a comical operation of dismemberment.

One can play games with the comical (that is, contemporize it); serving as the objects of the game we have the primordial artistic symbols of space and time—above, below, in front of, behind, earlier, later, first, last, past, present, brief (momentary), long and so forth. What reigns supreme here is the artistic logic of analysis, dismemberment, turning things into dead objects.

We possess a remarkable document that reflects the simultaneous birth of scientific thinking and of a new artistic prose model for the novel. These are the Socratic dialogues. For our purposes, everything in this remarkable genre, which was born just as classical antiquity was drawing to a close, is significant. Characteristically it arises as *pomnemoneumata*,[①] that is, as a genre of the memoir type, as transcripts based on personal memories of real conversations among contemporaries;[②] characteristic, also, is the fact that a speaking and conversing man is the central image of the genre. Characteristic, too, is the combination of the image of Socrates, the central hero of the genre, wearing the popular mask of a bewildered fool (almost a *Margit*)[③] with the image of a wise man of the most elevated sort (in the spirit of legends about seven wise men); this combination produces the ambivalent image of wise ignorance. Characteristic also is the ambivalent self-praise in the Socratic dialogue: I am wiser than everyone, because I know that I know nothing. In the image

---

① [Emerson and Holquist] *Apomnemoneumata*, or *Hypomnemata* (literally, "recollections"). It is thought by some that a work of this title ascribed to Ion of Chios may be identical with the *Epidémiai*.

② [Bakhtin] "Memory" in memoirs and autobiographies is of a special sort: it is memory of one's own contemporaniety and of one's own self. It is a deheroizing memory; there is an element of the mechanical in it, of mere transcription (nonmonumental). What results is personal memory without preexisting chronological pattern, bounded only by the termini of a single personal life (there are no fathers or generations). This "memoir quality" was already inherent in Socratic dialogue.

③ [Emerson and Holquist] *Margit*, Greek "fool," subject of a work frequently cited by Bakhtin, the *Margites (q. v.)*.

of Socrates one can detect a new type of prose heroization. Around this image, carnivalized legends spring up (for example, Socrates' relationship with Xanthippe);① the hero turns into a jester (compare the more recent carnivalization of legends surrounding Dante, Pushkin,② etc.).

Characteristic, even canonic, for the genre is the spoken dialogue framed by a dialogized story. Characteristic also is the proximity of its language to popular spoken language, as near as was possible for classical Greece; these dialogues in fact opened the path to Attic prose, and are connected with the essential renovation of the literary-prose language—and with a shift in languages in general. Characteristically this genre is at the same time a rather complex system of styles and dialects, which enter it as more-or-less parodied models of languages and styles (we have before us therefore a multi-styled genre, as is the authentic novel). Moreover the figure of Socrates himself is characteristic for the genre—he is an outstanding example of heroization in novelistic prose (so very different from epic heroization). It is, finally, profoundly characteristic—and for us this is of utmost importance—that we have laughter, Socratic irony, the entire system of Socratic degradations combined with a serious, lofty and for the first time truly free investigation of the world, of man and of human thought. Socratic laughter (reduced of irony) and Socratic

---

① Xanthippe, wife of Socrates.

② Dante Alighieri (1265–1321), Italian poet. [Emerson and Holquist] A good example of what Bakhtin has in mind here is provided by the leader of the *Oberuity,* Daniil Kharms (1905–1942), "Anecdotes about Pushkin." They are difficult to appreciate in translation, but are all similar to the following: "Pushkin loved to throw rocks. As soon as he saw a rock, he would throw it. Sometimes he became so excited that he stood, all red in the face, waving his arms, throwing rocks, simply something awful."—from *Russia's Lost Literature of the Absurd*, tr. and ed. by George Gibian (New York, 1974), 67.

degradations (an entire system of metaphors and comparisons borrowed from the lower spheres of life—from tradespeople, from everyday life, etc.) bring the world closer and familiarize it in order to investigate it fearlessly and freely. As our starting point we have contemporary reality, the living people who occupy it together with their opinions. From this vantage point, from this contemporary reality with its diversity of speech and voice, there comes about a new orientation in the world and in time (including the "absolute past" of tradition) through personal experience and investigation. It is canonical for the genre that even an accidental and insignificant pretext can ordinarily and deliberately serve as the external and most immediate starting point for a dialogue; the "todayness" of the day was emphasized in all its randomness (accidental encounters, etc.).

In other serio-comical genres we will come upon other aspects, nuances and consequences of this radical shift of the temporally valorized center of artistic orientation, and of the revolution in the hierarchy of times. A few words now about Menippean satire. Its folklore roots are identical with those of the Socratic dialogue, to which it is genetically related (it is usually considered a product of the disintegration of the Socratic dialogue). The familiarizing role of laughter is here considerably more powerful, sharper and coarser. The liberty to crudely degrade, to turn inside out the lofty aspects of the world and world views, might sometimes seem shocking. But to this exclusive and comic familiarity must be added an intense spirit of inquiry and a utopian fantasy. Nothing is left of the distant epic image of the absolute past; the entire world and everything sacred in it is offered to us without any distancing at all, in a zone of crude contact, where we can grab at everything with our own hands. In this world, utterly familiarized, the subject moves with extreme and fantastic freedom; from heaven to earth, from earth to the nether world, from the present into the past, from the past into the future.

In the comic afterlife visions of Menippean satire, the heroes of the absolute past, real-life figures from various eras of the historic past (for example, Alexander of Macedonia[①]) and living contemporaries jostle one another in a most familiar way, to talk, even to brawl; this confrontation of times from the point of view of the present is extremely characteristic. In Menippean satire the unfettered and fantastic plots and situations all serve one goal—to put to the test and to expose ideas and ideologues. These are experimental and provocative plots.

The appearance of the utopian element in this genre is symptomatic, although it is, to be sure, timid and shallow. The inconclusive present begins to feel closer to the future than to the past, and begins to seek some valorized support in the future, even if this future is as yet pictured merely as a return to the Golden Age of Saturn (in Roman times, Menippean satire was closely associated with the Saturnalia and with the freedom of Saturnalian laughter).

Menippean satire is dialogic, full of parodies and travesties, multi-styled, and does not fear elements of bilingualism (in Varro,[②] and especially in Boethius' *The Consolation of Philosophy*). The *Satyricon* of Petronius is good proof that Menippean satire can expand into a huge picture, offering a realistic reflection of the socially varied and heteroglot world of contemporary life.

For almost all the above-mentioned genres, the "serio-comical" is characterized by a deliberate and explicit autobiographical and

---

① Alexander the Great (356 B.C.E.–323 B.C.E.), Macedonian king.

② [Emerson and Holquist] Marcus Terentius Varro (fl. first century B.C.E.), politician and scholar, a pupil of Stilo—the first Roman philologist—who had made himself known through research on the genuineness of Plautus' comedies. Varro wrote numerous works on the Latin language, but Bakhtin refers to him as author of the lost work *Statuarum Menippearum Iibri*, humorous essays in the Menippean style satirizing the luxury of his age.

memoirist approach. The shift of the temporal center of artistic orientation, which placed on the same temporally valorized plane the author and his readers (on the one hand) and the world and heroes described by him (on the other), making them contemporaries, possible acquaintances, friends, familiarizing their relations (we again recall the novelistic opening of *Onegin*), permits the author, in all his various masks and faces, to move freely onto the field of his represented world, a field that in the epic had been absolutely inaccessible and closed.

The field available for representing the world changes from genre to genre and from era to era as literature develops. It is organized in different ways and limited in space and time by different means. But this field is always specific.

The novel comes into contact with the spontaneity of the inconclusive present; this is what keeps the genre from congealing. The novelist is drawn toward everything that is not yet completed. He may turn up on the field of representation in any authorial pose, he may depict real moments in his own life or make allusions to them, he may interfere in the conversations of his heroes, he may openly polemicize with his literary enemies and so forth. This is not merely a matter of the author's image appearing within his own field of representation—important here is the fact that the underlying, original formal author (the author of the authorial image) appears in a new relationship with the represented world. Both find themselves now subject to the same temporally valorized measurements, for the "depicting" authorial language now lies on the same plane as the "depicted" language of the hero, and may enter into dialogic relations and hybrid combinations with it (indeed, it cannot help but enter into such relations).

It is precisely this new situation, that of the original formally present author in a zone of contact with the world he is depicting, that makes possible at all the appearance of the authorial image on the field of representation. This new positioning of the author must be considered one of the most important results of surmounting epic (hierarchical) distance. The enormous formal, compositional and stylistic implications this new positioning of the author has for the specific evolution of the novel as a genre require no further explanation.

* * *

We will summarize with some conclusions.

The present, in its all openendedness, taken as a starting point and center for artistic and ideological orientation, is an enormous revolution in the creative consciousness of man. In the European world this reorientation and destruction of the old hierarchy of temporalities received its crucial generic expression on the boundary between classic antiquity and Hellenism, and in the new world during the late Middle Ages and Renaissance. The fundamental constituents of the novel as a genre were formed in these eras, although some of the separate elements making up the novel were present much earlier, and the novel's roots must ultimately be sought in folklore. In these eras all other major genres had already long since come to completion, they were already old and almost ossified genres. They were all permeated from top to bottom with a more ancient hierarchization of temporalities. The novel, from the very beginning, developed as a genre that had at its core a new way of conceptualizing time. The absolute past, tradition, hierarchical distance played no role in the formation of the novel as a genre (such spatiotemporal categories did play a role, though insignificant, in certain periods of the novel's development, when it was slightly influenced by the epic—for example in the Baroque novel). The novel took shape precisely at the point when epic distance was disintegrating, when both the world and man were assuming a degree of comic familiarity, when the object of artistic representation was being degraded to the level of a contemporary reality that was inconclusive and fluid. From the very beginning the novel was structured not in the distanced image of the absolute past but in the zone of direct contact with inconclusive present-day reality. At its core lay personal experience and free creative imagination. Thus a new, sober artistic-prose novelistic image and a new critical scientific perception came into being simultaneously. From the very beginning, then, the novel was made of different clay than the other already completed genres; it is a different breed, and with it and in it is born the future of all literature. Once it came into being, it could never be merely one genre among others, and it could not erect rules for interrelating with others in peaceful and harmonious coexistence. In the presence of the novel, all other genres somehow have a different resonance. A lengthy battle for the novelization of the other genres began, a battle to drag them into a zone of contact with reality. The course of this battle has been complex and tortuous.

The novelization of literature does not imply attaching to already completed genres a generic canon that is alien to them, not theirs. The novel, after all, has no canon of its own. It is, by its very nature, not canonic. It is plasticity itself. It is a genre that is ever questing, ever examining itself and subjecting its established forms to review. Such, indeed, is the only possibility open to a genre that structures itself in a zone of direct contact with developing reality. Therefore, the novelization of other genres does not imply their subjection to an alien generic canon; on the contrary, novelization implies their liberation from all that serves as a brake on their unique development, from all that would change them along with the novel into some sort of stylization of forms that have outlived themselves.

I have developed my various positions in this essay in a somewhat abstract way. There have been few illustrations, and even these were taken only from an ancient period in the novel's development. My choice was determined by the fact that the significance of that period has been greatly underestimated. When people talk about the ancient period of the novel they have traditionally had in mind the "Greek novel" alone. The ancient period of the novel is enormously significant for a proper understanding of the genre. But in ancient times the novel could not really develop all its potential; this potential came to light only in the modern world. We indicated that in several works of antiquity, the inconclusive present begins to sense a greater proximity to the future than to the past. The absence of a temporal perspective in ancient society assured that this process of reorientation toward a real future could not complete itself; afterall, there was no real concept of a future. Such a reorientation occurred for the first time during the Renaissance. In that era, the present (that is, a reality that was contemporaneous) for the first time began to sense itself not only as an incomplete continuation of the past, but as something like a new and heroic beginning. To reinterpret reality on the level of the contemporary present now meant not only to degrade, but to raise reality into a new and heroic sphere. It was in the Renaissance that the present first began to feel with great clarity and awareness an incomparably closer proximity and kinship to the future than to the past.

The process of the novel's development has not yet come to an end. It is currently entering a new phase. For our era is characterized by an extraordinary complexity and a deepening in our perception of the world; there is an unusual growth in demands on human discernment, on mature objectivity and the critical faculty. These are features that will shape the further development of the novel as well.

11.3 Key Words

① Erwin Rohde 欧文·罗德

Erwin Rohde (1845–1898) was one of the great classical German scholars of the 19th century. He is known today chiefly for his friendship and correspondence with fellow-philologist Friedrich Nietzsche. His *Psyche* (1890–1894) remains a standard reference work for Greek cult practices and beliefs related to the soul. His work, *Der Griechische Roman und seine Vorläufer* (1876), was considered by Mikhail Bakhtin to be "the best book on the history of the ancient novel," and it is still regarded as one of the greatest "monuments of 19th century classics scholarship in Germany."

② Golden Age of Roman literature 古罗马文学黄金时代

Classical Latin is the form of Latin language recognized as a standard by writers of the late Roman Republic and Roman Empire. In some later periods, it was regarded as good or proper Latin, with following versions viewed as debased, degenerate, vulgar, or corrupted. The word Latin is now understood by default to mean "classical Latin"; for example, modern Latin textbooks almost exclusively teach classical Latin.

③ Horace 贺拉斯

Quintus Horatius Flaccus (65 B.C.E.–8 B.C.E.), known in the English-speaking world as Horace, was the leading Roman lyric poet during the time of Augustus (also known as Octavian). Horace also crafted elegant hexameter verses (Satires and Epistles) and caustic iambic poetry (Epodes).

④ The Hellenistic period, the Middle Ages and Renaissance 希腊化时期、中世纪和文艺复兴时期

The Hellenistic period covers the period of Mediterranean history between the death of Alexander the Great in 323 B.C.E. and the emergence of the Roman Empire as signified by the Battle of Actium in 31 B.C.E. and the conquest of Ptolemaic Egypt (埃及托勒

密) the following year. The ancient Greek word Hellas is the original word for Greece, from which the word Hellenistic was derived. In the history of Europe, the Middle Ages or Medieval Period lasted from the 5th to the 15th century. It began with the fall of the Western Roman Empire and merged into the Renaissance and the Age of Discovery. The Middle Ages is the middle period of the three traditional divisions of Western history: classical antiquity, the medieval period, and the modern period. The Renaissance was a period in European history marking the transition from the Middle Ages to Modernity and covering the 15th and 16th centuries. It occurred after the Crisis of the Late Middle Ages and was associated with great social change. The traditional view focuses more on the early modern aspects of the Renaissance and argues that it was a break from the past, but many historians today focus more on its medieval aspects and argue that it was an extension of the Middle Ages.

⑤ Rousseau 卢梭

Jean-Jacques Rousseau (1712–1778) was a Genevan philosopher, writer and composer. His political philosophy influenced the progress of the Enlightenment throughout Europe, as well as aspects of the French Revolution and the development of modern political, economic and educational thought. His *A Discourse on Inequality* (《论人类不平等的起源》) and *The Social Contract* (《社会契约论》) are cornerstones in modern political and social thought. Rousseau's sentimental novel *Julie, or the New Heloise* (《新爱洛伊丝》) was important to the development of Preromanticism and Romanticism in fiction. His *Emile or on Education* (《爱弥儿》) is an educational treatise on the place of the individual in society. Rousseau's autobiographical writings—the posthumously published *Confessions* (《忏悔录》), which initiated the modern autobiography, exemplified the late 18th century "Age of Sensibility," and featured an increased focus on subjectivity and introspection that later characterized modern writing.

⑥ Polyglossia 多语种

Polyglossia is a noun that refers to the coexistence of multiple languages (or distinct varieties of the same language) in one society or area. It was first used in the 1970s in the academic journal *International Migration Review*. Polyglossia is a useful term for describing situations where more than two distinct varieties are used for clearly distinct purposes.

⑦ Menippean satire 梅尼普斯式讽刺

The genre of Menippean satire is a form of satire, usually in prose, which has a length and structure similar to a novel and is characterized by attacking mental attitudes rather than specific individuals or entities. Other features found in Menippean satire are different forms of parody and mythological burlesque, a critique of the myths inherited from traditional culture, a rhapsodic nature, a fragmented narrative, the combination of many different targets, and the rapid moving between styles and points of view.

⑧ Schlegel 施莱格尔

Karl Wilhelm Friedrich Schlegel (1772–1829) was a German poet, literary critic, philosopher, philologist and indologist. With his older brother, August Schlegel, he was one of the main figures of Jena Romanticism.

11.4 Extensive Explorations

① Why is it difficult to study the novel as a genre, according to Bakhtin?

② Can you give some examples of "characteristics with reservations" of the novel as a genre?

③ How many genres of novels did Bakhtin mention in the text? What are the differences between various genres?

④ When talking about "historians of literature usually reduce this struggle between the novel and other already completed genres," what did he mean and indicate about the struggle?

⑤ What are the positive characteristic prerequisites of the series of novels opened by Fielding?

⑥ According to Bakhtin, what are the three basic characteristics that fundamentally distinguish the novel in principle from other genres?

⑦ What are the three constitutive features characterizing the epic as a genre?

⑧ What does "absolute past" in the text literally mean?

⑨ Can you recite the major difference narrated by Bakhtin between Epic and Novel?

⑩ What are the "serio-comical genres" in the text?

12. William Empson's *Seven Types of Ambiguity*

12.1 Lead-in

William Empson (1906–1984) was an English literary critic and poet, one of the representative critics of the school—New Criticism. He acquired world popularity in the domain of literary study for his first book, *Seven Types of Ambiguity* (《含混的七种形态》), which was published in 1930.

Empson was excellent in maths and won an entrance scholarship to Winchester College. In 1925 he won a scholarship to Magdalene College, Cambridge, where he read Mathematics, then went on to pursue a second degree in English, and at the end of the first year he was offered a Bye Fellowship, a position in academia and post-secondary education at several British universities who "may or may not have fewer privileges when compared to a full fellow." Under the supervision of I. A. Richards (理查兹), he was once enlightened by a work on modernist poetry, which germinated his creation of *Seven Types of Ambiguity* which earned him worldly reputation.

He left Cambridge after a servant found condoms among Empson's possessions and claimed to have caught him in flagrante delicto with a woman. As a result, he lost his fellowship, revoked and banned from the city. He worked in Tokyo for couple of years, then, in 1937, he came to Peking University as an English teacher. During Japanese invasion of China, he joined the exodus of the university's staff, with little more than a typewriter and a suitcase, and ended up in Kunming, working in the National Southwest Associated

University (西南联合大学) till 1939. He then worked for a year on the *Daily Digest* of foreign broadcasts and in 1941 met George Orwell (乔治·奥威尔). Just after the war Empson returned to China. He taught at Peking University, befriending David Hawkes, who later became a noted sinologist and chair of Chinese at Oxford University. Then, in the late 1940s and early 1950s, he taught a summer course for the intensive study of literature at the Kenyon School of English at Kenyon College in Ohio. He then became head of the English Department at the University of Sheffield until his retirement in 1972. He was knighted in 1979, the same year his old college, Magdalene, awarded him an honorary fellowship some 50 years after his expulsion. Professor Sir William Empson died in 1984.

Seven Types of Ambiguity is a work of literary criticism by William Empson. It was one of the most influential critical works of the 20th century and was a key foundation work in the formation of the New Criticism school. The book is organized around seven types of ambiguity that Empson finds in the poetry he criticizes. The book was revised twice in 1947 and 1953. It also ushered in New Criticism in the United States.

According to Empson, the seven types of ambiguity are as follows:

1. The first type of ambiguity is the metaphor, that is, when two things are said to be alike which have different properties. This concept is similar to that of metaphysical conceit. 2. Two or more meanings are resolved into one. Empson characterizes this as using two different metaphors at once. 3. Two ideas that are connected through context can be given in one word simultaneously. 4. Two or more meanings that do not agree but combine to make clear a complicated state of mind in the author. 5. When the author discovers his idea in the act of writing. Empson describes a simile that lies halfway between two statements made by the author. 6. When

a statement says nothing and the readers are forced to invent a statement of their own, most likely in conflict with that of the author. 7. Two words that within context are opposites that expose a fundamental division in the author's mind.

Among all texts, the chapter on the first type of ambiguity is selected, not only because it is the first one, but it introduced the metaphor, which is one of the major rhetoric practices in the Western verses and poems and also inclusive of almost the rest of the six types.

12.2 Text

Seven Types of Ambiguity

(Chapter 1)

An ambiguity, in ordinary speech, means something very pronounced, and as a rule witty or deceitful. I propose to use the word in an extended sense, and shall think relevant to my subject any verbal nuance, however slight, which gives room for alternative reactions to the same piece of language.[①] Sometimes, especially in this first chapter, the word may be stretched absurdly far, but it is descriptive because it suggests the analytical mode of approach, and with that I am concerned.

---

① *Seven Types of Ambiguity* was first published in England in 1930. It appeared revised in 1947. The selection is from the 1947 edition (New York: New Directions, 1947).

[Empson] In the first edition I made it 'adds some nuance to the direct statement of prose.' This, as was pointed out, begs a philosophical question and stretches the term 'ambiguity' so far that it becomes almost meaningless. The new phrase is not meant to be decisive but to avoid confusing the reader; naturally the question or what would be the best definition of 'ambiguity' (whether the example in hand should be called ambiguous) crops up all through the book.

In a sufficiently extended sense any prose statement could be called ambiguous. In the first place it can be analyzed. Thus, 'The brown cat sat on the red mat' may be split up into a series: 'This is a statement about a cat. The cat the statement is about is brown,' and so forth. Each such simple statement may be translated into a complicated statement which employs other terms; thus you are now faced with the task of explaining what a 'cat' is; and each such complexity may again be analyzed into a simple series; thus each of the things that go to make up a 'cat' will stand in some spatial relation to the 'mat.' 'Explanation,' by choice of terms, may be carried in any direction the explainer wishes; thus to translate and analyze the notion of 'sat' might involve a course of anatomy; the notion of 'on' a theory of gravitation. Such a course, however, would be irrelevant not only to my object in this essay but to the context implied by the statement, the person to whom it seems to be addressed, and the purpose for which it seems to be addressed to him; nor would you be finding out anything very fundamental about the sentence by analyzing it in this way; you would merely be making another sentence, stating the same fact, but designed for a different purpose, context, and person. Evidently, the literary critic is much concerned with implications of this last sort, and must regard them as a main part of the meaning. There is a difference (you may say that between thought and feeling) between the fact stated and the circumstance of the statement, but very often you cannot know one without knowing the other, and an apprehension of the sentence involves both without distinguishing between them. Thus I should consider as on the same footing the two facts about this sentence, that it is about a cat and that it is suited to a child. And I should only isolate two of its 'meanings,' to form an ambiguity worth notice; it has contradictory associations, which might cause some conflict in the child who heard it, in that it might come out of a fairy story and might come out of *Reading without Tears*.

In analyzing the statement made by a sentence (having, no doubt, fixed on the statement by an apprehension of the implications of the sentence), one would continually be dealing with a sort of ambiguity due to metaphors, made clear by Mr. Herbert Read① in *English Prose Style*; because metaphor, more or less far-fetched, more or less complicated, more or less taken for granted (so as to be unconscious), is the normal mode of development of a language. 'Words used as epithets are words used to analyze a direct statement,' whereas 'metaphor is the synthesis of several units of observation into one commanding image; it is the expression of a complex idea, not by analysis, nor by direct statement, but by a sudden perception of an objective relation.' One thing is said to be like another, and they have several different properties in virtue of which they are alike. Evidently this, as a verbal matter, yields more readily to analysis than the social ambiguities I have just considered; and I shall take it as normal to the simplest type of ambiguity, which I am considering in this chapter. The fundamental situation, whether it deserves to be called ambiguous or not, is that a word or a grammatical structure is effective in several ways at once. To take a famous example, there is no pun, double syntax, or dubiety of feeling, in

*Bare ruined choirs, where late the sweet birds sang,*②

but the comparison holds for many reasons; because ruined monastery choirs are places in which to sing, because they involve sitting in a row, because they are made of wood, are carved into knots and so forth, because they used to be surrounded by a sheltering building crystallized out of the likeness of a forest, and coloured with stained

---

① Herbert Read (1893–1968), English poet and critic.

② Sonnet by William Shakespeare (1564–1616).

glass and painting like flowers and leaves, because they are now abandoned by all but the grey walls coloured like the skies of winter, because the cold and Narcissistic charm suggested by choirboys suits well with Shakespeare's feeling for the object of the Sonnets, and for various sociological and historical reasons (the protestant destruction of monasteries; fear of puritanism), which it would be hard now to trace out in their proportions; these reasons, and many more relating the simile to its place in the Sonnet, must all combine to give the line its beauty, and there is a sort of ambiguity in not knowing which of them to hold most clearly in mind. Clearly this is involved in all such richness and heightening of effect, and the machinations of ambiguity are among the very roots of poetry.

Such a definition of the first type of ambiguity covers almost everything of literary importance, and this chapter ought to be my longest and most illuminating, but it is the most difficult. The important meanings of this sort, as may be seen from the example about the cat, are hard to isolate, or to be sure of when you have done so; and there is a sort of meaning, the sort that people are thinking of when they say 'this poet will mean more to you when you have had more experience of life,' which is hardly in reach of the analyst at all. They mean by this not so much that you will have more information (which could be given at once) as that the information will have been digested; that you will be more experienced in the apprehension of verbal subtleties or of the poet's social tone; that you will have become the sort of person that can feel at home in, or imagine, or extract experience from, what is described by the poetry; that you will have included it among the things you are prepared to apprehend. There is a distinction here of the implied meanings of a sentence into what is to be assimilated at the moment and what must already be part of your habits; in arriving at the second of these the educator (that mysterious figure) rather than the analyst would be helpful. In a sense it cannot be explained in language, because to a person who does not understand it any statement of it is as difficult as the original one, while to a person who does understand it a statement of it has no meaning because no purpose.

Meanings of this kind, indeed, are conveyed, but they are conveyed much more by poets than by analysts; that is what poets are for, and why they are important. For poetry has powerful means of imposing its own assumptions, and is very independent of the mental habits of the reader; one might trace its independence to the ease with which it can pass from the one to the other of these two sorts of meaning. A single word, dropped where it comes most easily, without being stressed, and as if to fill out the sentence, may signal to the reader what he is meant to be taking for granted; if it is already in his mind the word will seem natural enough and will not act as an unnecessary signal. Once it has gained its point, on further readings, it will take for granted that you always took it for granted; only very delicate people are as tactful in this matter as the printed page. Nearly all statements assume in this way that you know something but not everything about the matter in hand, and would tell you something different if you knew more; but printed commonly differ from spoken ones in being intended for a greater variety of people, and poetical from prosaic ones in imposing the system of habits they imply more firmly or more quickly.

As examples of the things that are taken for granted in this way, and assume a habit, rather than a piece of information, in the reader, one might give the fact that a particular section of the English language is being used; the fact that English is being used, which you can be conscious of if you can use French; the fact that a European language is used, which you can be conscious of if you can use Chinese. The first of these 'facts' is more definite than it sounds; a word in a speech which falls outside the expected vocabulary will cause an uneasy stir in all but the soundest sleepers; many sermons use this with painful frankness. Evidently such a section is defined by its properties rather than by enumeration, and so alters the character of the words it includes; for instance, one would bear it in mind when considering whether the use of a word demands that one should consider its derivation. Regional or dialect poets are likely to use words flatly from that point of view. No single example of so delicate and continuous a matter can be striking; I shall take one at random out of the Synge *Deirdre*, to make clear that a word need not be unpoetical merely because its meaning has been limited:

> *DEIRDRE. ... It should be a sweet thing to have what is best and richest, if it's for a short space only.*
>
> *NAISI. And we've a short space only to be triumphant and brave.*[①]

The language here seems rich in implications; it certainly carries much feeling and conveys a delicate sense of style. But if one thinks of the Roman or medieval associations of *triumphant*, even of its normal use in English, one feels a sort of unexplained warning that these are irrelevant; the word here is a thin counter standing for a notion not fully translated out of Irish; it is used to eke out that alien and sliding speech-rhythm, which puts no weight upon its single words.[②]

The process of becoming accustomed to a new author is very much that of learning what to exclude in this way, and this first of the three 'facts,' hard as it may be to explain in detail, is one with which appreciative critics are accustomed to deal very effectively. But

① From *Deirdre of the Sorrows* by J. M. Synge (1871–1909), Anglo-Irisb dramatist.

② [Empson] Not a clear example, and I am not sure that what I said is true; but a borderline example was needed here to show that fine shades can be concerned.

the other two are more baffling; one can say little about the quality of a language, if only because the process of describing it in its own language is so top-heavy, and the words of another language will not describe it. The English prepositions, for example, from being used in so many ways and in combination with so many verbs, have acquired not so much a number of meanings as a body of meaning continuous in several dimensions; a tool-like quality, at once thin, easy to the hand, and weighty, which a mere statement of their variety does not convey. In a sense all words have a body of this sort; none can be reduced to a finite number of points, and if they could the points could not be conveyed by words.

Thus a word may have several distinct meanings; several meanings connected with one another; several meanings which need one another to complete their meaning; or several meanings which unite together so that the word means one relation or one process. This is a scale which might be followed continuously. 'Ambiguity' itself can mean an indecision as to what you mean, an intention to mean several things, a probability that one or other or both of two things has been meant, and the fact that a statement has several meanings.① It is useful to be able to separate these if you wish, but it is not obvious that in separating them at any particular point you will not be raising more problems than you solve. Thus I shall often use the ambiguity of 'ambiguity,' and pronouns like 'one,' to make statements covering both reader and author of a poem, when I want to avoid raising irrelevant problems as to communication. To be less ambiguous would be like analyzing the sentence about the cat into

---

① [Empson] It would seem pedantic to alter the phrase 'has several meanings.' But it is treacherous. If the simplest statement has a subject and a predicate it may be said to include two meanings. There would be no point in calling it ambiguous unless it gave room for alternative reactions.

a course of anatomy. In the same way the words of the poet will, as a rule, be more justly words, what they represent will be more effectively a unit in the mind, than the more numerous words with which I shall imitate their meaning so as to show how it is conveyed.

And behind this notion of the word itself, as a solid tool rather than as a collection of meanings, must be placed a notion of the way such a word is regarded as a member of the language; this seems still darker and less communicable in any terms but its own. For one may know what has been put into the pot, and recognize the objects in the stew, but the juice in which they are sustained must be regarded with a peculiar respect because they are all in there too, somehow, and one does not know how they are combined or held in suspension. One must feel the respect due to a profound lack of understanding for the notion of a potential, and for the poet's sense of the nature of a language.

These examples of the 'meanings' of an English sentence should make clear that no explanation, certainly no explanation written in English, can be conceived to list them completely; and that there may be implications (such as I should call meanings) of which a statement would be no use. Neither of these are objections to my purpose, because I can assume that my readers already understand and enjoy the examples I shall consider, and I am concerned only to conduct a sufficient analysis of their enjoyment to make it seem more understandable.

It is possible that there are some writers who write very largely with this sense of a language as such, so that their effects would be almost out of reach of analysis. Racine① always seems to me to write with the whole weight of the French language, to remind one always of the latent assumptions of French, in a way that I am

① Jean Baptiste Racine (1639–1699), French dramatist.

not competent to analyze in any case, but that very possibly could not be explained in intelligible terms. Dryden is a corresponding English figure in this matter;① Miss Gertrude Stein,② too, at this point, implores the passing tribute of a sigh. To understand their methods one might have to learn a great deal about the mode of action of language which is not yet known, and it might always be quicker to use habit than analysis, to learn the language than to follow the explanation.

I propose, then, to consider a series of definite and detachable ambiguities, in which several large and crude meanings can be separated out, and to arrange them in order of increasing distance from simple statement and logical exposition. There is much danger of triviality in this, because it requires a display of ingenuity such as can easily be used to escape from the consciousness of one's ignorance; because it ignores the fact that the selection of meanings is more important to the poet than their multitude, and harder to understand; and because it gives no means of telling how much has been done by meanings latent in the mode of action of the language, which may be far more elaborate and fundamental than those that can be written up. My methods can only be applied at intervals; I shall frequently pounce on the least interesting aspect of a poem, as being large enough for my forceps; and the atoms which build up the compounds I analyze will always be more complex than they. But in so far as anything can be said about this mysterious and important matter, to say it ought not to require apology.

I shall almost always take poems that I admire, and write with pleasure about their merits; you might say that, from the scientific point of view, this is a self-indulgence, and that as much is to be learnt

① Dryden (*Critical Theory Since Plato*, p. 253).

② Gertrude Stein (1874–1946), American expatriate writer.

from saying why bad poems are bad. This would be true if the field were of a known size; if you knew the ways in which a poem might be good, there would be a chance of seeing why it had failed. But, in fact, you must rely on each particular poem to show you the way in which it is trying to be good; if it fails you cannot know its object; and it would be trivial to explain why it had failed at something it was not trying to achieve. Of course, it may succeed in doing something that you understand and hate, and you may then explain your hatred; but all you can explain about the poem is its success. And even then, you can only have understood the poem by a stirring of the imagination, by something like an enjoyment of it from which you afterwards revolt in your own mind. It is more self-centred, therefore, and so less reliable, to write about the poems you have thought bad than about the poems you have thought good.

But, before I start to do this, I must consider two fundamental objections to my purpose, which many critics would raise; the objection that the meaning of poetry does not matter, because it is apprehended as Pure Sound, and the objection that what really matters about poetry is the Atmosphere. These two opinions are very similar, but are best answered in different ways.

The main argument for Pure Sound is the extreme oddity of the way poetry acts; the way lines seem beautiful without reason; the way you can decide (or at any rate people in practice do decide) whether a poem deserves further attention by a mere glance at the way it uses its words. This certainly is an important piece of evidence, and makes one feel that very strange things may be true about the mode of action of poetry, but it shows very little as to what these things may be. I shall myself try to bully my readers into a belief in the importance of ambiguity, for just this same reason.

There was a period of the cult of Pure Sound when infants were read passages from Homer, and then questioned as to their impressions, not unlike Darwin[①] playing the trombone to his French beans. And, indeed, conclusive evidence was collected in this way that a vague impression as to the subject of a poem may be derived from a study of its reciter; one can only question how far this is relevant to the question at issue. There is a crux here (to revive a rather stale controversy) which makes experiment difficult; on the one hand, it is no use telling a person who does not know Greek to read Homer for himself, because he does not know how to pronounce it (even if he knows how to pronounce the words, he will not pronounce them as a sentence); on the other hand, if you tell him how to pronounce the sentence, it is impossible to be sure you have not told him how to feel about it by the tone of your voice. Certainly it is no use denying that feelings can be conveyed, even between animals of different species, by grunts and screams; and there are those who say that language itself was at first a self-explanatory symbolism, based on these expressions of feeling, on onomatopoeia, and on that use of the tongue to point at matters of interest, or to imitate and so define a difficult action, which may be seen in a child learning to write. Certainly, too, one would expect language in poetry to retain its primitive uses more than elsewhere. But this sort of thing is no use to the admirers of Pure Sound in poetry, because a grunt is at once too crude and too subtle to be conveyed by the alphabet at all. Any word can be either screamed or grunted, so if you have merely a word written on paper you have to know not only its meaning but something about its context before it can tell you whether to grunt or to scream. Most admirers of Pure Sound, indeed, will admit that you have to be experienced in the words used by a poet before their sound can be appreciated, and evidently this admission makes all the difference.

They are the more willing to admit this because they are usually

---

① Charles Darwin (1809–1882), English naturalist.

appreciative critics, persons of an extreme delicacy of sensibility who have to guard this delicacy in unusual ways. A first-rate wine-taster may only taste small amounts of wine, for fear of disturbing his palate, and I dare say it would really be unwise for an appreciative critic to use his intelligence too freely; but there is no reason why these specialized habits should be imposed on the ordinary drinker or reader. Specialists usually have a strong Trades Union sense, and critics have been perhaps too willing to insist that the operation of poetry is something magical, to which only their own method of incantation can be applied, or like the growth of a flower, which it would be folly to allow analysis to destroy by digging the roots up and crushing out the juices into the light of day. Critics, as 'barking dogs,' on this view, are of two sorts: those who merely relieve themselves against the flower of beauty, and those, less continent, who afterwards scratch it up. I myself, I must confess, aspire to the second of these classes; unexplained beauty arouses an irritation in me, a sense that this would be a good place to scratch; the reasons that make a line of verse likely to give pleasure, I believe, are like the reasons for anything else; one can reason about them; and while it may be true that the roots of beauty ought not to be violated, it seems to me very arrogant of the appreciative critic to think that he could do this, if he chose, by a little scratching.

One reason, by the way, that the belief in Pure Sound is plausible seems interesting; it is that people often test it by experiments within their own family of languages. They know, say, a novel-reading amount of French, a public-school amount of Latin, half-forgotten, and a smattering of Italian; they try reading the *Oxford Book of Spanish Verse*, and are impressed by the discovery that they can get a great deal of pleasure out of individual lines without understanding the 'meaning' at all. Now such poetry is in a tradition to which they are accustomed; they know roughly what to look for in the poetry of a

Latin language; they know what the syntax connecting one or two large words is likely to be; and they are almost sure to know the root meaning (though not the precise meaning) of the one or two large words. It seems to be true that with this equipment one has a very fair chance of seeing what I may call the 'lyrical point' of one or two lines. This may be an important piece of evidence about the mode of action of poetry, but as far as it concerns Pure Sound one must remember that such people will be pronouncing the lines entirely wrong. (And Vergil[①] remains the most melodious of poets through all the vagaries of official pronunciation.)

Such points would be admitted by most reasonable people, and it may seem an evasion on my part to attack Pure Sound as a defence of the opposite fallacy of Pure Meaning. But the situation about Pure Sound is like that about crude materialism; both beliefs lead a sort of underground existence, and at a low level of organization have much vitality. Crude materialism is the first rough idea that people tumble into when they are interested in the sciences. In the same way, if you ask people in general about the interpretation of poetry, they are likely to say that it is no use talking because what they like is the sheer beauty of the sound.

The official, and correct, view, I take it, is that 'the sound must be an echo to the sense,' that we do not know what this condition may be, but that if we knew a great deal it could be analyzed in detail. Thus

Tendebantque manus ripae ulterioris amore
(Aeneid, VI.*)*

(the stock line to try on the dog) is beautiful because *ulterioris,* the

---

① Publius Virgilius Maro (70 B.C.E.–19 B.C.E.), Roman poet.

word of their banishment, is long, and so shows that they have been waiting a long time; and because the repeated vowel-sound (itself the moan of hopeless sorrow) in *ioris amore* connects the two words as if of their own natures, and makes desire belong necessarily to the unattainable. This I think quite true, but it is no use deducing from it Tennyson's① simple and laborious cult of onomatopoeia. Once you abandon the idea that sounds are valuable in themselves you are thrown far towards the other extreme; you must say that the sounds are valuable because they suggest incidental connections of meaning. If this be true, one can do a great deal to make poetry intelligible by discussing the variety of resultant meanings, without committing oneself very deeply as to how they have been suggested by the sounds.

In claiming so much for analysis I shall seem to be aligning myself with the 'scientific' mode of literary criticism, with 'psychological' explanations of everything, and columns of a reader's sensitivity-coefficients. There is coming into existence a sort of party-system among critics; those critics will soon be considered mere shufflers who are not either only interested in Truth or only interested in Beauty; and Goodness, the third member of that indissoluble trinity, has somehow got attached only to Truth, so that aesthetes are expected to profess a playful indifference to the principles on which they in fact (one is to assume) order their own lives. It is odd, and I think harmful, that this *fin-de-siècle* squabble is still going on. Somewhere in the eighties of the last century the idea got about that Physics, and those sciences that might be conceived as derivatives of Physics, held a monopoly of Reason; aesthetes had therefore to eschew Reason. Now there are serious difficulties about applying the scientific view of truth to the arts; I shall attempt to restate them in my last chapter. But the

① Alfred Lord Tennyson (1809–1992), English poet.

belief that Reason can be applied to the arts is as old as criticism, and fundamental to it; there is no more materialism about it than there is about Aristotle. And if one is to be forced to take sides, as a matter of mere personal venom, I must confess I find the crudity and latent fallacy of a psychologist discussing verses that he does not enjoy less disagreeable than the blurred and tasteless refusal to make statements of an aesthete who conceives himself to be only interested in Taste.

Johnson's[①] remarks about the correspondence theory are not to be despised, particularly in the 92nd *Rambler*:

> *There is nothing in the art of versifying so much exposed to the power of imagination as the accommodation of the sound to the sense. It is scarcely to be doubted that on many occasions we make the music that we imagine ourselves to hear, that we modulate the poem by our own disposition, and ascribe to the numbers the effects of the sense.*

But on the other hand:

> *The measure of time in pronouncing may be varied so as very strongly to represent, not only the modes of external motion, but the quick or slow succession of ideas, and consequently the passions of the mind.*

His examples certainly show very clearly that there is no single mode of correspondence; that very similar devices of sound may correspond effectively to very different meanings. And often enough in Milton, for instance, it is the opposite of onomatopoeia which is employed; thus in the lines about Vulcan—

---

① Johnson (*Critical Theory Since Plato*, p. 357).

From Heav'n, they fabl'd, thrown by angry Jove
Sheer o'er the crystal battlements; from morn
To noon he fell, from noon to dewy eve,
A summer's day; and with the setting sun
Dropped from the zenith —[①]

Milton is extremely cool about the matter; one is made to sit with him pleasantly in the shade, all day long, needing no further satisfaction; it is delightfully soothing to feel that the devil is all the time falling faster and faster. But this is only to say that a sound effect must be interpreted. I think myself its most important mode of action is to connect two words by similarity of sound so that you are made to think of their possible connections.

Another of Johnson's remarks brings up some questions which deserve mention:

> *Dionysius himself tells us, that the sound of Homer's verses sometimes exhibits the idea of corporal bulk: is not this a discovery nearly approaching to that of the blind man, who, after long enquiry into the nature of the scarlet colour, found that it represented nothing so much as the clangour of a trumpet?*

The blind man seems to have anticipated Miss Sitwell,[②] who has actually used this comparison, I think very justly. She also writes

The light is braying like an ass,

---

① John Milton (1608–1674), *Paradise Lost* I, 741-745.

② Edith Sitwell (1887–1964), English poet.

which of course depends for its effect on the whole scene described. In such cases, apprehension in terms of one of the senses is described in terms of, or compared with, one of the others; this has been called synaesthesia, and is clearly sometimes effective. It throws back the reader upon the undifferentiated affective states which are all that such sensations have in common; perhaps recalls him to an infantile state before they had been distinguished from one another; and may actually induce a sort of rudimentary disorder into his modes of sensation (so that the 'images' of the visualizer are transformed sounds) like those due to migraine or epilepsy or drugs like mescal. Mescal-eaters have just that impression common among readers of 'pure' poetry, that they are seeing very delightful but quite new colours, or knowing something which would be very important and interesting if they could make out just what it was. But how such a disturbance can be of serious importance to a reader of poetry it is not easy to see; or how one is to be sure when it is occurring. Often it is no more than a device for insisting on ambiguities of the first type; the main comparison is neither true nor false, and one is thrown back on a series of possible associations, as to the social setting in which these sensations would be expected, or the mood in which they would be sought out. Miss Sitwell seemed often to use the device rather as a flag of defiance, to insist that the main meaning is not what she valued, and the reader must put himself into a poetic or receptive frame of mind. ('These two things are alike in that, for quite different reasons, they harmonize with my mood.') But in a way this is only to push the notion of correspondence further back; how do these sensations come to seem proper to their social setting or their mood? Poe often seems excited about colours in a way that reminds one of people's reports from mescal, but then it is a Mexican drug and he had probably tried it; one cannot deduce anything very profound about poetry from that. And Swinburne[①] often uses devices that seem to demand synaesthesia;

Thy voice is an odour that fades in a flame,

and suchlike; but that is only part of his diffused use of grammar, by which several precise conceits can be dissolved into a vagueness; it would probably be a misreading here to confuse the modes of sensation. Nor, so far as I can see, is his use of the device at all similar to that made of it by Miss Sitwell.

Of course, when a poet is describing paintings, as Spenser[②] does so often, the colours mentioned are supposed to act on one as they would do in a painting. Now, it is naturally harder to analyze the visual arts than poetry, because their modes of satisfaction are further removed from the verbal system on which the discursive intelligence usually supports itself. In any case, I am not competent to do such a thing and shall not attempt it here; I mention this mysterious matter as a way in which poetry might be taking effect, but which I shall assume I can ignore. And it seems worth uttering the pious hope that such effects do not really depend on an obscure physiological perversion, which could be exploited separately, so as to 'deceive'; but that there is a field for analysis in the way the paintings admired by a particular school of poets are assumed as elements of sensibility, and referred to covertly, in their poetry.

So the *discovery of the blind man* may have its importance, but we must now turn to what *Dionysius himself said*, which may be very important indeed. I mentioned a moment ago the theory that language is fundamentally a system of gestures with the tongue;

① Algernon Charles Swinburne (1837–1909), English poet and critic.

② Edmund Spenser (c. 1552–1599), English poet.

there is no doubt that, once the advocate of Pure Sound has admitted that sound has some connection with meaning, Sir Richard Paget's[①] method of interpretation gives him a great deal of rational support. Everyone feels that, quite apart from words like 'pop' which are like their meaning, there are words like 'wee' which are fitted to their meaning; the Paget theory would explain this (taking only the vowel, for this brief example) by saying that while 'huge' moves the tongue back from the teeth so as to make as large a space as it can, 'wee' moves the tongue near to the teeth so as to leave as small a space as it can. In this way, not the sound itself, but our experience of the way it is produced, does, in fact, continually *exhibit the idea of corporal bulk*, which is just what Johnson thought impossible. All the sounds may be reduced to gestures in this way, more or less fancifully; they all, then, carry some suggestion of size, or shape, or movement, or pressure, up, down, forward, or backward, and, in themselves, that is all they can convey. This theory would have a peculiar charm for the materialists who wanted to explain everything in terms of Euclid and Newton; it offers a sort of guarantee that the explanation will be a picture on the blackboard. It is rather bad luck that it should be developed so late, when the faith even of physicists in pictures on the blackboard is not what it was, but that it explains some part of the effect of language it would be hard to deny.

Evidently there is here another field for the future analysis of poetry; when it becomes possible to list the root notions that the words must by their own nature be suggesting, it will be possible and profitable to discuss in some detail how far their sound is an echo to their sense. But such a process will always be subject to curious limitations;

---

① Richard Paget (b. 1869), English language scholar.

... owing to the comparative paucity of different mouth-gestures, each mouth-gesture which produces its own particular sound or root word has to stand for a considerable number of hand-(or other bodily) gestures; to put it in another way, each root word is naturally liable to bear many different meanings. ... One other point may be noted; the same mouth-gesture may be naturally construed in several different ways. Thus, the movement of tongue or lips may represent a pantomimic movement, symbolizing a real movement, or a spatial relation of some kind, e.g. above, below, around, or it may represent a shape of some kind drawn in outline. Finally, any of these meanings may be used figuratively instead of concretely.

(Sir RICHARD PAGET, *Human Speech*.)

Apart, then, from the ambiguities in the fully-developed language, such as I propose to consider, one would have also to consider the ambiguities (of the same sort, but entirely different in their details) which are always latent in the fundamental symbolism of the sound.

This suggests that the process of analyzing the effect of a poem, not indeed completely, but sufficiently to be any use, must be one of altogether impossible complexity; that one must instead give up all hope of doing such a thing, and fall back on a doctrinaire irrationalism. It is true that no explanation can be adequate, but, on the other hand, any one valid reason that can be found is worth giving; the more one understands one's own reactions the less one is at their mercy.

Thus it seems to be fairly true, as a matter of introspection, that one judges the quality of a poem by something felt as 'sound' and something felt as 'rhythm' but there are no necessary deductions from this fact, and it is liable to be misleading. One might use a spatial metaphor and a tautology to make it seem less important; 'the sound of words does not enter that part of the mind where it is effective, except in so far as the words take effect as words.' What this 'taking effect' may be like I shall try to discuss in my last chapter.

It has been deduced from the belief in Pure Sound that the resultant meaning of the words need not be known, that it is enough to know the meaning of the words in isolation and enough of their syntax to read them aloud rightly. In a degree this is often true, but it is better to regard this state of limited knowledge as a complicated state of indecision which involves much estimating of probabilities, and is less ignorance than an ordered suspension of judgment. Secondly, and more seriously, it has been deduced from this belief that you are liable to destroy the poem if its meaning is discovered, that it is important to preserve one's innocence about the meaning of verses, that one must use sensibility, and as little intelligence as possible. This, also, is often true, but I take a moral line here, and say it is true only of bad poetry. People suspect analysis, often rightly, as the refuge of the emotionally sterile, but that is only to say that analysis is often done badly. In so far as such a destruction occurs because you have used your intelligence it must be accepted, and you may reasonably expect to become interested in another poem, so that the loss is not permanent, because that is the normal process of learning to appreciate poetry.

As for the belief in Atmosphere, about which I shall now make some inadequate remarks, it may be viewed as a third deduction from the belief in Pure Sound. Critics often say or imply casually that some poetic effect conveys a direct 'physical' quality, something mysteriously intimate, something which it is strange a poet could convey, something like a sensation which is not attached to any one of the senses. This may only be a statement of how they themselves applied their conscious attention when reading the poem; thus a musical chord is a direct sensation, but not therefore unanalyzable into its separate notes even at the moment of sensing. It can be either felt or thought; the two things are similar but different; and it requires practice to do both at once. Or the statement might, one cannot deny, mean that there has been some confusion of the senses. But it may mean something more important, involving a distinction between 'sensation' and 'feeling'; that what the poet has conveyed is no assembly of grammatical meanings, capable of analysis, but a 'mood,' an 'atmosphere,' a 'personality,' an attitude to life, an undifferentiated mode of being.

Probably it is in this way, as a sort of taste in the head, that one remembers one's own past experiences, including the experience of reading a particular poet. Probably, again, this mode of apprehension is connected with the condition of the whole body, and is as near as one can get to an immediate self-knowledge. You may say, then, that any grammatical analysis of poetry, since it must ignore atmosphere, is trivial; that atmosphere is conveyed in some unknown and fundamental way as a by-product of meaning; that analysis cannot hope to do anything but ignore it; and that criticism can only state that it is there.

This belief may in part explain the badness of much nineteenth-century poetry, and how it came to be written by critically sensitive people. They admired the poetry of previous generations, very rightly, for the taste it left in the head, and, failing to realize that the process of putting such a taste into a reader's head involves a great deal of work which does not feel like a taste in the head while it is being done, attempting, therefore, to conceive a taste in the head and put it straight on to their paper, they produced tastes in the head which were in fact blurred, complacent, and unpleasing. But to say that the consequences of a critical formula have been unfortunate is not to say that it is untrue or even unusable; it is very necessary for a critic to remember about the atmosphere, chiefly because he must concentrate on the whole of the poem he is talking about rather than on the particular things that he can find to say.

In wishing to apply verbal analysis to poetry the position of the critic is like that of the scientist wishing to apply determinism to the world. It may not be valid everywhere; though it be valid everywhere it may not explain everything; but in so far as he is to do any work he must assume it is valid where he is working, and will explain what he is trying to explain. I assume, therefore, that the 'atmosphere' is the consciousness of what is implied by the meaning, and I believe that this assumption is profitable in many more cases than one would suppose.

I shall try to recommend this opinion by giving what seems to me a striking example; a case, that is, where an affective state is conveyed particularly vividly by devices of particular irrelevance. Macbeth, in these famous lines, may easily seem to be doing something physiological and odd, something outside the normal use of words. It is when he is spurring on his jaded hatred to the murder of Banquo and Fleance.

Come, seeling Night,
Skarfe up the tender Eye of pitiful Day
And with thy bloddie and invisible Hand
Cancel and teare to pieces that great Bond
That keepes me pale.
Light thickens, and the Crow
Makes Wing to th' Rookie Wood.
Good things of Day begin to droope, and drowse,
While Night's black Agents to their Prey's doe rowse,
Thou marvell'st at my words, but hold thee still;
Things bad begun, make strong themselves by ill:
So prythee go with me.

(III. ii. 50.)

The condition of his skin (By the pricking of my thumbs Something wicked this way comes), the sense of being withdrawn far within his own flesh (like an old lecher, a small fire at his heart, all the rest on's body cold), the sense that the affair is prosaic, it need not be mentioned, and yet an occasional squawking of the nerves (Hobbididance croaks in Tom's belly), in short the whole frame of body, as I read the lines, is lit up and imposed upon the reader, from which Macbeth lashes his exhausted energies into a new, into the accustomed, readiness for murder.

I have tried by these almost irrelevant quotations to show how much work the reader of Shakespeare is prepared to do for him, how one is helped by the rest of his work to put a great deal into any part of it, but this seems to explain very little. Various similar sound effects or associations may be noted; there is a suggestion of witches' broth, or curdling blood, about *thickens*, which the vowel sound of *light*, coming next to it, with the movement of stirring treacle, and the cluck of the k-sounds, intensify; a suggestion, too, of harsh, limpid echo, and, under careful feet of poachers, an abrupt crackling of sticks. The vowel sounds at the end make an increasing darkness as the crow goes forward. But, after all, one would be very surprised if two people got the same result from putting a sound-effect into words in this way.

It is safer to point out that *rooks* were, in any case, creatures of foreboding:

> *Augurs, and understood Relations, have*
> *By Magot-Pyes, and Choughes, and Rookes, brought forth*
> *The secret'st man of Blood;*
>
> (III. iv. 125.)

that Macbeth looked out of the window because Banquo was to be killed soon after dusk, so he wanted to know how the time was going; and that a dramatic situation is always heightened by breaking off the dialogue to look out of the window, especially if some kind of Pathetic Fallacy[①] is to be observed outside. But to notice this particular pathetic fallacy you must withdraw yourself from the apprehension of its effect, and be ready to notice irrelevant points which may act as a clue. I believe it is that the peaceful solitary *crow*, moving towards bed and the other crows, is made unnaturally like Macbeth and a murderer who is coming against them; this is suggested by the next lines, which do not say whether the *crow* is one of the *good things of day* or one of *night's black agents* (it is, at any rate, black), by the eerie way that *light* itself is *thickening*, as a man turns against men, *a crow* against *crows*, perhaps by the portentous way a *crow's* voice will carry at such a time, and by the sharpness of its wings against the even glow of a sky after sundown; but mainly, I think, by the use of the two words *rook* and *crow*.

Rooks live in a crowd and are mainly vegetarian; *crow* may be either another name for a *rook*, especially when seen alone, or it may mean the solitary Carrion crow. This subdued pun is made to imply here that Macbeth, looking out of the window, is trying to see himself as a murderer, and can only see himself as in the position of the *crow*, that his *day* of power, now, is closing; that he has to distinguish himself from the other *rooks* by a difference of name, *rook-crow*, like the kingly title, only; that he is anxious, at bottom, to be at one with the other *rooks*, not to murder them; that he can no longer, or that he may yet, be united with the rookery; and that he is murdering Banquo in a forlorn attempt to obtain peace of mind.[②]

---

① A term coined by the English art critic John Ruskin (1819–1900) to mean a figure of speech that attributes human feelings to inanimate things.

② [Empson] It was stupid of me to present this example as a sort of test case, with a tidy solution drawn from the names of birds. Obviously the passage is still impressive if you have no opinions at all about the difference between crows and rooks. But it is at least a good example of a heavy Atmosphere, and I don't think my treatment of it was wrong as far as it went.

Interest in 'atmospheres' is a critical attitude designed for, and particularly suited to, the poets of the nineteenth century; this may tell us something about them, and in part explain why they are so little ambiguous in the sense with which I am concerned. For a variety of reasons, they found themselves living in an intellectual framework with which it was very difficult to write poetry, in which poetry was rather improper, or was irrelevant to business, especially the business of becoming Fit to Survive, or was an indulgence of one's lower nature in beliefs the scientists knew were untrue. On the other hand, they had a large public which was as anxious to escape from this intellectual framework, on holiday, as they were themselves. Almost all of them, therefore, exploited a sort of tap-root into the world of their childhood, where they were able to conceive things poetically, and whatever they might be writing about they would suck up from this limited and perverted world an unvarying sap which was their poetical inspiration. Mr. Harold Nicolson① has written excellently about Swinburne's fixation on to the excitements of his early reading and experience, and about the unique position in the life of Tennyson occupied by the moaning of cold wind round a child frightened for its identity upon the fens. Wordsworth frankly had no inspiration other than his use, when a boy, of the mountains as a totem or father-substitute, and Byron only at the end of his life, in the first cantos of *Don Juan* in particular, escaped from the infantile incest-fixation upon his sister which was till then all that he had got to say. As for Keats's desire for death and his mother, it has become a byword among the learned. Shelley, perhaps, does not strike one as keeping so sharp a distinction between the world he considered real and the world from which he wrote poetry, but this did not in his case improve either

① Harold Nicolson (1886–1968), English writer.

of them; while Browning and Meredith,[①] who did write from the world they lived in, affect me as novel-writers of merit with no lyrical inspiration at all. Coleridge, it is true, relied on opium rather than the nursery. But of all these men an imposed excitement, a sense of uncaused warmth, achievement, gratification, a sense of hugging to oneself a private dream-world, is the main interest and material.[②]

In that age, too, began the doubt as to whether this man or that was 'grown-up,' which has ever since occupied so deeply the minds of those interested in their friends. Macaulay complains somewhere that in his day a man was sure to be accused of a child-mind if no doubt could be cast 'either on the ability of his intelligence or the innocence of his character'; now nobody seems to have said this in the eighteenth century. Before the Romantic Revival the possibilities of not growing up had never been exploited so far as to become a subject for popular anxiety.

Of course, these pat little theories are ridiculously simple; fantasy gratifications and a protective attitude towards one's inner life are in some degree essential for the production of poetry, and I have no wish to pretend the Romantics were not great poets. But I think this will be admitted, that they were making a use of language very different from that of their predecessors; imagine Shakespeare or Pope keeping a tap-root in this way. One might expect, then, that they would not need to use ambiguities of the kind I shall consider to give vivacity to their language, or even ambiguities with which the student of language, as such, is concerned; that the mode of approach to them should be psychological rather than grammatical, and that

① Wordsworth, George Gordon Lord Byron, John Keats, Shelley, English poets of the Romantic Age.

② [Empson] Byron I understand did not meet his half-sister at all until he was grown up. It seems no good trying to improve this paragraph, and I still think that the last sentence summing it up is sufficiently true.

their distortions of meaning will belong to darker regions of the mind.

This introduction has grown too long and too portentous; it is time I settled down to the little I can do in this chapter, which is to list a few examples of ambiguity of the first type. Many of the preceding paragraphs are designed merely for defence; if it is said that the verbal analyst is a crude irrelevant fellow who should be thinking about the atmosphere, the reply is that though there may be an atmosphere to which analysis is irrelevant, it is not necessarily anything very respectable.

I have already considered the comparison of two things which does not say in virtue of what they are to be compared. Of the same sort, though less common, is the ornamental use of false antithesis, which places words as if in opposition to one another without saying in virtue of what they are to be opposed. Cases in which several ways of opposing them are implied will be found in my later chapters as examples of more advanced ambiguity; but the device may be used to deny such an antithesis altogether. There is a rather trivial example of this in Peacock's[1] *War Song*:

We there, in strife bewildring,
Spitt blood enough to swim in;
We orphaned many children
And widowed many women.
The eagles and the ravens
We glutted with our foemen;
The heroes and the cravens,
The spearmen and the bowmen.

① Thomas Love Peacock (1785–1866), English novelist and poet.

In the last two lines he is not concerned to be thinking, to decide something or convince somebody; he makes a cradle and rocks himself in it; it is the tone of a man imagining himself in a mood wholly alien to him, and looking round with an amused complacent absence of reflection. The lines also give finality in that the impulse is shown to be dying away; some reflection has been implied on the difference between *heroes* and *cravens*, on their equal deaths, and on the relations between *eagles* and *heroes*, *r*avens and *cravens*, but the irrelevant calm of the last line says 'these distinctions may be made at other times, but they are irrelevant to our slaughter and the reaction to it of Nature,' he proceeds to another merely technical way of separating the dead into classes, and by the failure of the antithesis shows he is merely thinking of them as a huge pile.

How loved, how honoured once, avails thee not,
To whom related, or by whom begot;
A heap of dust is all remains of thee;
'Tis all thou art, and all the proud shall be.

(POPE, *Unfortunate Lady*.)①

The two parts of the second line make a claim to be alternatives which is not obviously justified, and this I think implies a good deal. If the antithesis is to be serious, or must mean 'one of her relations was grand but her father was humble,' or the other way about; thus one would take *how* to mean 'whether much or little' (it could mean 'though you were so greatly'), and the last line to contrast her with the *proud*, so as to imply that she is humble (it could unite her with the *proud*, and deduce the death of all of them from the death of one). This obscurity is part of the 'Gothic' atmosphere that Pope wanted:

---

① Pope (*Critical Theory Since Plato*, p. 297).

'her birth was high, but there was a mysterious stain on it'; or 'though you might not think it, her birth was high'; or 'her birth was high, but not higher than births to which I am accustomed.' Here, however, the false antithesis is finding another use, to convey the attitude of Pope to the subject. 'How simple, how irrelevant to the merits of the unfortunate lady, are such relationships; everybody has had both a relation and a father; how little I can admire the arrogance of great families on this point; how little, too, the snobbery of my reader, who is unlikely to belong to a great family; to how many people this subject would be extremely fruitful of antithesis; how little fruitful of antithesis it seems to an independent soul like mine.' What is important about such devices is that they leave it to the reader vaguely to invent something, and make him leave it at the back of his mind.

Not unlike the use of a comparison which does not say in virtue of what the two things are to be compared is the use of a comparative adjective which does not say what its noun is to be compared with; since all adjectives are in a sense comparative, this source of ambiguity is a sufficiently general one. In particular, it is the chief source of euphuistic conceits and the paradoxes cultivated in the nineties, which give a noun two contradictory adjectives and leave it to the reader to see how the adjectives are used.① Examples of this sort are too well known, and are generally thought too trivial, to be worth quoting. I shall give an example from one of Mr. Waley's② Chinese translations,

① [Empson] Such a trick has usually one meaning which is the answer of the puzzle, but while you are puzzling the words have possible alternative meanings, and even to those who see the answers at once the alternatives are in a way present as being denied. They may appear as the views of commonplace people, who are thereby snubbed; but they can also make a real ambiguity when the denial is not felt to be complete.

② Arthur Waley (1889–1966), English translator.

to insist upon the profundity of feeling which such a device may enshrine.

> *Swiftly the years, beyond recall.*
> *Solemn the stillness of this spring morning.*

The human mind has two main scales on which to measure time. The large one takes the length of a human life as its unit, so that there is nothing to be done about life, it is of an animal dignity and simplicity, and must be regarded from a peaceable and fatalistic point of view. The small one takes as its unit the conscious moment, and it is from this that you consider the neighbouring space, an activity of the will, delicacies of social tone, and your personality. The scales are so far apart as almost to give the effect of defining two dimensions; they do not come into contact because what is too large to be conceived by the one is still too small to be conceived by the other. Thus, taking the units as a century and the quarter of a second, their ratio is ten to the tenth and their mean is the standard working day; or taking the smaller one as five minutes, their mean is the whole of summer. The repose and self-command given by the use of the first are contrasted with the speed at which it shows the years to be passing from you, and therefore with the fear of death; the fever and multiplicity of life, as known by the use of the second, are contrasted with the calm of the external space of which it gives consciousness, with the absolute or extra-temporal value attached to the brief moments of self-knowledge with which it is concerned, and with a sense of security in that it makes death so far off.

Both these time-scales and their contrasts are included by these two lines in a single act of apprehension, because of the words *swift* and *still*. Being contradictory as they stand, they demand to be conceived in different ways; we are enabled, therefore, to meet the open skies with an answering stability of self-knowledge; to meet the brevity of human life with an ironical sense that it is morning and springtime, that there is a whole summer before winter, a whole day before night.

I call *swift* and *still* here ambiguous, though each is meant to be referred to one particular time-scale, because between them they put two time-scales into the reader's mind in a single act of apprehension. But these scales, being both present, are in some degree used for each adjective, so that the words are ambiguous in a more direct sense; the *years* of a man's life seem *swift* even on the small scale, like the mist from the mountains which 'gathers a moment, then scatters'; the morning seems still even on the large scale, so that this moment is apocalyptic and a type of heaven.

Lacking rhyme, metre, and any overt device such as comparison, these lines are what we should normally call poetry only by virtue of their compactness; two statements are made as if they were connected, and the reader is forced to consider their relations for himself. The reason why these facts should have been selected for a poem is left for him to invent; he will invent a variety of reasons and order them in his own mind. This, I think, is the essential fact about the poetical use of language.

Among metaphors effective from several points of view one may include, by no great extension, those metaphors which are partly recognized as such and partly received simply as words in their acquired sense. All languages are composed of dead metaphors as the soil of corpses, but English is perhaps uniquely full of metaphors of this sort, which are not dead but sleeping, and, while making a direct statement, colour it with an implied comparison. The school rule against mixed metaphor, which in itself is so powerful a weapon, is largely necessary because of the presence of these sleepers, who must be treated with respect; they are harder to use than either plain word or metaphor because if you mix them you must show you are conscious of their meaning, and are not merely being insensitive to the possibilities of the language.

Beauty is but a flower
Which wrinkles will devour.
Brightness falls from the air.
Queens have died young and fair.
Dust hath closed Helen's eye.
I am sick, I must die.
Lord, have mercy upon us.
*(NASH, Summer's Last Will and Testament.)*①

I call it a subdued metaphor here that *devour* should mean 'remove' or 'replace,' with no more than an overtone of cruelty and the unnatural. This may seem very different from the less evident subdued metaphor in the derivation of a word like 'apprehension,' say, but a reader may ignore the consequences even of so evident a metaphor as *devour.* If you go into the metaphor it may make Time the *edax rerum,* and wrinkles only time's tooth-marks; more probably it compares long curving wrinkles on the face to rodent ulcers, caterpillars on petals, and the worms that are to gnaw it in the grave. Of these, the caterpillar (from *flower*) are what the comparison insists upon, but the Elizabethan imagination would let slip no chance of airing its miraculous corpse-worm.

On the other hand

Brightness falls from the air

---

① Thomas Nashe (1567–1601), English dramatist.

is an example of ambiguity by vagueness, such as was used to excess by the Pre-Raphaelites. Evidently there are a variety of things the line may be about. The sun and moon pass under the earth after their period of shining, and there are stars falling at odd times; Icarus and the prey of hawks, having soared upwards towards heaven, *fall* exhausted or dead; the glittering turning things the sixteenth century put on the top of a building may have *fallen* too often. In another sense, hawks, lightning, and meteorites *fall* flashing from heaven upon their prey. Taking *brightness* as abstract, not as meaning something bright, it is as a benefit that light *falls*, diffusely reflected, from the sky. In so far as the sky is brighter than the earth (especially at twilight), brightness is natural to it; in so far as the earth may be bright when the clouds are dark, *brightness* falls from the sky to the earth when there is a threat of thunder. 'All is unsafe, even the heavens are not sure of their brightness,' or 'the qualities in man that deserve respect are not natural to him but brief gifts from God; they fall like manna, and melt as soon.' One may extract, too, from the oppression in the notion of thunder the idea that now, 'in time of pestilence,' the generosity of Nature is mysteriously interrupted; even at the scene of brilliant ecclesiastical festivity for which the poem was written there is a taint of darkness in the very *air*.

It is proper to mention a rather cynical theory that Nash wrote or meant 'hair'; still, though less imaginative, this is very adequate; oddly enough (it is electricity and the mysterious vitality of youth which have *fallen* from the *hair*) carries much the same suggestion as the other version; and gives the relief of a single direct meaning. Elizabethan pronunciation was very little troubled by snobbery, and it is conceivable that Nash meant both words to take effect in some way. Now that all this fuss has been made about aitches it is impossible to imagine what such a line would sound like.

For a final meaning of this line one must consider the line which follows it; there is another case of poetry by juxtaposition. In

Dust hath closed Helen's eye

one must think of Helen in part as an undecaying corpse or a statue; it is *dust* from outside which settles on her eyelids, and shows that it is long since they have been opened; only in the background, as a truth which could not otherwise be faced, is it suggested that the *dust* is generated from her own corruption. As a result of this ambiguity, the line imposes on *brightness* a further and more terrible comparison; on the one hand, it is the *bright* motes dancing in sunbeams, which *fall* and become dust which is dirty and infectious; on the other, the lightness, gaiety, and activity of humanity, which shall come to *dust* in the grave.

When a word is selected, as a 'vivid detail,' as particular for general, a reader may suspect alternative reasons why it has been selected; indeed the author might find it hard to say. When there are several such words there may be alternative ways of viewing them in order of importance.

Pan is our All, by him we breathe, we live,
We move, we are; ...
But when he frowns, the sheep, alas,
The shepherds wither, and the grass.
*(BEN JONSON, Pan's Anniversary.)*①

Alas, the word explaining which of the items in this list we are to take most seriously, belongs to the *sheep* by proximity and the break in the line, to the *grass* by rhyming with it, and to the *shepherds,* humble

① Ben Jonson (c. 1573–1637), English dramatist and poet.

though they may be, by the processes of human judgment; so that all three are given due attention, and the balance of the verse is maintained. The Biblical suggestions of *grass* as symbolic of the life of man ('in the mornings it is green and groweth up; in the evening it is cut down, dried up, and withered') add to the solemnity; or from another point of view make the passage absurdly blasphemous, because Pan here is James I. The grace, the pathos, the 'sheer song' of the couplet is given by an enforced subtlety of intonation, from the difficulty of saying it so as to bring out all the implications.

This last consideration is important, because it gives some hint as to why these devices belong to poetry rather than to prose, or indeed why poetry seems different from prose. A metrical scheme imposes a sort of intensity of interpretation upon the grammar, which makes it fruitful even when there is no 'song.'

I want to know a butcher paints,
A baker rhymes for his pursuit,
Candlestick-maker, much acquaints
His soul with song, or, haply mute,
Blows out his brains upon the flute.
(BROWNING.)

'I want to know that the whole class of butchers paints,' or 'I want to know that some one butcher paints,' or 'I want to know personally a butcher who paints'; any of these may be taken as the meaning, and their resultant is something like, 'I want to know that a member of the class of butchers is moderately likely to be a man who paints, or at any rate that he can do so if he wishes.' The demands of metre allow the poet to say something which is not normal colloquial English, so that the reader thinks of the various colloquial forms which are near to it, and puts them together; weighting their probabilities in proportion to their nearness. It is for such reasons as this that poetry can be more compact, while seeming to be less precise, than prose.

It is for these reasons, too, among others, that an insensitivity in a poet to the contemporary style of speaking, into which he has been trained to concentrate his powers of apprehension, is so disastrous, can be noticed so quickly, and produces that curious thinness or blurring of texture one finds in William Morris.[①] And that is why the practice of putting single words into italics for emphasis (again the Victorians are guilty) is so vulgar; a well-constructed sentence should be able to carry a stress on any of its words and should show in itself how these stresses are to be compounded. Both in prose and poetry, it is the impression that implications of this sort have been handled with more judgment than you yourself realize, that with this language as text innumerable further meanings, which you do not know, could be deduced, that forces you to feel respect for a style.

Also I have considered the 'implications' of sentences so far mainly as what they take for granted, as what must already be in mind if they are to be suitable. The stock example of this is, 'Have you stopped beating your wife?', which claims to know already that it has been your habit to do so. A complementary sort of implication may be defined: what must *not* be in mind if the sentence is to be suitable, what it leaves vague, or is not thinking about, or does not feel. The negative here assumes you might expect this particular thing to be in mind, because otherwise you would not have thought of it as an implication. You might think it lessened the importance of a negative implication that one is only conscious of it if its assumption is unjustified; but the mind is a destroyer; any assumption may chance to be questioned; and most people are conscious that they, therefore, can to some extent impose what they assume. In speaking

---

① William Morris (1834–1896), English poet and designer.

of 'implications' one thinks as much of negative as of positive ones, indeed it would often be difficult to make the distinction. One would notice, to discover a negative implication, the degree to which stock phrases were used which did not fit the situation very closely, as if it did not need to be, or could not safely be, defined further, or the degree to which a form of words had been selected which only said so much and no more. For such reasons as these, private letters often seem most exquisitely adapted to their setting when written most casually; it is exactly the extent to which their language is careless, the proportion of carelessness they give to the different matters in hand, which is so precise. Similarly in conversation this more refined sort of implication is very highly developed. It is comparable to the use of facial muscles, intended for different or immensely cruder uses (such as the muscles round the eyes designed to prevent them from being gorged with blood when you scream), to convey fine shades of 'expression.' They are comparable, again, in that there are fewer verbal devices, as there are fewer ways of moving facial muscles, than there are sorts of feeling to convey by them; this gives an inherent opportunity for ambiguity which is regularly exploited. The cult of careless ease in literature, where one is less sure of the audience, is more treacherous, but its advantages and dangers are of the same kind.

It is because of the wealth of implication which must be carried by sentences in poetry, because they must start from scratch and put the reader in possession of the entire attitude they assume, that the notion of 'sincerity' is important, and that it is so hard to imitate a style. A poem can be cross-questioned, and one must know, to feel sure that it will survive the process with undiminished reputation, that for a wide variety of possible assumptions in the reader the assumptions of the writer will seem reasonable enough to be adopted; and further that, for a hierarchy of degrees of care in the reader, the assumptions discovered in the writer will not show themselves to be self-conflicting in a way which to such a reader will seem absurd.

The reason, then, that ambiguity is more elaborate in poetry than in prose, other than the fact that the reader is trained to expect it, seems to be that the presence of metre and rhyme, admittedly irrelevant to the straightforward process of conveying a statement, makes it seem sensible to diverge from the colloquial order of statement, and so imply several colloquial orders from which the statement has diverged. But rhythm is a powerful weapon in itself, which needs to be considered separately; I have discussed negative implications here by way of a sidelong approach to it.

Rhythm allows one, by playing off the possible prose rhythms against the super-imposed verse rhythms, to combine a variety of statements in one order. Its direct effect seems a matter for physiology; in particular, a rhythmic beat taken faster than the pulse seems controllable, exhilarating, and not to demand intimate sympathy; a rhythmic beat almost synchronous with the pulse seems sincere and to demand intimate sympathy; while a rhythmic beat slower than the pulse, like a funeral bell, seems portentous and uncontrollable. But even if it is a simple rhythm which is apprehended, rather than something much more complex which involves the meaning, still it is the meaning which must show at what pace the verse is to be read. And, of course, it is not one rhythmical beat, like a bell tolling, which is apprehended; or if it is (since the ear insists on imposing rhythms, and cocaine can make one stroke into a series), then the word should be used in the plural; the foot, the grammatical clause, the line, the sentence, the stanza or paragraph, and the whole canto or subject-heading, are all rhythmical units; the total rhythmical line which results from them must be regarded as of an immense complexity entirely defined by the meaning; and even then it is the meaning which must imply how it is to be interpreted. So that rhythm is chiefly useful as a means of insisting upon, and then limiting, the possible implications; and though I may seem to be ignoring the rhythm through most of this book, I shall always be using it, so to speak, among the calculations on the margin, as a means of understanding the grammar.

However, one can oppose the use of rhythm to the use of ambiguity, because an interest in rhythm makes a poet long-winded, and ambiguity is a phenomenon of compression. Thus it is seldom that one finds relevant ambiguities in Spenser or Marlowe,① because their method is by a variety of means to sustain a poetic effect for so long that the poetic knot can be spread out at length, and one does not see that the separate uses of a word would be a pun if they were drawn together. When Marlowe brings off his triumphs of simplicity and the delight in rhythm it is often a matter of separating the implications of a sentence and using them at different times.

> *MEANDER. Your majesty shall shortly have your wish*
> *And ride in triumph through Persepolis.*
> *(Exeunt all except TAMBURLANE and his followers.)*
> *TAMBURLANE. And ride in triumph through Persepolis.*
> *Is it not brave to be a king, Techelles,*
> *Usumcasane and Theridamas,*
> *Is it not passing brave to be a king,*
> *And ride in triumph through Persepolis?*

Tamburlane can only use the same words again and again, because his mind is glutted with astonishment at them; Marlowe's idea of the heroic soul has extreme simplicity and unbounded appetite, so that after however great an expression of his desire for glory, after one

① Christopher Marlowe (1564–1593), English dramatist.

subordinate clause has opened out of another, with unalterable energy, it can still roar at the close with the same directness as in its opening line. Thus the lack of variety in his rhythm is in itself a device of some rhythmical subtlety. It is for this sort of reason that the same line is repeated here in three tones, of obsequiousness, of astonishment, and of triumph, which Shakespeare could have included in a single line.

Faustus, these books, thy wit, and our experience,
Shall make all nations to canonise us.
As Indian Moors obey their Spanish lords
So shall the spirits of every element
Be always serviceable to us three;
Like lions shall they guard us when we please,
Like Almain rutters, with their horsemen's staves,
Or Lapland giants, trotting by our sides;
Sometimes like women, or unwedded maids,
Shadowing more beauty in their airy brows
Than have the white breasts of the Queen of Love:
From Venice shall they drag huge argosies,
And from America the golden fleece
That yearly stuffs old Philip's treasury;
If learned Faustus will be resolute.

At first sight the last line is an afterthought expressing anxiety, but when immersed in the style one accepts it as a part of the sentence always intended, that might have been put in between the second line and the third. That a conditional clause should have been held back through all these successive lightnings of poetry, that after their achievement it should still be present with the same conviction and *resolution*, is itself a statement of heroic character. One's total impression of the character of Valdes is obtained by combining these two interpretations. Where so much can be said by the mere order of single mighty lines there is no need for much subtlety of implication within them.

I am considering here such ambiguities of rhythm as act without implying an ambiguity of grammar, or noticeable ambiguity in the use of words. This last example in result belongs to a later chapter, because it implies two different opinions of Valdes and leaves them to be reconciled; so does the following example, because it implies two different sentiments in the author. I put them here for the slightness of the machinery; it is a machinery continually used for ambiguities of the first type, and these examples may be prominent enough to show that it is powerful.

Aye, look, high heaven and earth ail from their prime foundation.
All thoughts to rive the heart are there, and all are vain;
Horror and scorn and hate and fear and indignation;
Oh why did I awake, when shall I sleep again?

*(A.E. HOUSMAN, Last Poems.)*①

The main rhythm of the third line (the crest of the wave) takes *hate* as its chief stress, and the first three nouns as a group together. *Fear* gives the second emphasis, allowed by the extra foot, *fear and indignation* act as a unit balancing the first three, and by attraction the *fear* meant is seen to be of a dignified kind. But behind the energy and determination of this treatment of the line as a unit, there is a rocking, broken, agitated, and impotent grouping, which takes the first four nouns as two pairs, associates *fear* with *hate* so as to make it weak and snarling, and throws in *indignation* as an isolated and squeaking disapproval.

---

① A. E. Housman (1859–1936), English poet.

I have mentioned Spenser, whom no discussion of rhythm can ignore. To show the scale of his rhythm, it may be enough to list some of the ways in which he gave movement to the stanza of the *Faerie Queene*; it is by the delicacy of this movement that he shows his attitude towards his sentences, rather than by devices of implication in the sentences themselves. At the same time, once such an attitude has been fixed, it is more easily described in terms of the meaning of the words than in terms of the meaning of the rhythm; in the next example, from Sidney, I shall use this other mode of approach.

Spenser concentrates the reader's attention on to the movement of his stanza: by the use of archaic words and constructions, so that one is at a safe distance from the exercise of an immediate judgment, by the steady untroubled flow of similar lines, by making no rapid change of sense or feeling, by sustained alliteration, parallel adjectives, and full statement of the accessories of a thought, and by the dreamy repetition of the great stanza perpetually pausing at its close. *Ababbcbcc* is a unit which may be broken up into a variety of metrical forms, and the ways in which it is successively broken up are fitted into enormous patterns. The first quatrain usually gratifies the ear directly and without surprise, and the stanzas may then be classified by the grammatical connections of the crucial fifth line, which must give a soft bump to the dying fall of the first quatrain, keep it in the air, and prevent it from falling apart from the rest of the stanza.

It may complete the sense of the quatrain, for instance, with a couplet, and the stanza will then begin with a larger, more narrative unit, *ababb* and wander garrulously down a perspective to the alexandrine. Or it may add to the quatrain as by an afterthought, as if with a childish earnestness it made sure of its point without regard to the metre, and one is relieved to find that the metre recovers itself after all. For more energetic or serious statements it will start a new quatrain at the fifth line, with a new sentence; there are then two smaller and tighter, repeatedly didactic, or logically opposed, or historically advancing, units, whose common rhyme serves to insist upon their contrast, which are summed up and reconciled in the final solemnity of the alexandrine. In times of excitement the fifth line will be connected both ways, so as to ignore the two quatrains, and, by flowing straight on down the stanza with an insistence on its unity, show the accumulated energy of some enormous climax; and again, by being connected with neither, it will make the stanza into an unstressed conversational device without overtones of rhythm, picking up stray threads of the story with almost the relief of prose. It would be interesting to take one of the vast famous passages of the work and show how these devices are fitted together into larger units of rhythm, but having said that every use of the stanza includes all these uses in the reader's apprehension of it I may have said enough to show the sort of methods Spenser had under his control; why it was not necessary for him to concentrate on the lightning flashes of ambiguity.

The size, the possible variety, and the fixity of this unit give something of the blankness that comes from fixing your eyes on a bright spot; you have to yield yourself to it very completely to take in the variety of its movement, and, at the same time, there is no need to concentrate the elements of the situation into a judgment as if for action. As a result of this, when there are ambiguities of idea, it is whole civilizations rather than details of the moment which are their elements; he can pour into the even dreamwork of his fairyland Christian, classical, and chivalrous materials with an air, not of ignoring their differences, but of holding all their systems of values floating as if at a distance, so as not to interfere with one another, in the prolonged and diffused energies of his mind.

Nowhere in English literature can this use of diffuseness as an alternative to, or peculiar branch of, ambiguity be seen more clearly than in those lovely sestines of Sidney, which are so curiously foreign to the normal modes or later developments of the language. This time I must do some serious quotation.

STREPHON. *KLAIUS.*

STREPHON. You Gote-heard Gods, that love the grassie mountaines,
You nimphes that haunt the springs in pleasant vallies,
You Satyrs joyd with free and quiet forrests,
Vouchsafe your silent eares to playning musique,
Which to my woes gives still an early morning:
And draws the dolor on till wery evening.

KLAIUS. O Mercurie, foregoer to the evening,
O heavenlie huntresse of the savage mountaines,
O lovelie starre, entitled of the morning,
While that my voice doth fill the woeful vallies
Vouchsafe your silent eares to playning musique,
Which oft hath Echo tir'd in secrete forrests.

STREPHON. I that was once free-burgess of the forrests
Where shade from Sunne, and sports I sought at evening,
I that was once esteemed for pleasant musique,
Am banisht now amongst the monstrous mountaines
Of huge despaire, and foul afflictions vallies,
Am growne a skrich-owle to myself each morning.

KLAIUS. I that was once delighted every morning,
Hunting the wild inhabiters of forrests,
I that was once the musique of these vallies,
So darkened am, that all my day is evening,

Hart-broken so, that mole-hills seem high mountaines,
And fill the vales with cries in stead of musique.

STREPHON. *Long since alas, my deadly Swannish musique*
Hath made itself a crier of the morning,
And hath with wailing strength climbed highest mountaines:
Long since my thoughts more desert be than forrests:
Long since I see my joyes come to their evening,
And state throwen down to over-troden vallies.

KLAIUS. *Long since the happie dwellers of these vallies,*
Have praide me leave my strange exclaiming musique,
Which troubles their dayes worke, and joyes of evening:
Long since I hate the night, more hate the morning:
Long since my thoughts chase me like beasts in forrests,
And make me wish myself laid under mountaines.

STREPHON. *Me seemes I see the high and stately mountaines,*
Transforme themselves to lowe dejected vallies:
Me seemes I heare in these ill-changed forrests,
The nightingales doo learne of Owles their musique:
Me seemes I feele the comfort of the morning
Turnde to the mortal serene of an evening.

KLAIUS. *Me seemes I see a filthie cloudie evening,*
As soone as Sunne begins to climbe the mountaines:
Me seemes I feel a noisome scent, the morning
When I do smell the flowers of these vallies:
Me seemes I heare, when I doo heare sweet musique,
The dreadful cries of murdered men in forrests.

STREPHON. I wish to fire the trees of all these forrests;
I give the Sunne a last farewell each evening;
I curse the fiddling finders out of musique:
With envy doo I hate the lofty mountaines;
And with despite despise the humble vallies:
I doo detest night evening, day, and morning.

KLAIUS. Curse to myself my prayer is, the morning:
My fire is more, than can be made with forrests;
My state more base, than are the basest vallies:
I wish no evenings more to see, each evening;
Shamed I have myself in sight of mountaines,
And stoppe mine eares, lest I go mad with musique.

STREPHON. For she, whose parts maintained a perfect musique,
Whose beauty shin'de more than the blushing morning,
Who much did pass in state the stately mountaines,
In straightness past the Cedars of the forrests,
Hath cast me wretch into eternal evening,
By taking her two Sunnes from these dark vallies.

KLAIUS. For she, to whom compared, the Alps are vallies,
She, whose lest word brings from the spheares their musique
At whose approach the Sunne rose in the evening,
Who, where she went, bare in her forehead morning,
Is gone, is gone from these our spoiled forrests,
Turning to deserts our best pastur'de mountaines.

STREPHON. These mountaines witness shall, so shall these vallies,
KLAIUS. These forrests eke, made wretched by our musique,
STREPHON. Our morning hymn is this,

KLAIUS. and song at evening.

(SIDNEY, *Arcadia.*)[①]

The poem beats, however rich its orchestration, with a wailing and immovable monotony, for ever upon the same doors in vain. *Mountaines, vallies, forrests; musique, evening, morning;* it is at these words only that Klaius and Strephon pause in their cries; these words circumscribe their world; these are the bones of their situation; and in tracing their lovelorn pastoral tedium through thirteen repetitions, with something of the aimless multitudinousness of the sea on a rock, we seem to extract all the meaning possible from these notions; we are at last, therefore, in possession of all that might have been implied by them (if we had understood them) in a single sentence; of all, in fact, that is implied by them, in the last sentence of the poem. I must glance, to show this, at the twelve other occasions on which each word is used.

Mountaines are haunts of Pan for lust and Diana for chastity, to both of these the lovers appeal; they suggest being shut in, or banishment; impossibility and impotence, or difficulty and achievement; greatness that may be envied or may be felt as your own (so as to make you feel helpless, or feel powerful); they give you the peace, or the despair, of the grave; they are the distant things behind which the sun rises and sets, the too near things which shut in your valley; deserted wastes, and the ample pastures to which you drive up the cattle for the summer.

Vallies hold nymphs to which you may appeal, and yet are the normal places where you live; are your whole world, and yet limited so that your voice can affect the whole of them; are opposed to *mountaines*, either as places of shelter and comfort, or as places of

① Sidney (*Critical Theory Since Plato*, p. 185).

humility and affliction; are rich with flowers and warmth, or are dark hollows between the hills.

Forests, though valuable and accustomed, are desolate and hold danger; there are both nightingales and owls in them; their beasts, though savage, give the strong pleasures of hunting; their burning is either useful or destructive; though wild and sterile they give freedom for contemplation, and their trunks are symbols of pride.

Music may express joy or sorrow; is at once more and less direct than talking, and so is connected with one's permanent feeling about the characters of pastoral that they are at once very rustic and rather over-civilized; it may please or distress the bystanders; and while belonging to despair and to the deaths of swans, it may share the living beauty of the lady, and be an inmate of the celestial spheres.

Morning brings hope, light and labour, *evening* rest, play and despair; they are the variety of Nature, or the tedious repetition of a day; their patrons Venus, whom one dare not name, and Mercury, who will bring no news of her. *Morning*, too, has often attached to it a meaning which, by an intelligent and illuminating misprint, is insisted upon in the eleventh (and subsequent) editions:

> *At whose approach the sun rose in the evening,*
> *Who where she went bore in her forehead mourning,*
> *Is gone, is gone, from these our spoiled forrests,*
> *Turning to deserts our best pastor'd mountaines.*

The form takes its effect by concentrating on these words and slowly building up our interest in them; all their latent implications are brought out by the repetitions; and each in turn is used to build up some simple conceit. So that when the static conception of the complaint has been finally brought into light (I do not mean by this to depreciate the sustained magnificence of its crescendo, but to praise the singleness of its idea), a whole succession of feelings about the local scenery, the whole way in which it is taken for granted, has been enlisted into sorrow and beats as a single passion of the mind.

I have put this poem at the end of a discussion ostensibly about rhythm, and shall mention its rhythm only to remark that it is magnificent; my point is that one can best illustrate its rhythm by showing the cumulative way it uses its words. It is seldom that the meaning of a poet's words is built up so flatly and steadily in the course of using them. And limited as this form may be, the capacity to accept a limitation so unflinchingly, the capacity even to conceive so large a form as a unit of sustained feeling, is one that has been lost since that age.

12.3 Key Words

① New Criticism 新批评

New Criticism was a formalist movement in literary theory that dominated American literary criticism in the middle decades of the 20th century. It emphasized close reading, particularly of poetry, to discover how a work of literature functioned as a self-contained, self-referential aesthetic object. The movement derived its name from John Crowe Ransom's 1941 book *The New Criticism*. The work of Cambridge scholar I. A. Richards, especially his *Practical Criticism* and *The Meaning of Meaning*, which offered what was claimed to be an empirical scientific approach, were important to the development of new critical methodology. Also very influential were the critical essays of T. S. Eliot, such as "Tradition and the Individual Talent" and "Hamlet and His Problems," in which Eliot developed his notion of the "objective correlative." Eliot's evaluative judgments, such as his condemnation of Milton and Dryden, his liking for the so-called metaphysical poets, and his insistence that poetry must be impersonal, greatly influenced the formation of the new critical canon.

② I. A. Richards 理查兹

Ivor Armstrong Richards (1893–1979), known as I. A. Richards, was an English educator, literary critic, and rhetorician. His work contributed to the foundations of New Criticism. Richards' intellectual contributions to the establishment of the literary methodology of New Criticism are presented in the books *The Meaning of Meaning: A Study of the Influence of Language upon Thought and of the Science of Symbolism* (1923), by C. K. Ogden and I. A. Richards, *Principles of Literary Criticism* (1924), *Practical Criticism* (1929), and *The Philosophy of Rhetoric* (1936).

③ George Orwell 乔治·奥威尔

Eric Arthur Blair (1903–1950), better known by his pen name George Orwell, was an English novelist and essayist, journalist and critic. His work is characterized by lucid prose, biting social criticism, opposition to totalitarianism, and outspoken support of democratic socialism. As a writer, Orwell produced literary criticism and poetry, fiction and polemical journalism; and is best known for the allegorical novella *Animal Farm* (1945) and the dystopian novel *Nineteen Eighty-Four* (1949). In 2008, *The Times* ranked George Orwell second among "The 50 greatest British writers since 1945."

④ Metaphor 隐喻

A metaphor is a figure of speech that, for rhetorical effect, directly refers to one thing by mentioning another. It may provide (or obscure) clarity or identify hidden similarities between two ideas. Metaphors are often compared with other types of figurative language, such as antithesis, hyperbole, metonymy and simile. One of the most commonly cited examples of a metaphor in English literature comes from the "All the world's a stage" monologue from *As You Like It* (《皆大欢喜》) by Shakespeare.

⑤ Synge's Deirdre 辛格的迪尔德

Deirdre of the Sorrows is a three-act play written by Irish playwright John Millington Synge in 1909. The play, based on Irish mythology, in particular the myths concerning Deirdre, Naoise, and Conchobar, was unfinished at the author's death in 1909. It was completed by William Butler Yeats and Synge's fiancée, Molly Allgood and first performed at the Abbey Theatre by the Irish National Theatre Society. Deirdre is the foremost tragic heroine in Irish legend and probably its best-known figure in modern times. She is known by the epithet "Deirdre of the Sorrows." Her story is part of the *Ulster Cycle*, the best-known stories of pre-Christian Ireland.

⑥ Vulcan 伏尔甘

Vulcan is the god of fire, volcanoes, metalworking, and the forge in Roman mythology.

⑦ Ben Jonson 本·琼森

Benjamin Jonson (1572–1637) was an English playwright and poet, whose artistry exerted a lasting impact upon English poetry and stage comedy. It was he who made the comedy of humours popular in the history of performance art. He is best known for the satirical plays *Every Man in His Humour* (1598), *Volpone* (1606), *The Alchemist* (1610) and *Bartholomew Fair* (1614) and for his lyric and epigrammatic poetry.

⑧ Richard Paget 理查·佩吉特

Sir Richard Horner Paget, 1st Baronet (1832–1908) was a British Conservative politician who sat in the House of Commons from 1865 to 1895.

⑨ A. E. Housman 豪斯曼

Alfred Edward Housman (1859–1936), usually known as A. E. Housman, was an English classical scholar and poet, best known to the general public for his cycle of poems *A Shropshire Lad*. Lyrical and almost epigrammatic in form, the poems wistfully evoke the dooms and disappointments of youth in the English countryside. Their beauty, simplicity and distinctive imagery appealed strongly to Edwardian taste, making him one of the foremost classicists of his age. He has been ranked as one of the greatest scholars who ever lived.

12.4 Extensive Explorations

① Why is metaphor the most important type of ambiguity? How did Empson describe it?

② Is there any good examples of metaphor in Chinese poetry? Is it comparable with the metaphors in any of Empson's quotations?

③ How did Empson analyze the metaphors in the quotation of "*Bare ruined choirs, where late the sweet birds sang*"? What does "*choirs*" here mean?

④ What example did Empson apply to introduce unpoetical word?

⑤ What is the relationship between the "scientific" mode of literary criticism and "psychological" explanations?

⑥ How did Pure Sound work in metaphors?

⑦ When mentioning Spenser, why did Empson stress that "no discussion of rhythm can ignore"? What is the function of rhythm in indications of a poem, according to Empson?

⑧ Try to analyze the series of metaphors in the quotation of Sydney's *Arcadia*.

13. M. H. Abrams' *The Mirror and the Lamp*

13.1 Lead-in

Meyer Howard "Mike" Abrams (1912–2015), usually cited as M. H. Abrams, was an American literary critic. His book *The Mirror and the Lamp* (《镜与灯》) made him worldly known in the 1950s. Edited by Abrams, *The Norton Anthology of English Literature* (《诺顿英国文学选集》) became the standard text for undergraduate survey courses across the U.S. and a major trendsetter in literary canon formation.

The same to Freud, Abrams was born in a European Jewish family in New Jersey. He entered Harvard University in 1930, then in 1934 he won a Henry Fellowship to Magdalene College, Cambridge, where he was supervised by I. A. Richards. He went back to Harvard for graduate school in 1935 and received a master's degree in 1937 and a Ph.D. in 1940.

In 1945, Abrams became a professor at Cornell University. The literary critics Harold Bloom, Gayatri Spivak and E. D. Hirsch, and the novelists William H. Gass and Thomas Pynchon, who were the major members of the school of New Criticism were his students at Cornell. He was elected a Fellow of the American Academy of Arts and Sciences in 1963.

As we know, Abrams had very close and direct ties to Anglo-American New Criticism, Of course, Empson is famous for his obscurity while Abrams famous for his conciseness, and that's why Abrams gained wide and long lasting reputation in his time. The

1st chapter of his *The Mirror and the Lamp* is selected in our textbook. Abrams started to compose *The Mirror and the Lamp* in the 1930s, and it was finally published in the 1950s. He emphasized that researchers need to focus on coordinates of literary theory before being obsessed by works of art. Actually, *The Mirror and the Lamp* concentrates on Romanticism and culture tradition. Therefore, the book provided good reference for the research into Wordsworth and Coleridge.

In the 1st chapter, Abrams concluded 4 coordinates of the world, the works, the authors and the readers. It's amazing to put forward coordinate as readers, for readers are aphasia in former types of literary theories. A number of theoreticians insist that it's only necessary to research on authors' personal life or on language of the work. And readers are of no importance, because they simply adopt the text provided by the author. Readers neither involve in creation nor in creating literary meanings. However, only readers convey the value of literary works. Such views are similar to reception aesthetic though reception aesthetic was established decades later. The 4 literary theories on the basis of the 4 coordinates, imitation theory, pragmatism theory, expression theory and objective theory are of great value in the history of literary theory as well. His theories are inspiring even today, especially for our study in Chinese literature, literary theory and literary criticism.

13.2 Text

Introduction: Orientation of Critical Theories[①]

I. Some Coordinates of Art Criticism

Four elements in the total situation of a work of art are discriminated and made salient, by one or another synonym, in almost all theories which aim to be comprehensive. First, there is the *work*, the artistic product itself. And since this is a human product, an artifact, the second common element is the artificer, the *artist*. Third, the work is taken to have a subject which, directly or deviously, is derived from existing things—to be about, or signify, or reflect something which either is, or bears some relation to, an objective state of affairs. This third element, whether held to consist of people and actions, ideas and feelings, material things and events, or super-sensible essences, has frequently been denoted by that word-of-all-work, 'nature'; but let us use the more neutral and comprehensive term, *universe*, instead. For the final element we have the *audience*: the listeners, spectators, or readers to whom the work is addressed, or to whose attention, at any rate, it becomes available.

On this framework of artist, work, universe, and audience I wish to spread out various theories for comparison. To emphasize the artificiality of the device, and at the same time make it easier to visualize the analyses, let us arrange the four coordinates in a convenient pattern. A triangle will do, with the work of art, the thing to be explained, in the center.

---

① 'Orientation of Critical Theories' is reprinted in part from *The Mirror and the Lamp: Romantic Theory and the Critical Tradition* (New York: Oxford University Press, 1953).

UNIVERSE

↑

WORK

↙ ↘

ARTIST AUDIENCE

Although any reasonably adequate theory takes some account of all four elements, almost all theories, as we shall see, exhibit a discernible orientation toward one only. That is, a critic tends to derive from one of these terms his principal categories for defining, classifying, and analyzing a work of art, as well as the major criteria by which he judges its value. Application of this analytic scheme, therefore, will sort attempts to explain the nature and worth of a work of art into four broad classes. Three will explain the work of art principally by relating it to another thing: the universe, the audience, or the artist. The fourth will explain the work by considering it in isolation, as an autonomous whole, whose significance and value are determined without any reference beyond itself.

To find the major orientation of a critical theory, however, is only the beginning of an adequate analysis. For one thing, these four co-ordinates are not constants, but variables; they differ in significance according to the theory in which they occur. Take what I have called the universe as an example. In any one theory, the aspects of nature which an artist is said to imitate, or is exhorted to imitate, may be either particulars or types, and they may be only the beautiful or the moral aspects of the world, or else any aspect without discrimination. It may be maintained that the artist's world is that of imaginative intuition, or of common sense, or of natural science; and this world may be held to include, or not to include, gods, witches, chimeras, and Platonic Ideas. Consequently, theories which agree in assigning to the represented universe the primary control over a legitimate work of art may vary from recommending the most uncompromising realism to the most remote idealism. Each of our other terms, as we shall see, also varies, both in meaning and functioning, according to the critical theory in which it occurs, the method of reasoning which the theorist characteristically uses, and the explicit or implicit 'world-view' of which these theories are an integral part.

It would be possible, of course, to devise more complex methods of analysis which, even in a preliminary classification, would make more subtle distinctions.① By multiplying differentiae, however, we sharpen our capacity to discriminate at the expense both of easy manageability and the ability to make broad initial generalizations. For our historical purpose, the scheme I have proposed has this important virtue, that it will enable us to bring out the one essential attribute which most early nineteenth-century theories had in common: the persistent recourse to the poet to explain the nature and criteria of poetry. Historians have recently been instructed to speak only of 'romanticisms,' in the plural, but from our point of vantage there turns out to be one distinctively romantic criticism, although this remains a unity amid variety.

II. Mimetic Theories

The mimetic orientation — the explanation of art as essentially an imitation of aspects of the universe — was probably the most primitive aesthetic theory, but mimesis is no simple concept by the time it makes its first recorded appearance in the dialogues of Plato. The arts of painting, poetry, music, dancing, and sculpture, Socrates says, are

---

① [Abrams] For a subtle and elaborate analysis of diverse critical theories, see Richard McKeon, 'Philosophic Bases of Art and Criticism,' *Critics and Criticism, Ancient and Modern,* ed. R. S. Crane (The University of Chicago Press, Chicago, 1952).

all imitations.[1] 'Imitation' is a relational term, signifying two items and some correspondence between them. But although in many later mimetic theories everything is comprehended in two categories, the imitable and the imitation, the philosopher in the Platonic dialogues characteristically operates with three categories. The first category is that of the eternal and unchanging Ideas; the second, reflecting this, is the world of sense, natural or artificial; and the third category, in turn reflecting the second, comprises such things as shadows, images in water and mirrors, and the fine arts.

Around this three-stage regress—complicated still further by various supplementary distinctions, as well as by his exploitation of the polysemism of his key terms—Plato weaves his dazzling dialectic.[2] But from the shifting arguments emerges a recurrent pattern exemplified in the famous passage in the tenth book of the *Republic*. In discussing the nature of art, Socrates makes the point that there are three beds: the Idea which 'is the essence of the bed' and is made by God, the bed made by the carpenter, and the bed found in a painting. How shall we describe the painter of this third bed?

> *I think, he said, that we may fairly designate him as the imitator of that which the others make.*
>
> *Good, I said; then you call him who is third in the descent from nature an imitator?*
>
> *Certainly, he said.*
>
> *And the tragic poet is an imitator, and therefore, like all other*

---

① [Abrams] *Republic* (trans. Jowett) x. 596-597; *Laws* ii. 667-668, vii. 814-816.

② [Abrams] See Richard McKeon, 'Literary Criticism and the Concept of Imitation in Antiquity,' *Critics and Criticism*, ed. Crane, pp. 147-149. The article exhibits those multiple shifts in Plato's use of the term 'imitation' which have trapped many later commentators as successfully as they once did the rash spirits who engaged Socrates in controversy.

imitators, he is thrice removed from the king and from the truth?
That appears to be so.[①]

From the initial position that art imitates the world of appearance and not of Essence, it follows that works of art have a lowly status in the order of existing things. Furthermore, since the realm of Ideas is the ultimate locus not only of reality but of value, the determination that art is at second remove from the truth automatically establishes its equal remoteness from the beautiful and good. Despite the elaborate dialectic—or more accurately, by means of it—Plato's remains a philosophy of a single standard; for all things, including art, are ultimately judged by the one criterion of their relation to the same Ideas. On these grounds, the poet is inescapably the competitor of the artisan, the lawmaker, and the moralist; indeed, any one of these can be regarded as himself the truer poet, successfully achieving that imitation of the Ideas which the traditional poet attempts under conditions dooming him to failure. Thus the lawmaker is able to reply to the poets seeking admission to his city, Best of strangers—

> *we also according to our ability are tragic poets, and our tragedy is the best and noblest; for our whole state is an imitation of the best and noblest life, which we affirm to be indeed the very truth of tragedy. You are poets and we are poets ... rivals and antagonists in the noblest of dramas ...*[②]

And the poor opinion of ordinary poetry to which we are committed on the basis of its mimetic character, is merely confirmed when Plato

① [Abrams] *Republic x*. 597 (*Critical Theory Since Plato*, p. 31).
② [Abrams] *laws* vii. 817.

points out that its effects on its auditors are bad because it represents appearance rather than truth, and nourishes their feelings rather than their reason; or by demonstrating that the poet in composing (as Socrates jockeys poor obtuse Ion into admitting) cannot depend on his art and knowledge, but must wait upon the divine afflatus and the loss of his right mind.[①]

The Socratic dialogues, then, contain no aesthetics proper, for neither the structure of Plato's cosmos nor the pattern of his dialectic permits us to consider poetry as poetry—as a special kind of product having its own criteria and reason for being. In the dialogues there is only one direction possible, and one issue, that is, the perfecting of the social state and the state of man; so that the question of art can never be separated from questions of truth, justice, and virtue. 'For great is the issue at stake,' Socrates says in concluding his discussion of poetry in the *Republic*, 'greater than appears, whether a man is to be good or bad.'[②]

Aristotle in the *Poetics* also defines poetry as imitation. 'Epic poetry and Tragedy, as also Comedy, Dithyrambic poetry, and most flute-playing and lyre-playing, are all, viewed as a whole, modes of imitation'; and 'the objects the imitator represents are actions...'[③] But the difference between the way the term 'imitation' functions in Aristotle and in Plato distinguishes radically their consideration of art. In the *Poetics*, as in the Platonic dialogues, the term implies that a work of art is constructed according to prior models in the nature of things, but since Aristotle has shorn away the other world

① [Abrams] *Republic* x. 603-605 (*Critical Theory Since Plato*, p. 29); *Ion* 535-536 (*Critical Theory Since Plato*, p. 13); *Apology* 22.

② [Abrams] *Republic* x. 608 (*Critical Theory Since Plato*, p. 36).

③ [Abrams] *Poetics* (trans. Ingram Bywater) I. 1447a, 1448a (*Critical Theory Since Plato*, p. 52). On imitation in Aristotle's criticism see McKeon, 'The Concept of Imitation,' op. cit., pp. 160-168.

of criterion-Ideas, there is no longer anything invidious in that fact. Imitation is also made a term specific to the arts, distinguishing these from everything else in the universe, and thereby freeing them from rivalry with other human activities. Furthermore, in his analysis of the fine arts, Aristotle at once introduces supplementary distinctions according to the objects imitated, the medium of imitation, and the manner—dramatic, narrative, or mixed, for example—in which the imitation is accomplished. By successive exploitation of these distinctions in object, means, and manner, he is able first to distinguish poetry from other kinds of art, and then to differentiate the various poetic genres, such as epic and drama, tragedy and comedy. When he focuses on the genre of tragedy, the same analytic instrument is applied to the discrimination of the parts constituting the individual whole: plot, character, thought, and so on. Aristotle's criticism, therefore, is not only criticism of art as art, independent of statesmanship, being, and morality, but also of poetry as poetry, and of each kind of poem by the criteria appropriate to its particular nature. As a result of this procedure, Aristotle bequeathed an arsenal of instruments for technical analysis of poetic forms and their elements which have proved indispensable to critics ever since, however diverse the uses to which these instruments have been put.

A salient quality of the *Poetics* is the way it considers a work of art in various of its external relations, affording each its due function as one of the 'causes' of the work. This procedure results in a scope and flexibility that makes the treatise resist a ready classification into any one kind of orientation. Tragedy cannot be fully defined, for example, nor can the total determinants of its construction be understood, without taking into account its proper effect on the audience: the achievement of the specifically 'tragic pleasure,' which is 'that of pity and fear.'[1] It is apparent, however, that the mimetic concept—the reference of a work to the subject matter which it imitates—is primary in Aristotle's critical system, even if it is *primus inter pares*.[2] Their character as an imitation of human actions is what defines the arts in general, and the kind of action imitated serves as one important differentia of an artistic species. The historical genesis of art is traced to the natural human instinct for imitating, and to the natural tendency to find pleasure in seeing imitations. Even the unity essential to any work of art is mimetically grounded, since 'one imitation is always of one thing,' and in poetry 'the story, as an imitation of action, must represent one action, a complete whole...'[3] And the 'form' of a work, the presiding principle determining the choice and order and internal adjustments of all the parts, is derived from the form of the object that is imitated. It is the fable or plot 'that is the end and purpose of tragedy,' its 'life and soul, so to speak,' and this because

> *tragedy is essentially an imitation not of persons but of action and life... We maintain that Tragedy is primarily an imitation of action, and that it is mainly for the sake of the action that it imitates the personal agents.*[4]

If we refer again to our analytic diagram, one other general aspect of the *Poetics* presses on our attention, particularly when we have the distinctive orientation of romantic criticism in mind. While Aristotle makes a distribution (though an unequal one) among the objects

---

① [Abrams] *Poetics* 6. 1449b, 14. 1453b (*Critical Theory Since Plato*, p. 55).

② First among equals.

③ [Abrams] *Poetics* 8. 1451a (*Critical Theory Since Plato*, p. 57).

④ [Abrams] Ibid., 6. 1450a-1450b (*Critical Theory Since Plato*, p. 55).

imitated, the necessary emotional effects on an audience, and the internal demands of the product itself, as determinants of this or that aspect of a poem, he does not assign a determinative function to the poet himself. The poet is the indispensable efficient cause, the agent who, by his skill, extracts the form from natural things and imposes it upon an artificial medium; but his personal faculties, feelings, or desires are not called on to explain the subject matter or form of a poem. In the *Poetics*, the poet is invoked only to explain the historical divergence of comic from serious forms, and to be advised of certain aids toward the construction of plot and the choice of diction.① In Plato, the poet is considered from the point of view of politics, not of art. When the poets make a personal appearance all the major ones are dismissed, with extravagant courtesy, from the ideal Republic; upon later application, a somewhat greater number are admitted to the second-best state of the *Laws*, but with a radically diminished repertory.②

'Imitation' continued to be a prominent item in the critical vocabulary for a long time after Aristotle—all the way through the eighteenth century, in fact. The systematic importance given to the term differed greatly from critic to critic; those objects in the universe that art imitates, or should imitate, were variously conceived as either actual or in some sense ideal; and from the first, there was a tendency to replace Aristotle's 'action' as the principal object of imitation with such elements as human character, or thought, or even inanimate things. But particularly after the recovery of the *Poetics* and the great burst of aesthetic theory in sixteenth-century Italy, whenever a critic was moved to get down to fundamentals and frame a comprehensive definition of art, the predicate usually included the word 'imitation,' or else one of

① [Abrams] *Poetics*. 4. 1448b, 17. 1455a-1455b (*Critical Theory Since Plato*, p. 27).

② [Abrams] *Republic* iii. 398, x. 606-608 (*Critical Theory Since Plato*, p. 27); *Laws* vii. 817.

those parallel terms which, whatever differences they might imply, all faced in the same direction: 'reflection,' 'representation,' 'counterfeiting,' 'feigning,' 'copy,' or 'image.'

Through most of the eighteenth century, the tenet that art is an imitation seemed almost too obvious to need iteration or proof. As Richard Hurd said in his 'Discourse on Poetical Imitation,' published in 1751, 'All *Poetry*, to speak with Aristotle and the Greek critics (if for so plain a point authorities be thought wanting) is, properly, *imitation*. It is, indeed, the noblest and most extensive of the mimetic arts; having all creation for its object, and ranging the entire circuit of universal being.'① Even the reputedly radical proponents of 'original genius' in the second half of the century commonly found that a work of genius was no less an imitation for being an original. '*Imitations*,' Young wrote in his *Conjectures on Original Composition*, 'are of two kinds: one of nature, one of authors. The first we call *Originals*...' The original genius in fact turns out to be a kind of scientific investigator: 'The wide field of nature lies open before it, where it may range unconfined, make what discoveries it can ... as far as visible nature extends...'② Later the Reverend J. Moir, an extremist in his demand for originality in poetry, conceived genius to lie in

① [Abrams] *The Works of Richard Hurd* (London, 1811), II, 111-112.

② [Abrams] Edward Young, *Conjectures on Original Composition*, ed. Edith Morley (Manchester, 1918), pp. 6, 18. See also William Duff, *Essay on Original Genius* (London, 1767), p. 192n. John Ogilvie reconciles creative genius and original invention with 'the great principle of poetic imitation' (*Philosophical and Critical Observations on the Nature, Characters, and Various Species of Composition*, London, 1774, I, 105-107). Joseph Warton, familiar proponent of a 'boundless imagination,' enthusiasm, and 'the romantic, the wonderful, and the wild,' still agrees with Richard Hurd that poetry is 'an art, whose essence is imitation,' and whose objects are 'material or animate, extraneous or internal' (*Essay on the Writings and Genius of Pope*, London, 1756, I, 89-90). Cf. Robert Wood, *Essay on the Original Genius and Writings of Homer* (1769), London, 1824, pp. 6-7, 178.

the ability to discover 'a thousand new variations, distinctions, and resemblances' in the 'familiar phenomena of nature,' and declared that original genius always gives 'the identical impression it receives.'[①] In this identification of the poet's task as novelty of discovery and particularity of description we have moved a long way from Aristotle's conception of mimesis, except in this respect, that criticism still looks to one or another aspect of the given world for the essential source and subject matter of poetry.

Instead of heaping up quotations, it will be better to cite a few eighteenth-century discussions of imitation that are of special interest. My first example is the French critic, Charles Batteux, whose *Les Beaux Arts réduits à un même principe (1747*) found some favor in England and had immense influence in Germany, as well as in his native country. The rules of art, Batteux thought, which are now so numerous, must surely be reducible to a single principle. 'Let us,' he cries, 'imitate the true physicists, who assemble experiments and then on these found a system which reduces them to a principle.'

That Batteux proposes for his procedure 'to begin with a clear and distinct idea' —a principle 'simple enough to be grasped instantly, and extensive enough to absorb all the little detailed rules'—is sufficient clue that he will follow in method not Newton, the physicist, but rather Euclid and Descartes.[②] In pursuance of his clear and distinct idea, he burrowed industriously through the standard French critics until, he says ingenuously, 'it occurred to me to open Aristotle, whose *Poetics* I had heard praised.' Then came the revelation; all details fell neatly into place. The source of

① [Abrams] 'Originality,' *Gleanings* (London, 1785), I, 107, 109.

② Isaac Newton (1643-1727), English mathematician and physicist; Euclid (fl. 300 B.C.E.), Greek mathematician; René Descartes (1596-1650), French mathematician and philosopher.

illumination?—none other than ‘the principle of imitation which the Greek philosopher established for the fine arts.’① This imitation, however, is not of crude everyday reality, but of ‘la belle nature’; that is, ‘le vrai-semblable,’ formed by assembling traits taken from individual things to compose a model possessing ‘all the perfections it is able to receive.’② From this principle Batteux goes on, lengthily and with great show of rigor, to extract one by one the rules of taste—both the general rules for poetry and painting and the detailed rules for the special genres. For

> *the majority of known rules refer back to imitation, and form a sort of chain, by which the mind seizes at the same instant consequences and principle, as a whole perfectly joined, in which all the parts are mutually sustained.*③

Next to this classic instance of a priori and deductive aesthetics I shall set a German document, Lessing’s *Laokoon,* published in 1776.④ Lessing undertook to undo the confusion in theory and practice between poetry and the graphic and plastic arts which, he believed, resulted from an uninquisitive acceptance of Simonides’ maxim that ‘painting is dumb poetry and poetry a speaking painting.’⑤ His own procedure, he promises, will be continually to test abstract theory against ‘the individual instance.’ Repeatedly he derides German

---

① [Abrams] Charles Batteux, *Les Beaux Arts réduits á un même principe* (Paris, 1747), pp. i-viii.

② [Abrams] Ibid., pp. 9-27.

③ [Abrams] Ibid., p. xiii. For the important place of imitation in earlier French neo-classic theories, see René Bray, *La Formation de la doctrine classique en France* (Lausanne, 1931), pp. 140ff.

④ Lessing (*Critical Theory Since Plato*, p. 379).

⑤ Simonides (fl. fifth century B.C.E.), Greek poet.

critics for their reliance on deduction. 'We Germans have no lack of systematic books. We are the most expert of any nation in the world at deducing, from a few given verbal explanations, and in the most beautiful order, anything whatever that we wish.' 'How many things would prove incontestable in theory, had not genius succeeded in proving the contrary in fact!'① Lessing's intention, then, is to establish aesthetic principles by an inductive logic which is deliberately opposed to the procedure of Batteux. Nevertheless, like Batteux, Lessing concludes that poetry, no less than painting, is imitation. The diversity between these arts follows from their difference in medium, which imposes necessary differences in the objects each is competent to imitate. But although poetry consists of a sequence of articulate sounds in time rather than of forms and colors fixed in space, and although, instead of being limited, like painting, to a static but pregnant moment, its special power is the reproduction of progressive action, Lessing reiterates for it the standard formula: 'Nachahmung' is still for the poet the attribute 'which constitutes the essence of his art.'②

As the century drew on, various English critics began to scrutinize the concept of imitation very closely, and they ended by finding (Aristotle to the contrary) that differences in medium between the arts were such as to disqualify all but a limited number from being classed as mimetic, in any strict sense. The trend may be indicated by a few examples. In 1744 James Harris still maintained, in 'A Discourse on Music, Painting, and Poetry,' that imitation was common to all three arts. 'They agree, by being all mimetic or imitative. They differ,

---

① [Abrams] Lessing, *Laokoon*, ed. W. G. Howard (New York, 1910), pp.23-25, 42.

② [Abrams] Ibid., pp. 99-102, 64.

as they imitate by different media...'[1] In 1762 Kames declared that 'of all the fine arts, painting only and sculpture are in their nature imitative'; music, like architecture, 'is productive of originals, and copies not from nature'; while language copies from nature only in those instances in which it 'is imitative of sound or motion.'[2] And by 1789, in two closely reasoned dissertations prefixed to his translation of the *Poetics,* Thomas Twining confirmed this distinction between arts whose media are 'iconic' (in the later terminology of the Chicago semiotician, Charles Morris[3]), in that they resemble what they denote, and those which are significant only by convention. Only works in which the resemblance between copy and object is both 'immediate' and 'obvious,' Twining says, can be described as imitative in a strict sense. Dramatic poetry, therefore, in which we mimic speech by speech, is the only kind of poetry which is properly imitation; music must be struck from the list of imitative arts; and he concludes by saying that painting, sculpture, and the arts of design in general are 'the only arts that are *obviously* and *essentially* imitative.'[4]

The concept that art is imitation, then, played an important part in neo-classic aesthetics; but closer inspection shows that it did not, in most theories, play the dominant part. Art, it was commonly said, is an imitation — but an imitation which is only instrumental toward producing effects upon an audience. In fact, the near-unanimity with

---

① [Abrams] *Three Treatises in The Works of James Harris* (London, 1803), I, 58. Cf. Adam Smith, 'Of the Nature of That Imitation Which Takes Place in What Are Called the Imitative Arts,' *Essays Philosophical and Literary* (London, n.d.), pp. 405ff.

② [Abrams] Henry Home, Lord Kames (*Critical Theory Since Plato,* p. 369), *Elements of Criticism* (Boston, 1796), II, I (chap. xviii).

③ Charles Morris (1903–1979).

④ [Abrams] Thomas Twining, ed., *Aristotle's Treatise on Poetry* (London, 1789). pp. 4, 21-22, 60-61.

which post-Renaissance critics lauded and echoed Aristotle's *Poetics* is deceptive. The focus of interest had shifted, and, on our diagram, this later criticism is primarily oriented, not from work to universe, but from work to audience. The nature and consequences of this change of direction is clearly indicated by the first classic of English criticism, written sometime in the early 1580's, Sir Philip Sidney's *The Apologie for Poetry*.

III. Pragmatic Theories

*Poesy therefore [said Sidney] is an arte of imitation, for so Aristotle termeth it in the word Mimesis, that is to say, a representing, counterfetting, or figuring foorth—to speake metaphorically, a speaking picture: with this end, to teach and delight.*①

In spite of the appeal to Aristotle, this is not an Aristotelian formulation. To Sidney, poetry, by definition, has a purpose—to achieve certain effects in an audience. It imitates only as a means to the proximate end of pleasing, and pleases, it turns out, only as a means to the ultimate end of teaching; for 'right poets' are those who 'imitate both to delight and teach, and delight to move men to take that goodnes in hande, which without delight they would flye as from a stranger...'② As a result, throughout this essay the needs of the audience become the fertile grounds for critical distinctions and standards. In order 'to teach and delight,' poets imitate not 'what is, hath been, or shall be,' but only 'what may be, and should be,' so that the very objects of imitation become such as to guarantee the

① [Abrams] Sir Philip Sidney (*Critical Theory Since Plato*, p. 189), 'An Apology for Poetry,' *Elizabethan Critical Essays*, ed. G. Gregory Smith (London, 1904), I, 158.

② [Abrams] Ibid., I, 159 (*Critical Theory Since Plato*, p. 189).

moral purpose, The poet is distinguished from, and elevated above, the moral philosopher and the historian by his capacity to move his auditors more forcefully to virtue, since he couples 'the general notion' of the philosopher with 'the particular example' of the historian; while by disguising his doctrine in a tale, he entices even 'harde harted evill men,' unaware, into the love of goodness, 'as if they tooke a medicine of Cherries.' The genres of poetry are discussed and ranked from the point of view of the moral and social effect each is suited to achieve: the epic poem thus demonstrates itself to be the king of poetry because it 'most inflameth the mind with desire to be worthy,' and even the lowly love lyric is conceived as an instrument for persuading a mistress of the genuineness of her lover's passion.[①] A history of criticism could be written solely on the basis of successive interpretations of salient passages from Aristotle's *Poetics*. In this instance, with no sense of strain, Sidney follows his Italian guides (who in turn had read Aristotle through the spectacles of Horace, Cicero, and the Church fathers) in bending one after another of the key statements of the *Poetics* to fit his own theoretical frame.[②]

For convenience we may name criticism that, like Sidney's, is ordered toward the audience, a 'pragmatic theory,' since it looks at the work of art chiefly as a means to an end, an instrument for getting something done, and tends to judge its value according to its success

---

① [Abrams] Sir Philip Sidney, 'An Apology for Poetry,' *Elizabethan Critical Essays*, ed. G. Gregory Smith (London, 1904), I, 159, 161-164, 171-180, 201 [*Critical Theory Since Plato*, p. 197].

② [Abrams] See, e.g., his use of Aristotle's statement that poetry is more philosophical than history (I, 167-168) (*Critical Theory Since Plato*, p. 57), and that painful things can be made pleasant by imitations (p. 171) (*Critical Theory Since Plato*, p. 58); and his wrenching of Aristotle's central term, *praxis* — the actions which are imitated by poetry — to signify the moral action which a poem moves the spectator to practice (p.171).

in achieving that aim. There is, of course, the greatest variance in emphasis and detail, but the central tendency of the pragmatic critic is to conceive a poem as something made in order to effect requisite responses in its readers; to consider the author from the point of view of the powers and training he must have in order to achieve this end; to ground the classification and anatomy of poems in large part on the special effects each kind and component is most competent to achieve; and to derive the norms of the poetic art and canons of critical appraisal from the needs and legitimate demands of the audience to whom the poetry is addressed.

The perspective, much of the basic vocabulary, and many of the characteristic topics of pragmatic criticism originated in the classical theory of rhetoric. For rhetoric had been universally regarded as an instrument for achieving persuasion in an audience, and most theorists agreed with Cicero that in order to persuade, the orator must conciliate, inform, and move the minds of his auditors.① The great classical exemplar of the application of the rhetorical point of view to poetry was, of course, the *Ars Poetica* of Horace. As Richard McKeon points out, 'Horace's criticism is directed in the main to instruct the poet how to keep his audience in their seats until the end, how to induce cheers and applause, how to please a Roman audience, and by the same token, how to please all audiences and win immortality.'②

In what became for later critics the focal passage of the *Ars Poetica*, Horace advised that 'the poet's aim is either to profit or to please, or to blend in one the delightful and the useful.' The context shows that Horace held pleasure to be the chief purpose of poetry, for he recommends the profitable merely as a means to give pleasure to the elders, who, in contrast to the young aristocrats, 'rail at what

① [Abrams] *Cicero* (*Critical Theory Since Plato*, p. 74), *De oratore* II. xxviii.

② [Abrams] 'The Concept of Imitation,' op. cit. p. 173.

contains no serviceable lesson.'[1] But *prodesse* and *delectare*, to teach and to please, together with another term introduced from rhetoric, *movere*, to move, served for centuries to collect under three heads the sum of aesthetic effects on the reader. The balance between these terms altered in the course of time. To the overwhelming majority of Renaissance critics, as to Sir Philip Sidney, the moral effect was the terminal aim, to which delight and emotion were auxiliary. From the time of the critical essays of Dryden through the eighteenth century, pleasure tended to become the ultimate end, although poetry without profit was often held to be trivial, and the optimistic moralist believed with James Beattie that if poetry instructs, it only pleases the more effectually.[2]

Looking upon a poem as a 'making,' a contrivance for affecting an audience, the typical pragmatic critic is engrossed with formulating the methods—the 'skill, or Crafte of making' as Ben Jonson called it—for achieving the effects desired. These methods, traditionally comprehended under the term *poesis*, or 'art' (in phrases such as 'the art of poetry'), are formulated as precepts and rules whose warrant consists either in their being derived from the qualities of works whose success and long survival have proved their adaptation to human nature, or else in their being grounded directly on the psychological laws governing the responses of men in general. The rules, therefore, are inherent in the qualities of each excellent work of art, and when excerpted and codified these rules serve equally to guide the artist in making and the critics in judging any future product. 'Dryden,' said Dr. Johnson, 'may be properly considered

① [Abrams] Horace, *Ars Poetica*, trans. E. H. Blakeney, in *Literary Criticism, Plato to Dryden*, ed. Allan H. Gilbert (New York, 1940), p. 139 (*Critical Theory Since Plato*, p. 83).

② [Abrams] *Essays on Poetry and Music* (third ed.; London, 1779), p. 10.

as the father of English criticism, as the writer who first taught us to determine upon principles the merit of composition.'[①] Dryden's method of establishing those principles was to point out that poetry, like painting, has an end, which is to please; that imitation of nature is the general means for attaining this end; and that rules serve to specify the means for accomplishing this end in detail:

> *Having thus shewn that imitation pleases, and why it pleases in both these arts, it follows, that some rules of imitation are necessary to obtain the end; for without rules there can be no art, any more than there can be a house without a door to conduct you into it.*[②]

Emphasis on the rules and maxims of an art is native to all criticism that grounds itself in the demands of an audience, and it survives today in the magazines and manuals devoted to teaching fledgling authors 'how to write stories that sell.' But rulebooks based on the lowest common denominator of the modern buying public are only gross caricatures of the complex and subtly rationalized neo-classic ideals of literary craftsmanship. Through the early part of the eighteenth century, the poet could rely confidently on the trained taste and expert connoisseurship of a limited circle of readers, whether these were Horace's Roman contemporaries under Emperor Augustus, or Vida's at the papal court of Leo X,[③] or Sidney's fellow-courtiers under Elizabeth, or the London audience of Dryden and

---

① [Abrams] 'Dryden,' *Lives of the English Poets*, ed. Birkbeck Hill (Oxford, 1905), I, 410.

② [Abrams] 'Parallel of Poetry and Painting' (1695), *Essays*, ed. W. P. Ker (Oxford, 1926), II, 138. See Hoyt Trowbridge, 'The Place of Rules in Dryden's Criticism,' *Modern Philology*, XLIV (1946), 84ff.

③ Augustus (63 B.C.E.–14 A.D.), first Roman Emperor; Marco Giraloma Vida (c. 1490–1556) Italian Latin poet; Leo X (1475–1521), Pope.

Pope; while, in theory, the voices even of the best contemporary judges were subordinated to the voice of the ages. Some neo-classic critics were also certain that the rules of art, though empirically derived, were ultimately validated by conforming to that objective structure of norms whose existence guaranteed the rational order and harmony of the universe. In a strict sense, as John Dennis made explicit what was often implied, Nature 'is nothing but that Rule and Order, and Harmony, which we find in the visible Creation'; so 'Poetry, which is an imitation of Nature,' must demonstrate the same properties. The renowned masters among the ancients wrote not

> *to please a tumultuous transitory Assembly, or a Handful of Men, who were call'd their Countrymen; They wrote to their Fellow-Citizens of the Universe, to all Countries, and to all Ages... They were clearly convinc'd, that nothing could transmit their Immortal Works to Posterity, but something like that harmonious Order which maintains the Universe...*[①]

Although they disagreed concerning specific rules, and although many English critics repudiated such formal French requisites as the unity of time and place, and the purity of comedy and tragedy, all but a few eccentrics among eighteenth-century critics believed in the validity of some set of universal rules. At about mid-century, it became popular to demonstrate and expound all the major rules for poetry, or even for art in general, in a single inclusive critical system. The pattern of the pragmatic reasoning usually employed may conveniently be

---

① [Abrams] *The Advancement and Reformation of Modern Poetry* (1701), in *The Critical Works of John Dennis,* ed. E. N. Hooker (Baltimore, 1939), I, 202-203. For Dennis' derivation of specific rules from the end of art, which is 'to delight and reform the mind,' see *The Grounds of Criticism in Poetry* (1704), ibid., pp. 336ff.

studied in such a compendious treatment as James Beattie's *Essay on Poetry and Music as they affect the Mind* (1762), or more succinctly still, in Richard Hurd's 'Dissertation of the Idea of Universal Poetry' (1766). Universal poetry, no matter what the genre, Hurd says, is an art whose end is the maximum possible pleasure. 'When we speak of poetry, as an *art*, we mean *such a way or method of treating a subject, as is found most pleasing and delightful to us*.' And this idea 'if kept steadily in view, will unfold to us all the mysteries of the poetic art. There needs but to evolve the philosopher's idea, and to apply it, as occasion serves.' From this major premise Hurd evolves three properties, essential to all poetry if it is to effect the greatest possible delight: figurative language, 'fiction' (that is to say, a departure from what is actual, or empirically possible), and versification. The mode and degree in which these three universal qualities are to be combined in any one species of poetry, however, will depend on its peculiar end, because each poetic kind must exploit that special pleasure which it is generically adapted to achieve. 'For the art of every *kind* of poetry is only this general art so modified as the *nature* of each, that is, its more immediate and subordinate end, may respectively require.'

> *For the name of poem will belong to every composition, whose primary end is to please, provided it be so constructed as to afford all the pleasure, which its kind or sort will permit.*①

On the basis of isolated passages from his *Letters on Chivalry and Romance*, Hurd is commonly treated as a 'preromantic' critic. But in the summation of his poetic creed in the 'Idea of Universal Poetry,'

① [Abrams] 'Dissertation on the Idea of Universal Poetry,' *Works*, II, 3-4, 25-27. For a parallel argument see Alexander Gerard. *An Essay on Taste* (London, 1759), p. 40.

the rigidly deductive logic which Hurd employs to 'unfold' the rules of poetry from a primitive definition, permitting 'the reason of the thing' to override the evidence of the actual practice of poets, brings him as close as anyone in England to the geometric method of Charles Batteux, though without that critic's Cartesian apparatus. The difference is that Batteux evolves his rules from the definition of poetry as the imitation of *la belle nature*, and Hurd, from its definition as the art of treating a subject so as to afford the reader a maximum pleasure; and this involves his assuming that he possesses an empirical knowledge of the psychology of the reader. For if the end of poetry is to gratify the mind of the reader, Hurd says, knowledge of the laws of mind is necessary to establish its rules, which are 'but so many MEANS, which experience finds most conducive to that end.'① Since Batteux and Hurd, however, are both intent on rationalizing what is mainly a common body of poetic lore, it need not surprise us that, though they set out from different points of the compass, their paths often coincide.②

But to appreciate the power and illumination of which a refined and flexible pragmatic criticism is capable, we must turn from these

① [Abrams] 'Idea of Universal Poetry,' *Works*, II, 3-4. On the rationale underlying the body of Hurd's criticism, see the article by Hoyt Trowbridge, 'Bishop Hurd, A Reinterpretation,' *PMLA*, LVIII (1943), 450ff.

② [Abrams] Batteux 'deduces' from the idea that poetry is the imitation, not of unadorned reality, but of *la belle nature*, that its end can only be 'to please, to move, to touch. in a word, pleasure' (*Les Beaux Arts*, pp. 81, 151). Conversely, Hurd infers from the fact that the end of poetry is pleasure that the poet's duty is to 'illustrate and adorn' reality, and to delineate it 'in the most taking forms' ('Idea of Universal Poetry,' *Works*, II, 8). For purposes of a specialized investigation into the evidences for plagiarism among poets, Hurd himself, in another essay, shifts his ground, and like Batteux, sets out from a definition of poetry as an imitation, specifically, of 'the fairest forms of things' ('Discourse on Poetic Imitation,' *Works*, II, 111).

abstract systematizers of current methods and maxims to such a practical critic as Samuel Johnson. Johnson's literary criticism assumes approximately the frame of critical reference I have described, but Johnson, who distrusts rigid and abstract theorizing, applies the method with a constant appeal to specific literary examples, deference to the opinions of other readers, but ultimately, reliance on his own expert responses to the text. As a result Johnson's comments on poets and poems have persistently afforded a jumping-off point for later critics whose frame of reference and particular judgments differ radically from his own. For an instance of Johnson's procedure which is especially interesting because it shows how the notion of the imitation of nature is coordinated with the judgment of poetry in terms of its end and effects, consider that monument of neo-classic criticism, Johnson's *Preface to Shakespeare*.

Johnson undertakes in his *Preface* to establish Shakespeare's rank among poets, and to do so, he is led to rate Shakespeare's native abilities against the general level of taste and achievement in the Elizabethan age, and to measure these abilities in turn 'by their proportion to the general and collective ability of man.'① Since the powers and excellence of an author, however, can only be inferred from the nature and excellence of the works he achieves, Johnson addresses himself to a general examination of Shakespeare's dramas. In this systematic appraisal of the works themselves, we find that mimesis retains for Johnson a measure of authority as criterion. Repeatedly Johnson maintains that 'this therefore is the praise of *Shakespeare*, that his drama is the mirrour of life,' and of inanimate nature as well: 'He was an exact surveyor of the inanimate world... *Shakespeare*, whether life or nature be his subject, shews plainly, that

① [Abrams] Johnson on Shakespeare, ed. Walter Raleigh (Oxford, 1908), pp. 10, 30-31.

he has seen with his own eyes...'[1] But, Johnson also claims,'The end of writing is to instruct; the end of poetry is to instruct by pleasing.'[2] It is to this function of poetry, and to the demonstrated effect of a poem upon its audience, that Johnson awards priority as aesthetic criterion. If a poem fails to please, whatever its character otherwise, it is, as a work of art, nothing; though Johnson insists, with a strenuous moralism that must already have seemed old-fashioned to contemporary readers, it must please without violating the standards of truth and virtue. Accordingly, Johnson discriminates those elements in Shakespeare's plays which were introduced to appeal to the local and passing tastes of the rather barbarous audience of his own time ('He knew,' said Johnson, 'how he should most please'),[3] from those elements which are proportioned to the tastes of the common readers of all time. And since in works 'appealing wholly to observation and experience, no other test can be applied than length of duration and continuance of esteem,' Shakespeare's long survival as a poet 'read without any other reason than the desire for pleasure' is the best evidence for his artistic excellence. The reason for this survival Johnson explains on the subsidiary principle that 'nothing can please many, and please long, but just representations of general nature.' Shakespeare exhibits the eternal 'species' of human character, moved by 'those general passions and principles by which all minds are agitated.'[4] Thus Shakespeare's excellence in holding up the mirror to general nature turns out, in the long run, to be justified by the superior criterion of the appeal this achievement holds for the enduring tastes of the general literary public.

---

① [Abrams] *Johnson on Shakespeare*, ed. Walter Raleigh (Oxford, 1908), pp. 14, 39. Cf. pp. 11, 31, 33, 37, etc.

② [Abrams] Ibid., p. 16.

③ [Abrams] Ibid., pp. 31-33, 41.

④ [Abrams] Ibid., pp. 9-12.

A number of Johnson's individual observations and judgments exhibit a play of the argument between the two principles of the nature of the world the poet must reflect, and the nature and legitimate requirements of the poet's audience. For the most part the two principles co-operate toward a single conclusion. For example, both the empirical nature of the universe and of the universal reader demonstrate the fallacy of those who censure Shakespeare for mixing his comic and tragic scenes. Shakespeare's plays, Johnson says, exhibit 'the real state of sublunary nature, which partakes of good and evil, joy and sorrow, mingled with endless variety.' In addition, 'the mingled drama may convey all the instruction of tragedy or comedy' by approaching nearer 'to the appearance of life'; while the objection that the change of scene 'wants at last the power to move' is a specious reasoning 'received as true even by those who in daily experience feel it to be false.'① But when the actual state of sublunary affairs conflicts with the poet's obligation to his audience, the latter is the court of final appeal. It is Shakespeare's defect, says Johnson,

> *that he seems to write without any moral purpose ... He makes no just distribution of good or evil, nor is always careful to shew in the virtuous a disapprobation of the wicked ... It is always a writer's duty to make the world better, and justice is a virtue independant on*

① [Abrams] *Johnson on Shakespeare*, ed. Walter Raleigh (Oxford, 1908), pp. 15-17. See Johnson's defense of Shakespeare for violating the decorum of character-types, by the appeal to 'nature' as against 'accident'; and for breaking the unities of time and place, by the appeal both to the actual experience of dramatic auditors, and to the principle that 'the greatest graces of a play, are to copy nature and instruct life' (ibid., pp. 14-15, 25-30). Cf. *Rambler* No. 156.

time or place.[1]

The pragmatic orientation, ordering the aim of the artist and the character of the work to the nature, the needs, and the springs of pleasure in the audience, characterized by far the greatest part of criticism from the time of Horace through the eighteenth century. Measured either by its duration or the number of its adherents, therefore, the pragmatic view, broadly conceived, has been the principal aesthetic attitude of the Western world. But inherent in this system were the elements of its dissolution. Ancient rhetoric had bequeathed to criticism not only its stress on affecting the audience but also (since its main concern was with educating the orator) its detailed attention to the powers and activities of the speaker himself—his 'nature,' or innate powers and genius, as distinguished from his culture and art, and also the process of invention, disposition, and expression involved in his discourse.[2] In the course of time, and particularly after the psychological contributions of Hobbes and Locke[3] in the seventeenth century, increasing attention was given to the mental constitution of the poet, the quality and degree of his 'genius,' and the play of his faculties in the act of

---

① [Abrams] *Johnson on Shakespeare*, ed. Walter Raleigh (Oxford, 1908), pp. 20-21. The logic appears even more clearly in Johnson's early paper on 'works of fiction,' in *Rambler* No. 4, 1750 (*The Works of Samuel Johnson*, ed. Arthur Murphy, London, 1824, IV, 23): 'It is justly considered as the greatest excellency of art, to imitate nature; but it is necessary to distinguish those parts of nature which are most proper for imitation,' etc. For a detailed analysis of Johnson's critical methods, see W. R. Keast, 'The Theoretical Foundations of Johnson's Criticism,' *Critics and Criticism*, ed. R. S. Crane, pp. 389-407.

② [Abrams] See the masterly précis of the complex movements within English neo-classic criticism by R. S. Crane, 'English Neoclassical Criticism,' *Critics and Criticism*, pp. 372-388.

③ Thomas Hobbes (1588–1679), English philosopher; John Locke (1632–1704).

composition. Through most of the eighteenth century, the poet's invention and imagination were made thoroughly dependent for their materials—their ideas and 'images'—on the external universe and the literary models the poet had to imitate; while the persistent stress laid on his need for judgment and art—the mental surrogates, in effect, of the requirements of a cultivated audience—held the poet strictly responsible to the audience for whose pleasure he exerted his creative ability. Gradually, however, the stress was shifted more and more to the poet's natural genius, creative imagination, and emotional spontaneity, at the expense of the opposing attributes of judgment, learning, and artful restraints. As a result the audience gradually receded into the background, giving place to the poet himself, and his own mental powers and emotional needs, as the predominant cause and even the end and test of art. By this time other developments, which we shall have occasion to talk about later, were also helping to shift the focus of critical interest from audience to artist and thus to introduce a new orientation into the theory of art.

IV. Expressive Theories

'Poetry,' Wordsworth announced in his Preface to the *Lyrical Ballads* of 1800, 'is the spontaneous overflow of powerful feelings.'[①] He thought well enough of this formulation to use it twice in the same essay, and on this, as the ground-idea, he founded his theory of the proper subjects, language, effects, and value of poetry. Almost all the major critics of the English romantic generation phrased definitions or key statements showing a parallel alignment from work to poet. Poetry is the overflow, utterance, or projection of the thought and feelings of the poet; or else (in the chief variant formulation) poetry

---

① Wordsworth (*Critical Theory Since Plato*, p. 490).

is defined in terms of the imaginative process which modifies and synthesizes the images, thoughts, and feelings of the poet. This way of thinking, in which the artist himself becomes the major element generating both the artistic product and the criteria by which it is to be judged, I shall call the expressive theory of art.

Setting the date at which this point of view became predominant in critical theory, like marking the point at which orange becomes yellow in the color spectrum, must be a somewhat arbitrary procedure. As we shall see, an approach to the expressive orientation, though isolated in history and partial in scope, is to be found as early as Longinus' discussion of the sublime style[①] as having its main sources in the thought and emotions of the speaker; and it recurs in a variant form in Bacon's brief analysis of poetry as pertaining to the imagination and 'accommodating the shows of things to the desires of the mind.'[②] Even Wordsworth's theory, it will appear, is much more embedded in a traditional matrix of interests and emphases, and is, therefore, less radical than are the theories of his followers of the 1830's. The year 1800 is a good round number, however, and Wordsworth's Preface a convenient document, by which to signalize the displacement of the mimetic and pragmatic by the expressive view of art in English criticism.

In general terms, the central tendency of the expressive theory may be summarized in this way: A work of art is essentially the internal made external, resulting from a creative process operating under the impulse of feeling, and embodying the combined product of the poet's perceptions, thoughts, and feelings. The primary source and subject matter of a poem, therefore, are the attributes and actions of the poet's own mind; or if aspects of the external

---

① Longinus. (*Critical Theory Since Plato*, p. 94).

② Bacon (*Critical Theory Since Plato*, p. 234).

world, then these only as they are converted from fact to poetry by the feelings and operations of the poet's mind. ('Thus the Poetry...' Wordsworth wrote, 'proceeds whence it ought to do, from the soul of Man, communicating its creative energies to the images of the external world.')① The paramount cause of poetry is not, as in Aristotle, a formal cause, determined primarily by the human actions and qualities imitated; nor, as in neo-classic criticism, a final cause, the effect intended upon the audience; but instead an efficient cause—the impulse within the poet of feelings and desires seeking expression, or the compulsion of the 'creative' imagination which, like God the creator, has its internal source of motion. The propensity is to grade the arts by the extent to which their media are amenable to the undistorted expression of the feelings or mental powers of the artist, and to classify the species of an art, and evaluate their instances, by the qualities or states of mind of which they are a sign. Of the elements constituting a poem, the element of diction, especially figures of speech, becomes primary; and the burning question is, whether these are the natural utterance of emotion and imagination or the deliberate aping of poetic conventions. The first test any poem must pass is no longer, 'Is it true to nature?' or 'Is it appropriate to the requirements either of the best judges or the generality of mankind?' but a criterion looking in a different direction; namely, 'Is it sincere? Is it genuine? Does it match the intention, the feeling, and the actual state of mind of the poet while composing?' The work ceases then to be regarded as primarily a reflection of nature, actual or improved; the mirror held up to nature becomes transparent and yields the reader insights into the mind and heart of the poet himself. The exploitation of literature as an index to personality first manifests itself in the early

① [Abrams] *Letters of William and Dorothy Wordsworth: The Middle Years*, ed. E. de Selincourt (Oxford, 1937), II, 705; 18 Jan. 1816.

nineteenth century; it is the inevitable consequence of the expressive point of view.

The sources, details, and historical results of this reorientation of criticism, in its various forms, will be a principal concern of the rest of this book. Now, while we have some of the earlier facts fresh in mind, let me indicate what happened to salient elements of traditional criticism in the essays 'What Is Poetry?' and 'The Two Kinds of Poetry,' written by John Stuart Mill in 1833. Mill relied in large part on Wordsworth's Preface to the *Lyrical Ballads,* but in the intervening thirty years the expressive theory had emerged from the network of qualifications in which Wordsworth had carefully placed it, and had worked out its own destiny unhindered. Mill's logic in answering the question, 'What Is Poetry?' is not *more geometrico,* like that of Batteux, nor stiffly formal, like Richard Hurd's; nonetheless, his theory turns out to be just as tightly dependent upon a central principle as theirs. For whatever Mill's empirical pretensions, his initial assumption about the essential nature of poetry remains continuously though silently effective in selecting, interpreting, and ordering the facts to be explained.

The primitive proposition of Mill's theory is: Poetry is 'the expression or uttering forth of feeling.'① Exploration of the data of aesthetics from this starting point leads, among other things, to the following drastic alterations in the great commonplaces of the critical tradition:

(1)*The poetic kinds.* Mill reinterprets and inverts the neo-classic ranking of the poetic kinds. As the purest expression of feeling, lyric poetry is 'more eminently and peculiarly poetry than any other...' Other forms are all alloyed by non-poetic elements, whether descriptive, didactic, or narrative, which serve merely as convenient

---

① [Abrams] *Early Essays by John Stuart Mill,* ed. J. W. M. Gibbs (London, 1897), p. 208.

occasions for the poetic utterances of feeling either by the poet or by one of his invented characters. To Aristotle, tragedy had been the highest form of poetry, and the plot, representing the action being imitated, had been its 'soul'; while most neo-classic critics had agreed that, whether judged by greatness of subject matter or of effect, epic and tragedy are the king and queen of poetic forms. It serves as an index to the revolution in critical norms to notice that to Mill, plot becomes a kind of necessary evil. An epic poem 'in so far as it is epic (i.e. narrative) ... is not poetry at all,' but only a suitable frame for the greatest diversity of genuinely poetic passages; while the interest in plot and story 'merely as a story' characterizes rude stages of society, children, and the 'shallowest and emptiest' of civilized adults.① Similarly with the other arts; in music, painting, sculpture, and architecture Mill distinguishes between that which is 'simple imitation or description' and that which 'expresses human feeling' and is, therefore, poetry.②

(2)*Spontaneity as criterion.* Mill accepts the venerable assumption that a man's emotional susceptibility is innate, but his knowledge and skill—his art—are acquired. On this basis, he distinguishes poets into two classes: poets who are born and poets who are made, or those who are poets 'by nature,' and those who are poets 'by culture.' Natural poetry is identifiable because it 'is Feeling itself, employing Thought only as the medium of its utterance'; on the other hand, the poetry of 'a cultivated but not naturally poetic mind,' is written with 'a distinct aim,' and in it the thought remains the conspicuous object, however surrounded by 'a halo of feeling.' Natural poetry, it turns out, is 'poetry in a far higher sense, than any other; since ... that

---

① [Abrams] *Early Essays by John Stuart Mill*, ed. J. W. M. Gibbs (London, 1897), pp. 228, 205-206, 213, 203-204.

② [Abrams] Ibid., pp. 211-217.

which constitutes poetry, human feeling, enters far more largely into this than into the poetry of culture.' Among the moderns, Shelley represents the poet born and Wordsworth the poet made; and with unconscious irony Mill turns Wordsworth's own criterion, 'the spontaneous overflow of feeling,' against its sponsor. Wordsworth's poetry 'has little even of the appearance of spontaneousness: the well is never so full that it overflows.'①

(3)*The external world.* In so far as a literary product simply imitates objects, it is not poetry at all. As a result, reference of poetry to the external universe disappears from Mill's theory, except to the extent that sensible objects may serve as a stimulus or 'occasion for the generation of poetry,' and then, 'the poetry is not in the object itself,' but 'in the state of mind' in which it is contemplated. When a poet describes a lion he 'is describing the lion professedly, but the state of excitement of the spectator really,' and the poetry must be true not to the object, but to 'the human emotion.'② Thus severed from the external world, the objects signified by a poem tend to be regarded as no more than a projected equivalent—an extended and articulated symbol—for the poet's inner state of mind. Poetry, said Mill, in a phrasing which anticipates T. E. Hulme and lays the theoretical groundwork for the practice of symbolists from Baudelaire through T. S. Eliot, embodies 'itself in symbols, which are the nearest possible representations of the feeling in the exact shape in which it exists in the poet's mind.'③ Tennyson, Mill wrote in a review of that poet's early poems, excels in 'scene-painting, in the higher sense of the term';

---

① [Abrams] *Early Essays by John Mill*, ed. J. W. M. Gibbs (London, 1897), pp. 222-231.

② [Abrams] Ibid., pp. 206-207.

③ [Abrams] Ibid., pp. 208-209. Cf. Hulme (English 1888–1917), 'If it is sincere in the accurate sense ... the whole of the analogy is necessary to get out the exact curve of the feeling or thing you want to express ...' ('Romanticism and Classicism,' *Speculations*, London, 1936, p. 138).

and this is

> *not the mere power of producing that rather vapid species of composition usually termed descriptive poetry ... but the power of creating scenery, in keeping with some state of human feeling; so fitted to it as to be the embodied symbol of it, and to summon up the state of feeling itself, with a force not to be surpassed by anything but reality.*①

And as an indication of the degree to which the innovations of the romantics persist as the commonplaces of modern critics—even of those who purport to found their theory on anti-romantic principles—notice how striking is the parallel between the passage above and a famous comment by T. S. Eliot:

> *The only way of expressing emotion in the form of art is by finding an 'objective correlative'; in other words, a set of objects, a situation, a chain of events which shall be the formula of that particular emotion; such that when the external facts, which must terminate in sensory experience, are given, the emotion is immediately evoked.*②

(4)*The audience.* No less drastic is the fate of the audience. According to Mill, 'Poetry is feeling, confessing itself to itself in moments of solitude...' The poet's audience is reduced to a single member, consisting of the poet himself. 'All poetry,' as Mill puts it, 'is of the nature of soliloquy.' The purpose of producing effects upon other men, which for centuries had been the defining character of the

---

① [Abrams] Review, written in 1835, of Tennyson's *Poems Chiefly Lyrical* (1830) and *Poems* (1833), in *Early Essays*, p. 242.

② [Abrams] 'Hamlet,' *Selected Essays* 1917-1932 (London, 1932), p. 145.

art of poetry, now serves precisely the opposite function: it disqualifies a poem by proving it to be rhetoric instead. When the poet's

> *act of utterance is not itself the end, but a means to an end—viz. by the feelings he himself expresses, to work upon the feelings, or upon the belief, or the will, of another,—when the expression of his emotions ... is tinged also by that purpose, by that desire of making an impression upon another mind, then it ceases to be poetry, and becomes eloquence.*[①]

There is, in fact, something singularly fatal to the audience in the romantic point of view. Or, in terms of historical causes, it might be conjectured that the disappearance of a homogeneous and discriminating reading public fostered a criticism which on principle diminished the importance of the audience as a determinant of poetry and poetic value. Wordsworth still insisted that 'Poets do not write for Poets alone, but for Men,' and that each of his poems 'has a worthy purpose'; even though it turns out that the pleasure and profit of the audience is an automatic consequence of the poet's *spontaneous* overflow of feeling, provided that the appropriate associations between thoughts and feelings have been established by the poet in advance.[②] Keats, however, affirmed roundly that 'I never wrote one

---

① [Abrams] *Early Essays*, pp. 208-209. Cf. John Keble, *Lectures on Poetry* (1832-1841), trans. E. K. Francis (Oxford, 1912), I, 48-49: 'Cicero is always the orator' because 'he always has in mind the theatre, the benches, the audience'; whereas Plato is 'more poetical than Homer himself' because 'he writes to please himself, not to win over others.'

② [Abrams] Preface to the *Lyrical Ballads*, *Wordsworth's Literary Criticism*, ed. N. C. Smith (London, 1905), pp. 30, 15-16.

single line of Poetry with the least Shadow of public thought.'① 'A poet is a nightingale,' according to Shelley, 'who sits in darkness and sings to cheer its own solitude with sweet sounds; his auditors are as men entranced by the melody of an unseen musician...'② For Carlyle, the poet utterly replaces the audience as the generator of aesthetic norms.

> *On the whole, Genius has privileges of its own; it selects an orbit for itself; and be this never so eccentric, if it is indeed a celestial orbit, we mere star-gazers must at last compose ourselves; must cease to cavil at it, and begin to observe it, and calculate its laws.*③

The evolution is complete, from the mimetic poet, assigned the minimal role of holding a mirror up to nature, through the pragmatic poet who, whatever his natural gifts, is ultimately measured by his capacity to satisfy the public taste, to Carlyle's Poet as Hero, the chosen one who, because he is 'a Force of Nature,' writes as he must, and through the degree of homage he evokes, serves as the measure of his *reader's* piety and taste.④

---

① [Abrams] *Letters*, ed. Maurice Buxton Forman (third ed.; New York, 1948), p. 131 (to Reynolds, 9 April, 1818).

② [Abrams] 'Defence of Poetry,' *Shelley's Literary and Philosophical Criticism*, ed. John Shawcross (London, 1909), p. 129.

③ Thomas Carlyle (1795–1881), Scottish writer. [Abrams] 'Jean Paul Friedrich Richter' (1827), *Works*, ed. H. D. Traill (London, 1905), XXVI, 20.

④ [Abrams] See *Heroes, Hero-Worship, and the Heroic in History*, in *Works*, V, esp. pp. 80-85, 108-112. Cf. Jones Very's indignant denial of the inference that because the general ear takes delight in Shakespeare, 'his motive was to please ... We degrade those whom the world has pronounced poets, when we assume any other cause of their song than the divine and original action of the soul in humble obedience to the Holy Spirit upon whom they call.' ['Shakespeare' (1838), *Poems and Essays*, Boston and New York, 1886, pp. 45-46].

V. Objective Theories

All types of theory described so far, in their practical applications, get down to dealing with the work of art itself, in its parts and their mutual relations, whether the premises on which these elements are discriminated and evaluated relate them primarily to the spectator, the artist, or the world without. But there is also a fourth procedure, the 'objective orientation,' which on principle regards the work of art in isolation from all these external points of reference, analyzes it as a self-sufficient entity constituted by its parts in their internal relations, and sets out to judge it solely by criteria intrinsic to its own mode of being.

This point of view has been comparatively rare in literary criticism. The one early attempt at the analysis of an art form which is both objective and comprehensive occurs in the central portion of Aristotle's *Poetics*. I have chosen to discuss Aristotle's theory of art under the heading of mimetic theories, because it sets out from, and makes frequent reference back to the concept of imitation. Such is the flexibility of Aristotle's procedure, however, that after he has isolated the species 'tragedy,' and established its relation to the universe as an imitation of a certain kind of action, and to the audience through its observed effect of purging pity and fear, his method becomes centripetal, and assimilates these external elements into attributes of the work proper. In this second consideration of tragedy as an object in itself, the actions and agents that are imitated re-enter the discussion as the plot, character, and thought which, together with diction, melody, and spectacle, make up the six elements of a tragedy; and even pity and fear are reconsidered as that pleasurable quality proper to tragedy, to be distinguished from the pleasures characteristic of comedy and other forms.[①] The tragic work itself can now be analyzed formally as a self-determining whole made up of parts, all organized around the controlling part, the tragic plot—itself a unity in which the component incidents are integrated by the internal relations of 'necessity or probability.'

As an all-inclusive approach to poetry, the objective orientation was just beginning to emerge in the late eighteenth and early nineteenth century. We shall see later on that some critics were undertaking to explore the concept of the poem as a heterocosm, a world of its own, independent of the world into which we are born, whose end is not to instruct or please but simply to exist. Certain critics, particularly in Germany, were expanding upon Kant's formula that a work of art exhibits *Zweckmässigkeit ohne Zweck* (purposiveness without purpose),[②] together with his concept that the contemplation of beauty is disinterested and without regard to utility, while neglecting Kant's characteristic reference of an aesthetic product to the mental faculties of its creator and receptor. The aim to consider a poem, as Poe expressed it, as a 'poem *per se*... written solely for the poem's sake,'[③] in isolation from external causes and ulterior ends, came to constitute one element of the diverse doctrines usually huddled together by historians under the heading 'Art for Art's Sake.' And with differing emphases and adequacy, and in a great variety of theoretical contexts, the objective approach to poetry has become one of the most prominent elements in the innovative criticism of the last two or three decades. T. S. Eliot's dictum of 1928, that 'when

① [Abrams] 'Not every kind of pleasure should be required of a tragedy, but only its own proper pleasure. The tragic pleasure is that of pity and fear...' (*Poetics* 14. 1453b).

② *Critical Theory Since Plato*, p. 428.

③ [Abrams] 'The Poetic Principle,' *Representative Selections*, ed. Margaret Alterton and Hardin Craig (New York, 1935), pp. 382-383.

we are considering poetry we must consider it primarily as poetry and not another thing' is widely approved, however far Eliot's own criticism sometimes departs from this ideal; and it is often joined with MacLeish's verse aphorism, 'A poem should not mean But be.'①
The subtle and incisive criticism of criticism by the Chicago Neo-Aristotelians and their advocacy of an instrument adapted to dealing with poetry as such have been largely effective toward a similar end.②
In his 'ontological criticism,' John Crowe Ransom has been calling for recognition of 'the autonomy of the work itself as existing for its own sake';③ campaigns have been organized against 'the personal heresy,' 'the intentional fallacy,' and 'the affective fallacy';④ the widely influential handbook, *The Theory of Literature*, written by René Wellek and Austin Warren, proposes that criticism deal with a poem *qua* poem, independently of 'extrinsic' factors; and similar views are being expressed, with increasing frequency, not only in our literary but in our scholarly journals. In America, at least, some form of the objective point of view has already gone far to displace its rivals as the reigning mode of literary criticism.

According to our scheme of analysis, then, there have been four major orientations, each one of which has seemed to various acute minds adequate for a satisfactory criticism of art in general. And by and large the historic progression, from the beginning through the early nineteenth century, has been from the mimetic theory of Plato and (in a qualified fashion) Aristotle, through the pragmatic theory,

---

① Archibald MacLeish (1892-1982), 'Ars Poetica.'

② A group at the University of Chicago. See R. S. Crane, ed. *Critics and Criticism* (1952).

③ [Abrams] See John Crowe Ransom (1888–1974), *The World's Body* (New York, 1938), esp. pp. 327ff., and 'Criticism as Pure Speculation,' *The Intent of the Critic*, ed. Donald Stauffer (Princeton, 1941).

④ See Wimsatt and Beardsley (*Critical Theory Since Plato*, p. 1026).

lasting from the conflation of rhetoric with poetic in the Hellenistic and Roman era almost through the eighteenth century, to the expressive theory of English (and somewhat earlier, German) romantic criticism.

13.3 Key Words

① *The Norton Anthology of English Literature*《诺顿英国文学选集》

The Norton Anthology of English Literature is an anthology of English literature published by the W. W. Norton Company. First published in 1962, it has gone through ten editions; as of 2006 there are over eight million copies in print, making it the publisher's best-selling anthology. M. H. Abrams, a critic and scholar of Romanticism, served as General Editor for its first seven editions, before handing the job to Stephen Greenblatt, a Shakespearean scholar and Harvard professor. The anthology provides an overview of poetry, drama, prose fiction, essays, and letters from *Beowulf* to the beginning of the 21st century.

② *Republic*《理想国》

Republic is a Socratic dialogue, authored by Plato around 375 B.C.E., concerning justice, the order and character of the just city-state, and the just man. It is Plato's best-known work, and has proven to be one of the world's most influential works of philosophy and political theory, both intellectually and historically. In the dialogue, Socrates talks with various Athenians and foreigners about the meaning of justice and whether the just man is happier than the unjust man. They consider the natures of existing regimes and then propose a series of different, hypothetical cities in comparison, culminating in Kallipolis, a utopian city-state ruled by a philosopher king. They also discuss the theory of forms, the immortality of the soul, and the role of the philosopher and of poetry in society. The dialogue's setting seems to be during the Peloponnesian War (伯罗奔尼撒战争).

③ Charles Batteux 查尔斯·巴托

Charles Batteux (1713–1780) was a French philosopher and writer on aesthetics. His 1746 treatise *Les Beaux Arts réduits à un même principe* (*The Fine Arts Reduced to a Single Principle*) was an attempt to find a unity among existing theories of beauty and taste on 'a single principle,' and its views were widely accepted, not only in France but throughout Europe.

④ Lessing 莱辛

Gotthold Ephraim Lessing (1729–1781), one of the most prominent philosophers of the Enlightenment era, recognized as the world's first dramaturgy, Germany's first dramatist and comedy playwright, champion of religious tolerance, translator and Shakespearean scholar. Today his own works appear as prototypes of the later developed bourgeois German drama. His theoretical writings *Laokoon* (《拉奥孔》) and *Hamburg Dramaturgy* (《汉堡剧评》) set the standards for the discussion of aesthetic and literary theoretical principles. Laokoon, is a figure in Greek and Roman mythology and the Epic Cycle. He was a Trojan priest who was attacked, with his two sons, by giant serpents sent by the gods. The story of Laokoon has been the subject of numerous artists, both in ancient and in more contemporary times.The death of Laokoon was famously depicted in a much-admired marble *Laokoon and His Sons*, attributed by Pliny the Elder to the Rhodian sculptors Agesander, Athenodoros, and Polydorus, which stands in the Vatican Museums, Rome. The marble *Laokoon* provided the central image for Lessing's *Laokoon*, 1766, an aesthetic polemic directed against Winckelmann and the comte de Caylus.

⑤ *Ars Poetica*《论诗艺》

"*Ars Poetica,*" or "*The Art of Poetry,*" is a poem written by Horace (贺拉斯), in which he advises poets on the art of writing poetry and drama. *Ars Poetica* has "exercised a great influence in later ages on European literature, notably on French drama" and has inspired poets and authors since it was written. Although it has been well-known since the Middle Ages, it has been used in literary criticism since the Renaissance.

⑥ Rhetoric 修辞

Rhetoric is the art of persuasion, which along with grammar and logic, is one of the three ancient arts of discourse. Rhetoric aims to study the capacities of writers or speakers needed to inform, persuade, or motivate particular audiences in specific situations. Aristotle defines rhetoric as "the faculty of observing in any given case the available means of persuasion" and since mastery of the art was necessary for victory in a case at law; or for passage of proposals in the assembly; or for fame as a speaker in civic ceremonies; he calls it "a combination of the science of logic and of the ethical branch of politics." Rhetoric typically provides heuristics for understanding, discovering, and developing arguments for particular situations, such as Aristotle's three persuasive audience appeals: logos, pathos, and ethos. The five canons of rhetoric or phases of developing a persuasive speech were first codified in classical Rome: invention, arrangement, style, memory, and delivery. From Ancient Greece to the late 19th century, rhetoric played a central role in Western education in training orators, lawyers, counsellors, historians, statesmen, and poets.

13.4 Extensive Explorations

① What are the four elements in the total situation of a work of art that make a comprehensive integrity of literature?

② With reference to the text about Ion, what do you think of the example of bed in depiction of imitation?

③ How did Aristotle discuss on imitation in his *Poetics*?

④ What is Lessing's attitude on imitation?

⑤ What does Sydney mean when he refers to imitation?

⑥ Why did Abrams indicate that pragmatic criticism originated in the classical theory of rhetoric?

⑦ What is the major aim of the critics of the pragmatic theory?

⑧ How did Samuel Johnson correlate the pragmatic theory when arguing on Shakespeare's plays?

14. H. R. Jauss' *Literary History as a Challenge to Literary Theory*

14.1 Lead-in

Hans Robert Jauss (1921–1997) was a German aesthetician and philosopher, notable for his declaration on the establishment of reception theory with his speech *Literary History as a Challenge to Literary Theory* (《文学史作为向文学理论的挑战》) in 1967. As the student of Hans-Georg Gadamer (伽达默尔), his field also concerns medieval and modern French literature. Jauss was born in Württemberg, Germany, and died in 1997 in Constance, Germany.

Jauss pursued his study at the University of Heidelberg (海德堡大学), his doctoral dissertation was on Marcel Proust. After working in various European universities, he moved to North America and continued his study with scholars of new criticism till his death. The text selected for the textbook is originally a speech given by Jauss in 1967 in Constance University, the title being *Literaturgeschichte als Provokation der Literaturwissenschaft*, which is better-known as the "Challenge," short for *Literary History as a Challenge to Literary Theory*. The speech given in 1967 once attracted great attention as well as response from contemporary scholars. Several years later, Wolfgang Iser (沃尔夫冈·伊泽尔) discussed about the pattern of communication of this text. Jauss and Iser were soon regarded as the binary star of reception aesthetics. Reception aesthetics was spread to China in late 1970s and early 1980s, which aroused great attention in the academic field during the 2nd Methodology Heat (第二次美学大

讨论) in China.

Hermeneutics has a straight impact on Jauss. As we know, terms appeared in his speech, such as horizons of expectation (期待视野), fusions of horizons (视野融合) and aesthetic distance (审美距离) are the key terms of reception aesthetics. Besides, phenomenological aesthetics also influenced Jauss and Iser. Wolfgang Iser, the other of the binary stars, was the student of Roman Ingarden (罗曼·英加登), the remarkable scholar on phenomenology. Actually, Jauss' "Challenge" also displayed influences other than hermeneutics and phenomenology, such as Marxism theory (马克思主义文论), formalism theory (形式主义文论) and structuralism theory (结构主义文论).

The text is an excerpt from the "Challenge," starting from the 5th chapter. His speech was originally a salute to Schiller (席勒), who lived 150 years earlier than Jauss. What Jauss was most concerned about were intentions and reasons for literary history research. While Schiller discussed in the same way on world history, Jauss' speech only replaced world history with literary history. As we know, those theories confine literature on relationships between world and humans like imitation theory were formed back in ancient Greek times. And expression theory with Wordsworth as the major representation concentrates on the author. Formalism analyzes on the basis of text itself. Formalists insist that the aesthetic value of literary works have nothing to do with authors' personal life. In a word, readers weren't given any attention to in the past, they never play the decisive part. Readers are almost totally mute in former theories. As Jauss suggested, only the fusion between readers' horizon and literature could fulfill the aesthetic value of literary works. As was pointed out, a literary work is not an object which stands by itself and which offers the same face to each reader in each period. It is not a monument which reveals its timeless essence in a monologue.

It is much more like an orchestration which strikes ever new chords among its readers and which frees the text from the substance of the words and makes it meaningful for the time: "words which must, at the same time that they speak to him create an interlocutor capable of listening." And his theory was inspiring. Former researchers pursued those static essence so that they finally neglect readers' effect. And in the 2nd part, Jauss had an important quotation. He said, a literary work, even if it seems fresh, does not appear as something absolutely new in an informational vacuum, but predisposes its readers to a very definite type of reception by textual strategies, overt and covert signals, familiar characteristics or implicit allusions. It awakens memories of the familiar, stirs particular emotions in the reader and with its "beginning" arouses expectations for the "middle and end," which can then be continued intact, changed, re-oriented or even ironically fulfilled in the course of reading according to certain rules of the genre or type of text. Jauss further suggested that even a newly created literary work is not unrelated to the past, on the contrary, it actually consists horizons and expectations of the past. Which is to say, there was never a literary work consisting an objective essence. It will always consist subjective essence which gave influences to the author in the past. And the formalism way that only concentrates on pattern itself is incorrect, because history was cut off. And static analyses like reflection theories neglected one's subjective effect as well. In their view, such subjective interpretation is actually misleading. In Jauss' theory, to create a literary work is to influence, awaken and attract readers to regain their past and new understandings. And such experience cannot be formed only by text itself, but fusions of horizons between readers and literary works that manage to work and accomplish new understandings, and so-called literary reception under horizons of expectation. Such theory promoted readers' status for the first time among the four factors of literature and only this time relationships between these four factors start to complete.

14.2 Text

Literary History as a Challenge to Literary Theory

(Chapter 5-8)

V

The theory of the aesthetics of reception not only allows the understanding of the meaning and form of a literary work within the historical development of its reception. It also demands the ordering of the individual work in its "literary series" so that its historical position and significance in the context of literary experience can be recognized. Literary history based on the history of reception and impact will reveal itself as a process in which the passive reception of the reader and critic changes into the active reception and new production of the author, or in which—stated differently—a subsequent work solves formal and moral problems that the last work raised and may then itself present new problems.

How can the individual work, which determines chronological order in positivistic literary history and thereby superficially turns it into a "fact," be brought back into its historical order and thus be understood as an "event" again? The theory of the formalist school seeks to solve this problem with its principle of "literary evolution." In this theory the new work appears against a background of previous or competing works, reaches the "high ridge" of a literary epoch as a successful form, is reproduced and thereby continuously automated so that finally, when the next form has won out, it vegetates on as a worn-out genre and thus as a part of commonplace literature. If one analyzed and described a literary period according to this program which so far has hardly been begun[①] one might expect a result far superior to the conventional literary history. It would relate the separate categories, which stand side by side unconnected or at least connected only by a sketchy general history (for example, works of one author, one direction or one style, as well as different genres) to each other and disclose the evolutionary give and take of function and form.[②] Works either striking, related, or inter-dependent would appear as factors in a process which would no longer have to be aimed at one central point because, as a dialectic producing new forms, the process requires no teleology. Seen in this way, the dynamics of literary evolution would eliminate the dilemma of selective criteria. The unique criterion is the work entering the literary series as a new form, not the reproduction of worn-out forms, styles and genres which now move to the background until a new turn in the evolutionary development makes them perceptible again. Finally, in the formalist plan of literary history, which is understood as "evolution" and, contrary to the normal meaning of this term, rejects every directed course, the historical character of a work would remain the same as its artistic character. The evolutionary meaning and characteristics of a literary work presuppose innovation as the decisive feature just as does the

---

① In the 1927 article, "Über literarische Evolution," by Jurii Tynjanov [*Die literarischen Kunstmittel und die Evolution in der Literatur* (Frankfort, 1967), pp. 37-60], this program is presented most exactly. It was only partially fulfilled—as J. Striedter informed me—in the treatment of problems of structural change in the history of literary genres, as in the volume *Russkaja proza*, Voprosy poetiki, VIII (Leningrad, 1926). See also J. Tynjanov, "Die Ode als rhetorische Gattung" (1922), *Texte der russischen Formalisten*, II, ed. J. Striedter (Munich, 1970).

② J. Tynjanov, "Über literarische Evolution," p. 59.

tenet that the work of art is to be perceived against the background of other artistic works.①

The formalist theory of "literary evolution" is certainly one of the most significant beginnings in the renovation of literary history. The recognition that historical changes are also occurring within a system in the field of literature, the attempt to functionalize literary development, and last but not least the theory of automation are achievements which must be retained, even if the one-sided canonization of the changes requires correction. Criticism has sufficiently pointed out the weaknesses of the formalist theory of evolution: mere opposition or aesthetic variation is not enough to explain the growth of literature; the question of the direction of the change of literary forms remains unanswered; innovation alone cannot assure artistic value; and the relationship between literary evolution and social change cannot be dispensed with by simple negation.② My thesis VII answers the last question; the other questions demand that the descriptive literary theory of the formalists be opened up to the dimension of historical experience by means of the aesthetics of reception. The historical position of the present observer as literary historian would have to be included in this experience.

The description of literary evolution as a never-ending fight of the new with the old or as the alternation of canonizing and automation of forms reduces the historical character of literature to the one-dimensional reality of its changes and limits historical understanding

---

① "A work of art is viewed as a positive value if it changes the structure of the preceding period; it is seen as a negative value if it adopts the structure without changing it." (J. Mukarovsky, cited by R. Wellek, "Der Begriff der Evolution," op. cit. pp. 42 ff.)

② See V. Erlich, *Russischer Formalismus*, pp. 284-287, and R. Wellek, "Der Begriff der Evolution," op cit. pp. 42 ff. See also J. Striedter, *Texte der russischen Formalisten*, I (Munich, 1969), Introduction, Section X.

to recognition of these changes. The changes of the literary order do not become a historical process until along with the opposition of old and new forms is recognized its specific mutual mediation. This mutual mediation, including the step from the old to the new form in the interaction of work and recipient (public, critic, new producer), past events and successive receptions, can be conceived of formally and substantially as the problem "which every work of art as a horizon of possible solutions creates and leaves behind." ① But the mere description of the structural changes and new artistic means of a work does not necessarily lead to this problem, nor back to the work's function within the historical order. In order to determine this function, that is, in order to recognize the remaining problem which the new work answers in the historical succession, the interpreter must call upon his own experience, because the past horizon of old and new forms, problems and solutions, can only be recognized after it has been further mediated by the present horizon of the work. Literary history as "literary evolution" presupposes the historical process of aesthetic reception and production up to the observer's time as a condition for the communicating of all formal contrasts or "qualities of difference."②

Founding "literary evolution" on an aesthetics of reception not only restores its lost direction by making the position of the literary historian the temporary term of this process. This procedure also emphasizes the fundamentally historical dimension of literary experience by stressing the variable distance between the immediate

---

① H. Blumenberg in *Poetik und Hermeneutik*, III, p. 692.

② According to V. Erlich.*Russischer Formalismus*, p. 281, this concept means three things to the formalists: "on the level of the representation of reality 'quality of difference' stands for the 'avoidance' of the real, thus for creative deformation. On the level of language the expression means the avoidance of usual speech usage. On the level of literary dynamics finally ... a change in the prevailing artistic standard."

and the potential meaning of a literary work. This means that the artistic character of a work, whose potential importance as criterion is reduced to that of innovation by formalism, does not by any means have to be immediately perceivable in the horizon of its first appearance, nor does it have to be exhausted by the opposition between old and new forms. The distance between the immediate first perception of a work and its potential meanings, or, to put it differently, the opposition between the new work and the expectations of its first readers, can be so great that a long process of reception is necessary in order to catch up with what first was unexpected and unusable. It can happen that the potential significance of a work may remain unrecognized until the evolution of a newer form widens the horizon and only then opens up the understanding of the misunderstood earlier form. Thus the dark lyrics of Mallarmé and his school prepared the way for a re-evaluation of baroque poetry, which had long been neglected and forgotten, and especially for the new philosophical interpretation and "rebirth" of Góngora. There are many examples of how a new literary form can open an approach to forgotten literature; they include the so-called "renaissances"—so-called because the term implies the appearance of an automatic rebirth and often obscures the fact that literary tradition does not transmit itself. That is, the literary past can only return when a new reception has brought it into the present again—whether it be that a different aesthetic attitude has intentionally taken up the past, or that a new phase of literary evaluation has expectedly illuminated past works.①

The new is not only an *aesthetic* category. It cannot be explained

① For the first possibility the (anti-romantic) re-evaluation of Boileau and the classic *contrainte* poetics through Gide and Valéry can be introduced; for the second the tardy discovery of Hölderlin's Hymns or Novalis's concept of future poetry [for the last see H. R. Jauss in *Romanische Forschungen*, LXXVII (1965), 174–183].

completely by the factors of innovation, surprise, surpassing, rearrangement and alienation, to which the formalist theory assigned utmost importance. The new becomes an historical category when the diachronic analysis of literature is forced to face the questions of which historical forces really make the literary work new, to what degree this newness is recognizable in the historical moment of its appearance, what distance, route, or circumlocution of understanding were required for its full realization, and whether the moment of this realization was so effective that it could change the perspective of the old and thereby the canonization of the literary past.① How the relationship of poetic theory and aesthetically productive practice appears in this light has already been discussed in another context.② Certainly the possibilities of the interaction between production and reception in the historical change of aesthetic attitude are not exhausted by these remarks. I only want to indicate the dimension into which a diachronic study of literature would move, since it can no longer remain satisfied with considering a chronological series of literary "facts" as the historical appearance of literature.

VI

The results which the separation and methodological complementariness of diachronic and synchronic analysis have achieved in the study of language provide grounds for improving upon the diachronic observation which until now has been the

---

① Thus, since the reception of the "minor romantic" Nerval, whose Chimères only attracted attention under the influence of Mallarmé, the canonized "major romantics," Lamartine, Vigny, Musset and a large part of the "rhetorical" lyrics of Victor Hugo have been forced more and more into the background.

② *Poetik und Hermeneutik*, II (*Immanente Aesthetik-Aesthetische Reflexion*), ed. W. Iser (Munich, 1966), esp. pp. 395–418.

customary method in the study of literary history. Since it reveals changes in aesthetic attitudes the perspective of the history of reception always discovers functional connections between the understanding of new works and the meaning of old works. This perspective can also make it possible to take a synchronic cross-section of a moment in the process, to arrange heterogeneous, contemporaneous works into equivalent, opposing, and hierarchical groups, and thereby to discover a general system of relationships in the literature of one historical moment. A new literary history could be developed from this if other cross-sections were made earlier and later to illustrate the literary changes of structure in epoch-making moments.

Siegfried Kracauer has questioned most decisively the primacy of diachronic observation in history. His study on "Time and History"[①] challenges the claim of general history that, within the homogeneous medium of chronological time, it can make events of all areas of life comprehensible as a unified process consistent in every historical moment. This understanding of history, still under the influence of Hegel's idea of the "objective spirit" (*objektiver Geist*), presupposes that everything which happens at one time is determined to the same degree by the meaning of this moment and thus conceals the fact that things which occur at the same time are not really simultaneous.[②]

---

① In *Zeugnisse—Theodor W. Adorno zum 60. Geburtstag* (Frankfort, 1963), pp. 50-64, and also in "General History and the Aesthetic Approach," *Poetik und Hermeneutik*, III. See also *History: The Last Things Before the Last* (New York, 1969), esp. Chap. VI: "Ahasverus, or The Riddle of Time," pp. 139-163.

② "First, in identifying history as a process in chronological time, we tacitly assume that our knowledge of the moment at which an event emerges from the flow of time will help us to account for its appearance. The date of the event is a value-laden fact. Accordingly, all events in the history of a people, a nation, or a civilization which take place at a given moment are supposed to occur then and there for reasons bound up, somehow, with that moment." (Kracauer, History, p. 141.)

For the variety of events of one historical moment, which the universal historian, as an exponent of a unified system, believes that he grasps, are *de facto* moments of completely different time curves, determined by the laws of their special history,[①] as becomes obvious in the discrepancies of the different "histories"—of art, of law, of economics, political history, etc.: "The shaped times of the diverse areas overshadow the uniform flow of time. Any historical period must therefore be imagined as a mixture of events which emerge at different moments of their own time."[②]

It is not the question here whether this assertion presupposes a primary inconsistency in history—which would mean that the consistency of general history only appears retrospectively from the viewpoint and presentation of the historian who imparts unity to it—or whether the radical skepticism of "historical reason" which leads Kracauer from the pluralism of a chronological and morphological passage of time to the basic antinomy of the general and the special in history, really proves that universal history is philosophically untenable today. However, it can be said for the field of literature that Kracauer's insights into the "co-existence of the simultaneous and the unsimultaneous,"[③] far from leading historical knowledge into a dilemma, emphasize the possibility and necessity

---

① This concept is discussed by H. Foccillon, *The Life of Forms in Art* (New York, 1948), and G. Kubler, *The Shape of Time: Remarks on the History of Things* (New Haven and London, 1962).

② S. Kracauer, *History*, p. 53.

③ *Poetik und Hermeneutik*, III, p. 569. The term "simultaneity of different things," with which F. Sengle, "Aufgaben der heutigen Literaturgeschtsschreibung," *Archiv für das Studium der neueren Sprachen*, CC (1964), pp. 247 ff., refers to the same phenomenon, fails to consider one dimension of the problem which becomes evident from his belief that this difficulty of literary history can be solved by simply combining comparative methods and modern interpretation ("that is, carrying out comparative interpretations on a wider base," p. 249).

of uncovering the historical dimension of literary appearances in synchronic cross-sections. For it follows from these insights that the chronological fiction of the moment which determines all simultaneous occurrences corresponds as little to the concept of the historicity of literature as does the morphological fiction of a homogeneous literary order in which all occurrences follow immanent laws one after the other. Purely diachronic observation, no matter how carefully it can explain changes in the history of a genre according to the immanent logic of innovation and automation, problem and solution, only reaches a truly historical dimension when it transcends the morphological canon, confronts the work important in the history of reception with the forgotten conventional works of the genre yet does not ignore its relationship to the literary surroundings in which it had to assert itself among works in other genres.

The historical character of literature appears exactly at the intersection of the diachronic and synchronic approaches. It must be possible to analyze the literary horizon of a certain historical moment as that synchronic system in which simultaneously appearing works can be received diachronically in relation, and in which the work can appear as of current interest or not, as fashionable, out-dated or of lasting value, or before its time or after it.[①] If simultaneously appearing literature—seen from the point of view of the aesthetics of production—breaks down into a heterogeneous variety of the

---

① In 1960 R. Jakobson developed similar assertions in a lecture which is now Chap. XI, "Linguistique et poétique," of his book, *Essais de linguistique générale* (Paris, 1963). See especially p. 212: "La description synchronique envisage non seulement la production littéraire d'une époque donnée, mais aussi cette partie de la tradition littéraire qui est restée vivante ou a été ressuscitée à l'époque en question. ... La poétique historique, tout comme l'histoire du language, si elle se veut vraiment compréhensive, doit être conçue comme une superstructure, bâtie sur une série de descriptions synchroniques successives."

unsimultaneous, that is, of works formed by the different moments of the "shaped time" of their genre (as the apparently present starry sky moves apart astronomically at very different rates), then this variety of literary works moves together again for readers who perceive them as works of their present and relate them to each other in a meaningful unity of a common horizon of literary expectations, memories, and anticipations.

Since every synchronic system must keep its past and its future as indivisible structural elements,① the synchronic cross-section analysis of the literary production at one historical point implies further cross-sections earlier and later. Analogous to the history of the language, constant and variable factors can then be localized as functions of the system. For literature is also a sort of grammar or syntax with relatively firm relationships of its own: the structure of the traditional and uncanonized genres, styles of expression, and rhetorical figures. Opposed to this is the more variable field of semantics: the literary themes, archetypes, symbols, and metaphors. This is why one can attempt to draw an analogy for literary history to what Hans Blumenberg has postulated, explained through examples of the changes in epochs and especially the resulting relations of Christian theology and philosophy, and established with his historical logic of question and answer for the history of philosophy: a "formal system of the interpretation of reality ... within the structure of which the changes can be localized which constitute the process of history

① J. Tynjanov and R. Jacobson, "Probleme der Literatur und Sprachforschung" (1928), *Kursbuch*, V (Frankfurt, 1966), 75: "The history of the system itself presents another system. Pure synchrony proves to be illusory: each synchronic system has its past and its future as an inseparable structural element of this system."

up to the radicalness of the change of epochs."[1] Once the substantial conception of a self-continuing literary tradition has been replaced by a functional explanation of the process relationship of production and reception, it must be possible to see behind the transformation of literary forms and content that change of positions in a literary system of the interpretation of reality which makes the change of horizons in the process of aesthetic experience intelligible.

On these premises a principle of presentation of a literary history could be developed which would neither have to follow the all too familiar high route of the traditional classics nor wander in the valleys of the complete descriptions of all texts which can no longer be historically articulated. The problem of the selection of the works significant for a new history of literature can be solved with the help of the synchronic view in a way which has not yet been tried: a change of horizon in the historical process of the "literary evolution" need not be seen throughout the whole complex of diachronic fact and relations, but can also be determined by the altered make-up of the synchronic literary system and by further cross-section analyses. In principle a presentation of literature in the historical succession of such systems, analyzed at arbitrary points of time, would be possible. The historical dimension of literature, its eventful continuity which is lost in traditionalism as in positivism, can only be rediscovered if the literary historian finds cross-sections and points out works which articulate the process character of "literary evolution" in its history-making moments and epochal caesuras. But it is neither statistics nor subjective caprice on the part of the literary historian which decide about this historical articulation but the history of impact, that is, what results from the event and what from the present perspective

---

① First in "Epochenschwelle und Rezeption," *Philosophische Rundschau*, VI (1958), 101 ff., most recently in *Die Legitimitiät der Neuzeit* (Frankfort, 1966), see esp. pp. 41 ff.

constitutes the continuity of literature as the historical explanation of its present status.

VII

The task of literary history is not completed until the literary work is not only synchronically and diachronically presented in the sequence of its systems but also seen as *special history* in its own unique relationship to *general history*. The fact that the historian can find in the literature of all times a typified, idealized, satirized, or utopian picture of social existence does not completely explain this relationship. The social function becomes manifest only where the literary experience of the reader enters the horizon of expectations of his life, forms his interpretation of the world, and thereby has an effect on his social actions.

The functional relationship of literature and society is usually demonstrated by traditional literary sociology within the narrow confines of a method that has only outwardly replaced the classical principle of *imitatio naturae* with the definition that literature is the representation of a given reality and that was forced to sanction a period-determined concept of style—"Realism" of the nineteenth century the literary category *par excellence*. Even the presently fashionable literary "structuralism," which is, often with doubtful justification, founded on the archetypal criticism of Northrop Frye or on the structural anthropology of Claude Lévi-Strauss, retains the basically classical aesthetics of representation and its schematization of "reflection" (*Widerspiegelung*) and "typification."[①] By interpreting the

① C. Lévi-Strauss himself testifies to this involuntarily but extremely impressively in his attempt to "interpret" one of R. Jakobson's linguistic descriptions of Baudelaire's poem *Les chats* with the help of his structural method; see in *L'Homme*, II (1962), 21.

findings of structural linguistics and literary scholarship as archaic, anthropological constants clothed in literary myths (an interpretation often made possible only by the allegorization of the text) it reduces historical existence to structures of an age-old social nature and literature to its mythic or symbolic expression. Thus exactly the predominantly social, or society-*forming* function of literature is missed. Literary structuralism does not ask—just as Marxist and formalist literary scholarship before it did not ask—how literature "itself helps to determine the idea of society which is its prerequisite" and which it has already helped to determine through the process of history. With these words Gerhard Hess in his lecture, "Das Bild der Gesellschaft in der französischen Literatur" (1954), formulated the unsolved problem of the connection between literary history and sociology and thereby explained to what degree literature can claim to have first discovered certain laws of social existence.[①] Answering the question of the society-forming function of literature from the point of view of the aesthetics of reception exceeds the competence of the traditional aesthetics of representation. The attempt to close the gap between literary-historical and sociological research by using the methods of the aesthetics of reception is simplified by the fact that the concept of the *horizon of expectations*,[②] has also played a role in the axioms of sociology since Karl Mannheim.[③] It is also the main point of a methodological essay, "Naturgesetze und theoretische Systeme" by Karl R. Popper, who anchors the scholarly forming of theories in

---

① Now in *Gesellschaft—Literatur—Wissenchaft: Gesammelte Schriften 1938–1966*, ed. by H. R. Jauss and C. Mueller-Daehn (Munich, 1967), pp. 1-13, esp. pp. 2 and 4.

② I have introduced this concept first in *Untersuchungen zur mittelalterlichen Tierdichtung* (Tübingen, 1959), see esp. pp. 153, 180, 225, 271; further *Archiv für das Studium der neueren Sprachen*, CXCVII (1961), 223-225.

③ K. Mannheim, *Mensch und Gesellschaft in Zeitalter des Umbaus* (Darmstadt, 1958), pp. 212 ff.

the pre-scholarly experience of life. Popper develops the problem of observation from the presupposition of a "horizon of expectations" and thus provides a basis of comparison for any attempt to determine the specific achievement of literature within the general process of experience and to define its relationships with other forms of social behavior.[①]

According to Popper, the procedure of scholarship shares with prescholarly experience the fact that every hypothesis, like every observation, always presupposes expectations: "namely those that constitute the horizon of expectations, a horizon that for the first time makes the observations significant and consequently gives them their place within the order of observations."[②] For in the procedure of scholarship as in the experience of life, the most significant moment is the "disappointment of expectations": "it resembles the experience of a blind man running into an obstacle and thereby learning of its existence. We gain contact with 'reality' by disproving our assumptions. The refutation of our errors in the positive experience that we gain from reality."[③] This model of course does not exhaustively explain the process of the scholarly formation of theories[④] though it certainly illustrates the "productive meaning of

① In *Theorie und Realität*, ed. by H. Albert (Tübingen, 1964), pp. 87-102.

② Ibid., p. 91.

③ Ibid., p. 102.

④ Popper's example of the blind man does not distinguish between the two possibilities of a simple reaction and experimental action assuming certain hypotheses. If the second possibility is characteristic of the reflective scholarly attitude in distinction to the unreflective attitude in life, the scholar would be "creative" on his part, that is he could be placed higher than the "blind man" and could better be compared with the poet as a creator of new expectations.

negative experience" of life.[①] It can, however, shed more light on the specific function of literature within social life. For the reader has one advantage over the (hypothetical) non-reader, that he — to adhere to Popper's metaphor — does not have to run into a new obstacle to gain new experience of reality. The experience of reading can free him from adaptations, prejudice, and predicaments in his life by forcing him to a new perception of things. The horizon of expectations of literature is differentiated from the horizon of expectations of historical life by the fact that it not only preserves real experiences but also anticipates unrealized possibilities, widens the limited range of social behavior by new wishes, demands, and goals, and thereby opens avenues for future experience.

The orientation of our experience by the creative capability of literature rests not only on its artistic character, which by virtue of a new form helps us surmount the mechanical process of everyday perception. The new form of art is not only "perceived against the background of other works of art and through association with

---

① Buck, *Lernen und Erfahrung*, pp. 70 ff. "[Negative experience] teaches not solely by leading us to revise the context of our subsequent experience so that the new fits into the corrected unity of an objective interpretation. ... Not only is the object of the experience represented differently, but the experiencing consciousness changes. The action of a negative experience is one of becoming conscious of oneself. Whatever one becomes conscious of are the motifs which have been guiding experience and which have remained unquestioned in this guiding function. Negative experience has primarily the character of self-experience, which frees one for a qualitatively new kind of experience." From these premises G. Buck developed the concept of hermeneutics, which as a "principle of practical life that is guided by the highest interest in practical living; the actors' understanding of each other" legitimizes the specific experience of the so-called humanities in contrast to the scientific empire. See "Bildung durch Wissenchaft," in *Wissenschaft, Bildung und pädagogische Wirklichkeit* (Heidenheim, 1969), p. 24.

them." Viktor Sklovskij is right in this famous sentence, the heart of the formalist credo, insofar as he turns away from the prejudice of classical aesthetics that defines beauty as harmony of form and content and accordingly reduces the new form to the secondary function shaping a given content. But the new form appears not only "in order to replace the old form, which is no longer artistic," it can also make possible a new perception of things by forming the content of an experience which first appears in the form of literature. The relationship of literature and reader can be realized in the sensuous realm as stimulus to aesthetic perception as well as in the ethical realm as a stimulation to moral reflection.① The new literary work is received and judged against the background of other art forms as well as the background of everyday experience of life. From the point of view of the aesthetics of reception its social function in the ethical realm is equally to be understood in the modality of question and answer, problem and solution, through which it enters the horizon of its historical effect.

How a new aesthetic form can simultaneously have moral consequences, how it can give a moral question the greatest conceivable social impact, is impressively demonstrated by the trial of Flaubert after the pre-publication of *Madame Bovary in the Révue de Paris* in 1857. The new literary form which forced Flaubert's readers to an unfamiliar perception of the "worn-out fable" was the principle of the impersonal (or uninvolved) narration in conjunction with the so-called "erlebte Rede," a stylistic device which Flaubert handled like

① J. Striedter has pointed out that in the diaries and examples from the prose of Leo Tolstoy, to which Sklovskij referred in his first explanation of the process of "Verfremdung," the purely aesthetic aspect was still connected with a theory of knowledge and an ethical aspect: "however, Sklovskij was interested—in contrast to Tolstoy—primarily in the artistic 'process' and not in the question of its ethical prerequisites and effects." (*Poetik und Hermeneutik*, II, pp. 288 ff.)

a virtuoso and with a consistent perspective. What is meant by this can be seen in a description which the prosecuting attorney Pinard claimed in his indictment was immoral in the highest degree. In the novel it follows Emma's first "misstep" and tells how she looked at herself in a mirror:

> *En s'aper çevant dans la glace, elle s'étonna de son visage. Jamais elle n'avait eu les yeux si grands, si noirs, ni d'une telle profondeur. Quelque chose de subtil épandu sur sa personne la transfigurait.*
>
> *Elle se repétait: J'ai un amant! un amant! se délectant à cette idée comme à celle d'une autre puberté qui lui serait survenue. Elle allait donc enfin posséder ces plaisirs de l'amour, cette fièvre de bonheur dont elle avait désespéré. Elle entrait dans quelque chose de merveilleux, où tout serait passion, extase, délire...*

The prosecuting attorney regarded the last sentences as an objective description which included the judgment of the narrator and was upset over this "glorification of adultery" which he considered to be even more dangerous and immoral than the misstep itself.① In this Flaubert's accuser fell victim to an error as the defense immediately pointed out. The incriminating sentences are not an objective determination of the narrator, which the reader can believe, but a subjective opinion of a person characterized by her feelings that are formed from novels. The scientific device consists in revealing the inner thoughts of this person without the signals of direct statement *(Fe vais donc enfin posséder...)* or indirect statement *(Elle se disait qu'elle*

---

① Flaubert, *Oeuvres*, I, 657: "thus, as early as this first mistake, as early as this first fall, she glorified adultery, its poetry, its voluptuousness. Voilà gentlemen, what for me is much more dangerous, much more immoral than the fall itself!"

allait donc enfin posséder...). The effect is that the reader must decide for himself whether he should accept this sentence as a true statement or as an opinion characteristic of this person. Indeed, Emma Bovary is actually "condemned merely by the explicit description of her existence and by her own feelings."① This modern analysis of style agrees exactly with the refutation of the defense attorney Senard, who stressed that disillusion begins for Emma as early as the second day: "The denouement for morality is to be found in every line of the book."② (Senard himself could not, however, name this artistic device which had not yet been recorded at this time.) The consternating effect of the formal innovation in Flaubert's narrative style was obvious in the trial: the impersonal narrative form forces his readers not only to perceive things differently — "photographically exact" according to the judgment of the time — but it also forced them into an alienating insecurity about their judgment. Since the new stylistic device broke with an old novelistic convention — unequivocal description and well-founded moral judgment about the characters — *Madame Bovary* could radicalize or raise questions of life, which during the trial caused the original motive for the accusation, alleged lasciviousness, to recede into the background. The defense attorney began his counter-attack by turning the charge that the novel does not present anything but the *Histoire des adultères d'une femme de province* into the question of whether the subtitle of *Madame Bovary* should not properly read *Histoire de l'education trop souvent donnée en province.*③ But the question with which the *Réquisitoire* of the prosecuting attorney reaches its high point has not yet been answered:

---

① E. Auerbach, *Mimesis*: Dargestellte Wirklichkeit in der abendländischen Literatur (Bern, 1946), p. 430.

② Flaubert, *Oeuvres,* I, 673.

③ Ibid., p. 670.

> *Qui peut condamner cette femme dans le livre? Personne. Telle est la conclusion. Il n'y a pas dans le livre un personnage qui puisse la condamner. Si vous y trouvez un personnage sage, si vous y trouvez un seul principe en vertu duquel l'adultère soit stigmatisé, j'ai tort.*[①]

If no character presented in the novel could condemn Emma Bovary and if no moral principle is asserted in whose name she could be condemned, is not general "public opinion" and its basis in "religious feeling" questioned along with the principle of "marital fidelity"? To what authority should the case of *Madame Bovary* be presented if the previously valid standards of society, "opinion publique, sentiment religieux, morale publique, bonnes moeurs," are no longer sufficient for judging this case?[②] These open and implicit questions do not by any means indicate an aesthetic lack of understanding or moral philistinism on the part of the prosecuting attorney. Rather, there is expressed in them the unsuspected influence of a new art form which can by means of a new *manière de voir les choses* jolt the reader of *Madame Bovary* out of the belief that his moral judgment is self-evident and reopen the long-closed question of public morals. Inasmuch as Flaubert, thanks to his impersonal style, did not provide an opportunity for the banning of his novel on grounds of immorality, the court acted consistently when it acquitted Flaubert as author but damned the literary school which they supposed him to represent, but which in reality was his stylistic device, as yet not recognized:

> *Attendu qu'il n'est pas permis, sous prétexte de peinture de caractère ou de couleur locale, de reproduire dans leurs écarts les*

---

① Flaubert, *Oeuvres*, p. 666.

② Cf. ibid., pp. 666-667.

faits, dits et gestes des personnages qu'un écrivain s'est donnée mission de peindre; qu'un pareil système, appliqué aux oeuvres de l'esprit aussi bien qu'aux productions des beaux-arts, conduit à un réalisme qui serait la négation du beau et du bon et qui, enfantant des oeuvres également offensantes pour les regards et pour l'esprit, commettrait de continuels outrages à la morale publique et aux bonnes moeurs.[①]

Thus a literary work with an unusual aesthetic form can shatter the expectations of its reader and at the same time confront him with a question which cannot be answered by religiously or publicly sanctioned morals. Instead of further examples, a word of reminder is in order here: it was not Bertolt Brecht but the Enlightenment which first proclaimed the competitive relationship between literature and canonized morals. Friedrich Schiller bears witness to this when he makes this express claim in regard to bourgeois drama: "the rules of the stage begin where the realm of worldly laws ends."[②] The literary work can also—and in the history of literature this possibility characterizes the most recent period of modernity—reverse the relationship of question and answer and in an artistic medium confront the reader with a new "opaque" reality which can no longer be understood from the previous horizon of expectations. Thus the newest form of the novel, the much discussed *nouveau roman*, is a form of modern art which—according to Edgar Wind's formulation—presents the paradoxical case "that the solution is provided, the problem, however, is given up in order that the solution

① Flaubert, *Oeuvres*, p. 717.

② Die Schaubühne als eine moralische Anstalt betrachtet, Säkular-Ausgabe, XI, 99. See also R. Koselleck, *Kritik und Krise* (Freiburg and Munich, 1959), pp. 82 ff.

can be understood as the solution."[1] Here the reader is excluded from the position of the immediate audience and placed in the position of an uninitiated third person, who in the face of a still meaningless reality must himself find the question which will enable him to discover the perception of the world and the interpersonal problem to which the work's answer is directed.

It follows from all of this that the specific achievement of literature in society can be found only when the function of literature is not understood as one of imitation. If one looks at the moments in history when literary works toppled the taboos of the prevailing morality or offered the reader new solutions for the moral casuistry of his life which later would be sanctioned by the consensus of all readers in a society, a little-studied area of research opens for the literary historian. The chasm between literature and history, between aesthetic and historical knowledge, can be bridged if literary history does not simply once again describe literary works as a reflection of the process of general history, but rather discovers in the course of "literary evolution" that truly socially formative function which belongs to literature as it competes with other arts and social forces in the emancipation of man from his natural, religious, and social ties.

If the literary critic is willing to overcome his lack of historical sense for the sake of this task, then it can provide an answer to the questions, why and to what ends one can still—or again—study literary history.

UNIVERSITAT KONSTANZ

(Translated by Elizabeth Benzinger)

---

① "Zur Systematik der künstlerischen Probleme," *Fahrbuch für Asthetik* (1925), 440; for the application of this principle to works of the art of the present see M. Imdahl, *Poetik und Hermeneutik*, III, pp. 493-505, 663-664.

14.3 Key Words

① Gadamer 伽达默尔

Hans-Georg Gadamer (1900–2002) was a German philosopher of the continental tradition, best known for his 1960 magnum opus *Truth and Method* (《真理与方法》) on hermeneutics. In addition to his work in hermeneutics, Gadamer is also well known for a long list of publications on Greek philosophy. Indeed, while *Truth and Method* became central to his later career, much of Gadamer's early life centered on studying Greek thinkers, Plato and Aristotle specifically. He was generally regarded as the major philosopher of hermeneutics who helped to establish the solid basis for the theory, also introducing a solution to the famous puzzle of "hermeneutic circle" (阐释的循环).

② Wolfgang Iser 沃尔夫冈·伊泽尔

Wolfgang Iser (1926–2007) was a German aesthetician and literary scholar. Iser is known for his reader-response criticism (读者反应批评) in literary theory. This theory began to evolve in 1967, while he was working in the University of Konstanz, which he helped to found in the 1960s. Together with Hans Robert Jauss, he is considered to be the founder of the Constance School of reception theory and also the reception aesthetics. In his approach to reader-response theory, Iser describes the process of first reading, the subsequent development of the text into a "whole," and how the dialogue between the reader and the text takes place. In his study of Shakespeare's histories, in particular *Richard II*, Iser interprets Richard's continually changing legal policy as expression of the desire for self-assertion. After retirement, Iser moved to North America and continued his debate and research with scholars of new criticism.

③ Roman Ingarden 罗曼·英加登

Roman Witold Ingarden (1893–1970) was a Polish philosopher who worked in phenomenology, ontology and aesthetics. Before World War II, Ingarden published his works mainly in the German language.

During the war, he switched to Polish, and as a result his major works in ontology went largely unnoticed by the wider world philosophical community. His most renowned works of literary or aesthetic theory included *The Literary Work of Art* (1963) and *The Cognition of the Literary Work of Art* (1968).

④ Marxism theory 马克思主义文论

Western Marxism is a current of Marxist theory arising from Western and Central Europe in the aftermath of the 1917 October Revolution (十月革命) in Russia. The term denotes a loose collection of theorists who advanced an interpretation of Marxism distinct from that codified by the Soviet Union. The Western Marxists placed more emphasis on Marxism's philosophical and subjective aspects, as well as the origins of Karl Marx's thought in the philosophy of Georg Wilhelm Friedrich Hegel (黑格尔), and what they called the "Young Marxism" (青年马克思主义). Although some early figures such as György Lukács (卢卡奇) and Antonio Gramsci (葛兰西) were prominent in political activities, Western Marxism became primarily the reserve of academia, especially after 1950s. Prominent figures included Walter Benjamin, Theodor Adorno (阿多诺), Max Horkheimer (霍克海默), and Herbert Marcuse (马尔库塞).

⑤ formalism theory 形式主义文论

In literary theory, formalism refers to critical approaches that analyze, interpret, or evaluate the inherent features of a text. These features include not only grammar and syntax but also literary devices such as meter and tropes. The formalistic approach reduces the importance of a text's historical, biographical, and cultural context. Formalism rose to prominence in the early twentieth century as a reaction against Romanticist theories of literature, which centered on the artist and individual creative genius, and instead placed the text itself back into the spotlight to show how the text was indebted to forms and other works that had preceded it. The formalist literary criticism developed from Russian formalism, including Russian and Soviet scholars such as Viktor Shklovsky (维克多·什克洛夫斯基), Yuri Tynianov (尤里·蒂尼亚诺夫), Vladimir Propp (弗拉基米尔·普罗普), Boris Eichenbaum (鲍里斯·艾亨鲍姆), Roman Jakobson (罗曼·雅各布森), Boris Tomashevsky (鲍里斯·托马舍夫斯基), Grigory Gukovsky (格里戈里·古可夫斯基), and was followed by Anglo-American New Criticism, with I. A. Richards, T. S. Eliot, William Empson, René Wellek (勒内·韦勒克) and so forth as the representatives.

⑥ structuralism theory 结构主义文论

Structuralism is the methodology that implies elements of human culture must be understood by way of their relationship to a broader, overarching system or structure. It works to uncover the structures that underlie all the things that humans do, think, perceive, and feel. Structuralism in Europe developed in the early 1900s, mainly in France and Russian Empire, in the structural linguistics of Ferdinand de Saussure (索绪尔) and the subsequent Prague, Moscow and Copenhagen schools of linguistics. In the late 1950s and early 1960s, when structural linguistics were facing serious challenges from thinkers and philosophers such as Noam Chomsky (诺姆·乔姆斯基) and thus fading in importance, an array of scholars in the humanities borrowed Saussure's concepts for use in their respective fields of study. French anthropologist Claude Lévi-Strauss (列维·施特劳斯) was arguably the first such scholar, sparking a widespread interest in structuralism.

⑦ Schiller 席勒

Johann Christoph Friedrich von Schiller (1759–1805) was a German poet, philosopher, physician, historian, and playwright. During the last seventeen years of his life, Schiller developed a productive, if complicated, friendship with the already famous and influential Johann Wolfgang von Goethe (歌德). They frequently discussed issues concerning aesthetics, and Schiller encouraged

Goethe to finish works he left as sketches. This relationship and these discussions led to a period now referred to as Weimar Classicism (魏玛古典主义). They also worked together on *Xenien*, a collection of short satirical poems in which both Schiller and Goethe challenge opponents of their philosophical vision. Schiller gave a speech titled as a professor of history. He also wrote many philosophical papers on ethics and aesthetics.

14.4 Extensive Explorations

① What is Jauss' attitude to the literary revolution?

② What is the difference between reception aesthetics and hermeneutics?

③ According to Jauss, what is the role of reader in the process of reading?

④ What is the purpose of introducing *Madame Bovary* in the discussion?

⑤ What is the relationship between *special history* and *general history*?

⑥ How do you understand literary history as "literary evolution"?

⑦ In conclusion, what do you think of the "Challenge" mean, according to Jauss?

15. Susan Sontag's *Against Interpretation*

15.1 Lead-in

Susan Sontag (1933–2004) was an American writer, filmmaker, philosopher, and political activist. Sontag was born in New York. Her father had a trading business in China. In 1951, her work appeared in print for the first time in the winter issue of the *Chicago Review*. She studied at Chicago University, Harvard University, Paris University, Oxford University and UC Berkeley and her first job was to teach freshman English at the University of Connecticut. She was awarded an American Association of University Women's fellowship in 1957 to St Anne's College, Oxford. During her work, she published series of essays as a critic, and as a battlefield journalist. In her time, Sontag was unique among her contemporaries. Her work on cultural research is more shocking than her success in novel spreading. Sontag had close relationships with scholars in America, Britain and France.

The text in our textbook, *Against Interpretation* was published in the 1960s. Social unrest and campaigns were rampant globally. Unrest was even harsher in America and Europe. Of course, even today, there're still misunderstandings on her *Against Interpretation*. Many readers were lost in translation of the concept "interpretation." Actually, Sontag was against those binary-opposite (二元对立的), metaphysical interpretations, while the German philosophical hermeneutics emphasized on the Horizontverschmelzung (视域融合), or the intervention of one's subjective horizon. For this reason,

Sontag almost never mentioned the philosophical hermeneutics in her article. As a contemporary scholar, Sontag also had a passion for art. Therefore, her rival on interpretation was to defend art. Sontag even mentioned at the end of *Against Interpretation*: We need an art exoticism.

15.2 Text

AGAINST INTERPRETATION

"Content is a glimpse of something, an encounter like a flash. It's very tiny—very tiny, content."

—Willem De Kooning, in an interview

"It is only shallow people who do not judge by appearances. The mystery of the world is the visible, not the invisible."

—Oscar Wilde, in a letter

1

The earliest experience of art must have been that it was incantatory, magical; art was an instrument of ritual. (Cf. the paintings in the caves at Lascaux, Altamira, Niaux, La Pasiega, etc.) The earliest theory of art, that of the Greek philosophers, proposed that art was mimesis, imitation of reality.

It is at this point that the peculiar question of the value of art arose. For the mimetic theory, by its very terms, challenges art to justify itself.

Plato, who proposed the theory, seems to have done so in order to rule that the value of art is dubious. Since he considered ordinary material things as themselves mimetic objects, imitations of transcendent forms or structures, even the best painting of a bed would be only an "imitation of an imitation." For Plato, art is neither particularly useful (the painting of a bed is no good to sleep on), nor, in the strict sense, true. And Aristotle's arguments in defense of art do not really challenge Plato's view that all art is an elaborate trompe l'oeil, and therefore a lie. But he does dispute Plato's idea that art is useless. Lie or no, art has a certain value according to Aristotle because it is a form of therapy. Art is useful, after all, Aristotle counters, medicinally useful in that it arouses and purges dangerous emotions.

In Plato and Aristotle, the mimetic theory of art goes hand in hand with the assumption that art is always figurative. But advocates of the mimetic theory need not close their eyes to decorative and abstract art. The fallacy that art is necessarily a "realism" can be modified or scrapped without ever moving outside the problems delimited by the mimetic theory.

The fact is, all Western consciousness of and reflection upon art have remained within the confines staked out by the Greek theory of art as mimesis or representation. It is through this theory that art as such—above and beyond given works of art—becomes problematic, in need of defense. And it is the defense of art which gives birth to the odd vision by which something we have learned to call "form" is separated off from something we have learned to call "content," and to the well-intentioned move which makes content essential and form accessory.

Even in modern times, when most artists and critics have discarded the theory of art as representation of an outer reality in favor of the theory of art as subjective expression, the main feature of the mimetic theory persists. Whether we conceive of the work of art on the model of a picture (art as a picture of reality) or on the model of a statement (art as the statement of the artist), content still comes first. The content may have changed. It may now be less figurative, less lucidly realistic. But it is still assumed that a work of art is its content. Or, as it's usually put today, that a work of art by definition says something. ("What X is saying is...,""What X is trying to say is...," "What X said is..." etc., etc.)

2

None of us can ever retrieve that innocence before all theory when art knew no need to justify itself, when one did not ask of a work of art what it said because one knew (or thought one knew) what it did. From now to the end of consciousness, we are stuck with the task of defending art. We can only quarrel with one or another means of defense. Indeed, we have an obligation to overthrow any means of defending and justifying art which becomes particularly obtuse or onerous or insensitive to contemporary needs and practice.

This is the case, today, with the very idea of content itself. Whatever it may have been in the past, the idea of content is today mainly a hindrance, a nuisance, a subtle or not so subtle philistinism. Though the actual developments in many arts may seem to be leading us away from the idea that a work of art is primarily its content, the idea still exerts an extraordinary hegemony. I want to suggest that this is because the idea is now perpetuated in the guise of a certain way of encountering works of art thoroughly ingrained among most people who take any of the arts seriously. What the overemphasis on the idea of content entails is the perennial, never consummated project of interpretation. And, conversely, it is the habit of approaching works of art in order to interpret them that sustains the fancy that there really is such a thing as the content of a work of art.

3

Of course, I don't mean interpretation in the broadest sense, the sense in which Nietzsche (rightly) says, "There are no facts, only interpretations." By interpretation, I mean here a conscious act of the mind which illustrates a certain code, certain "rules" of interpretation. Directed to art, interpretation means plucking a set of elements (the X, the Y, the Z, and so forth) from the whole work. The task of interpretation is virtually one of translation. The interpreter says, Look, don't you see that X is really—or, really means—A? That Y is really B? That Z is really C?

What situation could prompt this curious project for transforming a text? History gives us the materials for an answer. Interpretation first appears in the culture of late classical antiquity, when the power and credibility of myth had been broken by the "realistic" view of the world introduced by scientific enlightenment. Once the question that haunts post-mythic consciousness—that of the seemliness of religious symbols—had been asked, the ancient texts were, in their pristine form, no longer acceptable. Then interpretation was summoned, to reconcile the ancient texts to "modern" demands. Thus, the Stoics, to accord with their view that the gods had to be moral, allegorized away the rude features of Zeus and his boisterous clan in Homer's epics. What Homer really designated by the adultery of Zeus with Leto, they explained, was the union between power and wisdom. In the same vein, Philo of Alexandria interpreted the literal historical narratives of the Hebrew Bible as spiritual paradigms. The story of the exodus from Egypt, the wandering in the desert for forty years, and the entry into the promised land, said Philo, was really an allegory of the individual soul's emancipation, tribulations, and final deliverance. Interpretation thus presupposes a discrepancy between the clear meaning of the text and the demands of (later) readers. It seeks to resolve that discrepancy. The situation is that for some reason a text has become unacceptable; yet it cannot be discarded. Interpretation is a radical strategy for conserving an old text, which is thought too precious to repudiate, by revamping it. The interpreter, without actually erasing or rewriting the text, is altering it. But he can't admit to doing this. He claims to be only making it intelligible, by disclosing its true meaning. However far the interpreters alter the text (another notorious example is the Rabbinic and Christian "spiritual" interpretations of the clearly erotic Song of Songs), they must claim to be reading off a sense that is already there.

Interpretation in our own time, however, is even more complex. For the contemporary zeal for the project of interpretation is often prompted not by piety toward the troublesome text (which may conceal an aggression), but by an open aggressiveness, an overt contempt for appearances. The old style of interpretation was insistent, but respectful; it erected another meaning on top of the literal one. The modern style of interpretation excavates, and as it excavates, destroys; it digs "behind" the text, to find a sub-text which is the true one. The most celebrated and influential modern doctrines, those of Marx and Freud, actually amount to elaborate systems of hermeneutics, aggressive and impious theories of interpretation. All observable phenomena are bracketed, in Freud's phrase, as manifest content. This manifest content must be probed and pushed aside to find the true meaning — the latent content — beneath. For Marx, social events like revolutions and wars; for Freud, the events of individual lives (like neurotic symptoms and slips of the tongue) as well as texts (like a dream or a work of art) — all are treated as occasions for interpretation. According to Marx and Freud, these events only seem to be intelligible. Actually, they have no meaning without interpretation. To understand is to interpret. And to interpret is to restate the phenomenon, in effect to find an equivalent for it.

Thus, interpretation is not (as most people assume) an absolute value, a gesture of mind situated in some timeless realm of capabilities. Interpretation must itself be evaluated, within a historical view of human consciousness. In some cultural contexts, interpretation is a liberating act. It is a means of revising, of transvaluing, of escaping the dead past. In other cultural contexts, it is reactionary, impertinent, cowardly, stifling.

4

Today is such a time, when the project of interpretation is largely reactionary, stifling. Like the fumes of the automobile and of heavy industry which befoul the urban atmosphere, the effusion of interpretations of art today poisons our sensibilities. In a culture whose already classical dilemma is the hypertrophy of the intellect at the expense of energy and sensual capability, interpretation is the revenge of the intellect upon art.

Even more. It is the revenge of the intellect upon the world. To interpret is to impoverish, to deplete the world—in order to set up a shadow world of "meanings." It is to turn the world into this world. ("This world"! As if there were any other.) The world, our world, is depleted, impoverished enough. Away with all duplicates of it, until we again experience more immediately what we have.

5

In most modern instances, interpretation amounts to the philistine refusal to leave the work of art alone. Real art has the capacity to make us nervous. By reducing the work of art to its content and then interpreting that, one tames the work of art. Interpretation makes art manageable, comformable.

This philistinism of interpretation is more rife in literature than in any other art. For decades now, literary critics have understood it to be their task to translate the elements of the poem or play or novel or story into something else. Sometimes a writer will be so uneasy before the naked power of his art that he will install within the work itself — albeit with a little shyness, a touch of the good taste of irony — the clear and explicit interpretation of it. Thomas Mann is an example of such an overcooperative author. In the case of more stubborn authors, the critic is only too happy to perform the job.

The work of Kafka, for example, has been subjected to a mass ravishment by no less than three armies of interpreters. Those who read Kafka as a social allegory see case studies of the frustrations and insanity of modern bureaucracy and its ultimate issuance in the totalitarian state. Those who read Kafka as a psychoanalytic allegory see desperate revelations of Kafka's fear of his father, his castration anxieties, his sense of his own impotence, his thralldom to his dreams. Those who read Kafka as a religious allegory explain that K. in *The Castle* is trying to gain access to heaven, that Joseph K. in *The Trial* is being judged by the inexorable and mysterious justice of God. ... Another oeuvre that has attracted interpreters like leeches is that of Samuel Beckett. Beckett's delicate dramas of the withdrawn consciousness — pared down to essentials, cut off, often represented as physically immobilized — are read as a statement about modern man's alienation from meaning or from God, or as an allegory of psychopathology.

Proust, Joyce, Faulkner, Rilke, Lawrence, Gide ... one could go on citing author after author; the list is endless of those around whom thick encrustations of interpretation have taken hold. But it should be noted that interpretation is not simply the compliment that mediocrity pays to genius. It is, indeed, the modern way of understanding something, and is applied to works of every quality. Thus, in the notes that Elia Kazan published on his production of *A Streetcar Named Desire*, it becomes clear that, in order to direct the play, Kazan had to discover that Stanley Kowalski represented the sensual and vengeful barbarism that was engulfing our culture, while Blanche Du Bois was Western civilization, poetry, delicate apparel, dim lighting, refined feelings and all, though a little the worse for wear to be sure. Tennessee Williams' forceful psychological melodrama now became intelligible: it was about something, about the decline of Western civilization. Apparently, were it to go on being a play about a handsome brute named Stanley Kowalski and a faded mangy belle named Blanche Du Bois, it would not be manageable.

6

It doesn't matter whether artists intend, or don't intend, for their works to be interpreted. Perhaps Tennessee Williams thinks *Streetcar* is about what Kazan thinks it to be about. It may be that Cocteau in *The Blood of a Poet* and in *Orpheus* wanted the elaborate readings which have been given these films, in terms of Freudian symbolism and social critique. But the merit of these works certainly lies elsewhere than in their "meanings." Indeed, it is precisely to the extent that Williams' plays and Cocteau's films do suggest these portentous meanings that they are defective, false, contrived, lacking in conviction.

From interviews, it appears that Resnais and Robbe-Grillet consciously designed *Last Year at Marienbad* to accommodate a multiplicity of equally plausible interpretations. But the temptation to interpret *Marienbad* should be resisted. What matters in *Marienbad* is the pure, untranslatable, sensuous immediacy of some of its images, and its rigorous if narrow solutions to certain problems of cinematic form.

Again, Ingmar Bergman may have meant the tank rumbling down the empty night street in *The Silence* as a phallic symbol. But if he did, it was a foolish thought. ("Never trust the teller, trust the tale," said Lawrence.) Taken as a brute object, as an immediate sensory equivalent for the mysterious abrupt armored happenings going on inside the hotel, that sequence with the tank is the most striking moment in the film. Those who reach for a Freudian interpretation of the tank are only expressing their lack of response to what is there on the screen.

It is always the case that interpretation of this type indicates a dissatisfaction (conscious or unconscious) with the work, a wish to replace it by something else.

Interpretation, based on the highly dubious theory that a work of art is composed of items of content, violates art. It makes art into an article for use, for arrangement into a mental scheme of categories.

7

Interpretation does not, of course, always prevail. In fact, a great deal of today's art may be understood as motivated by a flight from interpretation. To avoid interpretation, art may become parody. Or it may become abstract. Or it may become ("merely") decorative. Or it may become non-art.

The flight from interpretation seems particularly a feature of modern painting. Abstract painting is the attempt to have, in the ordinary sense, no content; since there is no content, there can be no interpretation. Pop Art works by the opposite means to the same result; using a content so blatant, so "what it is," it, too, ends by being uninterpretable.

A great deal of modern poetry as well, starting from the great experiments of French poetry (including the movement that is misleadingly called Symbolism) to put silence into poems and to reinstate the magic of the word, has escaped from the rough grip of interpretation. The most recent revolution in contemporary taste in poetry—the revolution that has deposed Eliot and elevated Pound—represents a turning away from content in poetry in the old sense, an impatience with what made modern poetry prey to the zeal of interpreters.

I am speaking mainly of the situation in America, of course. Interpretation runs rampant here in those arts with a feeble and negligible avant-garde: fiction and the drama. Most American novelists and playwrights are really either journalists or gentlemen sociologists and psychologists. They are writing the literary equivalent of program music. And so rudimentary, uninspired, and stagnant has been the sense of what might be done with form in fiction and drama that even when the content isn't simply information, news, it is still peculiarly visible, handier, more exposed. To the extent that novels and plays (in America), unlike poetry and painting and music, don't reflect any interesting concern with changes in their form, these arts remain prone to assault by interpretation.

But programmatic avant-gardism—which has meant, mostly, experiments with form at the expense of content—is not the only defense against the infestation of art by interpretations. At least, I hope not. For this would be to commit art to being perpetually on the run. (It also perpetuates the very distinction between form and content which is, ultimately, an illusion.) Ideally, it is possible to elude the interpreters in another way, by making works of art whose surface is so unified and clean, whose momentum is so rapid, whose address is so direct that the work can be ... just what it is. Is this possible now? It does happen in films, I believe. This is why cinema is the most alive, the most exciting, the most important of all art forms right now. Perhaps the way one tells how alive a particular art form is, is by the latitude it gives for making mistakes in it, and still being good. For example, a few of the films of Bergman—though crammed with lame messages about the modern spirit, thereby inviting interpretations—still triumph over the pretentious intentions of their director. In *Winter Light* and *The Silence*, the beauty and visual sophistication of the images subvert before our eyes the callow pseudo-intellectuality of the story and some of the dialogue. (The most remarkable instance of this sort of discrepancy is the work of D. W. Griffith.) In good films, there is always a directness that entirely frees us from the itch to interpret. Many old Hollywood films, like those of Cukor, Walsh, Hawks, and countless other directors, have this liberating anti-symbolic quality, no less than the best work of the new European directors, like Truffaut's *Shoot the Piano Player* and *Jules and Jim*, Godard's *Breathless* and *Vivre Sa Vie*, Antonioni's *L'Avventura*, and Olmi's *The Fiancés*.

The fact that films have not been overrun by interpreters is in part due simply to the newness of cinema as an art. It also owes to the happy accident that films for such a long time were just movies; in other words, that they were understood to be part of mass, as opposed to high, culture, and were left alone by most people with minds. Then, too, there is always something other than content in the cinema to grab hold of, for those who want to analyze. For the cinema, unlike the novel, possesses a vocabulary of forms—the explicit, complex, and discussable technology of camera movements, cutting, and composition of the frame that goes into the making of a film.

8

What kind of criticism, of commentary on the arts, is desirable today? For I am not saying that works of art are ineffable, that they cannot be described or paraphrased. They can be. The question is how. What would criticism look like that would serve the work of art, not usurp its place?

What is needed, first, is more attention to form in art. If excessive stress on content provokes the arrogance of interpretation, more extended and more thorough descriptions of form would silence. What is needed is a vocabulary—a descriptive, rather than prescriptive, vocabulary—for forms.[①] The best criticism, and it is uncommon, is of this sort that dissolves considerations of content into those of form. On film, drama, and painting respectively, I can think of Erwin Panofsky's essay, "Style and Medium in the Motion Pictures," Northrop Frye's essay "A Conspectus of Dramatic Genres," Pierre Francastel's essay "The Destruction of a Plastic Space." Roland Barthes' book *On Racine* and his two essays on Robbe-Grillet are examples of formal analysis applied to the work of a single author. (The best essays in Erich Auerbach's *Mimesis*, like "The Scar of Odysseus," are also of this type.) An example of formal analysis applied simultaneously to genre and author is Walter Benjamin's essay, "The Story Teller: Reflections on the Works of Nicolai Leskov."

Equally valuable would be acts of criticism which would supply a really accurate, sharp, loving description of the appearance of a work of art. This seems even harder to do than formal analysis. Some of Manny Farber's film criticism, Dorothy van Ghent's essay "The

---

① One of the difficulties is that our idea of form is spatial (the Greek metaphors for form are all derived from notions of space). This is why we have a more ready vocabulary of forms for the spatial than for the temporal arts. The exception among the temporal arts, of course, is the drama; perhaps this is because the drama is a narrative (i.e., temporal) form that extends itself visually and pictorially, upon a stage. ... What we don't have yet is a poetics of the novel, any clear notion of the forms of narration. Perhaps film criticism will be the occasion of a breakthrough here, since films are primarily a visual form, yet they are also a subdivision of literature.

Dickens World: A View from Todgers," Randall Jarrell's essay on Walt Whitman are among the rare examples of what I mean. These are essays which reveal the sensuous surface of art without mucking about in it.

9

Transparence is the highest, most liberating value in art—and in criticism—today. Transparence means experiencing the luminousness of the thing in itself, of things being what they are. This is the greatness of, for example, the films of Bresson and Ozu and Renoir's *The Rules of the Game.*

Once upon a time (say, for Dante), it must have been a revolutionary and creative move to design works of art so that they might be experienced on several levels. Now it is not. It reinforces the principle of redundancy that is the principal affliction of modern life.

Once upon a time (a time when high art was scarce), it must have been a revolutionary and creative move to interpret works of art. Now it is not. What we decidedly do not need now is further to assimilate Art into Thought, or (worse yet) Art into Culture.

Interpretation takes the sensory experience of the work of art for granted, and proceeds from there. This cannot be taken for granted, now. Think of the sheer multiplication of works of art available to every one of us, superadded to the conflicting tastes and odors and sights of the urban environment that bombard our senses. Ours is a culture based on excess, on overproduction; the result is a steady loss of sharpness in our sensory experience. All the conditions of modern life—its material plenitude, its sheer crowdedness—conjoin to dull our sensory faculties. And it is in the light of the condition of our senses, our capacities (rather than those of another age), that the task of the critic must be assessed.

What is important now is to recover our senses. We must learn to *see* more, to *hear* more, to *feel* more.

Our task is not to find the maximum amount of content in a work of art, much less to squeeze more content out of the work than is already there. Our task is to cut back content so that we can see the thing at all.

The aim of all commentary on art now should be to make works of art—and, by analogy, our own experience—more, rather than less, real to us. The function of criticism should be to show *how it is what it is*, even *that it is what it is*, rather than to show *what it means*.

10

In place of a hermeneutics we need an erotics of art.

[1964]

15.3 Key Words

① Philistinism 庸俗主义

In the fields of philosophy and aesthetics, the derogatory term philistinism describes the "manners, habits and character" of a person whose anti-intellectual social attitude undervalues and despises art and beauty, spirituality and intellect. A philistine person is of smugly narrow mind, and of conventional morality whose materialistic views and tastes indicate a lack of and an indifference to cultural and aesthetic values.

② Nietzsche 尼采

Friedrich Wilhelm Nietzsche (1844–1900) was a German philosopher, cultural critic, composer, poet, and philologist whose works have exerted a profound influence on modern intellectual history. He became the youngest ever to hold the Chair of Classical

Philology at the University of Basel (巴塞尔大学) in 1869. In 1889, he suffered a collapse and afterward a complete loss of his mental faculties and died in 1900. Nietzsche's writing spans philosophical polemics, poetry, cultural criticism, and fiction while displaying a fondness for aphorism and irony. Prominent elements of his philosophy include his radical critique of truth in favor of perspectivism; his genealogical critique of religion and Christian morality and his related theory of master-slave morality; his aesthetic affirmation of existence in response to the "death of God" and the profound crisis of nihilism; his notion of the Apollonian and Dionysian; and his characterization of the human subject as the expression of competing wills, collectively understood as the will to power. He also developed influential concepts such as the Übermensch (超人) and the doctrine of eternal return. In his later works, he became increasingly preoccupied with the creative powers of the individual to overcome social, cultural and moral contexts in pursuit of new values and aesthetic health.

③ Thomas Mann 托马斯·曼

Thomas Mann (1875–1955) was a German novelist, short story writer, social critic, philanthropist, essayist, and laureate of the 1929 Nobel Prize in Literature. His highly symbolic and ironic epic novels and novellas are noted for their insight into the psychology of the artist and the intellectual. His analysis and critique of the European and German soul used modernized versions of German and Biblical stories, as well as the ideas of Johann Wolfgang von Goethe, Friedrich Nietzsche and Arthur Schopenhauer.

④ Kafka 卡夫卡

Franz Kafka (1883–1924) was a German-speaking Bohemian (波西米亚的) novelist and short-story writer, widely regarded as one of the major figures of 20th-century literature. His works fuse elements of realism and the fantastic. They typically feature isolated protagonists facing bizarre or surrealistic predicaments and incomprehensible socio-bureaucratic powers. They have been interpreted as exploring themes of alienation, existential anxiety, guilt, and absurdity. His best-known works include *Die Verwandlung* (《变形记》), *Der Proceß* (《审判》), and *Das Schloß* (《城堡》). The term Kafkaesque has entered the English language to describe situations like those found in his writing.

⑤ Ingmar Bergman 英格玛·伯格曼

Ingmar Bergman (1918–2007) was a Swedish director, writer, and producer who worked in film, television, and theatre. Considered to be among the most accomplished and influential filmmakers of all time, Bergman's films include *Smiles of a Summer Night* (《夏夜的微笑》, 1955), *The Seventh Seal* (《第七封印》, 1957), *Wild Strawberries* (《野草莓》, 1957), *Persona* (《假面》, 1966), *Cries and Whispers* (《哭泣与耳语》, 1972), *Scenes from a Marriage* (《婚姻生活》, 1973), and *Fanny and Alexander* (《芬妮与亚力山大》, 1982); the last two exist in extended television versions.

⑥ Pop Art 波普艺术

Pop Art is an art movement that emerged in the United Kingdom and the United States during the 1950s. The movement presented a challenge to traditions of fine art by including imagery from popular and mass culture, such as advertising, comic books and mundane mass-produced cultural objects. One of its aims is to use images of popular (as opposed to elitist) culture in art, emphasizing the banal or kitschy elements of any culture, most often through the use of irony. It is also associated with the artists' use of mechanical means of reproduction or rendering techniques. In Pop Art, material is sometimes visually removed from its known context, isolated, or combined with unrelated material.

⑦ The avant-garde 先锋派

The avant-garde are people or works that are experimental,

radical, or unorthodox with respect to art, culture, or society. It is frequently characterized by aesthetic innovation and initial unacceptability. The avant-garde pushes the boundaries of what is accepted as the norm or the status quo, primarily in the cultural realm. Many artists have aligned themselves with the avant-garde movement, and still continue to do so, tracing their history from Dada (达达主义) through the situationists to postmodern artists such as the language poets around 1981. The avant-garde also promotes radical social reforms.

⑧ Hermeneutics 解释学

Hermeneutics is derived from the Greek word ἑρμηνεύω, and from Hermes (赫 尔 墨 斯), the mythological Greek deity who was the "messenger of the gods," and also considered to be the inventor of language and speech, an interpreter, a liar, a thief and a trickster. Now it is the theory and methodology of interpretation, especially the interpretation of Biblical texts, wisdom literature, and philosophical texts. Hermeneutics is more than interpretive principles or methods we resort to when immediate comprehension fails. Rather, hermeneutics is the art of understanding and of making oneself understood. Modern hermeneutics includes both verbal and non-verbal communication as well as semiotics, presuppositions, and pre-understandings. Hermeneutics has been broadly applied in the humanities, especially in law, history and theology. Hermeneutics was initially applied to the interpretation, or exegesis, of scripture, and has been later broadened to questions of general interpretation. The terms hermeneutics and exegesis are sometimes (incorrectly) used interchangeably. Hermeneutics is a wider discipline which includes written, verbal, and non-verbal communication. Exegesis focuses primarily upon the word and grammar of texts. Hermeneutic, as a count noun in the singular, refers to some particular method of interpretation (see, in contrast, double hermeneutic).

15.4 Extensive Explorations

① Why did Sontag also mention mimesis? Is it theoretically related to the texts about Plato, Aristotle and Abrams?

② What does the "main feature of the mimetic theory" mean when she indicated that it persisted in modern times?

③ On the targeting of interpretation, what is the difference between Sontag's definition and that of Nietzsche?

④ According to Sontag, what does interpretation mean in art?

⑤ What does the instance of the interpretation of Kafka's work indicate?

⑥ What is the source of dissatisfaction mentioned in Chapter 6?

⑦ What is the behavior of art in America in Sontag's perspective?

⑧ Why cannot we take for granted on the work of art as sensory experience?

⑨ In summary, why and how did Sontag oppose interpretation?

16. Edward Said's *Orientalism*

16.1 Lead-in

Edward Wadie Said (1935–2003) was a professor of literature at Columbia University (哥伦比亚大学), a public intellectual, and a founder of the academic field of postcolonial studies. He is a Palestinian American born in Palestine, grew up in Egypt and received higher education in the United States. Said is most famous for his application of his education and bi-cultural perspective to illuminating the gaps of cultural and political understanding between the Western world and the Eastern world, especially about the Israeli–Palestinian conflict in the Middle East; and his best acknowledged work was *Orientalism* (《东方学》, 1978), on how the Western world perceives the Orient. Said died in 2003. The year 2003–2004 witnessed the loss of H. G. Gadamer, Susan Sontag and Richard Rorty (理查德·罗蒂), which partly aroused the writing of *After Theory* (《理论之后》, 2003) by Terry Eagleton (特里·伊格尔顿).

Orientalism (《东方学》) was first published in 1978. Said put forward three meanings of Orientalism in his book. First, he put forward the Orientalism in the domain of academic research. Asian study as well as East-Asian study is popular in Western academic world. Research on Oriental philosophy, literature and language is universal in the field of worldwide culture and philosophy, forming the first stratum of meaning of Orientalism. The second description of Orientalism is stated as a discourse pattern which conflicts with the West. The West is self-centered especially in culture field. In this sense, the Oriental is distinguished as a barbarian and even stupid, ugly image. The third stratum of Orientalism is depicted as a discourse of power, which is extremely emphasized by Said himself. In his narration, this Orientalism is the Orient which is exploited and controlled by the West. The theory of Said has its origins in the discourse theory (话语理论). Theory of Michel Foucault with the power of discourse and the hegemony theory of Antonio Gramsci, the remarkable theoretician of Western Marxism could both serve as the source of this theory. After setting up a self-centered pattern to exploit the whole world, the Orient actually became the weak side of discourse power and the power goes to the West. And the purpose of the integral Orientalism theory is to emphasize this loss of discourse power.

After the publication of *Orientalism*, a series of books was published as response or continuity of the theory. *Culture and Imperialism* (《文化与帝国主义》) is the best-known among these books. Edward Said put forward a strategy in *Culture and Imperialism* for resistance against the Western exploitation, and, in comparison, the Orientalism could be a startling statement. The text selected is the introduction of the book, outlining the theoretical structure of the book.

16.2 Text

Orientalism

(Introduction[①])

I

On a visit to Beirut during the terrible civil war of 1975–1976 a French journalist wrote regretfully of the gutted downtown area that

① [Said] This is the opening chapter, complete, reprinted from *Orientalism* (New York: Random House, 1978).

"it had once seemed to belong to ... the Orient of Chateaubriand and Nerval." [1] He was right about the place, of course, especially so far as a European was concerned. The Orient was almost a European invention, and had been since antiquity a place of romance, exotic beings, haunting memories and landscapes, remarkable experiences. Now it was disappearing; in a sense it had happened, its time was over. Perhaps it seemed irrelevant that Orientals themselves had something at stake in the process, that even in the time of Chateaubriand and Nerval Orientals had lived there, and that now it was they who were suffering; the main thing for the European visitor was a European representation of the Orient and its contemporary fate, both of which had a privileged communal significance for the journalist and his French readers.

Americans will not feel quite the same about the Orient, which for them is much more likely to be associated very differently with the Far East (China and Japan, mainly). Unlike the Americans, the French and the British—less so the Germans, Russians, Spanish, Portuguese, Italians, and Swiss—have had a long tradition of what I shall be calling *Orientalism,* a way of coming to terms with the Orient that is based on the Orient's special place in European Western experience. The Orient is not only adjacent to Europe; it is also the place of Europe's greatest and richest and oldest colonies, the source of its civilizations and languages, its cultural contestant, and one of its deepest and most recurring images of the Other. In addition, the Orient has helped to define Europe (or the West) as its contrasting image, idea, personality, experience. Yet none of this Orient is merely imaginative. The Orient is an integral part of European *material*

① Thierry Desjardins, *Le Martyre du Liban* (Paris: Plon, 1976), p. 14. [François-Auguste-Rene de Chateaubriand (1768–1848), French author; Gérard de Nerval (1808–1855), French poet.]

civilization and culture. Orientalism expresses and represents that part culturally and even ideologically as a mode of discourse with supporting institutions, vocabulary, scholarship, imagery, doctrines, even colonial bureaucracies and colonial styles. In contrast, the American understanding of the Orient will seem considerably less dense, although our recent Japanese, Korean, and Indochinese adventures ought now to be creating a more sober, more realistic "Oriental" awareness. Moreover, the vastly expanded American political and economic role in the Near East (the Middle East) makes great claims on our understanding of that Orient.

It will be clear to the reader (and will become clearer still throughout the many pages that follow) that by Orientalism I mean several things, all of them, in my opinion, interdependent. The most readily accepted designation for Orientalism is an academic one, and indeed the label still serves in a number of academic institutions. Anyone who teaches, writes about, or researches the Orient—and this applies whether the person is an anthropologist, sociologist, historian, or philologist—either in its specific or its general aspects, is an Orientalist, and what he or she does is Orientalism. Compared with *Oriental studies* or *area studies*, it is true that the term *Orientalism* is less preferred by specialists today, both because it is too vague and general and because it connotes the high-handed executive attitude of nineteenth-century and early-twentieth-century European colonialism. Nevertheless books are written and congresses held with "the Orient" as their main focus, with the Orientalist in his new or old guise as their main authority. The point is that even if it does not survive as it once did, Orientalism lives on academically through its doctrines and theses about the Orient and the Oriental.

Related to this academic tradition, whose fortunes, transmigrations, specializations, and transmissions are in part the subject of this study, is a more general meaning for Orientalism.

Orientalism is a style of thought based upon an ontological and epistemological distinction made between "the Orient" and (most of the time) "the Occident." Thus a very large mass of writers, among whom are poets, novelists, philosophers, political theorists, economists, and imperial administrators, have accepted the basic distinction between East and West as the starting point for elaborate theories, epics, novels, social descriptions, and political accounts concerning the Orient, its people, customs, "mind," destiny, and so on. *This* Orientalism can accommodate Aeschylus, say, and Victor Hugo, Dante and Karl Marx. A little later in this introduction I shall deal with the methodological problems one encounters in so broadly construed a "field" as this.

The interchange between the academic and the more or less imaginative meanings of Orientalism is a constant one, and since the late eighteenth century there has been a considerable, quite disciplined—perhaps even regulated—traffic between the two. Here I come to the third meaning of Orientalism, which is something more historically and materially defined than either of the other two. Taking the late eighteenth century as a very roughly defined starting point Orientalism can be discussed and analyzed as the corporate institution for dealing with the Orient—dealing with it by making statements about it, authorizing views of it, describing it, by teaching it, settling it, ruling over it: in short, Orientalism as a Western style for dominating, restructuring, and having authority over the Orient. I have found it useful here to employ Michel Foucault's notion of a discourse, as described by him in *The Archaeology of Knowledge* and in *Discipline and Punish*, to identify Orientalism.[①] My contention is that without examining Orientalism as a discourse one cannot

---

① Foucault (*Critical Theory Since Plato*, p. 1260), *The Archaeology of Knowledge* (trans. 1972); *Discipline and Punish* (trans. 1977).

possibly understand the enormously systematic discipline by which European culture was able to manage—and even produce—the Orient politically, sociologically, militarily, ideologically, scientifically, and imaginatively during the post-Enlightenment period. Moreover, so authoritative a position did Orientalism have that I believe no one writing, thinking, or acting on the Orient could do so without taking account of the limitations on thought and action imposed by Orientalism. In brief, because of Orientalism the Orient was not (and is not) a free subject of thought or action. This is not to say that Orientalism unilaterally determines what can be said about the Orient, but that it is the whole network of interests inevitably brought to bear on (and therefore always involved in) any occasion when that peculiar entity "the Orient" is in question. How this happens is what this book tries to demonstrate. It also tries to show that European culture gained in strength and identity by setting itself off against the Orient as a sort of surrogate and even underground self.

Historically and culturally there is a quantitative as well as a qualitative difference between the Franco-British involvement in the Orient and—until the period of American ascendancy after World War II—the involvement of every other European and Atlantic power. To speak of Orientalism therefore is to speak mainly, although not exclusively, of a British and French cultural enterprise, a project whose dimensions take in such disparate realms as the imagination itself, the whole of India and the Levant, the Biblical texts and the Biblical lands, the spice trade, colonial armies and a long tradition of colonial administrators, a formidable scholarly corpus, innumerable Oriental "experts" and "hands," an Oriental professorate, a complex array of "Oriental" ideas (Oriental despotism, Oriental splendor, cruelty, sensuality), many Eastern sects, philosophies, and wisdoms domesticated for local European use—the list can be extended more or less indefinitely. My point is that Orientalism derives from a particular closeness experienced between Britain and France and the Orient, which until the early nineteenth century had really meant only India and the Bible lands. From the beginning of the nineteenth century until the end of World War II France and Britain dominated the Orient and Orientalism; since World War II America has dominated the Orient, and approaches it as France and Britain once did. Out of that closeness, whose dynamic is enormously productive even if it always demonstrates the comparatively greater strength of the Occident (British, French, or American), comes the large body of texts I call Orientalist.

It should be said at once that even with the generous number of books and authors that I examine, there is a much larger number that I simply have had to leave out. My argument, however, depends neither upon an exhaustive catalogue of texts dealing with the Orient nor upon a clearly delimited set of texts, authors, and ideas that together make up the Orientalist canon. I have depended instead upon a different methodological alternative—whose backbone in a sense is the set of historical generalizations I have so far been making in this Introduction—and it is these I want now to discuss in more analytical detail.

II

I have begun with the assumption that the Orient is not an inert fact of nature. It is not merely *there*, just as the Occident itself is not just *there* either. We must take seriously Vico's[①] great observation that men make their own history, that what they can know is what they have made, and extend it to geography: as both geographical and cultural entities—to say nothing of historical entities—such locales,

---

① Vico (*Critical Theory Since Plato*, p. 313).

regions, geographical sectors as "Orient" and "Occident" are man-made. Therefore as much as the West itself, the Orient is an idea that has a history and a tradition of thought, imagery, and vocabulary that have given it reality and presence in and for the West. The two geographical entities thus support and to an extent reflect each other.

Having said that, one must go on to state a number of reasonable qualifications. In the first place, it would be wrong to conclude that the Orient was *essentially* an idea, or a creation with no corresponding reality. When Disraeli said in his novel *Tancred* that the East was a career, he meant that to be interested in the East was something bright young Westerners would find to be an all-consuming passion; he should not be interpreted as saying that the East was *only* a career for Westerners. There were—and are—cultures and nations whose location is in the East, and their lives, histories, and customs have a brute reality obviously greater than anything that could be said about them in the West. About that fact this study of Orientalism has very little to contribute, except to acknowledge it tacitly. But the phenomenon of Orientalism as I study it here deals principally, not with a correspondence between Orientalism and Orient, but with the internal consistency of Orientalism and its ideas about the Orient (the East as career) despite or beyond any correspondence, or lack thereof, with a "real" Orient. My point is that Disraeli's statement about the East refers mainly to that created consistency, that regular constellation of ideas as the pre-eminent thing about the Orient, and not to its mere being, as Wallace Stevens's phrase has it.

A second qualification is that ideas, cultures, and histories cannot seriously be understood or studied without their force, or more precisely their configurations of power, also being studied. To believe that the Orient was created—or, as I call it, "Orientalized"—and to believe that such things happen simply as a necessity of the imagination, is to be disingenuous. The relationship between Occident and Orient is a relationship of power, of domination, of varying degrees of a complex hegemony, and is quite accurately indicated in the title of K. M. Panikkar's classic *Asia* and *Western Dominance*.[①] The Orient was Orientalized not only because it was discovered to be "Oriental" in all those ways considered commonplace by an average nineteenth-century European, but also because it *could be*—that is, submitted to being—*made* Oriental. There is very little consent to be found, for example, in the fact that Flaubert's encounter with an Egyptian courtesan[②] produced a widely influential model of the Oriental woman; she never spoke of herself, she never represented her emotions, presence, or history. *He* spoke for and represented her. He was foreign, comparatively wealthy, male, and these were historical facts of domination that allowed him not only to possess Kuchuk Hanem physically but to speak for her and tell his readers in what way she was "typically Oriental." My argument is that Flaubert's situation of strength in relation to Kuchuk Hanem was not an isolated instance. It fairly stands for the pattern of relative strength between East and West, and the discourse about the Orient that it enabled.

This brings us to a third qualification. One ought never to assume that the structure of Orientalism is nothing more than a structure of lies or of myths which, were the truth about them to be told, would simply blow away. I myself believe that Orientalism is more particularly valuable as a sign of European-Atlantic power over the Orient than it is as a veridic discourse about the Orient (which is what, in its academic or scholarly form, it claims to be). Nevertheless, what we must respect and try to grasp is the sheer knitted-together strength

---

① [Said] K. M. Panikkar, *Asia and Western Dominance* (London: George Allen & Unwin, 1959).

② The source for this incident is Gustave Flaubert (1821–1880), *Flaubert in Egypt:*A *Sensibility on Tour;* A *Narrative Drawn from Gustave Flaubert's Travel Notes and Letters,* translated from French and edited by Francis Steegmuller (1972).

of Orientalist discourse, its very close ties to the enabling socio-economic and political institutions, and its redoubtable durability. After all, any system of ideas that can remain unchanged as teachable wisdom (in academies, books, congresses, universities, foreign-service institutes) from the period of Ernest Renan① in the late 1840s until the present in the United States must be something more formidable than a mere collection of lies. Orientalism, therefore, is not an airy European fantasy about the Orient, but a created body of theory and practice in which, for many generations, there has been a considerable material investment. Continued investment made Orientalism, as a system of knowledge about the Orient, an accepted grid for filtering through the Orient into Western consciousness, just as that same investment multiplied—indeed, made truly productive—the statements proliferating out from Orientalism into the general culture.

Gramsci has made the useful analytic distinction between civil and political society in which the former is made up of voluntary (or at least rational and noncoercive) affiliations like schools, families, and unions, the latter of state institutions (the army, the police, the central bureaucracy) whose role in the polity is direct domination. Culture, of course, is to be found operating within civil society, where the influence of ideas, of institutions, and of other persons works not through domination but by what Gramsci calls consent. In any society not totalitarian, then, certain cultural forms predominate over others, just as certain ideas are more influential than others; the form of this cultural leadership is what Gramsci has identified as *hegemony*, an indispensable concept for any understanding of cultural life in the industrial West.② It is hegemony, or rather the

---

① Ernest Renan (1823–1892), French writer, best known for his popular *Life of Jesus* (trans. 1927).

② Gramsci (*Critical Theory Since Plato*, p. 936).

result of cultural hegemony at work, that gives Orientalism the durability and the strength I have been speaking about so far. Orientalism is never far from what Denys Hay has called the idea of Europe,[①] a collective notion identifying "us" Europeans as against all "those" non-Europeans, and indeed it can be argued that the major component in European culture is precisely what made that culture hegemonic both in and outside Europe: the idea of European identity as a superior one in comparison with all the non-European peoples and cultures. There is in addition the hegemony of European ideas about the Orient, themselves reiterating European superiority over Oriental backwardness, usually overriding the possibility that a more independent, or more skeptical, thinker might have had different views on the matter.

In a quite constant way, Orientalism depends for its strategy on this flexible positional superiority, which puts the Westerner in a whole series of possible relationships with the Orient without ever losing him the relative upper hand. And why should it have been otherwise, especially during the period of extraordinary European ascendancy from the late Renaissance to the present? The scientist, the scholar, the missionary, the trader, or the soldier was in, or thought about, the Orient because he could be there, or could think about it, with very little resistance on the Orient's part. Under the general heading of knowledge of the Orient, and within the umbrella of Western hegemony over the Orient during the period from the end of the eighteenth century, there emerged a complex Orient suitable for study in the academy, for display in the museum, for reconstruction in the colonial office, for theoretical illustration in anthropological, biological, linguistic, racial, and historical theses about mankind and

---

① [Said] Denys Hay, *Europe: The Emergence of an Idea,* 2nd ed. (Edinburgh: Edinburgh University Press, 1968).

the universe, for instances of economic and sociological theories of development, revolution, cultural personality, national or religious character. Additionally, the imaginative examination of things Oriental was based more or less exclusively upon a sovereign Western consciousness out of whose unchallenged centrality an Oriental world emerged, first according to general ideas about who or what was an Oriental, then according to a detailed logic governed not simply by empirical reality but by a battery of desires, repressions, investments, and projections. If we can point to great Orientalist works of genuine scholarship like Silvestre de Sacy's *Chrestomathie arabe* or Edward William Lane's *Account of the Manners and Customs of the Modern Egyptians*,① we need also to note that Renan's and Gobineau's② racial ideas came out of the same impulse, as did a great many Victorian pornographic novels (see the analysis by Steven Marcus of "The Lustful Turk").③

And yet, one must repeatedly ask oneself whether what matters in Orientalism is the general group of ideas overriding the mass of material—about which who could deny that they were shot through with doctrines of European superiority, various kinds of racism, imperialism, and the like, dogmatic views of "the Oriental" as a kind of ideal and unchanging abstraction?—or the much more varied work produced by almost uncountable individual writers, whom one would

---

① Baron Silvestre de Sacy (1758–1838), French scholar of Arabic and Semitic languages, author of *Chrestomathie arabe* (in three volumes, 1806*); Grammaire arabe* (in two volumes, 1810). Edward William Lane (1801–1876), *Account of the Manners and Customs of the Modern Egyptians* (1833, trans. 1936).

② Joseph Arthur Comte de Gobineau (1816–1882), French novelist and essayist; focused frequently on Asiatic subjects.

③ [Said] Steven Marcus, *The Other Victorians: A Study of Sexuality and Pornography in Mid-Nineteenth-Century England* (1966; reprint ed., New York: Bantam Books, 1967), pp. 200-219.

take up as individual instances of authors dealing with the Orient. In a sense the two alternatives, general and particular, are really two perspectives on the same material: in both instances one would have to deal with pioneers in the field like William Jones,① with great artists like Nerval or Flaubert. And why would it not be possible to employ both perspectives together, or one after the other? Isn't there an obvious danger of distortion (of precisely the kind that academic Orientalism has always been prone to) if either too general or too specific a level of description is maintained systematically?

My two fears are distortion and inaccuracy, or rather the kind of inaccuracy produced by too dogmatic a generality and too positivistic a localized focus. In trying to deal with these problems I have tried to deal with three main aspects of my own contemporary reality that seem to me to point the way out of the methodological or perspectival difficulties I have been discussing, difficulties that might force one, in the first instance, into writing a coarse polemic on so unacceptably general a level of description as not to be worth the effort, or in the second instance, into writing so detailed and atomistic a series of analyses as to lose all track of the general lines of force informing the field, giving it its special cogency. How then to recognize individuality and to reconcile it with its intelligent, and by no means passive or merely dictatorial, general and hegemonic context?

III

I mentioned three aspects of my contemporary reality: I must explain and briefly discuss them now, so that it can be seen how I was led to a particular course of research and writing.

---

① Sir William Jones (1746–1794), English writer, traveler, and linguist; author of *Persian Grammar* (1771), among other works.

1. *The distinction between pure and political knowledge.* It is very easy to argue that knowledge about Shakespeare or Wordsworth is not political whereas knowledge about contemporary China or the Soviet Union is. My own formal and professional designation is that of "humanist," a title which indicates the humanities as my field and therefore the unlikely eventuality that there might be anything political about what I do in that field. Of course, all these labels and terms are quite unnuanced as I use them here, but the general truth of what I am pointing to is, I think, widely held. One reason for saying that a humanist who writes about Wordsworth, or an editor whose specialty is Keats, is not involved in anything political is that what he does seems to have no direct political effect upon reality in the everyday sense. A scholar whose field is Soviet economics works in a highly charged area where there is much government interest, and what he might produce in the way of studies or proposals will be taken up by policymakers, government officials, institutional economists, intelligence experts. The distinction between "humanists" and persons whose work has policy implications, or political significance, can be broadened further by saying that the former's ideological color is a matter of incidental importance to politics (although possibly of great moment to his colleagues in the field, who may object to his Stalinism or fascism or too easy liberalism), whereas the ideology of the latter is woven directly into his material—indeed, economics, politics, and sociology in the modern academy are ideological sciences—and therefore taken for granted as being "political."

Nevertheless the determining impingement on most knowledge produced in the contemporary West (and here I speak mainly about the United States) is that it be nonpolitical, that is, scholarly, academic, impartial, above partisan or small-minded doctrinal belief. One can have no quarrel with such an ambition in theory, perhaps, but in practice the reality is much more problematic. No one has ever devised a method for detaching the scholar from the circumstances of life, from the fact of his involvement (conscious or unconscious) with a class, a set of beliefs, a social position, or from the mere activity of being a member of a society. These continue to bear on what he does professionally, even though naturally enough his research and its fruits do attempt to reach a level of relative freedom from the inhibitions and the restrictions of brute, everyday reality. For there is such a thing as knowledge that is less, rather than more, partial than the individual (with his entangling and distracting life circumstances) who produces it. Yet this knowledge is not therefore automatically nonpolitical.

Whether discussions of literature or of classical philology are fraught with—or have unmediated—political significance is a very large question that I have tried to treat in some detail elsewhere.[①] What I am interested in doing now is suggesting how the general liberal consensus that "true" knowledge is fundamentally nonpolitical (and conversely, that overtly political knowledge is not "true" knowledge) obscures the highly if obscurely organized political circumstances obtaining when knowledge is produced. No one is helped in understanding this today when the adjective "political" is used as a label to discredit any work for daring to violate the protocol of pretended suprapolitical objectivity. We may say, first, that civil society recognizes a gradation of political importance in the various fields of knowledge. To some extent the political importance given a field comes from the possibility of its direct translation into economic terms; but to a greater extent political importance comes from the closeness of a field to ascertainable sources of power in political

① [Said] See my *Criticism Between Culture and System* (Cambridge, Mass.: Harvard University Press, 1983).

society. Thus an economic study of long-term Soviet energy potential and its effect on military capability is likely to be commissioned by the Defense Department, and thereafter to acquire a kind of political status impossible for a study of Tolstoi's[①] early fiction financed in part by a foundation. Yet both works belong in what civil society acknowledges to be a similar field, Russian studies, even though one work may be done by a very conservative economist, the other by a radical literary historian. My point here is that "Russia" as a general subject matter has political priority over nicer distinctions such as "economics" and "literary history," because political society in Gramsci's sense reaches into such realms of civil society as the academy and saturates them with significance of direct concern to it.

I do not want to press all this any further on general theoretical grounds: it seems to me that the value and credibility of my case can be demonstrated by being much more specific, in the way, for example, Noam Chomsky has studied the instrumental connection between the Vietnam War and the notion of objective scholarship as it was applied to cover state-sponsored military research.[②] Now because Britain, France, and recently the United States are imperial powers, their political societies impart to their civil societies a sense of urgency, a direct political infusion as it were, where and whenever matters pertaining to their imperial interests abroad are concerned. I doubt that it is controversial, for example, to say that an Englishman in India or Egypt in the later nineteenth century took an interest in those countries that was never far from their status in his mind as British colonies. To say this may seem quite different from saying that

---

① Tolstoy (*Critical Theory Since Plato*, p. 757).

② [Said] Principally in his *American Power and the New Mandarins: Historical and Political Essays* (New York: Pantheon Books, 1969) and *For Reasons of State* (New York: Pantheon Books, 1973). [Chomsky (*Critical Theory Since Plato*, p. 1166).]

all academic knowledge about India and Egypt is somehow tinged and impressed with, violated by, the gross political fact—and yet *that is what I am saying* in this study of Orientalism. For if it is true that no production of knowledge in the human sciences can ever ignore or disclaim its author's involvement as a human subject in his own circumstances, then it must also be true that for a European or American studying the Orient there can be no disclaiming the main circumstances of *his* actuality: that he comes up against the Orient as a European or American first, as an individual second. And to be a European or an American in such a situation is by no means an inert fact. It meant and means being aware, however dimly, that one belongs to a power with definite interests in the Orient, and more important, that one belongs to a part of the earth with a definite history of involvement in the Orient almost since the time of Homer.

Put in this way, these political actualities are still too undefined and general to be really interesting. Anyone would agree to them without necessarily agreeing also that they mattered very much, for instance, to Flaubert as he wrote *Salammbô*, or to H. A. R. Gibb as he wrote *Modern Trends in Islam*.[①] The trouble is that there is too great a distance between the big dominating fact, as I have described it, and the details of everyday life that govern the minute discipline of a novel or a scholarly text as each is being written. Yet if we eliminate from the start any notion that "big" facts like imperial domination can be applied mechanically and deterministically to such complex matters as culture and ideas, then we will begin to approach an interesting kind of study. My idea is that European and then American interest in the Orient was political according to some of the obvious historical

---

① Gustave Flaubert (1821–1880), French novelist; H[amilton] A. R. Gibb (1895–1971), British Arabic and Islamic scholar. *Modern Trends in Islam* was published in 1947.

accounts of it that I have given here, but that it was the culture that created that interest, that acted dynamically along with brute political, economic, and military rationales to make the Orient the varied and complicated place that it obviously was in the field I call Orientalism.

Therefore, Orientalism is not a mere political subject matter or field that is reflected passively by culture, scholarship, or institutions; nor is it a large and diffuse collection of texts about the Orient; nor is it representative and expressive of some nefarious "Western" imperialist plot to hold down the "Oriental" world. It is rather a *distribution* of geopolitical awareness into aesthetic, scholarly, economic, sociological, historical, and philological texts; it is an elaboration not only of a basic geographical distinction (the world is made up of two unequal halves, Orient and Occident) but also of a whole series of "interests" which, by such means as scholarly discovery, philological reconstruction, psychological analysis, landscape and sociological description, it not only creates but also maintains; it is, rather than expresses, a certain *will* or *intention* to understand, in some cases to control, manipulate, even to incorporate, what is a manifestly different (or alternative and novel) world; it is, above all, a discourse that is by no means in direct, corresponding relationship with political power in the raw, but rather is produced and exists in an uneven exchange with various kinds of power, shaped to a degree by the exchange with power political (as with a colonial or imperial establishment), power intellectual (as with reigning sciences like comparative linguistics or anatomy, or any of the modern policy sciences), power cultural (as with orthodoxies and canons of taste, texts, values), power moral (as with ideas about what "we" do and what "they" cannot do or understand as "we" do). Indeed, my real argument is that Orientalism is—and does not simply represent—a considerable dimension of modern political-intellectual culture, and as such has less to do with the Orient than it does with "our" world.

Because Orientalism is a cultural and a political fact, then, it does not exist in some archival vacuum; quite the contrary, I think it can be shown that what is thought, said, or even done about the Orient follows (perhaps occurs within) certain distinct and intellectually knowable lines. Here too a considerable degree of nuance and elaboration can be seen working as between the broad superstructural pressures and the details of composition, the facts of textuality. Most humanistic scholars are, I think, perfectly happy with the notion that texts exist in contexts, that there is such a thing as intertextuality, that the pressures of conventions, predecessors, and rhetorical styles limit what Walter Benjamin once called the "overtaxing of the productive person in the name of ... the principle of 'creativity,' " in which the poet is believed on his own, and out of his pure mind, to have brought forth his work.[①] Yet there is a reluctance to allow that political, institutional, and ideological constraints act in the same manner on the individual author. A humanist will believe it to be an interesting fact to any interpreter of Balzac that he was influenced in the *Comédie humaine* by the conflict between Geoffroy Saint-Hilaire and Cuvier,[②] but the same sort of pressure on Balzac of deeply reactionary monarchism is felt in some vague way to demean his literary "genius" and therefore to be less worth serious study. Similarly—as Harry Bracken has been tirelessly showing—philosophers will conduct their discussions of Locke, Hume, and empiricism without ever taking into

---

① [Said] Walter Benjamin (1892–1940), *Charles Baudelaire: A Lyric Poet in the Era of High Capitalism,* trans. Harry Zohn (London: New Left Books, 1973), p. 71.

② [Said] Honoré de Balzac (1799–1850), French novelist, author of the *Comédie humaine;* Étienne Geoffroy Saint-Hilaire (1772–1844), French naturalist, noted for studies of animal development, in some ways anticipating theories of organic evolution; Georges Cuvier (1769–1832), French zoologist and anatomist, whose views of anatomy diverged sharply from Saint-Hilaire's over the question of whether or not animal kinds were immutable.

account that there is an explicit connection in these classic writers between their "philosophic" doctrines and racial theory, justifications of slavery, or arguments for colonial exploitation.① These are common enough ways by which contemporary scholarship keeps itself pure.

Perhaps it is true that most attempts to rub culture's nose in the mud of politics have been crudely iconoclastic; perhaps also the social interpretation of literature in my own field has simply not kept up with the enormous technical advances in detailed textual analysis. But there is no getting away from the fact that literary studies in general, and American Marxist theorists in particular, have avoided the effort of seriously bridging the gap between the superstructural and the base levels in textual, historical scholarship; on another occasion I have gone so far as to say that the literary-cultural establishment as a whole has declared the serious study of imperialism and culture off limits.② For Orientalism brings one up directly against that question—that is, to realizing that political imperialism governs an entire field of study, imagination, and scholarly institutions—in such a way as to make its avoidance an intellectual and historical impossibility, yet there will always remain the perennial escape mechanism of saying that a literary scholar and a philosopher, for example, are trained in literature and philosophy respectively, not in politics or ideological analysis. In other words, the specialist argument can work quite effectively to block the larger and, in my opinion, the more intellectually serious perspective.

Here it seems to me there is a simple two-part answer to be given, at least so far as the study of imperialism and culture (or

① [Said] Harry Bracken, "Essence, Accident and Race," *Hermathena 116* (Winter 1973): 81-96. [Locke (*Critical Theory Since Plato*, p. 281); Hume (*Critical Theory Since Plato*, p. 322).]

② [Said] In an interview published in *Diacritics* 6, no. 3 (Fall 1976): 38.

Orientalism) is concerned. In the first place nearly every nineteenth-century writer (and the same is true enough of writers in earlier periods) was extraordinarily well aware of the fact of empire: this is a subject not very well studied, but it will not take a modern Victorian specialist long to admit that liberal cultural heroes like John Stuart Mill, Arnold, Carlyle, Newman, Macaulay, Ruskin, George Eliot, and even Dickens had definite views on race and imperialism, which are quite easily to be found at work in their writing. So even a specialist must deal with the knowledge that Mill, for example, made it clear in *On Liberty* and *Representative Government* that his views there could not be applied to India (he was an India Office functionary for a good deal of his life, after all) because the Indians were civilizationally, if not racially, inferior. The same kind of paradox is to be found in Marx, as I try to show in this book. In the second place, to believe that politics in the form of imperialism bears upon the production of literature, scholarship, social theory, and history writing is by no means equivalent to saying that culture is therefore a demeaned or denigrated thing. Quite the contrary: my whole point is to say that we can better understand the persistence and the durability of saturating hegemonic systems like culture when we realize that their internal constraints upon writers and thinkers were *productive*, not unilaterally inhibiting. It is this idea that Gramsci, certainly, and Foucault and Raymond Williams in their very different ways have been trying to illustrate. Even one or two pages by Williams on "the uses of the Empire" in *The Long Revolution* tell us more about nineteenth-century cultural richness than many volumes of hermetic textual analyses.[①]

Therefore I study Orientalism as a dynamic exchange between

① [Said] Raymond Williams (*Critical Theory Since Plato*, p. 1356), *The Long Revolution* (London: Chatto & Windus, 1961), pp. 66-67.

individual authors and the large political concerns shaped by the three great empires—British, French, American—in whose intellectual and imaginative territory the writing was produced. What interests me most as a scholar is not the gross political verity but the detail, as indeed what interests us in someone like Lane or Flaubert or Renan is not the (to him) indisputable truth that Occidentals are superior to Orientals, but the profoundly worked over and modulated evidence of his detailed work within the very wide space opened up by that truth. One need only remember that Lane's *Manners and Customs of the Modern Egyptians* is a classic of historical and anthropological observation because of its style, its enormously intelligent and brilliant details, not because of its simple reflection of racial superiority, to understand what I am saying here.

The kind of political questions raised by Orientalism, then, are as follows: What other sorts of intellectual, aesthetic, scholarly, and cultural energies went into the making of an imperialist tradition like the Orientalist one? How did philology, lexicography, history, biology, political and economic theory, novel-writing, and lyric poetry come to the service of Orientalism's broadly imperialist view of the world? What changes, modulations, refinements, even revolutions take place within Orientalism? What is the meaning of originality, of continuity, of individuality, in this context? How does Orientalism transmit or reproduce itself from one epoch to another? In fine, how can we treat the cultural, historical phenomenon of Orientalism as a kind of *willed human work*—not of mere unconditioned ratiocination—in all its historical complexity, detail, and worth without at the same time losing sight of the alliance between cultural work, political tendencies, the state, and the specific realities of domination? Governed by such concerns a humanistic study can responsibly address itself to politics and culture. But this is not to say that such a study establishes a hard-and-fast rule about the relationship between knowledge and politics.

My argument is that each humanistic investigation must formulate the nature of that connection in the specific context of the study, the subject matter, and its historical circumstances.

2. *The methodological question*. In a previous book I gave a good deal of thought and analysis to the methodological importance for work in the human sciences of finding and formulating a first step, a point of departure, a beginning principle.① A major lesson I learned and tried to present was that there is no such thing as a merely given, or simply available, starting point: beginnings have to be made for each project in such a way as to *enable* what follows from them. Nowhere in my experience has the difficulty of this lesson been more consciously lived (with what success—or failure—I cannot really say) than in this study of Orientalism. The idea of beginning, indeed the act of beginning, necessarily involves an act of delimitation by which something is cut out of a great mass of material, separated from the mass, and made to stand for, as well as be, a starting point, a beginning; for the student of texts one such notion of inaugural delimitation is Louis Althusser's idea of the *problematic*, a specific determinate unity of a text, or group of texts, which is something given rise to by analysis.② Yet in the case of Orientalism (as opposed to the case of Marx's texts, which is what Althusser studies) there is not simply the problem of finding a point of departure, or problematic, but also the question of designating which texts, authors, and periods are the ones best suited for study.

It has seemed to me foolish to attempt an encyclopedic narrative history of Orientalism, first of all because if my guiding principle was to be "the European idea of the Orient" there would be virtually no

① [Said] In my *Beginnings: Intention and Method* (New York: Basic Books, 1975).

② [Said] Louis Althusser (*Critical Theory Since Plato*, p. 1297), *For Marx*, trans. Ben Brewster (New York: Pantheon Books, 1969), pp. 65-67.

limit to the material I would have had to deal with; second, because the narrative model itself did not suit my descriptive and political interests; third, because in such books as Raymond Schwab's *La Renaissance orientale*, Johann Fück's *Die Arabischen Studien in Europa bis in den Anfang des 20. Jahrhunderts*, and more recently, Dorothee Metlitzki's *The Matter of Araby in Medieval England*① there already exist encyclopedic works on certain aspects of the European-Oriental encounter such as make the critic's job, in the general political and intellectual context I sketched above, a different one.

There still remained the problem of cutting down a very fat archive to manageable dimensions, and more important, outlining something in the nature of an intellectual order within that group of texts without at the same time following a mindlessly chronological order. My starting point therefore has been the British, French, and American experience of the Orient taken as a unit, what made that experience possible by way of historical and intellectual background, what the quality and character of the experience has been. For reasons I shall discuss presently I limited that already limited (but still inordinately large) set of questions to the Anglo-French-American experience of the Arabs and Islam, which for almost a thousand years together stood for the Orient. Immediately upon doing that, a large part of the Orient seemed to have been eliminated—India, Japan, China, and other sections of the Far East—not because these regions were not important (they obviously have been) but because one could discuss Europe's experience of the Near Orient, or of Islam, apart from its experience of the Far Orient. Yet at certain moments of that

① [Said] Raymond Schwab, *La Renaissance orientale* (Paris: Payot, 1950); Johann W. Fück, *Die Arabischen Studien in Europa bis in den Anfang des 20. Jahrhunderts* (Leipzig: Otto Harrassowitz, 1955); Dorothee Metlitzki, *The Matter of Araby in Medieval England* (New Haven, Conn.: Yale University Press, 1977).

general European history of interest in the East, particular parts of the Orient like Egypt, Syria, and Arabia cannot be discussed without also studying Europe's involvement in the more distant parts, of which Persia and India are the most important; a notable case in point is the connection between Egypt and India so far as eighteenth-and nineteenth-century Britain was concerned. Similarly the French role in deciphering the Zend-Avesta, the pre-eminence of Paris as a center of Sanskrit studies during the first decade of the nineteenth century, the fact that Napoleon's interest in the Orient was contingent upon his sense of the British role in India: all these Far Eastern interests directly influenced French interest in the Near East, Islam, and the Arabs.

Britain and France dominated the Eastern Mediterranean from about the end of the seventeenth century on. Yet my discussion of that domination and systematic interest does not do justice to (a) the important contributions to Orientalism of Germany, Italy, Russia, Spain, and Portugal and (b) the fact that one of the important impulses toward the study of the Orient in the eighteenth century was the revolution in Biblical studies stimulated by such variously interesting pioneers as Bishop Lowth, Eichhorn, Herder, and Michaelis.[①] In the first place, I had to focus rigorously upon the British-French and later the American material because it seemed inescapably true not only that Britain and France were the pioneer nations in the Orient and in Oriental studies, but that these vanguard positions were held by virtue of the two greatest colonial networks in pre-twentieth-century history; the American Oriental position since World War II has fit—I think, quite self-consciously—in the places excavated by the two

---

① Robert Lowth (1710–1787), English churchman, author of *The Sacred Poetry of the Hebrews;* Johann Gottfried Eichhorn (1752–1827), German Biblical scholar; Johann Gottfried Herder (1744–1803), German philosopher and theologian; Johann David Michaelis (1717–1791), German orientalist.

earlier European powers. Then too, I believe that the sheer quality, consistency, and mass of British, French, and American writing on the Orient lifts it above the doubtless crucial work done in Germany, Italy, Russia, and elsewhere. But I think it is also true that the major steps in Oriental scholarship were first taken in either Britain and France, then elaborated upon by Germans. Silvestre de Sacy, for example, was not only the first modern and institutional European Orientalist, who worked on Islam, Arabic literature, the Druze religion, and Sassanid Persia; he was also the teacher of Champollion and of Franz Bopp, the founder of German comparative linguistics. A similar claim of priority and subsequent pre-eminence can be made for William Jones and Edward William Lane.

In the second place—and here the failings of my study of Orientalism are amply made up for—there has been some important recent work on the background in Biblical scholarship to the rise of what I have called modern Orientalism. The best and the most illuminatingly relevant is E. S. Shaffer's impressive "*Kubla Khan*" and *The Fall of Jerusalem*,① an indispensable study of the origins of Romanticism, and of the intellectual activity underpinning a great deal of what goes on in Coleridge, Browning, and George Eliot. To some degree Shaffer's work refines upon the outlines provided in Schwab, by articulating the material of relevance to be found in the German Biblical scholars and using that material to read, in an intelligent and always interesting way, the work of three major British writers. Yet what is missing in the book is some sense of the political as well as ideological edge given the Oriental material by the British and French writers I am principally concerned with; in addition, unlike Shaffer

① [Said] E. S. Shaffer, "*Kubla Khan*" *and The Fall of Jerusalem: The Mythological School in Biblical Criticism and Secular Literature, 1770–1880* (Cambridge: Cambridge University Press, 1975).

I attempt to elucidate subsequent developments in academic as well as literary Orientalism that bear on the connection between British and French Orientalism on the one hand and the rise of an explicitly colonial-minded imperialism on the other. Then too, I wish to show how all these earlier matters are reproduced more or less in American Orientalism after the Second World War.

Nevertheless there is a possibly misleading aspect to my study, where, aside from an occasional reference, I do not exhaustively discuss the German developments after the inaugural period dominated by Sacy. Any work that seeks to provide an understanding of academic Orientalism and pays little attention to scholars like Steinthal, Müller, Becker, Goldziher, Brockelmann, Nöldeke[①]—to mention only a handful—needs to be reproached, and I freely reproach myself. I particularly regret not taking more account of the great scientific prestige that accrued to German scholarship by the middle of the nineteenth century, whose neglect was made into a denunciation of insular British scholars by George Eliot. I have in mind Eliot's unforgettable portrait of Mr. Casaubon in *Middlemarch*. One reason Casaubon cannot finish his Key to All Mythologies is, according to his young cousin Will Ladislaw, that he is unacquainted with German scholarship. For not only has Casaubon chosen a subject "as changing as chemistry: new discoveries are constantly making new points of view": he is undertaking a job similar to a refutation of

---

① Hegmann Steinthal (1823–1899), German philologist; Friedrick Max Müller (1823–1900), German orientalist; Wilhelm Adolph Becker (1796–1846), German classical archeologist; Ignás Goldziher (1850–1921), Hungarian scholar; Carl Brackelmann (1868–1956), German philologist; Theodor Nöldeke (1836–1930), German orientalist.

Paracelsus because "he is not an Orientalist, you know."①

Eliot was not wrong in implying that by about 1830, which is when *Middlemarch* is set, German scholarship had fully attained its European pre-eminence. Yet at no time in German scholarship during the first two-thirds of the nineteenth century could a close partnership have developed between Orientalists and a protracted, sustained *national* interest in the Orient. There was nothing in Germany to correspond to the Anglo-French presence in India, the Levant, North Africa. Moreover, the German Orient was almost exclusively a scholarly, or at least a classical, Orient: it was made the subject of lyrics, fantasies, and even novels, but it was never actual, the way Egypt and Syria were actual for Chateaubriand, Lane, Lamartine, Burton, Disraeli, or Nerval.② There is some significance in the fact that the two most renowned German works on the Orient, Goethe's *Westöstlicher Diwan* and Friedrich Schlegel's *Über die Sprache und Weisheit der Indier*, were based respectively on a Rhine journey and on hours spent in Paris libraries. What German Oriental scholarship did was to refine and elaborate techniques whose application was to texts, myths, ideas, and languages almost literally gathered from the Orient by imperial Britain and France.

Yet what German Orientalism had in common with Anglo-French and later American Orientalism was a kind of intellectual *authority* over the Orient within Western culture. This authority must in large part be the subject of any description of Orientalism, and it is so in this study. Even the name *Orientalism* suggests a serious, perhaps

---

① [Said] George Eliot, *Middlemarch: A Study of Provincial Life* (1872; reprint ed., Boston: Houghton Mifflin Co., 1956), p.164. [Paracelsus (Theophrastus von Hohenheim, 1493–1541), Swiss alchemist and physician.]

② Edward William Lane (1801–1876), English orientalist; Alphonse de Lamartine (1790–1869), French poet; Richard Francis Burton (1821–1890), English orientalist; Benjamin Disraeli (1804–1881), British statesman and novelist.

ponderous style of expertise; when I apply it to modern American social scientists (since they do not call themselves Orientalists, my use of the word is anomalous), it is to draw attention to the way Middle East experts can still draw on the vestiges of Orientalism's intellectual position in nineteenth-century Europe.

There is nothing mysterious or natural about authority. It is formed, irradiated, disseminated; it is instrumental, it is persuasive; it has status, it establishes canons of taste and value; it is virtually indistinguishable from certain ideas it dignifies as true, and from traditions, perceptions, and judgments it forms, transmits, reproduces. Above all, authority can, indeed must, be analyzed. All these attributes of authority apply to Orientalism, and much of what I do in this study is to describe both the historical authority in and the personal authorities of Orientalism.

My principal methodological devices for studying authority here are what can he called *strategic location*, which is a way of describing the author's position in a text with regard to the Oriental material he writes about, and *strategic formation*, which is a way of analyzing the relationship between texts and the way in which groups of texts, types of texts, even textual genres, acquire mass, density, and referential power among themselves and thereafter in the culture at large. I use the notion of strategy simply to identify the problem every writer on the Orient has faced: how to get hold of it, how to approach it, how not to be defeated or overwhelmed by its sublimity, its scope, its awful dimensions. Everyone who writes about the Orient must locate himself vis-à-vis the Orient; translated into his text, this location includes the kind of narrative voice he adopts, the type of structure he builds, the kinds of images, themes, motifs that circulate in his text—all of which add up to deliberate ways of addressing the reader, containing the Orient, and finally, representing it or speaking in its behalf. None of this takes place in the abstract, however. Every writer on the Orient (and this is true even of Homer) assumes some Oriental precedent, some previous knowledge of the Orient, to which he refers and on which he relies. Additionally, each work on the Orient affiliates itself with other works, with audiences, with institutions, with the Orient itself. The ensemble of relationships between works, audiences, and some particular aspects of the Orient therefore constitutes an analyzable formation—for example, that of philological studies, of anthologies of extracts from Oriental literature, of travel books, of Oriental fantasies—whose presence in time, in discourse, in institutions (schools, libraries, foreign services) gives it strength and authority.

It is clear, I hope, that my concern with authority does not entail analysis of what lies hidden in the Orientalist text, but analysis rather of the text's surface, its exteriority to what it describes. I do not think that this idea can be overemphasized. Orientalism is premised upon exteriority, that is, on the fact that the Orientalist, poet or scholar, makes the Orient speak, describes the Orient, renders its mysteries plain for and to the West. He is never concerned with the Orient except as the first cause of what he says. What he says and writes, by virtue of the fact that it is said or written, is meant to indicate that the Orientalist is outside the Orient, both as an existential and as a moral fact. The principal product of this exteriority is of course representation: as early as Aeschylus's play *The Persians* the Orient is transformed from a very far distant and often threatening Otherness into figures that are relatively familiar (in Aeschylus's case, grieving Asiatic women). The dramatic immediacy of representation in *The Persians* obscures the fact that the audience is watching a highly artificial enactment of what a non-Oriental has made into a symbol for the whole Orient. My analysis of the Orientalist text therefore places emphasis on the evidence, which is by no means invisible, for such representations *as representations*, not as "natural" depictions of the Orient. This evidence is found just as prominently in the so-called truthful text (histories, philological analyses, political treatises) as in the avowedly artistic (i.e., openly imaginative) text. The things to look at are style, figures of speech, setting, narrative devices, historical and social circumstances, *not* the correctness of the representation nor its fidelity to some great original. The exteriority of the representation is always governed by some version of the truism that if the Orient could represent itself, it would; since it cannot, the representation does the job, for the West, and *faute de mieux*, for the poor Orient. "Sie können sich nicht vertreten, sie müssen vertreten werden,"[①] as Marx wrote in *The Eighteenth Brumaire of Louis Bonaparte*.

Another reason for insisting upon exteriority is that I believe it needs to be made clear about cultural discourse and exchange within a culture that what is commonly circulated by it is not "truth" but representations. It hardly needs to be demonstrated again that language itself is a highly organized and encoded system, which employs many devices to express, indicate, exchange messages and information, represent, and so forth. In any instance of at least written language, there is no such thing as a delivered presence, but a re-presence, or a representation. The value, efficacy, strength, apparent veracity of a written statement about the Orient therefore relies very little, and cannot instrumentally depend, on the Orient as such. On the contrary, the written statement is a presence to the reader by virtue of its having excluded, displaced, made supererogatory any such *real thing* as "the Orient." Thus all of Orientalism stands forth and away from the Orient: that Orientalism makes sense at all depends more on the West than on the Orient, and this sense is directly indebted to various Western techniques of representation that make the Orient visible, clear, "there" in discourse about it. And these representations

① "They cannot represent themselves; they must be represented."

rely upon institutions, traditions, conventions, agreed-upon codes of understanding for their effects, not upon a distant and amorphous Orient.

The difference between representations of the Orient before the last third of the eighteenth century and those after it (that is, those belonging to what I call modern Orientalism) is that the range of representation expanded enormously in the later period. It is true that after William Jones and Anquetil-Duperron,① and after Napoleon's Egyptian expedition, Europe came to know the Orient more scientifically, to live in it with greater authority and discipline than ever before. But what mattered to Europe was the expanded scope and the much greater refinement given its techniques for receiving the Orient. When around the turn of the eighteenth century the Orient definitively revealed the age of its languages—thus outdating Hebrew's divine pedigree—it was a group of Europeans who made the discovery, passed it on to other scholars, and preserved the discovery in the new science of Indo-European philology. A new powerful science for viewing the linguistic Orient was born, and with it, as Foucault has shown in *The Order of Things*, a whole web of related scientific interests. Similarly William Beckford, Byron, Goethe, and Hugo② restructured the Orient by their art and made its colors, lights, and people visible through their images, rhythms, and motifs. At most, the "real" Orient provoked a writer to his vision; it very rarely guided it.

Orientalism responded more to the culture that produced it than to its putative object, which was also produced by the West.

---

① A. H. Anquetil-Duperron (1731–1805), French orientalist.

② Foucault (*Critical Theory Since Plato*, p. 1260); William Beckford (1760–1844), English novelist; George Gordon Lord Byron (1788–1824), English poet; Johann Wolfgang von Goethe (1749–1832), German poet and dramatist; Victor-Marie Hugo (1802–1885), French poet and novelist.

Thus the history of Orientalism has both an internal consistency and a highly articulated set of relationships to the dominant culture surrounding it. My analyses consequently try to show the field's shape and internal organization, its pioneers, patriarchal authorities, canonical texts, doxological ideas, exemplary figures, its followers, elaborators, and new authorities; I try also to explain how Orientalism borrowed and was frequently informed by "strong" ideas, doctrines, and trends ruling the culture. Thus there was (and is) a linguistic Orient, a Freudian Orient, a Spenglerian Orient, a Darwinian Orient, a racist Orient—and so on. Yet never has there been such a thing as a pure, or unconditional, Orient; similarly, never has there been a nonmaterial form of Orientalism, much less something so innocent as an "idea" of the Orient. In this underlying conviction and in its ensuing methodological consequences do I differ from scholars who study the history of ideas. For the emphases and the executive form, above all the material effectiveness, of statements made by Orientalist discourse are possible in ways that any hermetic history of ideas tends completely to scant. Without those emphases and that material effectiveness Orientalism would be just another idea, whereas it is and was much more than that. Therefore I set out to examine not only scholarly works but also works of literature, political tracts, journalistic texts, travel books, religious and philological studies. In other words, my hybrid perspective is broadly historical and "anthropological," given that I believe all texts to be worldly and circumstantial in (of course) ways that vary from genre to genre, and from historical period to historical period.

Yet unlike Michel Foucault, to whose work I am greatly indebted, I do believe in the determining imprint of individual writers upon the otherwise anonymous collective body of texts constituting a discursive formation like Orientalism. The unity of the large ensemble of texts I analyze is due in part to the fact that they frequently refer to each other: Orientalism is after all a system for citing works and authors. Edward William Lane's *Manners and Customs of the Modern Egyptians* was read and cited by such diverse figures as Nerval, Flaubert, and Richard Burton. He was an authority whose use was an imperative for anyone writing or thinking about the Orient, not just about Egypt: when Nerval borrows passages verbatim from *Modern Egyptians* it is to use Lane's authority to assist him in describing village scenes in Syria, not Egypt. Lane's authority and the opportunities provided for citing him discriminately as well as indiscriminately were there because Orientalism could give his text the kind of distributive currency that he acquired. There is no way, however, of understanding Lane's currency without also understanding the peculiar features of his text; this is equally true of Renan, Sacy, Lamartine, Schlegel,① and a group of other influential writers. Foucault believes that in general the individual text or author counts for very little; empirically, in the case of Orientalism (and perhaps nowhere else) I find this not to be so. Accordingly my analyses employ close textual readings whose goal is to reveal the dialectic between individual text or writer and the complex collective formation to which his work is a contribution.

Yet even though it includes an ample selection of writers, this book is still far from a complete history or general account of Orientalism. Of this failing I am very conscious. The fabric of as thick a discourse as Orientalism has survived and functioned in Western society because of its richness: all I have done is to describe parts of that fabric at certain moments, and merely to suggest the existence of a larger whole, detailed, interesting, dotted with fascinating figures, texts, and events. I have consoled myself with believing that this

---

① Joseph Ernest Renan (1823–1892), French philologist and historian; Schlegel (*Critical Theory Since Plato*, p. 473).

book is one installment of several, and hope there are scholars and critics who might want to write others. There is still a general essay to be written on imperialism and culture; other studies would go more deeply into the connection between Orientalism and pedagogy, or into Italian, Dutch, German, and Swiss Orientalism, or into the dynamic between scholarship and imaginative writing, or into the relationship between administrative ideas and intellectual discipline. Perhaps the most important task of all would be to undertake studies in contemporary alternatives to Orientalism, to ask how one can study other cultures and peoples from a libertarian, or a nonrepressive and nonmanipulative, perspective. But then one would have to rethink the whole complex problem of knowledge and power. These are all tasks left embarrassingly incomplete in this study.

The last, perhaps self-flattering, observation on method that I want to make here is that I have written this study with several audiences in mind. For students of literature and criticism, Orientalism offers a marvelous instance of the interrelations between society, history, and textuality; moreover, the cultural role played by the Orient in the West connects Orientalism with ideology, politics, and the logic of power, matters of relevance, I think, to the literary community. For contemporary students of the orient, from university scholars to policymakers, I have written with two ends in mind: one, to present their intellectual genealogy to them in a way that has not been done; two, to criticize—with the hope of stirring discussion—the often unquestioned assumptions on which their work for the most part depends. For the general reader, this study deals with matters that always compel attention, all of them connected not only with Western conceptions and treatments of the Other but also with the singularly important role played by Western culture in what Vico called the world of nations. Lastly, for readers in the so-called Third World, this study proposes itself as a step towards an understanding not so much of Western politics and of the non-Western world in those politics as of the *strength* of Western cultural discourse, a strength too often mistaken as merely decorative or "superstructural." My hope is to illustrate the formidable structure of cultural domination and, specifically for formerly colonized peoples, the dangers and temptations of employing this structure upon themselves or upon others.

The three long chapters and twelve shorter units into which this book is divided are intended to facilitate exposition as much as possible. Chapter One, "The Scope of Orientalism," draws a large circle around all the dimensions of the subject, both in terms of historical time and experiences and in terms of philosophical and political themes. Chapter Two, "Orientalist Structures and Restructures," attempts to trace the development of modern Orientalism by a broadly chronological description, and also by the description of a set of devices common to the work of important poets, artists, and scholars. Chapter Three, "Orientalism Now," begins where its predecessor left off, at around 1870. This is the period of great colonial expansion into the Orient, and it culminates in World War II. The very last section of Chapter Three characterizes the shift from British and French to American hegemony; I attempt there finally to sketch the present intellectual and social realities of Orientalism in the United States.

3. *The personal dimension*. In the *Prison Notebooks* Gramsci says: "The starting-point of critical elaboration is the consciousness of what one really is, and is 'knowing thyself' as a product of the historical process to date, which has deposited in you an infinity of traces, without leaving an inventory." The only available English translation inexplicably leaves Gramsci's comment at that, whereas in fact Gramsci's Italian text concludes by adding, "therefore it is imperative

at the outset to compile such an inventory."[1]

Much of the personal investment in this study derives from my awareness of being an "Oriental" as a child growing up in two British colonies. All of my education, in those colonies (Palestine and Egypt) and in the United States, has been Western, and yet that deep early awareness has persisted. In many ways my study of Orientalism has been an attempt to inventory the traces upon me, the Oriental subject, of the culture whose domination has been so powerful a factor in the life of all Orientals. This is why for me the Islamic Orient has had to be the center of attention. Whether what I have achieved is the inventory prescribed by Gramsci is not for me to judge, although I have felt it important to be conscious of trying to produce one. Along the way, as severely and as rationally as I have been able, I have tried to maintain a critical consciousness, as well as employing those instruments of historical, humanistic, and cultural research of which my education has made me the fortunate beneficiary. In none of that, however, have I ever lost hold of the cultural reality of, the personal involvement in having been constituted as, "an Oriental."

The historical circumstances making such a study possible are fairly complex, and I can only list them schematically here. Anyone resident in the West since the 1950s, particularly in the United States, will have lived through an era of extraordinary turbulence in the relations of East and West. No one will have failed to note how "East" has always signified danger and threat during this period, even as it has meant the traditional Orient as well as Russia. In the universities a growing establishment of area-studies programs and institutes

---

① [Said] Antonio Gramsci (*Critical Theory Since Plato*, p. 936), *The Prison Notebooks: Selections,* trans. and ed. Quintin Hoare and Geoffrey Nowell Smith (New York: International Publishers, 1971), p. 324. The full passage, unavailable in the Hoare and Smith translation, is to be found in Gramsci, *Quaderni del Carcere,* ed. Valentino Gerratana (Turin: Einaudi Editore, 1975), 2: 1363.

has made the scholarly study of the Orient a branch of national policy. Public affairs in this country include a healthy interest in the Orient, as much for its strategic and economic importance as for its traditional exoticism. If the world has become immediately accessible to a Western citizen living in the electronic age, the Orient too has drawn nearer to him, and is now less a myth perhaps than a place crisscrossed by Western, especially American interests.

One aspect of the electronic, postmodern world is that there has been a reinforcement of the stereotypes by which the Orient is viewed. Television, the films, and all the media's resources have forced information into more and more standardized molds. So far as the Orient is concerned, standardization and cultural stereotyping have intensified the hold of the nineteenth-century academic and imaginative demonology of "the mysterious Orient." This is nowhere more true than in the ways by which the Near East is grasped. Three things have contributed to making even the simplest perception of the Arabs and Islam into a highly politicized, almost raucous matter: one, the history of popular anti-Arab and anti-Islamic prejudice in the West, which is immediately reflected in the history of Orientalism; two, the struggle between the Arabs and Israeli Zionism, and its effects upon American Jews as well as upon both the liberal culture and the population at large; three, the almost total absence of any cultural position making it possible either to identify with or dispassionately to discuss the Arabs or Islam. Furthermore, it hardly needs saying that because the Middle East is now so identified with Great Power politics, oil economics, and the simple-minded dichotomy of freedom-loving, democratic Israel and evil, totalitarian, and terroristic Arabs, the chances of anything like a clear view of what one talks about in talking about the Near East are depressingly small.

My own experiences of these matters are in part what made me write this book. The life of an Arab Palestinian in the West, particularly in America, is disheartening. There exists here an almost unanimous consensus that politically he does not exist, and when it is allowed that he does, it is either as a nuisance or as an Oriental. The web of racism, cultural stereotypes, political imperialism, dehumanizing ideology holding in the Arab is very strong indeed, and it is this web which every Palestinian has come to feel as his uniquely punishing destiny. It has made matters worse for him to remark that no person academically involved with the Near East—no Orientalist, that is—has ever in the United States culturally and politically identified himself wholeheartedly with the Arabs; certainly there have been identifications on some level, but they have never taken an "acceptable" form as has liberal American identification with Zionism, and all too frequently they have been radically flawed by their association either with discredited political and economic interests (oil-company and State Department Arabists, for example) or with religion.

The nexus of knowledge and power creating "the Oriental" and in a sense obliterating him as a human being is therefore not for me an exclusively academic matter. Yet it is an *intellectual* matter of some very obvious importance. I have been able to put to use my humanistic and political concerns for the analysis and description of a very worldly matter, the rise, development, and consolidation of Orientalism. Too often literature and culture are presumed to be politically, even historically innocent; it has regularly seemed otherwise to me, and certainly my study of Orientalism has convinced me (and I hope will convince my literary colleagues) that society and literary culture can only be understood and studied together. In addition, and by an almost inescapable logic, I have found myself writing the history of a strange, secret sharer of Western anti-Semitism. That anti-Semitism and, as I have discussed it in its Islamic branch, Orientalism resemble each other very closely is a historical, cultural, and political truth that needs only to be mentioned to an Arab Palestinian for its irony to be perfectly understood. But what I should like also to have contributed here is a better understanding of the way cultural domination has operated. If this stimulates a new kind of dealing with the Orient, indeed if it eliminates the "Orient" and "Occident" altogether, then we shall have advanced a little in the process of what Raymond Williams has called the "unlearning" of "the inherent dominative mode."①

16.3 Key Words

① Palestine 巴勒斯坦

Palestine is a geographic region in Western Asia usually considered to include Israel, the West Bank, the Gaza Strip, and in some definitions, parts of western Jordan. The name was used by ancient Greek writers, and it was later used for the Roman province Syria Palaestina, the Byzantine Palaestina Prima, and the Islamic provincial district of Jund Filastin. Located at the junction of Egypt, Syria, and Arabia, and being the birthplace of Judaism and Christianity, the region has a tumultuous history as a crossroads for religion, culture, commerce, and politics. It has been controlled by numerous peoples, including ancient Egyptians, Canaanites, Israelites and Judeans, Assyrians (亚述), Babylonians (巴比伦), Achaemenids (阿契门尼德，波斯帝国), ancient Greeks, the Jewish Hasmonean Kingdom, Romans, Parthians (帕提亚，安息帝国), Sasanians (萨珊王朝), Byzantines, the Arab Rashidun, Umayyad (倭马亚王朝), Abbasid (阿拔斯王朝) and Fatimid (法蒂玛) caliphates, Crusaders (圣战), Ayyubids (阿尤布王朝), Mamluks (马穆鲁克), Mongols, Ottomans (奥斯曼), the British, and modern Israelis, Jordanians, Egyptians and Palestinians.

---

① [Said] Raymond Williams (*Critical Theory Since Plato*, p. 1356), *Culture and Society, 1780–1950* (London: Chatto & Windus, 1958), p. 376.

② East Asian Studies 东亚研究

East Asian Studies is a distinct multidisciplinary field of scholarly enquiry and education that promotes a broad humanistic understanding of East Asia past and present. The field includes the study of the region's culture, written language, history and political institutions. East Asian Studies is located within the broader field of Asian studies and is also interdisciplinary in character, incorporating elements of the social sciences (anthropology, economics, sociology, politics, etc.) and humanities (literature, history, art, film, music, etc.), among others. The field encourages scholars from diverse disciplines to exchange ideas on scholarship as it relates to the East Asian experience and the experience of East Asia in the world. In addition, the field encourages scholars to educate others to have a deeper understanding of and appreciation and respect for, all that is East Asia and, therefore, to promote peaceful human integration worldwide. At universities throughout North America and the Western world, the study of East Asian Humanities is traditionally housed in EALC (East Asian Languages and Civilizations or Cultures) departments, which run majors in Chinese and Japanese Language and Literature and sometimes Korean Language and Literature. East Asian Studies programs, on the other hand, are typically interdisciplinary centers that bring together literary scholars, historians, anthropologists, sociologists, political scientists, etc. from their various departments and schools to promote instructional programs, conferences and lecture series of common interest. East Asian Studies centers also often run interdisciplinary undergraduate and master's degree programs in East Asian Studies.

③ Discourse theory 话语理论

Discourse generally denotes written and spoken communications, though its usage differs between various disciplines and approaches. For instance, in semantics and discourse analysis, it is a conceptual generalization of conversation within each modality and context of communication. Moreover, in regard to semantics, discourse is understood as the totality of codified language (i.e., vocabulary) used in a given field of intellectual enquiry and of social practice, such as legal discourse, medical discourse, religious discourse, etc. In the work of philosopher Michel Foucault, and that of the social theoreticians Foucault inspired, discourse is described as "an entity of sequences, of signs, in that they are statements in conversation." As discourse, a statement is not a unit of semiotic signs, but an abstract construct that allows such signs to assign meaning, thus conveying specific, repeatable communications to, between, and among objects, subjects, and statements. As such, discourse is composed of semiotic sequences (relations among signs that communicate meaning) between and among objects, subjects, and statements. In simple terms, Foucault's analysis of discourse examines and determines the connections among language, as well as structure and agency. Foucault applied what he called "discursive formation," a term that conceptually describes the regular communications (written and spoken) that produce such discourse, in his analysis of large bodies of knowledge, such as political economy and natural history.

④ Beirut 贝鲁特

Beirut is the capital and largest city of Lebanon (黎巴嫩). Located on a peninsula at the midpoint of Lebanon's Mediterranean coast, Beirut is an important regional seaport. It is also one of the oldest cities in the world, having been inhabited for more than 5,000 years. Identified and graded for accountancy, advertising, banking, finance and law, Beirut is ranked as a Beta World City by the Globalization and World Cities Research Network.

⑤ the Near East 近东

The Near East is a Eurocentric geographical term which roughly encompasses a transcontinental region comprising Western Asia,

Turkey (both Anatolia and East Thrace), and Egypt (which is mostly located in North Africa). Despite having been defined variously within different academic circles, the term was originally applied to the maximum extent of the Ottoman Empire. The term has fallen into disuse in American English and has been replaced by the term "the Middle East."

⑥ Vico 维科

Giambattista Vico (1668–1744) was an Italian political philosopher and rhetorician, historian and jurist, of the Age of Enlightenment. He criticized the expansion and development of modern rationalism, was an apologist for classical antiquity, a precursor of systematic and complex thought, in opposition to Cartesian analysis and other types of reductionism, and was the expositor of the fundamentals of social science and of semiotics. Vico's intellectual magnum opus is the book *Scienza Nuova* (《新科学》, 1725), which attempts a systematic organization of the humanities as a single science that recorded and explained the historical cycles by which societies rise and fall.

⑦ Gramsci 葛兰西

Antonio Francesco Gramsci (1891–1937) was an Italian Marxist philosopher and Communist politician. He wrote on political theory, sociology and linguistics. He attempted to break from the economic determinism of traditional Marxist thought and so is considered a key neo-Marxist (新马克思主义). Gramsci is best known for his theory of cultural hegemony, which describes how the state and ruling capitalist class—the bourgeoisie—use cultural institutions to maintain power in capitalist societies.

⑧ Napoleon's Egyptian expedition 拿破仑征服埃及

The French campaign in Egypt and Syria (1798–1801) was Napoleon Bonaparte's campaign in the Ottoman territories of Egypt and Syria, proclaimed to defend French trade interests, seek further direct alliances with Tipu Sultan, weaken Britain's access to

India, and to establish scientific enterprise in the region. It was the primary purpose of the Mediterranean campaign of 1798, a series of naval engagements that included the capture of Malta (马耳他). The campaign ended in defeat for Napoleon, and the withdrawal of French troops from the region. On the scientific front, the expedition eventually led to the discovery of the Rosetta Stone (罗塞塔石碑), creating the field of Egyptology. Despite early victories and an initially successful expedition into Syria, Napoleon and his Armée d'Orient (东方远征军) were eventually defeated and forced to withdraw, especially after suffering the defeat of the supporting French fleet at the Battle of the Nile.

16.4 Extensive Explorations

① What does Said's "Orient" include in his *Orientalism*?

② What did the personal identity and experience of Said influence his theory of Orientalism?

③ In what way is the discourse theory related to Orientalism?

④ Describe the distinction between pure and political knowledge in the text.

⑤ What is the question of methodology in the text?

⑥ What is the function of the personal dimension in the text?

⑦ What is "orientalized" according to Said?

⑧ If you ever traveled or lived in Western countries, talk about your feelings in the Western societies as a foreigner.

后　记

《西方文论原典导读》是在国家精品在线课程、第一批国家级一流课程“西方文论原典导读”的讲义基础上编写完成的。在导言中介绍过，2014 年我们首次开设本课程，2015 年开始建设在线课程。在两学期的教学实践中，二十余万字的讲义在授课过程中逐渐形成。吉林大学文学院很多优秀的学生在选修了本门课之后，参与了课程视频的制作，分别对本课程的视频讲稿和文字讲义做出了贡献。她们的名字是：刘蕾（文学院新闻系 2016 届毕业生）、刘新悦（文学院新闻系 2018 届毕业生）、王一涵（文学院中文系 2017 届毕业生）、刘婉莹（文学院中文系 2017 届毕业生）、张蕾（文学院新闻系 2016 届毕业生）、田睿（文学院中文系 2017 届毕业生）、周雨轩（外国语学院 2018 届毕业生）等。我的硕士研究生赵欣扬参与了书稿的整理编订。本教材的出版，还得到了北京师范大学出版社的大力支持。周粟老师、谭徐锋老师对本教材的立项做出引导，周劲含老师、陈倩老师为书稿的审校、编排和修订付出了巨量的劳动。在众多师长朋友和优秀学生的努力下，本教材才得以问世。在此，我要向以上各位辛勤付出的学者和朋友们表示衷心的感谢。

本教材与混合式在线课程“西方文论原典导读”直接配套，欢迎大家在线学习本课程。大家可以在超星学银、中国大学 MOOC 和学习强国平台检索到这门课程，也欢迎大家通过站内信和邮件，交流学习心得、对本课程提出建议。

2021 年 4 月